WITCHCRAFT

WITCHCRAFT

Jayne Ann Krentz

This first world hardcover edition published 2010
in Great Britain and in the USA by
SEVERN HOUSE PUBLISHERS LTD of
9–15 High Street, Sutton, Surrey, England, SM1 1DF,
by arrangement with Harlequin Books.
First published 1985 in the USA in mass market format only.

British Library Cataloguing in Publication Data

Krentz, Jayne Ann.
Witchcraft.
1. Women novelists--Fiction. 2. Threats of violence--
Fiction. 3. Romantic suspense novels.
I. Title
813.5'4-dc22

ISBN-13: 978-0-7278-6902-9 (cased)

All Severn House titles are printed on acid-free paper.

Severn House Publishers support The Forest Stewardship Council [FSC], the leading international forest certification organisation. All our titles that are printed on Greenpeace-approved FSC-certified paper carry the FSC logo.

Printed and bound in Great Britain by
MPG Books Ltd., Bodmin, Cornwall.

1

THE ROSE with the needle thrust into its heart arrived on Kimberly Sawyer's doorstep that morning. Darius Cavenaugh, the man with the emerald eyes, arrived that evening. Both events shook her to the core.

There was nothing unusual at first about the rose, other than the fact it had been left without a note. Kimberly discovered it as she opened the door to walk down to the beach. Startled and then mildly intrigued, as any woman would have been, she picked up the blood-red flower and cheerfully stuck it into an old wine bottle. It would look nice sitting on the windowsill in front of her typewriter.

Not until midmorning, when the petals began to open, did Kimberly look up from her work and see the vicious shaft of the steel needle spearing the center of the rose. It had been carefully insinuated between the folded petals so that it would be revealed only when they gradually opened.

Kimberly froze at the subtle, deliberate violence. She sat very still, staring at the wicked needle, and tried to chase away the frisson of fear that flashed down her spine.

Then she remembered Darius Cavenaugh.

The image of his savagely hewn features and the gleaming emerald depths of his strangely compelling eyes appeared with shattering intensity in her mind. Her gaze never leaving the needle in the rose, Kimberly reached out a trembling hand

and picked up the receiver of her chromium-yellow telephone.

She found herself searching blindly for the little card Darius Cavenaugh had given her two months ago, her fingers shuffling awkwardly through the file on her desk. And then she was dialing the number without even pausing to think.

Halfway through the process, Kimberly suddenly realized how foolishly she was behaving. This was ridiculous. Someone was playing a joke on her, nothing more. But the phone had already started to ring. Before she could slam down the receiver a woman's voice answered.

"Hello?"

Frantically Kimberly tried to retreat. "I'm...I'm sorry, I have the wrong number."

"This phone is unlisted," the woman said coolly. "May I ask who's calling and where you got the number?"

"I'm sorry, I misdialed." Kimberly hastily replaced the receiver. Stupid. What on earth was she thinking of to call Cavenaugh's residence just because she'd had a small, but rather jolting experience?

She was back under control now. Kimberly frowned at the offending rose and tried to imagine which of her few neighbors might have played such a bizarre trick on her. There was gruff and dour Mr. Wilcox who lived farther down the beach. Then there was Elvira Eden, the aging flower child who had never quite evolved mentally beyond the era of the 1960s. She had a huge garden, Kimberly reminded herself. But it was hard to picture the perpetually serene and smiling Elvira doing something like this. And old Wilcox, while admittedly not possessed of a charming personality wasn't really the type, either.

Restlessly, Kimberly got to her feet, shoving her hands into the rear pockets of her snug, faded jeans and went to stand in front of the huge window that faced the ocean.

This was a particularly desolate and rugged stretch of California's northern coast. Few people lived here year-round, although the tourists would be pouring in from San Francisco and the Bay area when summer arrived. But it was early spring right now and there was only a handful of residents strung along the craggy coastline this far north of Fort Bragg.

None of the ones whom she'd met seemed the type to pull this little stunt with the rose.

"You're going soft in the brain, Kim," she lectured herself as she filled a teakettle and set it on the stove. "It's got to be someone's crazy idea of a joke."

Once again Cavenaugh's image flashed through her mind. She couldn't help wondering about the woman who had answered his phone. It could have been any one of his relatives or someone who worked on the estate. The Cavenaugh winery undoubtedly employed several people. As far as relatives went, there was his sister, Julia, Julia's son Scott, an aunt whom Kimberly vaguely remembered being named Millicent and who knew how many others?

Kimberly shuddered at the notion of so many people intimately involved in one's daily world. Extended families were not high on her list of life's pleasures. In fact, families of any size tended to make her wary.

That thought made Kimberly remember the buff-colored envelope that had arrived in her mailbox yesterday. It was still lying, unopened, on the kitchen counter. That envelope wasn't the first she had received, bearing the discreet address of a Los Angeles law firm. After opening the first several months ago, Kimberly had determined not to open any more.

Still, for some obscure reason, it was difficult for her to just toss it in the garbage.

The kettle came to a boil and Kimberly poured herself a huge mug of tea. She needed to get back to work. Her fictional characters were making more pressing demands on her than the silly incident with the rose. With a frown of concentration, she sat down to finish chapter three.

She worked for an hour before thinking again of the pierced rose. Kimberly looked up, gazing absently into the middle distance beyond her window, and found herself staring at the crimson flower instead of untangling the intricacies of her current plot.

That needle had been placed inside the petals deliberately. There was no point telling herself it had happened accidentally. And no mere accident had brought the flower to her doorstep.

A spark of sunlight glinted on the needle, illuminating it harshly. Then one of the storm clouds rolling in from the ocean blotted out the brief ray of light. The steel needle continued to gleam dully.

She ought to throw the rose into the garbage along with that letter from the lawyer, Kimberly told herself uneasily. But the unanswered questions surrounding the rose's presence on her doorstep seemed to make it impossible to just dismiss the incident.

Thoughts of Darius Cavenaugh brushed through her mind again, and before they had disappeared she found her eyes sliding toward the yellow telephone. Without stopping to think she picked up the receiver, dialing the number on the small card quickly, as though something beyond her own will drove her to do so.

"This is ridiculous," Kimberly muttered as she listened to the phone ringing a hundred miles away on the estate in the

Napa Valley. She took a deep breath and hurriedly disconnected herself before anyone could pick up the receiver.

But all afternoon as the storm began to gather itself out at sea for the assault on the coast, Kimberly's thoughts kept ricocheting back and forth between the rose on her windowsill and the image of Darius Cavenaugh. Twice more she found herself reaching for the phone as though an outside force were prompting her. Twice more she slammed the receiver back into the cradle with an exclamation of disgust. She could not call Cavenaugh. Not over something as trivial as this damned rose business.

Chapter three grudgingly ended shortly before five o'clock. With a feeling of relief Kimberly covered the typewriter. It had been terribly difficult to keep her mind on her work. Outside, the sky was already quite dark and the wind was beginning to howl demandingly around the small beachfront cottage.

Turning on a few more lights to ward off the pressing, storm-driven darkness, Kimberly built a small fire on the old stone hearth. It was not uncommon for the electricity to go off during a storm, and she didn't want to find herself without heat or light later on this evening.

A feeling of tension, real restless uneasiness, began to work on her nervous system as she lit the fire and went into the kitchen to see about dinner.

Long accustomed to eating alone, Kimberly normally viewed the prospect with a certain quiet pleasure. She poured herself a glass of Cavenaugh Merlot wine and sipped it slowly as she prepared a baked potato and a green salad. This evening would be a good time to finish that wonderfully trashy adventure novel she had started reading last night.

As usual she set a neat table for herself, preparing the baked potato exactly as she liked it with loads of sour cream and

salad dressing, grated cheese, chopped black olives, a sprinkling of peanuts and some sliced hot peppers. Setting out the bottle of hot sauce to which she was pleasantly addicted, she poured a bit more of the Merlot into her glass.

Kimberly had bought the Cavenaugh wine on a whim earlier that week when it showed up on the shelves of the tiny market in the nearby town. It had been an expensive whim, and not one she would indulge frequently. Writers living from one royalty statement to the next tended to become connoisseurs of wines that came in large bottles with screw tops. She'd actually had to dig out a genuine corkscrew for the Cavenaugh Vineyards bottle. The wine inside had proven to be excellent, but that didn't really surprise her. Anything Darius Cavenaugh did would be done well. No, she thought absently, more than just well. It would be done *right*. With all the loose ends tied up. She wasn't certain why she knew that on the basis of only having spent a few hours with him, but she didn't question the knowledge.

She had been hoping the extra half glass of wine that she'd allowed herself tonight might dispel some of the strange tension she was experiencing, but it didn't seem to be working.

Kimberly was just about to sink a fork into the elaborately decorated baked potato when the lights flickered and went out.

"Well, damn. There goes my chance to finish that novel tonight," she murmured with a sigh. Across the room the fire crackled. Picking up her plate, the hot sauce and the remaining glass of wine, Kimberly started toward it, intending to finish her meal while sitting in front of the hearth.

The purr of a sophisticated car's engine in her driveway captured her attention when she was halfway across the small room. The sound rose briefly above the increasing howl of

the wind and rain and then suddenly fell silent. Someone had chosen a miserable night to come visiting.

A moment later came the knock on her door. Kimberly had already set down her dinner and was peering through the tiny window set in the door panel. It was impossible to see who stood on the step because the porch light was not working.

"Who is it?" she called with a trace of unease. Except for that incident two months ago, crime was not a real problem around here. Nevertheless, Kimberly was instinctively wary tonight. That business with the rose had unsettled her more than she had realized.

There was no answer. Perhaps whoever it was couldn't hear her over the roar of the storm. Taking a deep breath and telling herself not to be so skittish, Kimberly unlocked the door, leaving the chain on, and opened it a couple of inches.

"Who's there?" she inquired coolly, peering through the small opening.

The man on her front step turned his head in that moment, and the faint light from the fire flared briefly on his roughly etched features. His gaze flicked over her shadowed face; a gaze that Kimberly knew would be emerald green in the full light of day.

"Cavenaugh," he said.

Kimberly closed her eyes with an odd sense of relief at the succinct answer. "Cavenaugh," she repeated. The rough texture of his voice brought back memories of the last time she had seen him. It also brought an indescribable wariness that she had never been able to properly identify or understand.

As she stared up at him the wind screamed eerily, just as it had that night two months ago when she had gotten herself involved in the incredible situation that had led to her meeting Darius Cavenaugh. She realized abruptly that he must be getting chilled out on her porch.

Without another word she closed the door, undid the chain lock and then allowed him inside. She stepped back as he moved into the firelit room, her eyes moving over him, trying to accept the fact he was here.

"What a coincidence that you should show up tonight," she finally managed politely as she motioned him to a comfortably overstuffed chair in front of the fire. "I was thinking about you today. What are you doing here? Have you come on business regarding that mess two months ago? Let me have your jacket. The electricity went off but the fire should keep the place warm. I was just about to eat. Have you had dinner?"

When he simply looked at her as he shrugged off the suede jacket he was wearing, Kimberly realized belatedly that she was babbling and wondered why. It wasn't at all like her. Annoyed with herself she hastily closed her mouth and silently accepted his jacket. It was still warm from the heat of his strong, lean body and the leather seemed to carry a trace of his scent. As soon as she caught the hint of the unique masculine essence, Kimberly knew she had never forgotten it.

How odd to have that surprisingly intimate realization about a man whom she barely knew; someone whom she'd had no relationship beyond the quite limited association brought on by the events of two months ago.

"I think," Cavenaugh said calmly as he sank down into the old chair, "that you did more than think about me today."

Startled, Kimberly finished hanging up his jacket and then started back across the room. "What on earth are you talking about?"

"That was you on the phone this morning, wasn't it? When Julia mentioned that a woman had called and then claimed to have misdialed I had a feeling—" He broke off with a

faintly slanting smile. "And later on the phone rang again but the person on the other end of the line had gotten cold feet by the time I picked up the receiver. That was you too, wasn't it?"

Slowly, her amber brows knit together in a small frown, Kimberly walked over to the kitchen and poured another glass of the Cavenaugh Merlot wine. "How did you know?"

"A hunch. The number's unlisted and people rarely misdial it. Two or three such hangups in one day were a little suspicious. Something told me it had to be you. Offhand I can't think of anyone else I know who would have hesitated to make the call." His mouth moved briefly, wryly. "Everyone else seems to have no qualms at all about contacting me for just about any reason."

"You didn't even call me back to make certain," she pointed out quietly as she walked back to her chair in front of the fire.

He reached up to accept the glass of wine she offered. Almost idly Cavenaugh held the glass so that the deep ruby liquid was lit by firelight. He perused the color with an expert's eye and then took a cautious taste.

"Very good," he pronounced, watching Kimberly over the rim.

"It should be. It's a Cavenaugh wine," she murmured dryly. "Cost me half a royalty check."

"I know." He swirled the wine in the glass and smiled faintly. "You must have known I was arriving tonight."

She blinked, mildly surprised. "How could I know that?"

"Beats me. The same way I realized it was you on the phone today, I suppose." He took another sip of the wine and continued to watch her.

"Coincidence," she assured him roundly. Kimberly found herself having to quash an unsettling sensation of intimacy caused by his words. She'd had that bottle of wine in the

kitchen cupboard for several days along with a few others. It was odd that she'd opened it tonight. Then again..."Well, maybe it was more than sheer coincidence," she admitted. "I did think about you several times today and you're right. It was me on the phone. I suppose I had Cavenaugh on the brain, and when I chose a wine tonight it was automatic to reach for the name."

"Automatic," he agreed blandly. "Subliminal advertising. I'll have to talk to my public relations consulting firm about the technique."

"That doesn't explain why you didn't try to phone me back to find out whether or not I was the mysterious caller," she pointed out. Kimberly reached for her plate. "And did you get any dinner?"

"No, I didn't get any dinner. I drove straight through."

"Want to split a baked potato and salad?"

"Is that what that is?" He eyed the heavily decorated baked potato as if it were some alien life form. "Well, I'm hungry enough to risk it."

She got up again to find another plate and then she carefully divided the still hot potato. "So?"

"So what?" He took the plate and fork from her and then watched, fascinated as Kimberly sprinkled hot sauce liberally over her own share of the food.

"Why didn't you call to find out if it had been me on the phone?"

"Because I'd been planning to drive over here for a week. Deciding it had probably been you on the phone just pushed me into making the trip tonight instead of this coming weekend." He forked up a chunk of potato warily. "What all have you got on this thing?"

"Everything I could think of."

"Well, it's interesting."

"A highly personalized baked potato," she said with a grin. "One of the many advantages of living alone. You can eat anything you want and have it fixed any way you like. Want some hot sauce?"

He considered the matter for a few seconds and then accepted the bottle. "Why not? In for a penny, in for a pound." Cavenaugh gave her an assessing glance. "You're very content living by yourself, aren't you? I realized that when I met you two months ago. You're quite self-contained. Have you always been alone?"

Kimberly shook her head with a small smile of amusement. "I don't really think of myself as being isolated. I'm just independent and used to doing things exactly as I like to do them; that's the way I was raised. When I was growing up there were only my mother and me. It must seem strange to you because you're always surrounded by family and all those people who work at the winery. From my point of view that kind of constant pressure would drive me crazy!"

"Pressure?"

She nodded. "Where there is a lot of family, there are a lot of demands. And in your case, you have the additional pressure and responsibility of supervising the winery staff. Many of them must be almost like family by now. You told me that the Cavenaugh winery had been around for a long time so I imagine many of the workers have, too."

Cavenaugh nodded slowly, emerald eyes appraising her features in the firelight. "You're right. There are certain demands in my situation."

"Well," Kimberly pointed out thoughtfully, "at least you're at the top of the pile instead of at the bottom. If one is going to have to live with so many other people it's probably best to be the one in charge."

"It has its moments," he agreed coolly. "But I get the feeling you wouldn't want to trade places with me."

Kimberly gave a mock shudder. "Not for the world. I'm afraid I've grown very accustomed to the freedom of being alone."

"But perhaps you wouldn't mind sharing your life with one other loner?"

Kimberly hesitated. "What makes you say that?"

"I've read the first two books in the Amy Solitaire series. *Vicious Circle* and *Unfinished Business*."

She smiled slowly. "You surprise me. I wouldn't have thought they would appeal to you."

"Being in the author's debt is bound to give me a certain curiosity about the author herself," Cavenaugh said sardonically. "Reading your books is a natural extension of that curiosity."

"Did you learn anything?" she quipped, wishing he wouldn't bring up the subject of being in her debt. Yet if she were perfectly honest with herself his promise of repayment had been on her mind today. She had thought of it the moment she had seen the petals of the rose unfolding to reveal the needle.

Kimberly could remember very clearly Darius Cavenaugh's last words to her two months ago. They had flickered in and out of her head along with his image all day long. *I want your word of honor that if there is ever anything I can do to repay you, you will call me. Anytime, anywhere. Do you understand, Kimberly Sawyer? I'll come to you wherever you are.*

She'd understood the shattering intensity of his gaze two months ago. Understood that he meant every word. But it had never occurred to her then that she might actually call on him. In fact, a part of her had warned that it would be very

dangerous to call on Darius Cavenaugh for repayment of the debt. That warning had caused her to hang up the phone repeatedly today.

"I learned in *Unfinished Business* that Miss Solitaire is quite capable of passion even while she's got her hands full trying to defeat a homicidal corporate executive. And since you didn't kill off her lover, Josh Valerian, at the end of the book I presume he's going to reappear in the next one?"

Kimberly's mouth twisted in rueful humor as she finished her potato and put aside her plate. "I rather liked him."

"So did Amy Solitaire."

"Umm." Deliberately she kept her answer noncommittal.

"Because he's so much like Amy herself? Another loner? You're going to make him your heroine's soul mate, aren't you? Two lovers united against the world, completely self-contained, independent and totally in tune with each other. They will live life on their own terms, having various and assorted adventures together, saving each other's necks occasionally. And they will not be bogged down with the demands and pressures of families, of real life."

"A perfect relationship, don't you think?" Kimberly retorted, thrusting her jeaned legs out toward the fire and leaning back into her chair. "The way I see it Amy Solitaire and Josh Valerian will have a rare degree of mutual understanding. Two people who know each other so intimately that they're aware of what the other is thinking without having to put it into words."

"Do you really believe that kind of perfect communication is possible between a man and a woman?" Cavenaugh asked quietly.

"Why not?"

"Men and women are fundamentally different, in case you haven't noticed. And I'm not talking about just the obvious biological differences. We. . .well, we *think* differently."

She slid him a sharp glance, wondering at the certainty in his words. "Perhaps in real life it's unrealistic to expect that kind of total understanding. But that's the great thing about being a writer of fiction, isn't it? I'm free to work out my fantasy of total intimacy with a member of the opposite sex to my own satisfaction."

Cavenaugh's hard mouth lifted in mocking amusement. "You see? There's a good example of why there can't be perfect communication between a man and woman in real life. You say the words 'total intimacy' and the first image that comes into my head is being in bed with you; having you completely nude and lost in passion. But that's not what you meant at all, is it?"

"No," she snapped, annoyed at the feeling of warmth that was flowing into her cheeks. She concentrated intently on the fire. "That's not what I meant."

"By total intimacy you mean something resembling telepathy, don't you? Being able to read each other's minds. And more than that; being in perfect agreement with what the other is thinking."

"I admit it's an ideal, not a realistic goal. As I said, I'm lucky to be a writer of fiction."

"Aren't you afraid of missing something good in real life while you pursue your fictional love affairs?"

"I choose to live alone, Cavenaugh. That does not mean I spend every moment alone," she informed him coldly.

"But until you find your soul mate, you don't intend to allow a man into your life on a permanent basis, right?"

She'd had enough of this insane conversation. "I think it's time we changed the subject. Why are you here?"

"Because you almost sent for me today," he said. "And because I want to be here. A week ago I decided I wouldn't delay matters much longer."

Kimberly shifted uneasily. "What matters?"

"You and me," he told her simply. "I've thought about you a great deal during the past two months, Kim." His eyes never left her face. The message in those emerald depths was very plain to read.

Kimberly stared at him, fiercely aware of the primitive light flickering on his coal-black hair. It illuminated the silver at his temples, making her think of moonlight on a dark ocean. Darius Cavenaugh was somewhere in his late thirties, and the years were heavily etched on his harsh features.

His body was lean, toughened by hard work in the Cavenaugh Vineyards, Kimberly imagined. But there was more to him than physical strength. The toughness went all the way through him, was a part of his emotional and intellectual makeup as well as the physical side of his nature. Briefly she wondered why a man who had made his living creating fine wines should have developed such a thoroughgoing, almost arrogant strength.

The white shirt, jeans and well-worn boots in which he was dressed tonight gave no indication of the financial resources she suspected he commanded, but the clothes did emphasize the fundamental impact he made on her senses.

"What are you thinking?" he asked when she didn't say anything for a moment.

"That somehow you don't come across as a jolly little old wine maker," she remarked dryly.

His eyes narrowed for an instant. "Maybe that's because I haven't always been a wine maker. But that's another matter. Let's get the business side of this out of the way first. What happened to make you think of calling me today?"

She sighed, unable to see the rose hidden in shadows on her windowsill when she automatically glanced in that direction. "It was silly, really."

"I doubt that. You may have some weird notions about the basic relationship between a man and a woman, but you're not silly. My family owes you more than it can ever repay, and I am more than willing to give you anything I can against that debt."

Kimberly stirred uneasily again. "I wish you wouldn't talk about it in such terms. I only did what seemed logical in the circumstances."

"You saved my nephew's life. He sends his best, by the way. When I told Scott I was going over to the coast to see you he asked me to tell you he'd like to play the 'escape' game again some dark night."

Kimberly groaned and lifted her gaze heavenward in mocking supplication. "You can tell him he'll have to play it alone next time. I was scared to death!"

She remembered all too vividly that night two months ago when she had looked out her window and seen the lights in the normally closed cottage a few hundred yards from her own. The old, two-story house on the bluff above her cottage was used primarily as a summer rental so the fact that it was occupied in winter had mildly interested Kimberly.

Other things had interested Kimberly about that house for three days preceding that fateful night. She had seen the car arrive with the woman and the small, dark-haired child. The little boy had been wearing a bright orange windbreaker. But

after they had disappeared inside the old house they had not emerged again. It made no sense to come to the coast and stay locked inside a shack of a cottage for three solid days. People who came to this part of the country wanted to walk on the beach, hunt for shells and generally immerse themselves in the stark drama of winter on the coast.

On the third day, Kimberly had decided to pay a visit to her neighbors. She had been rudely turned away at the door by a strikingly beautiful woman who had made it quite clear that the family did not want to be bothered. It was as she was walking back to her own cottage that Kimberly had happened to glance up at the second-story window and seen the face of the seven-year-old boy staring down at her.

In that moment she realized she had never seen such an expression of emptiness on any human's face, young or old. It had stunned her. As she had stood there looking up at the boy he had abruptly been yanked away from the window, presumably by one of the adults inside the cottage.

Instinctively alarmed but at a loss as to what might be happening, Kimberly had gone back to her own place and located the phone number of the real estate firm that handled rentals in the area. When she asked the agent if he had rented the house he told her that he hadn't.

Kimberly had explained there was someone staying there and the agent had agreed to check with the owners to see if they had rented it out on their own. When the word came back that the owners were in Jamaica and couldn't be reached, the agent had said he'd drive by his client's property the following day when he got a chance and see what was happening. Possibly some freeloaders had broken in to use the facilities.

That evening Kimberly had found herself watching the other cottage almost constantly. Something was wrong and she wasn't sure how to handle it. After all, she had no real evidence of any sort of criminal activity taking place.

The only thing she had to go on at all was the strange look on the face of the child in the window and the fact that she was almost certain there should be no one staying in the cottage at this time of year.

And then she had turned on the radio to catch the evening news and heard the bulletin about the kidnapping. It had taken place three days earlier but the family had tried to keep it quiet while they handled the situation. Someone had leaked the news to the press.

As she listened to the description of the missing boy, Kimberly had gone very, very still. He had dark hair and he had last been seen wearing a bright orange windbreaker. By the end of the news broadcast she knew that the child she'd seen in the upstairs window was little Scott Emery whose wealthy uncle, Darius Cavenaugh, had just received a ransom note.

There had been a storm brewing that night, just as there was tonight, Kimberly recalled. When she'd tried to call the local law-enforcement authorities she'd found her phone was out of order because of the high winds.

Her next thought had been to take her car and drive into the nearest town, which was several miles away. She'd pulled on a waterproof jacket and a pair of boots and stepped outside, keys in her hand. Instinctively she'd glanced over at the other cottage and seen the lights in the upstairs window go out. Perhaps, she remembered thinking, the boy had just been put to bed for the night.

She decided to take the risk of climbing up onto the porch roof of the old cottage. It wasn't such an outrageous idea.

After all, the storm would muffle any noise she might make as she approached the house under cover of darkness and climbed up on the shaky railing of the porch.

It was easy enough to swing herself up onto the porch roof, and from there she made her way to the darkened window where she had last seen the child.

Peering through the window she was able to make out the shape of a small boy lying quietly on the bed. He was alone in the room.

He'd been startled by Kimberly's soft knock on the window but he didn't cry out. Instead he simply stared at what must have been only a dark, shadowed face. Gently Kimberly knocked again.

With a bravery that exceeded his years, Scott Emery came slowly toward the window until he could see Kimberly smiling encouragingly at him. And then he recognized the lady he'd seen earlier that day.

Once the recognition was established Kimberly had no trouble at all getting Scott to cooperate. Together they raised the old window. The child's movements were slow and unusually awkward. It wasn't until the window had been forced open and Kimberly had gotten a whiff of the strange odor in the room that she realized he might be drugged. The penetrating fragrance of a burning herb stung her nostrils and she held her breath as she guided Scott out the window. He crawled out wearing a pair of cheap pajamas and nothing else. There wasn't time to search for the orange windbreaker. Following Kimberly's whispered instructions he kept very quiet as they made their way over the porch. Kimberly balanced precariously on the railing, lifting Scott down and then they ran through the storm toward her car. For once the

temperamental vehicle started relatively easily and Kimberly drove straight to the local authorities.

During the drive Scott Emery told her how his kidnappers were really witches. One good thing about the drugging effects of the herbs, Kimberly had reflected privately, was that they seemed to have mitigated the emotional trauma most kidnap victims suffered. Scott didn't appear to realize just how much time had elapsed since he'd been taken. He simply looked forward to seeing his uncle.

After that there was a time of confusion and chaos capped by the appearance of Darius Cavenaugh when he arrived to claim his nephew.

Whatever drugging influence Scott had been under evaporated quickly in the fresh air. He began to perk up almost at once and started chattering quite cheerfully about the "witches" who had held him captive. His uncle listened intently. The authorities arrived at the cottage to find it abandoned with virtually no clues as to the identity of the kidnappers.

Scott's tale of being held prisoner by witches had been dismissed as a child's fantasy, possibly induced by the drug. Only Darius Cavenaugh refused to dismiss Scott's story as an embroidery of the facts. He'd held his own counsel on the subject.

Kimberly had spent several hours with Cavenaugh that night. The paperwork and the questions had gone on seemingly forever. Cavenaugh had handled it all with a cool, relentless patience and efficiency that said a great deal about him. During that time she had sensed the strength, the total reliability of the man. No wonder little Scott was convinced his uncle would ultimately take care of things. Cavenaugh

was the kind of man who fulfilled his responsibilities, regardless of what it took to do so.

The kidnappers, as far as Kimberly knew, were still at large.

"Why did you almost send for me today, Kim?" Cavenaugh asked again.

She took a deep breath. "You won't believe this but I tried to call you because someone gave me a rose."

He was silent for a moment. "A rose?"

Without a word Kimberly got to her feet and went over to the windowsill. Gingerly she picked up the wine bottle and brought the flower over to where Cavenaugh sat watching her.

"Remember what Scott kept saying about being held captive by witches?" she whispered.

Cavenaugh contemplated the needle in the rose. "I remember."

Kimberly sat down again, her fingers lacing together tensely between her knees. "Do you think I'm letting my imagination run away with me?"

Cavenaugh met her eyes across the short distance separating them. "No. I think this little gift could quite properly be interpreted as a threat." He considered the rose once more. "That's why you called me, wasn't it? Or rather why you considered calling me. You're scared."

"Yes." It was a relief to admit it aloud. Then something struck her about the way he had asked the question. She gave him an uncertain glance. "Why else would I have gotten in touch with you?"

He smiled whimsically in the firelight. "It occurred to me that you might want to see me again for the same reason that I wanted to see you."

Kimberly felt the electrical charge that seemed to be coiling around her. It was a culmination of the growing tension she had been experiencing all day. "Why did you want to see me again, Cavenaugh?"

"I've never been sure how much of Scott's story I should take at face value," Cavenaugh said slowly. "But I do know one thing for certain. I did meet a real live witch that night I came to collect him from the local sheriff's office. I haven't been able to get her out of my head for nearly two months. But I told myself it would be wise to wait until she called in the debt I owe her. I was just about to give up and come to see you, anyway, Kim. Our timing was just about perfect, wasn't it? Almost like telepathy."

2

CAVENAUGH HAD ANTICIPATED a variety of circumstances under which Kimberly Sawyer might conceivably ask him for help. Most of the scenarios he had imagined involved money. He was used to people asking him for money.

It wouldn't have mattered to him if she'd needed money. After seeing the rather battered old Chevy in the drive and noting the general condition of the worn furniture, he would certainly have understood such a request. And since he had only been looking for an angle that would bring her to him, he'd decided that money was as good as any other reason.

After all, Cavenaugh acknowledged, the main goal was to bring her back into his life long enough for him to explore the strange attraction he'd experienced the first time he'd met her. He was thirty-eight years old and he knew damn well the curious hunger to see her again should have faded rapidly after he'd returned to the Napa Valley. But it hadn't. Something in her called to him and he wasn't going to be able to get her completely out of his mind until he'd satisfied the need to see her again.

It hadn't occurred to him that what Kim might ultimately ask for in repayment of the debt he owed her would be something as basic as protection. Now that she was tentatively raising the issue, Cavenaugh was startled at the rush of fiercely protective instincts he felt.

By now he had freely admitted to himself that he wanted her. He just hadn't been expecting the force of that desire to spill over into other areas of his basic instincts. The sudden, compelling need to protect her put a new light on what should have been an essentially simple situation.

After all, Cavenaugh reminded himself, he knew what it was to want a woman. He also knew how quickly superficial desire could burn itself out. Sexual attraction was a compelling, if frequently short-lived drive. That was something he could handle. But when the attraction became enmeshed with other emotions and instincts such as this strange protectiveness, it threatened to metamorphose into something much stronger and infinitely more dangerous.

Watching Kim now in the firelight, Cavenaugh admitted to himself that he wasn't quite certain why this particular woman held such fascination. He hadn't really been joking when he called her a witch.

Amber was the word that came into his head whenever he had conjured up her image in his mind. For example, there were the warm amber curls that she wore in a delightfully straggly knot at the back of her head. It was understandable that several of the twisting tendrils had been loose the night he had met her. She had been through a hectic adventure in a storm. But tonight the suggestion of disarray was present again and he sensed the style was simply part of her personality. All Cavenaugh knew for certain was that he felt a strong urge to unpin the amber knot and watch her hair tumble around her shoulders.

Amber described her eyes, too. Golden brown and quick to reflect emotion. More than once during the past two months Cavenaugh had wondered what that gaze would look like shadowed with passion.

There was nothing extraordinary about the rest of her features. There was strength in her face, intelligence in her glance. Cavenaugh sensed the willpower beneath the surface as well as an innate wariness, and wondered idly what had caused the latter. He guessed that she was in her late twenties, perhaps twenty-seven or twenty-eight.

Her body was pleasantly rounded and softly shaped with breasts that would perfectly fit the palm of his hand. He could see the outline of them beneath the butterscotch-and-black plaid sweater she wore. And that sweetly curved derriere so nicely revealed in the snug jeans made him want to reach out and squeeze.

While everything went together in a reasonably attractive package it didn't explain the compulsion he had been experiencing to see Kimberly Sawyer again. Something else was at work.

"Witchcraft," he murmured.

"Ridiculous," Kimberly declared, assuring herself that Cavenaugh was no longer alluding to the glimmering tension that had sprung up between them. "I overreacted to that damn rose. I'm sure it's someone's idea of a sick joke."

"But you called me today."

"I almost called you," she corrected firmly. "I kept changing my mind because I kept realizing how foolish it was to take that thing too seriously."

He sent her an assessing glance. "I'm here now."

"I told you two months ago that there was absolutely no need for you to feel you owed me anything!"

"I rather thought it would be money," he said musingly.

She glared at him. "I beg your pardon?"

"I somehow assumed that when you decided to collect on the debt, it would be money you'd want."

"I certainly don't need any of your money!" she exploded tightly.

"The Amy Solitaire books do all right?"

"They do just fine, thank you."

"I couldn't be sure," he explained gently, examining the inside of the beach cottage. "After all, you live way out here in the middle of nowhere, drive a ten-year-old car, dress in jeans that look about as ancient as the car—" He broke off with a shrug. "How was I to know your financial status?"

"I live out here because it suits me. Writers need lots of privacy and quiet, in case you didn't know. As for the car, well, I realize it's not exactly a late model Cadillac, but then I never did like Cadillacs. And the jeans happen to be very comfortable. Writers like comfortable clothes," she added far too sweetly.

"You're getting annoyed, aren't you?"

"Sharp of you to notice."

"You're also scared," he reminded her flatly. "Which brings us back to the issue at hand." He lifted the rose to examine it once again. "They haven't found the kidnappers, you know."

Kimberly licked her lower lip a bit nervously. "I'd been rather hoping something had turned up."

"Not a thing. No leads, no clues, no descriptions other than that one you gave of the woman and Scott's insistence that he was being held by witches. Nothing."

She heard the hint of controlled savagery in his voice and drew in her breath. "It must be very frustrating," she suggested uneasily.

The emerald eyes lifted from contemplation of the rose, and Kimberly found herself staring into the remorseless gaze of a predator. In that moment she almost pitied the kidnappers. The realization of just how implacable this man would

be when the people who had dared to threaten a member of his family were found was almost frightening.

"Frustrating is a mild term for what I feel whenever I consider the matter," Cavenaugh informed her very evenly.

Kimberly swallowed. "Yes. I can see that."

"Sooner or later I'll have them."

"The kidnappers? I certainly hope so. But if the authorities have nothing to go on..."

"I have my own people working on it."

"Your own people! What on earth do you mean?" she asked, startled.

"Never mind." He set down the wine bottle with the rose and reached for the glass of Merlot he had been drinking. "At the moment we should be discussing your situation. I don't think we'll take any chances. Someone may be out to punish you for having gotten involved. It's possible they know or have figured out who it was who rescued Scott that night. Regardless of what's going on you'll be safest at the estate. Can you be packed and ready to go early in the morning?"

Dumbfounded at the suggestion, Kimberly nearly choked on her own sip of wine. "Ready to go? That's impossible. I'm not going anywhere. I have eight chapters left to write on *Vendetta* and a deadline to meet. Furthermore, this is my home. I'm not about to leave it. I can't just pack up and move in with you until the kidnappers are found! For heaven's sake, this business with the rose is probably a totally unrelated incident."

"You can't be sure of that. If you had been sure you wouldn't have almost called me today. Even if the rose isn't related to the kidnapping, it's still quite deliberately vicious. You'll be safest at the estate."

"No," Kimberly answered with absolute conviction. "It's kind of you to offer, but—"

"This is hardly a matter of kindness. I owe you, remember?" he shot back harshly.

"Well, consider the debt canceled!"

"That's not possible. I always pay my debts."

"I haven't asked that you pay this one," she protested violently.

"You no longer have any choice in the matter."

"What on earth are you saying?" Kimberly leaped to her feet to confront him. "No one invited you here tonight. And no one is going to tell me what to do. I've been on my own a long time, Cavenaugh, and I like it that way. I like it very much. The last thing I intend to do is move into a crowded, busy household such as yours and stay indefinitely. It would drive me crazy and I'd never get any work done."

He stood up slowly, the light from the fire playing over the bluntly carved planes of his face. The shifting, golden shadows alternately revealed and veiled the visible signs of the force of his determination, but Kimberly could feel the impact of it on another level altogether and it made her shiver. She wished with all her heart she hadn't made that phone call today.

"It made little difference. I would have been here within a day or two, anyway," he assured her calmly as if he could read her mind.

Kimberly didn't care for the ease with which he seemed able to interpret her thoughts. "Look, Cavenaugh, don't you understand that what you're suggesting just isn't practical?"

"You can bring your typewriter and anything else you need. There's plenty of room."

She gritted her teeth. "I don't want to go with you."

"I can see that." He reached out a hand to touch one of the curling tendrils of hair that had escaped the amber knot. "Are

you more afraid of me than you are of whoever sent the rose?" he asked very softly.

Mutely Kimberly stared up at him, aware of the controlled desire lying just below the surface of that green gaze. She felt the answering response in her own body and shook her head wonderingly. "You want me, don't you?" she asked very carefully.

"Is that why you're afraid of me?" Cavenaugh released the curl of amber hair to let his fingertips gently graze the line of her throat.

Kimberly flinched at the intimate touch. "Yes."

His gaze narrowed. "You're an adult, self-confident woman. Why does my wanting you make you afraid?"

She answered starkly as the fundamental truth came into her head. "Because you can't have me. And I think you could be very dangerous, Cavenaugh, in a situation where you can't have something you want."

His hand fell away but even though he was no longer touching her, Kimberly could feel the faint menace in him. It was controlled but nonetheless formidable. It made her want to flee. Until today she had never known such an instinctive desire to run, least of all from a man.

"Why can't I have you, Kim?" The words were spoken with a deceptively silky edge.

She tried to keep her own voice calm and very matter-of-fact in an attempt to diffuse the stalking threat in him. "How about the trite, but true reason that you and I live in two different worlds?" Kimberly swung away from him, turning to face the hearth. "You are a man of property, community status, family responsibilities, commitments. You are tied to that winery and the people who live and work there just as much as they're tied to you. I understand how the demands of family and status and business all have to mesh for a man in your

situation. I operate differently. I'm free. You're not. Whatever we might have together would, of necessity, have to be short-lived and unsatisfying. At least from my point of view. Of course, from your angle a brief, passionate little affair with no future might be just what you'd like. But I'm not willing to play the role of casual mistress for any man."

She could feel the intensity of his gaze burning into her as he moved silently up behind her. His nearness made her tremble faintly. The knowledge annoyed her.

"You *are* afraid of me, aren't you? And you have the nerve to call yourself *free*? I don't think you know the meaning of the word."

Nervously Kimberly stepped away from him. "Please, Cavenaugh, this has gone far enough."

He hesitated and then shrugged. "Perhaps you're right. For now. We have a more pressing issue at hand."

"The rose?"

"I was referring to the little matter of where I'm going to sleep tonight," he retorted dryly. "Or did you intend to send me out into the storm?"

The wind howled with increased ferocity, and rain hammered against the windows as if to impress upon Kimberly what a cruel female she would be if she actually drove Darius Cavenaugh from her home on a night such as this. He gave her a small, crooked smile and all of a sudden her sense of perspective returned.

"I wouldn't throw my worst enemy out on a night like this and you're hardly in that category, are you?"

He shook his head, but the faint expression of amusement disappeared and he gave her a surprisingly serious look. "No. I'm not your enemy. Never that. We're bound together in some way, you and I."

"Because you feel you owe me something because of what I did for Scott."

"That's part of it. But who can always say why a man and a woman find themselves linked? There are other ties that bind," he reminded her softly.

"Uh-huh. Ties of family and responsibility and status. I've already mentioned them. And none of those ties exist between you and me."

Cavenaugh raised heavy black brows in sudden enlightenment. "You're looking for a real life Josh Valerian, aren't you? Another self-sufficient, self-contained loner with no emotional ties or responsibilities to anyone other than you and himself."

Kimberly was silent for a moment, mildly astonished at his perception, then she inclined her head austerely. "Every woman has a right to her fantasies."

"And your particular fantasy is of a man who will need and want only you," Cavenaugh hazarded roughly.

"A man whose loyalties are always one hundred percent with me," she agreed simply. "A man who is free to give me as much as I can give him." Kimberly shook off the assessing intent of his gaze and summoned a brisk smile. "And now about this little matter of where you will sleep tonight."

Cavenaugh looked as though he was going to pursue the discussion of her "fantasy" man but the forbidding expression in her amber eyes must have stopped him. He bit back whatever words had been poised to attack and nodded once. "As we've already decided, I don't fall into the category of enemy. And as I'm not yet your lover—"

Kimberly flushed at the easy way he began that last sentence and found herself rushing to interrupt. "I'll get some blankets from the closet. You can use the couch. I'll want your

word of honor, however, that I'm not going to have to kick you out of my bedroom at any time during the night."

"Your hospitality overwhelms me."

"Sorry, but you're a little overwhelming, yourself," she confessed wryly. "And I've had an unsettling day."

Humor flashed in the green eyes. "I take it you don't have many unsettling days?"

"Hardly. Another advantage to living alone, Cavenaugh. My days usually go exactly as I wish them to go."

"I think you're really quite spoiled, Kim."

"*Thoroughly* spoiled," she said with a quick laugh. "Believe me, I treasure the luxury of my independence. Now, back to your word of honor. Do I have it?"

"About not invading your bedroom? I would much prefer to be invited."

She let that pass, assuming it was as close to a promise as she was going to get and fully aware of the fact that she wasn't about to force him back out into the storm tonight. He was not her enemy even though he represented a very ancient form of danger. Walking to the hall closet she opened it and began pulling down sheets and blankets.

"One pillow or two?"

"One will do." He caught the pillow she tossed at him, his hand moving in an almost negligent gesture that betrayed an easy sense of coordination. "Kim, about your coming home with me in the morning," he began quietly.

"In the morning you'll be on your way back to the Cavenaugh Vineyards. Alone. How many quilts do you want?"

"One," he ordered, sounding irritated. "Kim, you were right to be nervous about that damn rose. We're going to take precautions."

"I'll take them."

"You called on me to protect you," he reminded her grimly.

"No, I did not call on you. I considered calling you, and at a few points during the day I almost did call you. But in the end I never actually asked for any help, did I, Cavenaugh? You keep forgetting that. You're here because you decided all on your own to drive over to the coast, not because I yelled for help."

"You're being unreasonable about this and with any luck by morning you'll have calmed down enough to realize it." Cavenaugh shoved his hands into the back pockets of his jeans and regarded her with ominous warning.

Kim refused to be browbeaten. She had been taking care of herself too long to allow herself to be intimidated by any man.

"That expression may be very effective on little Scott or on one of your employees who is late for work, but that's the limit of its usefulness, I'm afraid. It doesn't have any effect on me at all."

"I keep asking myself how Josh Valerian would handle this," Cavenaugh murmured just as Kimberly swept past the counter where the buff-colored envelope from the Los Angeles law office had been lying.

"He'd know when to stop pushing," Kimberly advised. The trailing corner of the quilt she was carrying in her arms caught the envelope and nudged it over the counter edge.

"He'd know when to stop because of this uncanny communication he shares with Amy Solitaire, I take it." Cavenaugh watched the envelope drop to the floor and moved forward to retrieve it.

"You don't have to sound so scornful. The relationship between Amy and Josh is going to help sell a lot of books."

"Not to men," Cavenaugh predicted as he studied the return address on the envelope.

"Women are the largest segment of my readers," Kimberly informed him grandly. "And I'll tell you right now they're going to love the sense of complete emotional and mental intimacy I'm building between Josh and Amy."

"Well, if you put enough sexual intimacy in the books, maybe you'll hang on to your male readership, too."

"I use the violence to keep my male readers interested," Kim gritted. "Men are really big on violence. Maybe it's a substitute for genuine intimacy for them. What are you doing with that letter?" She glanced up from preparing the couch and frowned as she saw the envelope in his hand.

"Wondering why you haven't opened it. Most people open letters from lawyers fast."

Kimberly's mouth curved grimly. "Not in my case. I've already had two letters from that law office. I know what's inside."

Cavenaugh eyed her intently. "Trouble, Kim?" he finally asked softly, tossing the envelope gently into the air and catching it absently. "Have you got other problems besides receiving roses impaled with needles?"

"No. The folks who employ those fancy lawyers are the ones with the problem. They created it themselves, however, and I have no intention of helping them solve it." She stepped back from the couch, examining her work. "There, that should do for tonight. It's going to be a bit cramped but it's better than sleeping on the floor."

"The floor is the only alternative you're offering?"

"I'm afraid so," she said cheerfully. "And since you're sleeping out here, you're in charge of the fire. I don't know how long the electricity will be off and it could get quite chilly by morning."

"I'll take care of the fire," he agreed, glancing down at the letter in his hand. "Are you sure this isn't something I can help you with, Kim?"

"What's inside that letter has nothing to do with you. It has nothing to do with me, either. That's what I told the lawyers after they sent the first one. You can toss that envelope into the garbage."

He set it back down on the counter instead. "You can be amazingly stubborn at times."

"Something tells me you can be just as stubborn," she retorted humorously. "But I think stubbornness in men is generally referred to as willpower."

"In the morning we'll have to see whether my willpower is stronger than your feminine stubbornness, won't we?" he queried easily. "Thanks for the bed, Kim."

"You're welcome. I'm sorry I don't have any extra toothbrushes or razors or whatever it is men need when they stay overnight."

"It's all right. I've got everything I need in the car."

"I see. You came prepared?" she asked a bit caustically.

"Going to hold it against me?" he challenged gently.

"Good night, Cavenaugh. Don't forget to keep an eye on the fire." Head held regally high, Kimberly swept past him to her small, comfortable bedroom. Damned if she was going to get into a useless argument about where he had originally intended to spend the night.

Half an hour later the house was quiet and Kimberly lay in bed under her huge feather quilt studying the ceiling. This had definitely not been one of her normal, pleasantly predictable days. She wasn't quite certain how to react to today.

No doubt about it, she was accustomed to having the unpredictable and the potentially dangerous confined within the pages of her manuscripts.

She turned over on her side, fluffed her pillow and considered the man in her living room. It was strange that he had shown up on her doorstep even though she had never actually summoned him. Darius Cavenaugh must be very anxious to pay off his debt to her.

Or else he was very anxious to get her into bed.

Kimberly glowered into the darkness. Men, in her experience, rarely pursued women quite this far, at least not ordinary women such as herself. She couldn't help wondering what it was that had brought Cavenaugh all the way from his vineyards to her front door.

She could understand that a man such as Darius Cavenaugh would be very conscious of the bonds of the debt he felt he was under. After all, he had undoubtedly grown up imbued with the notion of obligation and loyalty and family honor. The noble-sounding virtues were stamped all over his hard face. Kimberly remembered little Scott solemnly telling her all about the generations of Cavenaughs who had been in the wine business. The boy had chatted quite freely while they had waited together in the sheriff's offices for the arrival of his uncle. Scott was, even at his young age, quite aware of the importance of family heritage.

"That's why the witches kidnapped me," he had explained with a touch of pride. "They knew my uncle would pay anything he had to, to get me back. Uncle Dare wouldn't let anyone keep me."

"Dare?" Kimberly had questioned, wondering about the mysterious uncle who was on his way to collect his nephew.

"His real name is Darius. But we all call him Dare."

For some reason Kimberly had not felt sufficiently at ease with the tough, powerful man who had arrived later to call him by the shortened version of his first name. He had re-

mained Cavenaugh in her mind. And after tonight, that hadn't changed.

"Do you have an uncle who would pay lots of money to get you back?" Scott had demanded interestedly, kicking his feet as he sat on the wooden chair beside her. One of the men in the sheriff's office had bundled him up in an old leather flight jacket, which Scott had loved on sight.

"No, I'm afraid I don't have anyone who would shell out cold cash to get me back," Kimberly had told the boy, unprepared for the way it had upset him.

"How about your mom and dad?" he'd pressed anxiously.

"I never knew my father," Kimberly had said carefully, "and my mother died a few years ago."

"And you don't even have an uncle like mine?"

Kimberly had gently denied the existence of any such useful uncle in her life. Later, after meeting Darius Cavenaugh she'd privately decided there were very few little kids in the world with uncles like Cavenaugh.

She had thought the topic of who might pay her ransom should she ever be kidnapped had been closed. Certainly Scott's attention had been totally diverted the moment Darious Cavenaugh had walked through the door. The child had rushed forward with excitement and confidence in his greeting. Cavenaugh had swept him up and examined every inch of him with eyes of green ice. At last, satisfied that the boy was all right, he'd allowed Scott to make the introductions.

Eagerly Scott had explained who Kimberly Sawyer was and how she had come to his window that night.

"We went across the top of the porch and down the side and the witch never even knew we were gone, did she, Kim?"

"No," she agreed, smiling affectionately at the youngster. "She never even knew. Rather like Hansel and Gretel."

"I told Kim you would have paid anything to get me back, isn't that right, Uncle Dare?" Holding the hand of the green-eyed man with happy possessiveness, Scott looked up at his uncle for confirmation.

"Anything," Cavenaugh had agreed.

Kimberly had seen the grim protectiveness in the depth of the man's gaze and had known he spoke the truth. Cavenaugh would have done more than pay a ransom to get Scott back. He would have killed to save the boy. The stark realization of just how far this man would go to fulfill his obligations had sent an odd shiver down her spine.

"Kim doesn't have anyone who would pay to get her back if someone took her away," Scott went on before Kimberly realized what he was going to say. "But we would pay, wouldn't we, Uncle Dare?"

Cavenaugh had looked straight into Kimberly's embarrassed gaze and had said with absolute conviction, "We would do anything we could for Miss Sawyer. She has only to ask."

Later, after the long talk with the authorities, Cavenaugh had taken Kim aside and reiterated that vow.

Recognizing the powerful sense of obligation by which Cavenaugh had felt himself bound, Kimberly had quickly promised to call on him should she ever need help. At the time, of course, she had never anticipated such an occasion.

Yet his face was the first thing she had thought of when the arrival of the rose sent a shaft of fear through her. And now he was here.

But there was a new element in the situation. In addition to the sense of obligation he felt toward her, there was no mistaking the fact that Cavenaugh wanted her physically.

When it came to dealing with the sensual tension he evoked in her, Kimberly knew she was trying to handle something

just as strong as any witchcraft. But it was a comfort to know he was out there in her living room tonight. Normally she did not mind spending the nights alone. Tonight, she realized, would have been an exception. The knowledge that Cavenaugh was close by soothed the lingering fear the arrival of the rose had caused. She soon fell asleep.

When she awoke several hours later the storm had slackened somewhat but the wind continued to hurl rain against the windows behind the drawn shades.

Kimberly heard the sounds of the storm only vaguely. Her main awareness was of being thirsty. Too many salty black olives on the potato tonight. Hovering in that floating region between wakefulness and dreams, she wondered if she could get back to sleep without making a trip out to the kitchen for a glass of water.

But the growing thirst finally had its way. Still half asleep, Kimberly pushed back the quilt and padded barefoot to her bedroom door. Dimly she wondered why she had closed it tonight. She never closed her door. After all, there was hardly any need. She was always alone in the house.

Wrenching it open in annoyance, she continued on down the hall to the open kitchen. There was a faint flow of light from the fireplace and Kimberly vaguely remembered that the electricity was off.

It was getting cold, she realized. The oversized man's cotton T-shirt she habitually wore to bed barely covered her derriere. One of these days she was going to remember to buy some real pajamas. There was a robe hanging in her closet but it had seemed too much bother to drag it out just for a short trip to the kitchen.

With comfortable familiarity she found the cabinet door in the darkness and groped inside for a glass. Then she shuffled over to the sink and ran the water. The shade on the

kitchen window had been left up this evening, and as she stood barefoot in front of the sink, drinking her water, Kimberly stared disinterestedly out into the darkness. If she was careful she could stay in this half-asleep state until she crawled back into bed.

She had almost finished the contents of the glass when something moved outside the window.

Startled by shifting shadows where there should be nothing but open expanse between her and the view of the ocean, Kimberly belatedly began to come awake.

As her eyes widened, lightning crackled across the sky, obligingly illuminating the scene in front of the kitchen window. In that split second of atmospheric brilliance Kimberly stared in horror at the figure in a cowled robe who stood outside staring back at her.

She had no time to discern a face in the shadowy depths of the cowl. Kimberly's entire attention was riveted on the silver dagger the figure was holding upright in front of himself.

In that moment she knew the dagger was meant for her.

Although the scream that echoed through the small house was hers, Kimberly felt dissociated from the sound of unadulterated terror in her voice. She was more conscious of the glass sliding from her fingers and crashing into the sink.

"Kim!"

Cavenaugh. She had forgotten all about him. Half turning she saw him as he leaped over the back of the couch, rushing toward her.

"What the hell...?"

"Outside the window," she managed to gasp. "Someone outside the window with a knife. I, oh, my God!"

"Get down."

The command cracked violently through the air. He was right, Kimberly realized, stunned. She was standing silhou-

etted against the kitchen window. But she couldn't seem to move.

Then movement on her part became unnecessary. Cavenaugh reached her a second later, driving into her with the full weight of his half-naked body. He dragged her violently down onto the floor behind the protection of the counters and out of sight of anyone who might still be standing at the kitchen window.

3

"STAY DOWN," Cavenaugh gritted, sprawling along the length of Kimberly's body.

Crushed against the cold vinyl tile of the kitchen floor, Kimberly gasped for breath. "I can't do much else with you on top of me like this. You weigh a ton, Cavenaugh!"

He ignored that, his features a rigid mask of concern in the shadowy light. "Tell me exactly what you saw out there," he whispered roughly. He lifted his head so that he could meet her wide-eyed gaze.

"I told you. There was a man, at least I think it was a man. He was wearing a hooded robe or something. I couldn't see his face. But when the lightning flashed I saw a knife. A big silver dagger. It was horrible. I had the awful feeling he meant me to see it."

"Given the fact that the bastard was outside your window and not someone else's on the block, that's a fair guess," Cavenaugh mocked grimly. He shifted his weight and she realized he was going to get up off the floor. "Lie still. Don't move until I get back, understand? No one can see you down here behind the kitchen counters."

"Until you get back!" Kimberly repeated, horrified. "What's that supposed to mean? Where on earth do you think you're going?"

"I'm going to have a look around outside." He rolled off her, uncoiling easily to his feet.

"No, you can't go out there!" She grabbed for his jean-clad leg. It was like trying to hold on to a breaking wave. He slipped from her grasp as if he hadn't even been aware of it. "Cavenaugh, this is stupid," she hissed as she watched him stride across the room to find his boots. "You can't go out there. Who knows what might be waiting? For Pete's sake, come back here."

He didn't bother to answer. The golden afterglow of the fire flickered on the sleek planes of his bare back as he bent over briefly to shove his feet into the boots. And then he was at the door, slipping off the chain.

"Don't move," he ordered once again as he stepped cautiously outside. He shut the door softly behind himself.

"Cavenaugh, wait!"

She was appealing to an empty room. Angrily Kimberly sat up on the chilly floor, hugging her bare knees to her chest as she stared at the door. For what seemed an unbearably long time she continued to sit where she was, visions of the cowled figure holding the knife repeating themselves endlessly in her head. Suddenly, startlingly aware of her own near nudity as the icy vinyl finally made its presence known against her backside, she started to get to her feet. Halfway up she remembered Cavenaugh's injunction to stay where she was.

Astonished that she had allowed the force of his command to keep her there on the floor for even a few seconds, Kimberly stood up completely and peered cautiously out the kitchen window. She could see nothing, and the thought that Cavenaugh was out there somewhere, facing who knew what on her behalf, finally jolted her into action.

Turning away from the window, Kimberly started toward the hall to her bedroom. She needed to find her jeans and some shoes and a shirt before following her guest out into the stormy night.

She was nearly across the room when the door opened again and Cavenaugh stepped back inside. Whirling, she halted to demand anxiously, "Are you all right? I was terrified!"

He stood staring at her, eyes deep and unreadable in the dim glow of the firelight. The rain had dampened his shoulders and hair and the jeans rode low on his hips. Kimberly saw the glistening drops of moisture caught in the curling dark hair on his chest and was violently aware of the lingering hint of anger emanating from him.

"I told you to stay down on the floor." Cavenaugh fastened the catch on the door and then started toward her.

"I decided sitting on a cold vinyl floor wasn't doing anyone much good," Kimberly retorted, injecting a measure of irritation into her words. She found herself increasingly uneasy now and the sense of anxiety wasn't caused by what she had just seen through the window. "You didn't answer my question. I take it you're all right?"

"I'm fine." He stopped beside the couch and pried off his wet boots. "Got a towel? I'm soaked."

"Of course." Grateful for the small diversion, Kimberly reached into the hall closet nearby and yanked down a towel. She stepped forward to hand it to him and then remembered the short T-shirt she was wearing. "Here," she said quickly, tossing him the towel. "I'll go find my robe." She hurried to her bedroom door. "Did you see anything out there?" Opening the closet she pulled out the red terry cloth robe.

"No, I couldn't find a trace of anything or anyone. Hardly surprising with this rain and wind."

His voice came from her bedroom doorway. Startled that he had followed her down the hall, Kimberly fumbled with the robe. The darkness wasn't providing much privacy. She knew the pale length of her legs must be quite visible beneath the incredibly short hem of the T-shirt. Cavenaugh

stood watching her as though he had a right, idly drying his hair and the back of his neck.

"Perhaps in the morning we'll be able to find some signs," she suggested hesitantly, wondering why it was proving so difficult to get into the robe. Her fingers didn't seem to want to function properly. Although she had been quite chilled a few minutes ago her whole body now seemed unnaturally warm.

"I doubt it." He didn't move from her doorway and the vividness of his gaze seemed to burn over her. "Who owned that T-shirt originally?"

"I beg your pardon?"

"I just wondered what man left that T-shirt behind for you to wear to bed. Will he be coming back to collect it or you in the near future?"

Kimberly felt herself flushing and was glad he couldn't see the change in her skin color here in the darkness. Distractedly she managed to knot the red robe around her waist. "I always sleep in T-shirts. I buy them myself in packages of three. No one left it behind. Now, if you've finished commenting on my lingerie, I suggest we go back to the living room and talk over this situation."

He didn't move. Kimberly drew in a deep breath and decided on a firmly aggressive approach. She walked straight toward the door, giving every indication that she fully expected him to step aside. When he didn't, she was forced to halt a foot away.

"Excuse me," she said very politely. "You seem to be blocking the door."

Cavenaugh slowly lowered the hand holding the towel. "Why didn't you stay on the floor in the kitchen?"

"Because the floor was damn cold!" she exploded. "And because I didn't know what you were doing outside. I was

worried, Cavenaugh. I've had something of a shock this evening."

He searched her face in the darkness, his own gaze brooding and watchful.

"Pardon me, Cavenaugh, but you really are in the way." She put out a palm, flattened it boldly against his chest and shoved with all her strength. The situation was slipping out of control, and she was woman enough to know it.

She might as well have been pushing against a granite wall for all the good it did. Realizing belatedly that the forceful approach wasn't going to have much effect, Kimberly hastily tried to pull back her hand. She didn't move quickly enough; he managed to snag her wrist.

"You realize, of course, that what happened tonight clinches tomorrow's plans." He didn't move, just stood there chaining her wrist. "You're coming back to the estate with me in the morning."

Kimberly swallowed, violently aware of his strength and the absolute certainty with which he spoke. Her need to rebel was more of an instinct than a reasoned act. After all, she had been literally terrified tonight. Staying alone here in this house was about the last thing she wanted to do at the moment. But giving in to Darius Cavenaugh seemed almost as dangerous.

"I make my own decisions, Cavenaugh. Don't ever forget that," she asserted, lifting her chin defiantly. "I've been doing it a long time and I'm quite good at it."

"From now on," he grated softly as he pulled her closer, "you're going to get used to having a little help in the decision-making department. I'm responsible for you because of what you did for Scott two months ago. I have every intention of carrying out my duty."

"I'm sure you do. You're the kind of man who would always do what was expected of him, aren't you? And you're

accustomed to being in charge of other people. But I don't expect you to protect me, Cavenaugh, and I most certainly don't intend to take orders from you. I'll handle this in my own way." She was trembling now and not just from anger. Cavenaugh was too close, too big, too overwhelming dressed in nothing but a pair of jeans. Her earlier fears of the robed figure holding the dagger were being swamped with a new and altogether different type of trepidation.

"Don't be afraid of me, Kim," he said quietly.

She narrowed her eyes, angry that he had perceived her new nervousness. "If you don't want to frighten me any more than I've already been frightened this evening, I suggest you release my hand," she ordered coolly.

"I might be more willing to do that if I hadn't seen you running around in the firelight dressed in that skimpy little T-shirt," Cavenaugh told her in a husky voice as he dragged her half an inch closer. "And if I hadn't felt you lying half-naked under me out there on the floor. And if I hadn't just gone hunting for that bastard with the knife." He tugged her another half inch toward him. "Or if I hadn't been wondering off and on for two months what it would be like to take you to bed—"

"No!" But her protest was a breathless squeak of denial that held no real power. Mesmerized by the sensual tension crackling in the air around them, she found herself crushed against his bare chest, her fingers splayed wildly on his shoulders.

"Come here, witch," Cavenaugh growled softly as he lowered his head to find her mouth. "Let's find out just how strong your spells are."

Kimberly had an impression of emeralds that gleamed with a thoroughly dangerous fire and then her own eyes closed beneath the impact of Cavenaugh's mouth. The kiss was not

a gentle, tasting caress. Her lips were captured and parted; her inner warmth exploded with a hunger that astounded her.

As his hands slid down her back, sensing the shape of her through the robe, Kimberly felt a tantalizing heat flare to life in her body. She had been honest with herself earlier this evening when she'd privately admitted the effect his politely controlled desire had on her. She would be less than honest with herself now if she tried to deny that Cavenaugh's unleashed passion was devastating.

She heard the soft, feral groan deep in his throat and her pulse raced. His mouth was warm and marauding, unbelievably exciting. Kimberly cried out with stifled regret when he finally freed her lips. But almost immediately he was searching out the delicate skin of her throat and his hands slipped around her waist to find the sash of the red robe.

"Do you have any idea what you look like in that T-shirt?" Cavenaugh demanded hoarsely as he untwisted the knot of the sash. "What you felt like out there on the floor?"

"I felt cold," she tried to say, struggling for some self-control.

"You felt soft and warm and silky. Not cold at all. And you feel even warmer now. I knew it was going to be like this. For two months I've known—"

"Cavenaugh, wait," she managed on a thread of sound and then she caught her breath as his hands moved inside the parted edges of the robe.

"Why should I wait? You want this as much as I do."

The classic male reasoning provoked her as nothing else could have done. Kimberly slapped at his hand, trying to step away from his compelling touch.

"No, I'm not at all sure I want it. Everything's happening much too fast. I've been through a great deal this evening. I want time to think."

"If I give you time to think, you'll come up with a thousand reasons why you shouldn't get involved with me."

Kimberly gasped, both at the accuracy of his muttered analysis and at the feel of his palm as he pushed his hand up under the T-shirt to find her breast.

"Ah, Cavenaugh, please..." But the words were on a fine line between surrender and resistance and she knew instinctively that he realized it.

Dimly she tried to tell herself that her strong physical reaction to this man was the result of the scare she'd had. Heaven knew she'd used that rationale often enough to introduce a sex scene in her novels. After a scene of action or violence adrenaline and excitement were flooding the nervous systems of her characters. It seemed natural to channel it into sex on occasion.

But only within the confines of a book, she thought frantically. Surely that sort of thing didn't happen in real life! But how else could she explain her explosive reaction to Cavenaugh's touch?

And then the electricity was restored without any warning. Cavenaugh lifted his head abruptly as lights blazed around him. Kimberly saw the flash of impatience and irritation in his gaze.

"You must have had every light in the house on before you lost the electricity," he complained brusquely.

"Another advantage to living alone," Kimberly tossed back a little breathlessly. "There's no one around to lecture me about my electricity bills. Or anything else."

But the mood had been broken and they both knew it. Reluctantly, Cavenaugh let her slide from his grasp, the emerald fire of his eyes lingering on her flushed face. Kimberly busied herself retying the sash of the robe.

He studied her trembling fingers and understood how shaken she was. After hesitating a moment he decided to give

her the out she needed. If he didn't, matters were going to be a lot more difficult in the morning.

"I shouldn't have assaulted you like that," he told her quietly. "Hell, I was supposed to be the one protecting you, wasn't I?"

"These things happen," she surprised him by saying in a very distant tone.

"Do they?" He controlled the flicker of amusement her words caused.

"Oh, yes. I use this sort of scenario all the time in my books. Scenes of action often precipitate scenes of...of..."

"Passion?"

"Exactly. All that pent-up adrenaline and stuff. Very useful. I just hadn't realized it worked that way in real life, too." Her smile was rather forced but it was there as she faced him with casual challenge.

Cavenaugh felt a little stunned. "You've already got the whole thing neatly rationalized, haven't you?"

"As I said, it was just one of those things. Chalk it up to an odd quirk in human nature."

He struggled to restrain himself from taking hold of her and tossing her down on the bed. Cavenaugh was astonished at the force of the urge he felt to do exactly that. He'd show her the difference between one of her books and real life! Almost immediately, he realized the stupidity of that course of action. He had other, more immediate goals to work toward, he reminded himself grimly. After all, the most important matter at hand was to get her into the car without opposition in the morning. Humoring her now might make that task simpler. He smiled crookedly.

"I'll accept your analysis of the situation. From my point of view, I can only apologize for my actions. I appreciate your understanding."

There was an odd look of relief in her eyes as if she knew she had just come perilously close to an infinitely dangerous confrontation. A confrontation with herself or with him, Cavenaugh wondered fleetingly.

"Yes, well, it's been a hectic evening, hasn't it?" she remarked condescendingly.

Cavenaugh wanted to shake her. He'd like to show her just how "hectic" he could make her neat, self-contained world. Instead he said politely, "Yes, it has. I think I'll recheck all your locks before I go back to bed. And it might be a good idea if you left the door of your bedroom open."

"So that you can hear me if I get carried off by witches?"

"It's not really all that funny," he murmured.

"I know," she said with a sigh, toying nervously with the end of her red sash. "I was scared to death earlier. I'm glad you were here, Cavenaugh. Very glad."

Wisely he decided to let that ride without following it up with a demand that she let him continue to protect her. Given a few more hours alone in her room to think about the situation, she would come to her senses.

"Get some sleep, Kim. Everything will be fine. Whoever was out there knows you're not alone now."

"Good night, Cavenaugh," she nodded, sounding vaguely wistful.

He looked down at her, aware of the fierce restlessness in his body. She looked so intriguing with her amber hair in tumbled disarray. Her bare feet beneath the hem of the robe made her somehow charmingly vulnerable and he found himself wanting to pull her nervous fingers away from the sash that kept the old terry cloth robe close to her body. Taking a resolute grip on his senses, Cavenaugh stepped out into the hall. Then he thought of something.

"There's just one thing, Kim."

"What's that?" She frowned curiously.

"The next time I give you an order in a situation like the one we had tonight, I'll expect you to obey it."

Instantly he knew he'd made a mistake. The small frown on her face turned into a mask of feminine hauteur. "Since I don't expect too many more situations such as the one we experienced tonight, I don't see that as a problem. Good night, Cavenaugh."

He decided he'd better get out of her room before he said anything further to annoy her. Without a word he stalked down the hall, turning off lights as he went. Stopping in front of the fire, he poked at the embers, listening as Kimberly turned off the light in her own room and climbed into bed. A moment later the house was silent again.

There was one more light still blazing, the one in the kitchen area. Cavenaugh walked over to flip the switch and his eyes fell on the buff-colored envelope from the Los Angeles law firm. Idly he picked it up, wondering why Kim hadn't opened it. Perhaps she had trouble on her hands from another source besides Scott's "witches."

Long accustomed to dealing with trouble, Cavenaugh made his decision. He unsealed the envelope and lifted out the stiff, formal stationery. Then standing barefoot in Kimberly's kitchen, he read the letter without any compunction whatsoever. When he was finished he had even more questions about Kimberly Sawyer.

Thoughtfully Cavenaugh refolded the letter and stuffed it back into the envelope. Then he turned off the kitchen light and walked to the uncomfortable couch. In front of the fire he stepped out of the slightly damp jeans and spread them out so that they would dry by morning. As he slid under the blankets Kim had given him earlier he propped himself on his elbow and stared intently into the glowing coals of the fire.

Kimberly Sawyer was an intriguing woman. She was also proving to be something of a mystery. Above all, Caven-

augh reminded himself, he had an obligation to protect her. He owed her that much in return for what she had done two months ago. But it wasn't the sense of responsibility he felt that stayed on his mind as he allowed himself to go back to sleep. Nor was it the questions engendered by that letter in the kitchen.

The last, disturbing thought he had of Kimberly was a memory of the way she had begun to respond to him when he'd held her in his arms. If he'd had a little more time or a more appropriate set of circumstances, he decided, he could have had her in bed. That realization was deeply satisfying.

KIMBERLY AWOKE the next morning with a decidedly grim realization of her own. She knew she didn't want to face another night alone in this isolated house. Someone was deliberately trying to terrorize her. The man in the living room was offering shelter. She really had no logical choice but to accompany him back to the wine country until this business was all cleared up.

No sense fooling herself, she thought as she climbed out of bed and headed toward the bathroom. It wasn't going to be easy living in a house full of strangers. But handling figures in hooded robes who walked around carrying large silver daggers wasn't much more inviting. She could just imagine what the authorities would say if she tried to tell them what had happened last night. They would think she'd gone off her rocker. At least Cavenaugh hadn't questioned her story of what she'd seen through the window.

The closed door of her bathroom and the sound of running water inside brought her up short.

"Cavenaugh, are you in there?"

"Were you expecting anyone else?" he called back provokingly.

"Don't dawdle," she warned.

The door opened a minute later and he stood in front of her wiping the last of the shaving cream off his neck. He was naked from the waist up and it was obvious he had made himself quite at home. Emerald eyes glinted as he took in the disapproving way she peered around him into the interior of the bathroom.

"Your trouble is that you're simply not used to having a man in the house. Or anyone else for that matter. Don't worry, I'm fully trained. I won't leave my towels lying on the floor."

"Are you finished?" she demanded frostily, wondering if there would be any hot water left.

"Just about."

"Good. Then you can start breakfast," she informed him triumphantly, sweeping past him to commandeer the small bathroom. He allowed himself to be pushed out into the hall, but not before she'd caught sight of the half-amused twist of his mouth.

"A man would have his hands full teaching you the fine art of household compromise," he observed.

"When it comes to having enough hot water for my morning shower, I don't believe in compromise. Go start the eggs, Cavenaugh. I like them on the well-done side." She started to close the door and then stopped. "Oh, by the way, I've decided to take you up on your offer. At least for a few days."

He raised one dark brow. "No more arguments about returning to the estate with me this morning?"

"Is the offer still open?"

"It was never an offer, Kim," he explained gently. "It was more of a requirement. I can't stay here with you because I have too many other responsibilities at home. But I can't leave you alone here, either; not after what's been happening. The only alternative is for you to go home with me."

She tilted her head to one side, studying him coolly through narrowed lashes. "If I have a few things to learn about sharing the bathroom, allow me to inform you that you have a hell of a lot to learn about diplomacy."

"Meaning I ought to learn how to make commands sound like requests?" he drawled.

Disdaining to answer that before she'd even had her morning coffee, Kimberly slammed the door in his face.

Half an hour later when she strode into the kitchen dressed in a fresh pair of jeans and a peach-colored shirt, she sniffed appreciatively at the aroma that greeted her.

"Not bad, Cavenaugh. Not bad at all." She examined the eggs he was scrambling at the stove. A stack of toast was keeping warm in the oven.

"I do my best to please," he murmured.

Kimberly grinned. "Something tells me you just happened to be hungry yourself. Not that I'm complaining. I can't even remember the last time someone cooked breakfast for me. I'll enjoy it while I can." She opened the refrigerator. "What do you want on your eggs?"

"Anything but hot sauce."

She tossed him a disapproving glance. "You don't know what you're missing. I love it on my eggs." Pulling the huge bottle of pepper sauce from the refrigerator she carried it toward the counter. Actually, having Darius Cavenaugh around was rather interesting, she decided privately. What would it be like living in his house for a few days?

Setting down the hot sauce, Kimberly leaned across the counter to collect a couple of napkins. It was then her eyes fell on the opened envelope from the lawyers. Instantly the good mood she had been indulging evaporated as she realized that Cavenaugh must have read the letter.

"What's this all about?" she demanded softly, holding up the opened envelope.

Cavenaugh didn't pause in the act of dishing out the eggs. "That's what I was going to ask you."

"You opened this!"

He nodded, putting the frying pan into the sink and picking up the two plates.

She stared at him in stunned amazement. He didn't even appear mildly embarrassed. "You deliberately opened a private letter!"

"I was curious."

"Curious! My God, Cavenaugh, what gives you the right to be curious about my personal correspondence?" she flung furiously.

He still appeared unperturbed. "In my experience letters from lawyers often spell trouble. Since you didn't seem interested in opening it I thought I'd better."

She sat down weakly on the stool beside him, feeling more amazement than anything else. "I can't believe you had the nerve to do something like this."

He slanted her a glance. "Who are the Marlands, Kim?"

"To blithely open someone else's private mail. It's incredible. There are laws against that sort of thing," she went on, ignoring his question.

"Kim, who are the Marlands? Why have they hired that law firm to contact you? Why are they asking you to meet with them?"

"Are you this high-handed with all those people you have working for you and living with you? If so, I don't see how you keep your employees. Your relatives must find you absolutely infuriating."

"Kim," he interrupted patiently. "Just answer my questions."

"Why should I?"

He muttered something short and explicit under his breath. "Because if you don't answer my questions, I'm liable to contact that law firm myself and find out what's going on."

"First invasion of privacy and now threats," she gritted.

"Kim, just be reasonable about this, all right? I'm only trying to find out if you've got real trouble. Maybe it's got something to do with that character at the window last night. Maybe we're way off base thinking he was connected with the kidnapping."

Kimberly was too startled at his conclusions to restrain her answer. "Good Lord, no! I assure you that Mr. and Mrs. Wesley Marland would never dirty their well-manicured hands in something as nasty as kidnapping."

"So who are they?" he persisted gently. "Why do they want you to get in touch with them?"

Kimberly decided it really wasn't worth the battle. Besides, she reasoned, it wouldn't do any harm to tell him the truth. "My father's parents."

"Your grandparents?"

"Technically." She shrugged and began lacing her eggs with hot sauce. "I don't really think of myself as being related to them except in a strictly biological sense. I've never even met them."

"From the sound of that letter they want to meet you."

"It's a little late for them to play the role of loving grandparents."

"What happened?" Cavenaugh asked quietly.

"Breakfast is hardly the time to drag family skeletons out of the closet," Kimberly parried brightly.

"I've learned there aren't any good times to do it. Might as well be over breakfast," he retorted dryly.

Something in his tone caused her to send him a questioning glance. Whatever lay beneath the surface of the remark was destined to remain a mystery for now, however. Cav-

enaugh was on the trail of her secrets and had no intention of being sidetracked into revealing any of his own. Still, she found herself wondering suddenly about his past. What was it he had said last night? There had been some remark about him not always having made his living making wine.

"Tell me, Kim," he broke into her reverie to prod softly.

"It's short and sordid. Actually, given your own family background, you'll probably understand the Marlands' position completely. My father was their only son and heir. The Marlands own a big chunk of Pasadena, California, and have sizable investments throughout the state. The family goes back for generations. All the way back to Spanish land grant days. Lots of pride of heritage and lots of money. They had raised my father to be a worthy inheritor of the money and the name. He had been perfectly groomed for his role in life, as I understand it. Private schools, the best of everything money could buy. And then one day the noble son and heir committed a serious judgmental error. He felt in love with my mother."

"Let me guess," Cavenaugh inserted coolly. "Your mother didn't come from the right background?"

"My mother was an underpaid, overworked nurse. She lacked any sort of background at all, let alone the right one. She was an orphan. She met my father when he went into the hospital for some minor surgery. You know what they say about men falling in love with their nurses."

"No. What do they say?" Cavenaugh inquired.

"Never mind. Apparently it's a regular nursing syndrome. It usually wears off as soon as the man is discharged from the hospital. Only in my father's case, it didn't. He knew he'd never get his parents' approval to marry my mother so one night in the heat of passion he ran off with her to Las Vegas."

"Hoping to present his parents with a fait accompli?"

"Umm," Kimberly said, nodding. "It didn't quite work out that way. The Marlands were infuriated and demanded an immediate divorce. I gather my father tried to resist at first but they worked on him, pointing out his responsibility to the family name and fortune, forcing him to consider where his true loyalties lay. And then they cut off the money. My parents were divorced shortly thereafter," Kimberly concluded dryly.

"What happened when you were born?"

"Absolutely nothing. There was no contact from the Marlands."

"You don't even bear your father's name?"

"I refuse. I took my mother's."

"Scott said your mother died a few years ago," Cavenaugh said gently.

"She was killed in a car accident on an L.A. freeway," Kimberly explained bleakly.

Cavenaugh was silent for a while as he thoughtfully munched toast. Kimberly decided he had abandoned the topic but a moment later he asked, "Why do the Marlands want to contact you now after all these years?"

Kimberly allowed herself a savage little smile. "Because the noble son and heir, my father, never had any more children. He married well, mind you, but his wife proved unable to have children. My father was killed in a sailing accident a year after my mother died, according to those lawyers." Fleetingly she remembered the odd sensation of loss she'd had when she'd learned that the father she'd never known had died.

"So now the Marlands have no one except you."

"They don't have me," Kimberly said with cool finality. "As far as I'm concerned they made their bed twenty-eight years ago. Now they can sleep in it. They chose to wield all that family power and pressure then and they can damn well

live with the results. I'll never forgive them for what they did to my mother."

"That letter from their lawyer implies there would be a large settlement for you if you'll agree to a meeting with the Marlands."

"I don't need or want their money."

"How about the sense of having family ties?" Cavenaugh pointed out. "You're just as alone now as your grandparents are."

"I'm not a big fan of strong family ties," Kimberly told him wryly. "Not after what family ties did to my mother."

"Is that why you're so intent on finding a man who's as free as you are?"

Kimberly blinked. "Full marks for analysis. You've got it in one. If I ever decide to marry it will be to a man whose loyalty is one hundred percent with me. I won't share him with several generations of responsibility and clout and money."

"And of course he must share this deep sense of nonverbal communication with you, too."

"You find it humorous?" she asked coldly.

"I think you're living in a fantasy world. You want a man who will materialize out of nowhere with no ties to anyone but you, and who will think the same way you do."

"It's a pleasant enough fantasy," she returned negligently.

"You might like the real world just as well," he suggested.

"Not a chance."

"Are you sure there won't come a time when you'll need a real flesh-and-blood man?"

"Not on a permanent basis," she tossed back caustically. "Would you please pass the jam?"

"Is that a way of telling me you want to change the topic?" He handed her the jar of strawberry jam.

"I am continually amazed at your perceptive abilities." She gave him a brilliant smile.

"I have a few other abilities, too, but you have so many built-in prejudices against men in my position that you're not going to give yourself a chance to test them, are you?"

"If you're talking about the way you seemed to read my mind yesterday..."

He shook his head impatiently. "There was no telepathy involved yesterday. I just put a few facts together and realized it must be you calling the house. Since I had intended to drive over to the coast to see you soon, anyway, I decided to arrive sooner rather than later. No, Kim, I'm not referring to any supernatural abilities. I'm talking about more concrete ones. I'd like a chance to prove my ability to satisfy you in bed, for example."

Kimberly drained her coffee in a single, hot swallow and set the cup down with a sharp clatter. "Don't hold your breath. If you think that I'll sleep with you in exchange for your offer of protection, you might as well leave now. I'll take care of myself."

Cavenaugh's emerald eyes glittered with sudden proud fury. "When I decide to sleep with you, witch, it will be on my terms, not yours. And you can bet my terms won't include exchanging sex for protection. You're not the only one who has a few ironclad rules regarding relationships. I may choose to be generous in a relationship but I definitely will not resort to buying a woman, with either money or protection or anything else. Do we understand each other?"

Kimberly caught her lower lip briefly between her teeth as she considered the arrogant anger in him. "I didn't mean to insult you, Cavenaugh," she apologized aloofly. And it was the truth. She hadn't meant to antagonize him. It was just that he had pushed her a little too far.

"Terrific," he growled sardonically as he reached for the coffeepot. "Maybe we do share some mystical channel of communication. At least you understand me well enough to know when to back down."

THE CAVENAUGH VINEYARDS and winery could have served as a picture postcard of a Napa Valley wine estate. Gently rolling hills of neatly trimmed vines surrounded the chateau-style buildings in the center. A tree-lined drive led from the highway through the vineyards to the winery.

Kimberly sat in the passenger seat of Darius Cavenaugh's well-bred Jaguar as he turned off the highway and headed toward the main house. She was feeling very wary as she approached his home—more so than she had expected to feel.

"It looks as though it's all been here a couple of hundred years," she finally remarked, studying the vaguely French country house architecture of the two main buildings.

"Not quite," Cavenaugh said. "My father had the winery building constructed in the 1960s. It's open to the public three days a week. I had the main house built two years ago. So much for family history."

"But your family has been in the wine business here in California for several generations, hasn't it?"

"Off and on," Cavenaugh said cryptically.

Kimberly's brows came together in a small line. "Well, right now it looks like it's definitely on." The grounds appeared sleek and prosperous, well cared for and undoubtedly quite profitable.

Cavenaugh allowed himself a remote expression of satisfaction. "Yes. Right now, it's on."

The Cavenaugh home was set on a hill above the winery building, protected from tourists by a gated drive and a deceptively casual-looking low rock wall.

"I've had electronic equipment installed along the entire perimeter of the wall," Cavenaugh explained as he used a small gadget to open the gate automatically. "No one can get past without Starke knowing."

"Who's Starke?"

"A friend of mine. He's in charge of security around here. With all the tourists we get on weekends we've always had to exercise some controls. After what happened to Scott, we've really tightened things up." He threw her a grimly compelling glance as he halted the Jaguar in front of the house. "As long as you stay on the house grounds you'll be safe, Kim. I don't want you going beyond that wall without someone accompanying you. Is that very clear?"

Kimberly glanced uneasily around at the perimeter of her new jail and wondered what she'd gotten herself into. A trapped sensation began to nibble at her awareness. She wasn't certain how she should respond to Cavenaugh's orders and was therefore grateful for the distraction that came barreling through the main door of the house.

"Uncle Dare, Uncle Dare, you brought her! I knew you would!" Scott Emery's delighted face appeared at the window of the car on Cavenaugh's side. He looked past his uncle to examine Kimberly. "Hi, Miss Sawyer," he said, his voice lowering under a sudden attack of shyness. "Do you remember me?"

Kimberly grinned. "Believe me, Scott, I will never forget you!"

"Kim's going to be staying with us for a while," Cavenaugh began, opening his car door and pushing a hand affectionately through the youngster's shaggy black hair.

"Oh boy, I can show her my new train setup!"

"Miss Sawyer, we're so glad to have you. I told Dare he wasn't to return without you!"

Kimberly was sliding out of the Jaguar, not waiting for Cavenaugh to open the door for her when the new voice interrupted Scott's excited chatter. She looked up to see an attractive, black-haired woman with Cavenaugh-green eyes coming down the front steps. There was no doubt about who she was.

"Julia?" Kimberly held out her hand politely to Darius Cavenaugh's sister.

"I've been wanting to meet you since the night Dare brought Scott home and told us what happened. I'm sure he told you how very, very grateful we all are for what you did. I'm delighted he was able to talk you into visiting us!"

"Thank you," Kim began awkwardly, wondering how long she would be welcome when Cavenaugh's household discovered that she was there for an unspecified duration. Before she could think of anything else to say to the pretty young woman who was Scott's mother, Kimberly became aware of yet another person standing at the top of the steps.

"Hello, Starke," Cavenaugh said calmly as he nodded at the newcomer. "I'd like you to meet Kimberly Sawyer. We'll be looking after her for a while."

Kimberly managed a polite smile as the man came slowly down the steps. It wasn't the easiest task she had ever set herself. The man they called Starke suited his name. A forbidding face that Kimberly guessed rarely knew the tug of a smile was outlined in awesomely blunt planes and angles. There was a sense of restrained menace about the man, as if the layer of civilization was rather thin. Kimberly could see a raw, potentially violent intelligence deep in the dark pools of the brooding gaze under which he pinned her. She hid a shudder and wondered where on earth Cavenaugh had found him.

"It's about time you got here, Miss Sawyer," Starke said in a graveled riverbed voice as he inclined his iron-gray head austerely. "Cavenaugh needs you."

Before Kim could find a response to the outrageous remark, Starke had already turned and stalked back into the house.

"Don't mind Starke," Julia Emery exclaimed cheerfully as she urged Kimberly up the steps. "He's a little weird but he's nice."

"And no one will ever get past him to get at Scott again," Cavenaugh observed softly as he carried Kimberly's suitcase inside the house.

"You can say that again," Julia whispered confidentially to Kimberly. "Poor Starke took it very hard when Scott got kidnapped. I think he felt it was his fault, which of course it wasn't. Whoever took Scott got him on the way home from school. We used to let him ride his bike, you see. Not any more, naturally. Starke drives him back and forth now."

"I see," Kimberly said, glad that everyone was going to let Starke's nutty remark about Cavenaugh needing her slide by without comment. To make certain nothing more was said on the subject she hurried to exclaim over the beautiful interior of the house. "What a lovely home, Julia. It looks like an elegant old chateau."

"But fortunately has all the modern conveniences," Julia said, chuckling. "Including plenty of room. I'll take you upstairs to the bedroom you'll be using. We had it prepared just in case Dare succeeded in getting you to agree to stay with us for a while."

Another figure bustled forward as Julia guided Kimberly through the wide hall toward a large, curving staircase. "This is Mrs. Lawson. She takes care of us. Don't know what we'd do without her. The house would probably fall apart. Mrs. Lawson, this is Kimberly Sawyer."

The plump housekeeper held out her hand with a cheerful smile and a crinkle of genuine humor in her gray eyes. She was probably in her late fifties, Kimberly estimated, as she greeted the woman. Privately she wondered how many other people there were in the household. The sense of being surrounded grew.

She and Julia had reached the second floor of the house and were halfway down the hall toward the bedroom Kimberly was to use when two other figures popped out of a sunny sitting room with loud exclamations of pleasure.

"Ah, this must be Kim," the first declared. "So glad you could come, dear! I'm Dare's aunt, Milly Cavenaugh."

Kimberly smiled at the charmingly stately woman in her midsixties who swept up to her. Milly Cavenaugh had the now-familiar green eyes of the family but her once-black hair had silvered quite elegantly. She wore it in a regal bun at the back of her head. The queenly style suited the woman. Milly was tall and proudly built. Her eyes sparkled with animation and an unquenchable curiosity. Cavenaugh had mentioned that his aunt had lost her husband years ago and now divided her time between whatever projects happened to take her fancy.

Kimberly knew she was going to like the older woman, but she also knew she was going to thoroughly enjoy the creature in the purple turban and lime-green dress who stood behind her. For an instant she just stared at the brightly dressed woman. The robust, vividly attired lady was about the same age as Milly, but where Cavenaugh's aunt had an air of elegance about her, her companion appeared wonderfully eccentric and not a little scatterbrained. A good character for a book, Kimberly found herself thinking.

"Kim, this is my aunt's friend, Ariel Llewellyn," Julia said, making the introductions quickly. "Ariel and my aunt are inseparable."

"Rubbish," Ariel announced grandly, shaking Kimberly's hand with brisk enthusiasm. "Milly and I amuse each other and spend a good many afternoons together but we certainly aren't inseparable, are we, Milly?"

"Vile slander," Milly agreed lightly. "How long will you be staying, dear?"

"A few days, I think." Kimberly felt decidedly uneasy under the questioning. It was anyone's guess how long she could bring herself to stay in this energetic, well-populated household, even under the best of circumstances. Already she felt a wave of panic at the notion of having so little privacy. She realized she had become accustomed to privacy, living by herself most of her adult life. Vaguely she wondered how Cavenaugh stood having so many lively people surrounding him. But then, he had grown up in this environment, she reminded herself. And he was a man who carried out his responsibilities.

"Is that everyone in the house?" Kimberly asked Julia hesitantly as Scott's mother swept her on down the hall to the room assigned to her.

"For the moment," Julia assured her breezily. "We get a lot of people in and out during the day, of course. Mostly employees who come to see Dare or visit with Mrs. Lawson. Then there are the visits from Scott's friends. And Milly and Ariel are very fond of tea parties so they frequently entertain."

"It sounds rather, uh, hectic," Kimberly noted cautiously.

"You get used to it.'

"Oh." Kimberly said nothing more as Julia ushered her into a warm, sunny room that looked out over the vineyards. She headed at once for the window, peering out at the view.

"I hope you'll like this room," Julia remarked. "Dare will bring your suitcase up soon. He's busy talking to Starke down in the study at the moment."

Kimberly suddenly realized that Cavenaugh had not followed his sister and Kimberly up the stairs. "That's fine. I'm in no rush. I'll need to get my typewriter out of the car, too, and my supplies."

"Don't worry. Starke will take care of it." Julia smiled warmly. "You know, we really are glad you decided to come and visit for a while. We'll never be able to thank you enough for what you did two months ago."

"Please, don't keep mentioning that," Kimberly begged. "It really wasn't that big a deal."

"You'd feel differently if it were your son who had been taken," Julia assured her in heartfelt tones. "I was a nervous wreck during those three days. When the ransom note arrived I really went to pieces. Up until that point I had been telling myself that the kidnapper was probably Scott's father, and at least, being his father, Tony wouldn't have hurt Scott. After the note arrived we knew it had to be a real kidnapping. It was terrifying."

"You thought Scott's father might have taken him?" Kimberly asked in disbelief and then realized the full implications. "Oh, I see. A...a custody dispute?"

"Not really," Julia said wryly. "The last thing Tony would want is to be burdened with a child. He was furious when I got pregnant. But he was also furious when he left."

"He divorced you?"

"Not willingly." Julia's gentle mouth curved bleakly. "He wasn't about to divorce the tie to the Cavenaugh money. Then Dare informed him that there really wasn't any money except what Dare personally controlled."

Kimberly stirred uneasily as Julia confided the information. She wasn't at all sure she wanted to know too much about the Cavenaughs. "I see," she said again, a bit weakly, but Julia plowed on without any sign of hesitation.

"My father filed for bankruptcy three years ago. Then he and mother were killed in a light-plane crash on the way home from Tahoe. A few months later Dare came home and rescued the winery and the family."

"Came home from where?" Kimberly asked blankly. She had assumed Cavenaugh had always lived here.

"He had a business of his own. An import-export company that he operated out of San Diego. He spent a lot of time traveling abroad in connection with the business and we saw very little of him for a long time. But when he finally showed up in our lives again he was quite successful in his own right. He had the capital it took to get the Cavenaugh Vineyards back on its feet. He also sized up the situation with Tony, my husband, and kicked him out."

Kimberly stared at her. "Did you love Tony?"

"By the time he left I was more than glad to get rid of him," Julia admitted calmly. "He had been using me for years, hoping to inherit my father's money. I thought he cared about me, though. That's how completely he had me fooled. It took Dare to see through him. Dare and Starke are very good judges of human nature, by the way," Julia added lightly. "They've been together for years and they seem to have an instinct for people like Tony Emery. It was all very traumatic but I'm glad it's over."

Kimberly considered the absent Tony and wondered what had really happened. She couldn't help wondering if Tony Emery had found himself in the same situation in which her mother had found herself so many years ago. Kimberly wouldn't put it past Darius Cavenaugh to get rid of someone he deemed no more than a conniving gigolo who was unworthy of a member of the Cavenaugh family.

But even as she accepted the fact that Cavenaugh could probably be quite ruthless, she also found herself realizing that he must have had legitimate grounds for his actions. She

didn't want to believe Darius Cavenaugh would have done something as traumatic as throwing out Julia's husband unless there were real reasons. Julia herself seemed content with the situation, Kimberly had to admit.

The remainder of the afternoon was a hubbub of unfamiliar activity for Kimberly. She was taken on a tour of Scott's train land, introduced to Julia's new fiancé, Mark Taylor, the owner of a small winery nearby, shown around the grounds by Milly and Ariel and generally kept in constant motion by one member or another of the Cavenaugh household. A number of winery employees came and went from the study Cavenaugh used for an office on the first floor of the house.

She didn't see Cavenaugh himself until dinner. By then she was so tired she could barely hold up her end of the conversation. Ariel Llewellyn stayed for dinner, as did Mark Taylor. Scott was wound up with excitement and managed to dominate the conversation. By the time Mrs. Lawson had cleared away dessert, Kimberly was frantic for an excuse to escape. There seemed to be no letup of activity or conversation in the house and she simply wasn't used to being surrounded by so many people.

And there had been no hot sauce on the table at dinner. Depressing.

When she pleaded a headache and tiredness, she was allowed to flee up the stairs to the privacy of her own room. But not before Ariel had produced a special herb tea and given her strict instructions on drinking it before going to bed. Kimberly's sense of relief as she closed the door was overwhelming. In that moment she decided she would willingly accept a few more glimpses of people in cowled robes carrying silver daggers if it meant she could be alone again with unlimited quantities of hot sauce.

Wearing one of her comfortable T-shirts, Kimberly sank wearily onto the bed and sipped the tea Ariel had prescribed for her headache. It was bitter and unpleasant but for some reason she felt obliged to finish it. Ariel had been so anxious to help her. The knock on her door startled her so much she nearly spilled the contents of the cup.

Sighing, Kimberly pulled on her robe and went to answer the summons, half expecting Scott or Julia to be standing on the other side of the door. But it was Cavenaugh who stood there.

"Think you'll survive?" he asked wryly, stepping into her room without waiting for an invitation. He turned to run his eyes over her tousled figure.

She drew a breath and said carefully, "Cavenaugh, I'm not used to so many people and so much activity."

"I know. How do you think it was for me when I came back two years ago? I thought I'd go nuts."

Kimberly blinked in amazement at the unexpected confession. "You did?"

"All I can say is, you get used to it."

'That's what Julia says." She smiled.

"Well, personally I'm looking forward to the day Julia marries Mark and she and Scott move in with him," Cavenaugh said firmly. "And Aunt Milly and that wacky Ariel travel a bit. They're often gone for several days at a time. I'm more than happy to foot the bills for those trips, believe me." He hesitated and then said deliberately, "But even when a few of them are gone, it's never really *quiet* around here. The business side of things alone keeps everything in motion."

"I can imagine." She had the strangest impression he was trying to tell her something else, something oblique, but she was too tired to figure it out.

He prowled around the room, absently checking the windows. "I suppose you're tired..."

"Very," she mumbled in forceful tones. "Scott seems to have my entire day planned out for tomorrow. I suppose I'd better get prepared for it."

Cavenaugh stopped his restless prowling, coming to a halt in front of her. "You realize they all assume we're sleeping together."

"What!"

He nodded. "I'm afraid so. Except for Scott, of course, who hasn't gotten around to thinking about things like that in great detail yet."

"But...I...you...we hardly even know each other." Kimberly exploded. "How could anyone assume..." Words failed her.

"They know I've been planning on seeing you again. I didn't make any secret of it. There have been occasional business trips I've made during the past couple of months that I think they've interpreted as slipping away to find you. And since they know we spent last night together, it's natural for them to think we slept together. I just thought I'd warn you."

"Oh, gee, thanks," she said furiously. "Did you know everyone was going to assume that when you came over to the coast to collect me?"

He dismissed the question as unimportant. "There's no harm done, Kim. Relax. Is it really so terrible? The whole family is very anxious to see me married, I'm afraid. It's just harmless fantasizing on their part."

"Harmless for whom? I'm going to look like a fool!"

His mouth hardened and the green eyes flared dangerously for an instant. "Why should you look like a fool?"

"How else can you describe a woman who appears to be sleeping with a wealthy man in hopes of marrying him?"

"But you don't have any wish to marry someone like me, do you, Kim?" He moved toward her, catching her chin with his palm and studying her infuriated features broodingly.

"Just as you wouldn't wish to marry someone like me," she flung back tightly. "But in a situation like this, I'm the one who will look foolish, not you."

"Because you're a woman?"

"I doubt that has much to do with it. Being a man didn't protect Julia's first husband, did it? It's more a question of money and power and sheer clout. You have it, I don't."

He released her chin and thrust his hands into the back pockets of his jeans. "What do you know about Emery?"

"Nothing much. Julia just explained that you got rid of him a couple of years ago." Wishing fiercely that she'd never raised the subject, Kimberly chewed nervously on her lower lip. This was family business. Not her business.

"Tony Emery had been cheating on my sister for years. He couldn't have cared less about her or about Scott. Furthermore, he was swindling my father who had been soft enough to give him a job in the accounting department. He was garbage, and when he found out I controlled the financial side of things in the family, he left quite willingly. He knew I'd never support him the way my father had."

"I understand," she said stiffly, refusing to meet his hard gaze.

"Do you? I doubt it. You think poor old Tony was in the same position as your mother was when she found herself confronting your grandparents. But it wasn't like that at all. I'd have made sure Emery had a job and a future if I'd thought for one minute that he cared about Julia and Scott. But he didn't."

"So you got rid of him."

"As I said, it wasn't hard to convince him to go," Cavenaugh reiterated bluntly. "Kim, there's no similarity at all to your mother's position."

"Right," she agreed with unnatural briskness. "Well, it's getting late, Cavenaugh. I'm sure that even if your family

thinks we're sleeping together occasionally, they won't be expecting us to do so under the family roof. Please don't feel obliged to stay any longer just for appearances' sake!"

"You're a sarcastic little witch at times, aren't you?" he growled.

"Only when I'm feeling pressured."

"And you're feeling pressured now, aren't you?" he asked with a gentleness she wasn't expecting.

"Yes."

"Kim, everything's going to be all right. You'll be safe here. I swear it."

She heard the underlying vow in his words and nodded mutely. She would be safe enough here from people carrying silver daggers but that didn't guarantee her any safety at all from Darius Cavenaugh. And both she and Cavenaugh knew it. Their eyes clashed in sudden, mutual understanding and in that moment Kimberly would have sworn that they really could read each other's minds.

Slowly Cavenaugh shook his head. "No promises on the situation between us, Kim. Only that I'll protect you from others."

He walked out the door, closing it softly behind him before Kimberly could think of anything to say.

TWO DAYS LATER Cavenaugh stood at the curving window of his office-study and watched Kimberly as she surreptitiously left the house and made her way through the huge garden. She glanced back over her shoulder two or three times, her amber hair gleaming in the wintry sunshine. He knew she was checking to see whether or not she was being followed.

At the far end of the garden she unlatched the gate and stepped outside. He knew exactly what was going through her head in that moment.

Freedom.

She was escaping, he realized. Two days of constant, even if well-meant, attention from everyone in the household had finally taken their toll. He had watched her deal politely with Julia's eager hospitality, Scott's excited efforts to entertain and the invitations to Aunt Milly's zany afternoon tea-leaf reading activities with Ariel. In addition, everyone on the estate from Mrs. Lawson to the gardener had displayed unabashed interest in her. They all knew the role Kimberly had played in retrieving Scott from his ordeal.

And they all thought they could guess the role she was destined to play in Cavenaugh's life.

Cavenaugh's mouth hardened a bit at the edges as he followed her escape route. She was on the other side of the garden now, striding briskly toward the low, electronically wired rock wall that was supposed to be the farthest she could wander from the house without an escort.

He had a grim feeling that she wasn't going to follow the rules today. She wanted some peace and quiet and privacy and she'd go beyond the rock wall to get it.

Glancing down at the manuscript pages he had picked up from the desk in Kimberly's room a few minutes before, Cavenaugh skimmed over the lines of fast-paced dialogue and equally swift action. *Vendetta* was undoubtedly going to be another highly successful novel in the Amy Solitaire series. Cavenaugh rather liked Amy. It was Josh Valerian he wanted to have dumped into one of the huge fermentation tanks over in the main production building.

It was damn tough competing with a fictional "other man." Especially when that other man was probably Kimberly's secret fantasy. He was pondering Valerian's excellent timing, both in the matter of coming to Amy's rescue and in bed when Starke entered the room.

"She's left the house, Dare."

"I know."

"Want me to go after her?"

"No, I'll go and get her. She's a little desperate at the moment." Cavenaugh turned away from the window and smiled bleakly at his friend. "I don't blame her. At times I know how she feels. Any leads on that business of the dagger?"

Starke shook his iron-gray head. "I wish we had a better description of it. This whole thing keeps getting screwier by the minute. I have a couple of possibilities to check out, though. There aren't that many sources for handmade silver daggers in this part of California. It's beginning to look as though we may be dealing with a pack of real crazies."

"Scott's witches?"

"Yeah. The authorities aren't interested in that line of reasoning at all, however. Cranston prefers his own more straightforward theories. We'll have to keep following this one on our own."

Cavenaugh nodded. He and Starke were accustomed to doing things in their own way. "Have you got enough people working on it?"

"Three. But they're all good," Starke assured him.

"All right." Cavenaugh tossed down the manuscript pages he had been reading. "I'd better go bring back our wandering houseguest."

Starke eyed him thoughtfully. "You didn't stay with her last night."

Cavenaugh glanced up sharply. "Your job is to keep an eye on this household, but that doesn't mean you have to turn into a voyeur!"

Starke lifted one brow with mocking politeness. "Sorry."

"About what?" Cavenaugh growled.

"About overstepping the line between employer and employee," Starke said calmly.

Cavenaugh swore grittily and ran a hand through his hair. "Don't give me that. You know very well you're hardly an employee."

Starke relented. "I know. Dare, you've been as tight as a compressed spring ever since you brought her here. The problem isn't that you're sleeping with her like everyone on the estate thinks—the problem is that you're *not* sleeping with her."

"Stick to worrying about witches and daggers, Starke. I can do without the psychiatric advice." Back in front of the window Cavenaugh watched Kimberly disappear from sight. Behind him he sensed Starke shrugging.

"Whatever you say, *boss*."

"Damn it to hell, Starke, what are you trying to do? Make me explode?"

"Not me. I've been with you on a couple of occasions when you've lost your temper. I'd rather you take it out on Kim. Something tells me she can handle it. Go release some of that tension with her. Since everyone on the place already assumes you've taken her to bed, you might as well go ahead and do it."

Cavenaugh slanted his friend a violent glance. "Your theories on handling a woman like Kim leave me gasping in amazement." He scooped up the manuscript pages of *Vendetta* and shoved them across the desk. "Want to find out what women really want in a man? Here, read this."

"What's this?" Curiously Starke picked up the pages and leafed through them.

"Part of the book Kim's working on at the moment. Pay particular attention to Josh Valerian."

Starke looked up. "Why?"

"Because he's Kimberly's ideal man."

Starke grinned, one of his rare, wolfish grins. "I take it you don't fit the role of Josh Valerian?"

"Valerian enjoys total communication with the heroine," Cavenaugh said dangerously. "He always seems to know what she's thinking, how she's feeling. What's more, he understands her thoughts and feelings perfectly."

"So? What's so tricky about that? You've always been good at reading other people. Don't you have a pretty fair idea of what Kim's thinking a lot of the time?"

"Yes. Unfortunately, it doesn't do me a lot of good." Cavenaugh moved around his desk to grab his suede jacket.

"Why not?"

"Because I don't always agree with or approve of what she thinks or the way she thinks."

Starke gave him a mildly astonished look. "Why should you. You're a man. She's a woman. How could you possibly react the same way to everything?"

Cavenaugh smiled wryly as he pulled on the jacket. "You know, Starke, you have a way of going straight to the heart of the matter. You're absolutely right. Why should I worry about not being Josh Valerian? Kim's an adult female. She doesn't need some mystical other half of herself. She needs a man."

"You."

"Damn right." Cavenaugh paused as something crinkled in his jacket pocket. He removed the folded, buff-colored envelope from the L.A. law firm. "Valerian isn't the only obstacle in my path right now." He handed the envelope to Starke. "See what you can find out about this situation, will you? I want to talk to one of those lawyers."

"You're going after Kim now?" Starke accepted the envelope.

"Thought I'd work off some of this excess tension you're complaining about," Cavenaugh muttered, striding for the door.

"By yelling at her or by taking her to bed?"

At the door Cavenaugh turned, green eyes narrowed in a way Starke had learned to respect over the years. "I'd thought I'd try a little of each. See which method works best."

"Probably the second one," Starke said quite seriously.

Cavenaugh slammed the door of the study and stalked down the hall to the door that opened onto the garden.

5

THE BUILDING WAS NOTHING MORE than a storage shed tucked into the base of a hillside full of vineyards. But standing isolated and out of sight of the main house, it made an inviting refuge. When Kimberly spotted the shed after passing the forbidden rock wall she made straight for it. The day was deceptively moderate, considering the season. She'd only taken a light jacket with her when she left the house and after a few minutes of walking through the vineyards she had removed that.

Alone at last, she thought wryly, as she curiously plucked open the shed door and peered into the dark interior. She had realized this morning that if she didn't get away for a while she was liable to say or do something that would definitely border on the rude.

And heaven knew she didn't really want to risk that. Although the Cavenaugh household was overwhelming, she liked its various and assorted members, even the perennially visiting Ariel, who was constantly reading tea leaves, casting horoscopes or prescribing herb teas. She and Aunt Milly made quite a pair, Kimberly decided. Currently they had undertaken to plan a party. Julia was also involved, and when it looked as though they were all going to commandeer Kimberly, too, she had fled. She had finally reached a point where she needed to be alone for a while.

It was pleasantly warm inside the shed. Leaving the door swinging open on its hinges, Kimberly idly poked around amid the odd tools, stacked boxes and assorted equipment. Sunlight trickled through the cracks and chinks in the old wooden walls, providing a fuzzy sort of light here and there. Kimberly was examining an old leather harness, wondering what had happened to the horse who had worn it, when she became aware of a presence standing in the doorway behind her.

She swung around abruptly, Cavenaugh's warning about not going beyond the rock wall slamming into her head. For an instant as she stared at the figure silhouetted against the sun she couldn't see who it was. A shaft of fear sizzled through her. And then he moved.

"Cavenaugh! It's you." She smiled in relief. "You scared the daylights out of me."

He remained where he was, dark and rather intimidating as he filled the doorway. He had his familiar suede jacket hooked negligently over his shoulder. Dressed in jeans and a blue work shirt he could have passed for one of his own employees except for the air of grim command that emanated from him.

"Let's see how good our nonverbal communication is, Kim," he suggested sardonically. "Why don't you try reading my mind?"

Kimberly grimaced wryly. "Right now I can read you like an open book. You're angry because I disobeyed orders and went beyond the wall, aren't you? Going to yell at me?"

"I probably should. I didn't give those orders lightly, Kim. I gave them for your own protection."

"I know," she said, sighing. She slowly hung the old harness back on a rusty nail. "You'll have to make allowances for me. I've never been very good at taking orders from people

who thought they knew what was best for me. Go ahead and yell."

He stepped through the door, his face moving out of the shadows and into a ray of light streaming through a crack. Green eyes met hers with a flash of genuine understanding. "I have a feeling chewing you out wouldn't do a whole lot of good. Besides, I know why you disobeyed orders in the first place. And I guess that if I'm perfectly honest I can't say I blame you. It can get to be a bit much."

She smiled weakly. "Your family and your employees are all very nice, Cavenaugh."

'But they drive you crazy at times."

She looked at him with gratitude. "I'm just not used to big families."

"You're not used to any kind of family, are you?"

"No, I suppose not. For a long time there was just mom and me and then there was just me."

"And you like it that way."

"It's been pleasant."

"Lots of freedom," he observed, taking a step closer so that he could look directly down into her face.

"Yes."

"Don't you think I know what that feels like? Not having to worry about anyone but yourself? Not having to solve everyone else's problems? Being free to come and go as you like? Not being on call for everyone from your sister to your aunt's nutty friends?"

And suddenly Kimberly realized that she wasn't the only one who craved some time alone. Her stay in the household was only temporary. Cavenaugh, however, was trapped by the responsibilities he had undertaken. And being the man he was he would never walk away from them.

"Ah, Cavenaugh," she whispered softly, lifting a hand to touch the side of his face. "I hadn't realized, hadn't understood how it was for you." Her amber eyes brimmed with comprehension and gentleness.

"Kim," he muttered, letting the suede jacket slide to the dusty floor. "Kimberly, I..." He bit off the words, reaching out to pull her into his arms with a rough hunger that seemed to explode out of nowhere.

His sudden passion swamped her. Kimberly felt his arms close around her, his hands sweeping with aching longing over her body as his mouth captured hers. She parted her lips willingly when he demanded the intimacy. And when he cupped her hips, drawing her jeaned thighs against his own, she moaned softly. His body hardened violently as it encountered her gentle curves. Beneath the snug fabric of his clothing she could feel the unmistakable evidence of his arousal.

The primitive knowledge thrilled Kimberly, filling her with a rush of heady desire. She had been telling herself for the past three days that she didn't know this man well enough to even think of becoming involved with him. What she did know about him seemed to indicate that he was all wrong for her, in any event.

Yet this afternoon she had finally understood that they weren't so very different, after all. Cavenaugh had been trapped in a situation she'd always avoided, but that didn't mean his longings weren't the same as her own. He could never be really free the way she was, but she empathized totally with what his self-denial must have cost him.

"Can you read my mind now, Kim?" he demanded huskily as he drew his mouth reluctantly away from her own. His palms slid up under her cotton knit shirt, finding the clasp of her bra. When it came free he groaned and let his fingers

glide around her ribs until the fullness of her breasts rested on the edge of his hands. "You must know exactly what I'm thinking. I want you, Kim. I've been wanting you for two months. I *need* you."

"Yes," she managed breathlessly, answering all the questions he had asked, both implied and explicit. "Oh, yes, Cavenaugh."

"Oh, God, Kim. Come to me, lady, and let me make love to you. I've been aching for you. You don't know what it's been like having you in my house but not in my bed."

The ardent plea unlocked the last of her reserve. Kimberly wrapped her arms around him and made no protest when he pushed the cotton shirt up over her head. Her loosened bra fell to the floor and Cavenaugh inhaled sharply as he drank in the sight of her breasts.

"Firm and ripe." He ran his thumbs over her budding nipples. "Just like my grapes at harvest. I want you so much, sweetheart."

Nestling her head against his chest, Kimberly closed her eyes and let the enthralling sensations sweep through her. Vaguely she was aware of Cavenaugh lowering her to the floor. She felt him spread the suede jacket under her before he urged her onto her back. And then he was lying beside her, undoing the fastening of her jeans.

"We're all alone," he rasped. "Just you and me. It's perfect. Absolutely perfect. *You're* perfect."

She smiled up at him, her eyes glowing with feminine mystery behind her half-lowered lashes. "I didn't think it could ever work between us. . . ."

"Just let me do the thinking now, Kimberly. I'll take care of you. I'll make it good for you. I swear it." His palms tugged at the tight-fitting jeans until they were forced down over her hips. He dragged the bikini underpants along with them. A

moment later she lay naked. Her body flushed under the heat of the desire she could read in him.

Tremulously she put her fingers on the buttons of his work shirt. He rested his palm possessively on the flat of her stomach as she fumbled with the task of undressing him.

"You're shaking like a leaf," he observed with passionate amusement.

"I know."

"Are you afraid of me?"

"Do I look afraid?"

He lowered his head to taste one of her throbbing nipples. "You look beautiful."

"Cavenaugh, I'm not the only one who's shaking. Are you afraid of me?"

"I probably should be," he growled, letting his fingers glide down to the juncture of her thighs. "Any sane man is afraid of witches." He seemed fascinated with the way her body moved instinctively under his hand.

She pushed his shirt off his shoulders and then began to struggle with his jeans. But he grew impatient with her fumbling and sat up to finish the job.

Kimberly took in the sight of his completely nude body, fascinated by his obvious need. Strong and hard and powerful, he gathered her close, letting her feel every tough plane and angle of him.

His fingers shaped her curves, exploring the softness of her as if discovering something totally unique. His unabashed delight in her was intoxicating, Kimberly discovered. She'd never experienced such excitement and anticipation. It was all swirled into a pervasive warmth that captured her senses.

"I want you," she finally choked.

"You sound astonished," he murmured as he forced her legs provocatively apart with his hand.

"I am. I've never wanted someone like this," she admitted in absolute honesty.

"Oh, Kim!"

As if her words were more than he could resist, Cavenaugh moved, sprawling along the length of her, finding a place for himself between her thighs. The heat of him burned into her skin and the heaviness of his smoothly muscled body was a glorious, crushing weight that seemed to excite every inch of her.

Kimberly caught her breath on a sob of expectation mixed with a strange trepidation as she felt his hardness poised on the brink of her feminine core. His hand moved between them briefly, teasing the exquisitely sensitive region until she cried out and sank her nails into his shoulders.

"You're so sweet, so ready for me," Cavenaugh muttered in tones of masculine wonder. "Do you really want me so much, witch?"

"Yes, ah, Cavenaugh, *yes*!"

And then he was thrusting deeply into her, the impact of him making itself felt throughout her body. Hot, demanding, deliciously overpowering, Cavenaugh took possession of her in a way that made him as much her captive as she was his.

Kimberly clung to the man above her, holding him close with legs that wrapped around him and arms that were silken bonds. Cavenaugh moved into her, claiming her body with elemental passion, giving her all of himself in return. The rhythm of his lovemaking claimed her and she was meshed in perfect harmony with his own pulsating desire.

When her body tightened in warning of the impending climax, Kimberly called Cavenaugh's name and he buried his mouth against her breast. She felt his teeth against her skin and the sensation sent her over some invisible edge.

"Oh, my God, Cavenaugh!"

"Now, Kim. Give me everything *now*. I'll keep you safe."

She shimmered beneath him and before the delicate convulsions had rippled completely through her body he was following her, huskily shouting his own release.

Kimberly sank down into a gentle oblivion, unaware of the hard floor beneath her, unaware of the unromantic surroundings provided by the old shed. She knew only that she had shared the most profound sense of intimacy that she had ever experienced. It might prove a fleeting thing, but while it lasted it was incredible.

And in that warm, vulnerable moment she was certain that Darius Cavenaugh had felt everything she had felt. The relationship between them was changed for all time.

Cavenaugh slowly released himself from her body, moving onto his side so that he could gather her against him. His cradling arm felt warm and comfortable and strong.

"Are you going to be furious with me later?" he asked evenly, green eyes poring over her love-softened face.

Mutely she shook her head. "For making love to me? No, Cavenaugh. It felt. . .right."

His mouth crooked gently. "I knew it was going to be like this."

"Did you?" She twisted lazily in his arms. "You should have told me."

"I think I tried to on a couple of occasions but you weren't listening."

"Ah, Cavenaugh. How was I to know?" she asked simply.

He leaned down and brushed his mouth against her lips. "In the future you'll just have to trust me to know what's best for you."

She smiled mischievously. "I wouldn't dream of putting so much responsibility on your shoulders. You've already got more than enough to worry about."

"More than enough?"

"Ummm." She ran her fingers through his silver-tinged hair. "I've seen the way everyone in the household and on the estate turns to you for advice and help on even the most trivial matters. And you always stop and give it. It's a wonder you have time to get any of the winery's real business done."

He exhaled slowly, as if enjoying the lingering moment of total relaxation. "I suppose you're right in a sense. When I arrived two years ago everything was in such chaos that I had no option but to become totally involved both with what was left of the family and the business. People had been floundering. Julia's marriage was in a mess, Scott was having emotional problems because of his father's rejection of him, Aunt Molly was distraught over my father's death, the employees feared for their jobs and the wine wasn't doing well in the markets. On top of that, the estate was going into bankruptcy."

"So you stepped in and took over responsibility for everything and everyone. You did your family duty, and now you're trapped by that duty."

The brackets at the edges of his mouth tightened slightly. "I don't see myself as trapped, Kim. I chose to do it."

Instantly she was sorry she'd phrased her words the way she had. "It doesn't matter whether duty chose you or you chose it. Your life has been completely changed by it. What was it like during the days you ran that import-export business?"

"I'm sure you'd describe my life-style back then as considerably freer than it is now," he said easily. Absently he stroked slow circles on her arm. "A lot of traveling with basically only

myself and Starke to think about. And Lord knows Starke can take care of himself."

"Where on earth did you find him?"

"In the middle of a street riot in some miserable little country in the Middle East. I was in town making a deal for some rugs and Starke was there to make...well, another kind of deal. We were both in the wrong place at the wrong time. Things got nasty and by the time it was over we were partners. Two years ago when I decided to take over the winery after my father died, he opted to come with me."

"You must be close friends."

"Depends how you describe close friends, I guess. I probably know him as well as anyone, but there's a hell of a lot no one will ever know about Starke."

"Why did you go into business for yourself? How did you escape being groomed to take over the winery?" Kimberly asked.

"I had no interest in the winery when I was growing up. I wanted to do something more exciting with my life. I wanted adventure and action and the challenge of making my own fortune."

"And you found all that?"

"Oh, yes," Cavenaugh agreed with a cryptic smile. "I found it."

"But when the chips were down, you came back to assume your responsibilities to your family."

Some of the warm intimacy disappeared from Cavenaugh's green eyes. "You have a way of making family responsibilities sound like a grim fate to be avoided at all costs."

"Maybe it's just because I know how twisted they can become."

Cavenaugh appeared to be sorting through his next words. "Kim, if your father had really loved your mother he wouldn't

have given her up to please his family. And he wouldn't have spent the rest of his life pretending you didn't exist. He would have fought to make his parents accept you and your mother.... Blame his own weakness for what he did to her, not his sense of family responsibility."

Kimberly suddenly became very aware of a certain chill invading the old shed. "I think we're about to lose our sunny afternoon," she observed with a lightness she was far from feeling. "Clouds are starting to form."

Cavenaugh levered himself up beside her, slanting her a speculative glance. "Which, translated, means you don't want to talk about the situation regarding your grandparents, right?"

"Cavenaugh, I always said you do have some amazing powers of perception."

He finished pulling on his jeans and reached down to help her to her feet, his eyes lingering on her full breasts as she fastened her shirt. "You have some amazing powers, yourself, witch. I feel like a new man this afternoon."

His words halted her emotional withdrawal. Kimberly looked up at him and felt a return of the warmth she had been feeling earlier. But what she felt for him now, she thought fleetingly, went far beyond warmth or even passion for that matter. Deliberately she thrust the realization aside and smiled brilliantly.

"I hope I was a more interesting tonic than some of those concoctions Ariel is always serving up."

"You're much more than a tonic, Kim, and you know it." He took her hand. "Come on, honey, much as I hate to end this very satisfying idyll, I'm afraid we have to get back to the house. I've got a thousand and one things that have to be done this afternoon."

"Winery business?"

"Right. There's a new marketing plan that I've got to go over and a report from the accountant's office."

"It can't have been easy pulling the Cavenaugh Vineyards out of the red these past two years," Kimberly observed slowly as she allowed him to lead her back toward the house.

"It's been a challenge," he agreed dryly.

He didn't release her hand after they came within sight of the house. Instead he clasped her fingers tightly in his own all the way through the garden and up to the back door. Anyone watching from the house could not have missed the intimacy. And anyone watching would probably be able to guess how she and Cavenaugh had just spent the past hour, Kimberly realized uneasily. A part of her went on the defensive when she saw Julia hovering in the hall.

But Julia did not appear to be the slightest bit concerned that her brother might have just made love to their houseguest. She greeted them both cheerfully and glanced at Cavenaugh with obvious relief.

"Oh, there you are, Dare. I've been looking for you. Aunt Milly and Ariel want to invite half the world to this party we've been planning, and I said I'd check with you."

"No one gets invited who isn't personally known to either you or me, Julia, you know that. I don't want any strangers in the house until those kidnappers have been caught."

"That's what I told them you'd say. They're working up a guest list now for you to go over. Oh, and Scott has been scouring the place for you, too. He wants you to help him add a new section to his train track. And I was wondering if you'd talk to that car dealer for me. I'm not getting anywhere with him. He simply won't fix that problem in the transmission free of charge. Claims it's not under warranty. I know he'll back down if you deal with him."

"Uncle Dare, Uncle Dare," Scott interrupted excitedly, tearing around the corner with a miniature train tunnel in one hand. "I've been looking for you. Come and help me set up my new tunnel."

Before Cavenaugh could respond, Aunt Milly appeared in the hall, the ever-present Ariel right behind her. "Here's the preliminary guest list, Dare. Julia said you'd want to go over it. We have to get the invitations out soon so we were hoping you'd get a chance to look at it this afternoon."

Cavenaugh reluctantly extended his hand to take the list. "All right, Aunt Milly. Scott, let's take a quick look at that train track. Julia, get me the dealer's phone number and I'll—"

It was too much. After two full days in the Cavenaugh household, Kimberly knew things were always like this. It was time to put a stop to it. She stepped forward and removed the guest list from Cavenaugh's hand. When he glanced at her in surprise she smiled serenely and turned to the others.

"I'm afraid Cavenaugh doesn't have time to worry about the guest list or the car dealer this afternoon. He has to go over a marketing report and some papers from the accountant." She glanced pointedly at her watch. "It's only three-thirty on a Wednesday afternoon. A time when every other executive in the country is concentrating on business. And that's exactly what Cavenaugh is going to do today. Scott, you just got home from school. Go find something else to play with for now. Your uncle will help you with the train track later. Julia, you can take a look at the guest list, can't you? You will know who's familiar and who isn't. The car dealer can wait until tomorrow. Aunt Milly, I'm sure you and Ariel can begin filling out the invitations. They can be addressed later after the guest list is approved by Julia." She

glanced around at the circle of astonished faces. "There, I think that does it. Go to work, Cavenaugh. You have a winery to run. The rest of the household can get along without you this afternoon. No one will bother you until five o'clock. Personally," she added firmly, "I'm going to get some writing done." With a challenging smile she invited objections. There were none.

She shooed the others down the hall, leaving Cavenaugh standing alone.

He stood there for a long moment after Kimberly's amber head had disappeared, savoring the memory of her in his arms. And then he walked slowly toward his study, letting himself inside and closing the door behind him with a sense of satisfaction. He had an hour and a half of uninterrupted time ahead of him. He could accomplish a hell of a lot. Especially when he knew he wouldn't have to worry about dealing with every small family crisis that came along.

Picking up the copy of the marketing plan, Cavenaugh sat down behind the desk that had been his father's and went to work.

It was forty-five minutes later that he heard the knock on the window behind him. Glancing around he saw Starke staring back at him through the glass, hand poised to knock again. Cavenaugh leaned across and opened the window.

"What on earth are you doing out there in the garden?"

Starke's somber face twisted in a wry grimace. "Are you kidding?" He glanced furtively to the side, obviously checking to make sure the coast was clear. "This was the only way I could get to you. If she catches me out here, she'll probably skin me alive."

"Kim?"

"Yeah. She's given strict orders you aren't to be disturbed until five o'clock. No one's allowed near the study unless they

can claim a life-or-death emergency. What the heck's going on?"

"I'm working," Cavenaugh said with a grin.

Realization dawned on Starke's features. "And she's decided you need more privacy?"

"I'm an executive," Cavenaugh reminded him mockingly. "That means I get to set some rules about interruptions during working hours."

"Well, I'll be damned. The lady's going to get the household organized, isn't she? About time. I always did say you put yourself too much at the beck and call of everyone around here."

Cavenaugh glanced at his watch. "It's not five o'clock yet."

Starke arched one eyebrow. "So you want to know why I'm interrupting? Two reasons. The first is to tell you I set up a telephone call with one of those lawyers in L.A. for ten tomorrow morning."

"Thanks." Some of the quiet satisfaction left the emerald eyes as he contemplated the phone call. "What's the second reason you're standing outside my window?"

Starke grinned one of his rare grins. "I just wanted to see the results for myself."

"Results of what?"

"Your efforts to release a little tension this afternoon. Looks like it worked, Dare. You look real good. Nice and relaxed."

Cavenaugh gave him a sardonic expression and reached out to shut the window firmly in Starke's face. "Get lost, Starke, or I'll report you to Kim."

His grin wider than ever, Starke obediently disappeared into the garden.

UPSTAIRS IN HER ROOM Kimberly sat staring at the blank sheet of paper in her typewriter. She hadn't succeeded in typing a

single word for the past forty-five minutes. All her thoughts were on the man with whom she had shared the passionate interlude in the shed.

There was no point deluding herself. The white-hot fires of his desire had crystallized her feelings. If she hadn't made love with him perhaps she would have been able to go on pretending that what she felt was only a physical attraction.

Now she knew different. The incredibly, shatteringly intimate experience in the old shed had forced her to acknowledge the truth. She was falling in love with Darius Cavenaugh. No, even that statement didn't disclose the full truth. She was in love with him. Full stop.

Dazedly Kimberly stared at nothing, trying to sort through the ramifications of what had happened. She had been telling herself all along that he was the wrong kind of man for her. Yet at every turn the intimacy between them was growing deeper and more pervasive. There were times when she really did wonder if they were reading each other's minds. And the bonds that existed between them now after that scene in the shed were deeper than anything else she had ever known. She didn't understand how it could have happened so completely or so quickly. But she couldn't deny that it had happened. Love was not a matter of logic or rationality, Kimberly discovered.

With a heart full of trepidation she tried to picture her future. Cavenaugh was inseparable from this house and the wine business. If she became involved with him, she became involved with everything that went with him.

After all her years of avoiding anything that even hinted of competing loyalties and inescapable family obligations—two things that had the potential for destroying love—Kimberly wondered if she could learn to adjust to such a situation. There was no doubt that the Cavenaugh household was

a cheerful one. Cavenaugh himself might make the major decisions yet there was no denying he was also trapped by his role. Just look at the way the rest of the family felt free to impose on his time, Kimberly thought grimly. If she moved in here permanently, she'd certainly do some major reorganizing.

And then she realized just how far her thoughts had taken her. Moving in here permanently was an absolutely idiotic notion. No one, least of all Cavenaugh, had invited her to do so!

Just what had he felt after making love to her, she wondered. Some of the warm certainty that she had felt herself returned. Kimberly knew that for Cavenaugh the experience had been more than just a casual interlude. Surely she couldn't be deluding herself about something as crucial as that.

No, this growing sensation of sureness, of understanding and empathy between herself and Cavenaugh was very much for real. It was, Kimberly decided, almost like the invisible bonds she was building between Amy Solitaire and Josh Valerian.

And with that euphoric knowledge blazing in her mind, Kimberly finally managed to go back to work on *Vendetta*.

NO ONE SEEMED UPSET that evening at dinner. It was as though the entire household, including Starke, had accepted her right to rewrite the rules under which they all functioned. As promised, Cavenaugh disappeared after the meal to assist Scott with his railroad construction. Julia told Aunt Milly that she had gone over the guest list and recognized everyone on it.

"Wonderful," Aunt Milly enthused. "Ariel and I can address the envelopes in the morning. We wrote out all the in-

vitations this afternoon," she added as an aside to Kimberly who was quietly sipping tea near the fireplace.

"Will it be a large party?" Kimberly asked.

"Fairly large. We used to have parties all the time when Dare's father was alive, but since Dare has taken over we don't entertain nearly as often."

"No one felt much like having a party for quite some time after mom and dad died," Julia put in quietly. "And then I was going through that awful divorce." She smiled at Kimberly. "It's taken a while to put the family back on its feet emotionally as well as financially. You were right to step in this afternoon, you know. It made me realize how much we've all come to lean on Dare. He's been fulfilling a number of different roles for all of us during the past two years. I don't know how he does it at times."

"I think he finds it all worthwhile," Kimberly assured her gently.

"Of course he does," Aunt Milly put in with serene confidence. "After all, he's the head of the family. It's his duty to hold things together."

Kimberly said nothing but for some reason she happened to catch Starke's eye as he looked up from the newspaper he was reading across the room. She wasn't certain she could read the message in his quiet eyes but she thought she saw approval there.

"A man trying to hold things together for everyone else," Starke murmured softly, "needs a woman who can understand him and occasionally protect him from all that responsibility."

There was an embarrassed silence among the three women in front of the fire. Starke appeared oblivious to it as he went back to reading his newspaper.

"By the way," Aunt Milly announced forcefully, as if to distract everyone from Starke's comment, "Ariel said to tell you that she's ready to tell your fortune, Kim. She'll give you a reading tomorrow."

"I'll look forward to it," Kimberly replied ruefully, knowing there was no polite way to escape the promised session.

"She's very good at card reading, you know," Aunt Milly went on chattily. "She even predicted you'd be returning with Dare."

Julia laughed. "The whole household predicted that. We all know where he'd gone and why. I was the one who answered the phone that day you hung up, Kim. When I told Dare, he seemed to know immediately it was you. Why didn't you stay on the line?"

"I had a few second thoughts."

"Well, I'm certainly glad you're here now," Aunt Milly intoned. "You're going to be very good for Dare."

At ten o'clock Kimberly excused herself and climbed the stairs to her room. Cavenaugh, who had long since returned to the living room to read the paper, said a polite good-night. She felt his eyes on her as she made her way up the staircase. And in that moment she was very certain she knew exactly what was going through his head. He was remembering the passion they had shared that afternoon. Well, Kimberly, thought, so was she.

An hour later she heard the door to her room open. It was a small sound in the darkness, a sound fraught with inevitability.

Turning sleepily in bed she stared at the shadowy outline of the man who stood on the threshold. Her voice was a soft, husky whisper as she greeted him.

"Hello, Cavenaugh."

Without a word he closed the door behind him and walked across the room to stand looking down at her in darkness. Although she could not make out their emerald color in the shadows, Kimberly could see the way his eyes gleamed. She sensed the hunger in him because it was much the same as her own.

Kimberly held out her arms and he went to her with a heavy groan of need and desire.

6

CAVENAUGH LAY watching the dawn stream through an uncertain cloud cover and lazily contemplated the sense of satisfaction that permeated his body. He felt good. More than that, he felt great. He couldn't remember feeling quite like this ever in his life.

It was as though something vital had been missing in his world and now he had it in his grasp. He would be a fool to let it go. But he was also, he discovered, a very greedy and possessive man. He didn't just want to warm himself beside the fire that was Kim. He wanted that fire to engulf him.

Beside him Kimberly shifted as she began drifting awake. Her bare foot brushed against his leg and the curve of her hip was pressing his thigh with unconscious invitation. Cavenaugh told himself it was probably adolescent or, at the very least, ungentlemanly to wake up in a state of semiarousal but here he was, doing exactly that. And all because of the woman beside him.

With the practical approach of his sex, Cavenaugh had decided to stop trying to figure out why this particular woman exercised such power over him. He wanted her; he needed her. Having possessed her, it was now impossible to even think about the possibility of giving her up.

And he could make her want him. That thought brought a savage satisfaction. She was like hot, flowing amber in his arms, clinging to him as she surrendered to the intimate demands of his body and her own. Yet he lost himself in her even

at the moment when he claimed her most completely. It was a paradox which, being male, he decided not to waste time analyzing. It was the way things were and he was content to accept the situation. He was old enough and intelligent enough to realize that a relationship such as this came along once in a lifetime if a man was very, very lucky. Only a fool would question it or analyze it to death.

It was far more crucial to spend his time assessing the threats to the relationship. And when it came to dealing with threats, Cavenaugh was more than willing to spend time analyzing, evaluating and ultimately neutralizing them. He had already taken steps to protect Kimberly from the strange hints of physical menace that had cropped up around her. Certainly that battle was the most urgent one.

But there were other threats of a more subtle nature and therefore more difficult for a man to analyze and defeat. Number one on the list was the wariness she had of families and the responsibilities and pressures that went with them. He had to find a way to show her that the past could not be allowed to dictate how she lived and loved in the present. Once he had shown her that her grandparents were not the personification of callous, selfish arrogance she had always thought them to be, he could remove a large measure of her distrust of men who had family loyalties.

And then there was that damned Josh Valerian to deal with.

Cavenaugh felt his body harden into full arousal as Kimberly stirred in his arms. He watched her face as her lashes fluttered open and he smiled slightly. The momentary confusion in her gaze amused him. It also pleased him.

"You're not accustomed to waking up beside a man, are you?" he murmured. He turned on his side, hooking a hair-roughened thigh over her legs. "Better get used to it. There are going to be a lot more mornings like this one." He bent

his head to drop a small, possessive kiss on her warm shoulder.

"Are there?" she asked, looking up at him with unreadable mysteries in her eyes.

"Definitely." He let his palm glide luxuriously upward until it covered her breast, and the morning hunger in him escalated. "Most definitely," he repeated, aware that his voice had roughened. "What's more, I don't intend to share them with that other man."

She blinked in sleepy astonishment. "What other man?"

"Valerian."

"Josh Valerian?"

"Umm." He pushed his knee between her silky thighs and tasted the dark grape that tipped her breast. "I've been thinking about him."

"Come to any earthshaking conclusions?" she asked uncertainly.

"Only the obvious. I think the fastest, most effective way of getting one man out of your head is to keep reminding you that another, namely me, now possesses your body." He pushed himself forward until his manhood was at the soft gate of her femininity.

"Cavenaugh, are you joking?"

He smiled a little grimly as he met her questioning gaze. "What do you think?"

The tip of her tongue touched the corner of her mouth as she tried to assess just how serious he was. Cavenaugh didn't mind this evidence of female wariness. It meant she was focusing on him, not some illusion of a perfect man.

"I...I don't think you are joking."

Slowly he thrust into her, taking his time so that he could experience every centimeter of her clinging, velvety core. She grew hot and damp around him and the soft little gasp at the back of her throat sent ripples of satisfaction through him.

"You're right," he growled as she instinctively lifted herself against his loins. "I'm not joking. You see how well we're communicating these days?"

"Cavenaugh, you can be an arrogant beast at times," she managed as her body warmed and tightened beneath him. Her fingers were splayed on his shoulders and her legs twisted around his in growing demand.

"But I'm real. And you need a real man, not some fictional wimp who will never be able to hold you like this or make you come alive in his arms."

"Josh is not a wimp!"

"He's no good to you right now, is he? Right now you need *me*. Admit it," Cavenaugh rasped as the delicious tension built between them. "Tell me you need me!"

"I need you, Cavenaugh. Please. Now. All of you. *Ah, Cavenaugh!*"

A long time later Kimberly lay in bed and watched Cavenaugh pull on his jeans and thrust his arms into his shirt. He didn't bother to do up the buttons. As he had explained, he was only going to duck back across the hall to his bedroom.

"Not that there's any hope the entire household won't know where I spent the night," he growled humorously as he came to stand beside the bed. "But it might be easier for you to go down to breakfast if you can pretend that we observed the proprieties."

"That's very, uh, considerate of you," she said demurely, thankful for his understanding of just how awkward this sort of situation could be for a woman.

His emerald eyes gleamed with buried fire. "Lady, if I was only considering myself, I'd move you into my room today and say the hell with the proprieties. But I'm not totally insensitive. I also realize that I'm supposed to be protecting you, not taking advantage of you." He bent over the bed, plant-

ing a hand on either side of her body. "So I'm going to try very hard to behave myself until we get things sorted out between us. If that's the way you want me to behave, I suggest you don't tempt me too far."

"If you come to my room again in the middle of the night I'll have no one but myself to blame?" she taunted wryly.

"Right." He kissed her forehead and then straightened. "See you at breakfast." With a proprietary slap on her hip, Cavenaugh turned and strode out the door.

Kimberly watched him go, half amused, half enthralled by the self-assured, unabashedly male arrogance in him. He was feeling very good this morning, she decided. Men were probably at their most dangerous when they felt that good. On the other hand, it gave her an undeniable pleasure to know she was the cause of his wholly masculine satisfaction.

ARIEL'S CARD READING that morning was far from being a private affair. She arrived complete with a new burgundy turban for the occasion and a wonderfully clashing flowered dress in pea green. By the time she was ready to deal the deck of ordinary playing cards into a series of numbered squares, Julia, Mrs. Lawson and Aunt Milly were gathered around. Good-naturedly Kimberly sat in front of the inlaid table Ariel was using and waited to have her fortune told.

"She's really quite good," Julia confided cheerfully. "A few months ago she predicted Mark and I would become engaged and that's exactly what happened."

Aunt Milly nodded enthusiastically. "And she predicted I'd get sick at the little restaurant in Mexico last summer. She was right."

"Lots of people get ill eating unfamiliar food in foreign countries," Kimberly felt obliged to point out. "And after seeing Mark and Julia together, I think I could have predicted an engagement, too."

Julia laughed. "Don't ruin it all by being too analytical."

"Julia's absolutely right," Ariel declared roundly as she shuffled the cards. "You'll spoil all the fun if you start analyzing the whole thing."

"Okay, okay, I promise not to intellectualize about it."

"Have you ever had your fortune told?" Ariel asked.

"Nope."

"Well, once the cards are dealt they all have a relationship to one another in addition to their own independent meanings. It can get very complex. Each of these squares stands for a certain aspect of life. This square concerns prosperity. That one deals with projects you might be thinking of undertaking and that one is your love life."

"I can't wait to see what card turns up on that square," Julia said with a chuckle.

"As if we don't know," Mrs. Lawson put in with bland emphasis.

"Ready?" Ariel asked lightly as she began to deal the cards into the squares.

"Ready," Kimberly agreed in resignation.

Ariel became unexpectedly serious as she dealt the cards. When she began to turn them over and study them she seemed to become completely involved with the task.

"Excellent," Ariel murmured as she turned over a heart on the square representing prosperity. "You will enjoy success in your work. Money is no problem for you. This next square represents changes in your life. Here you have a spade. Hmmm. That's not so good. A spade indicates a change for the worse. Perhaps actual danger. However, it appears to be mitigated by the King of Hearts next to it in the square for happiness."

The card reading continued, largely a vague and ambivalent process as far as Kimberly could determine. Whenever a card representing misfortune turned up, Ariel seemed

to find one next to it that lessened or canceled out the first. There were good cards for such things as health, ambition, money and travel.

"A recent trip may lead to major changes in your life," Ariel noted as she turned over the card on the travel square.

Kimberly resisted the impulse to say "no kidding." But she caught Julia's eye and found the other woman grinning at her.

"And now we come to your love life," Ariel finally declared grandly. Her listeners leaned forward expectantly. Kimberly felt a wave of embarrassment and wondered if all the others were aware of how she had spent the night. She watched as Ariel turned over a King of Clubs.

"Hmm," the older woman said, eyeing the card. "He'll be faithful, at least."

"Well?" Kimberly pressured. "Is that all it indicates?"

"Not quite. It implies that although you can trust him implicitly, he will not be without faults."

"What man is?" Julia asked rhetorically.

"In fact," Ariel went on as she turned up another club, "he might prove quite infuriating at times."

"As Julia said," Mrs. Lawson interrupted, "what man isn't?"

Ariel bent over the cards, turning up others in the vicinity of the "lover" square. "There is more than that here," she said slowly. "There is danger again. You will know fear, Kim."

"Fear? Of what?"

Ariel ignored the question and turned up a diamond. "There is much pain from fraud and deceit."

"Probably refers to some of the royalty statements I've had from various and assorted publishers. Forget that one. Tell me what I'm supposed to be afraid of."

Ariel shook her head slowly. "It is difficult to say, Kim. I see darkness. Darkness and silver."

Kimberly froze as an image of the dark, cowled figure holding the silver dagger leaped into her head. "A man?" Her mouth suddenly felt quite dry.

"Perhaps, perhaps not." Ariel frowned and then turned over the next card. She gave a few more vague analyses and then sat back, collecting all the cards into a neat pile.

"Is that the end of it?" Aunt Milly asked cheerfully.

"That's it," Ariel said.

"Well, Kim, it sounds as though you'd better be wary of a dark, dangerous lover with silver in his hair," Julia commented, laughing.

"But who can be trusted," Aunt Milly put in firmly.

"Sounds to me like someone we all know very well," Mrs. Lawson declared happily.

"Yes, well, it's been fun, Ariel," Kimberly said, getting decisively to her feet. "Now, if you'll all excuse me, I really must get back to work. That dark, dangerous man sounds like the villain in my latest novel. I'd better go see how he's getting along."

The card reading party broke up as Julia and Mrs. Lawson went back to their own projects. Kimberly was halfway out the door of the sitting room they had all been using when Ariel stopped her with a small, fluttery hand on her arm. Kimberly was astonished by the intent look in the older woman's eyes.

"The cards should not be dismissed lightly, Kim. They are not always simply a parlor trick."

Kimberly smiled gently. "I'll remember that, Ariel. Thanks. Oh, by the way, how is the party planning going?"

"Wonderfully," Aunt Milly enthused. "The invitations go out today. The party is scheduled for this coming Saturday night."

"Rather short notice for everyone, isn't it?"

"Oh, we phoned everyone this morning to tell them about it. The invitations are just a formality," Ariel explained complacently, removing her hand from Kimberly's arm. "As it turns out, Saturday is an especially propitious time for the affair. Run along dear. Milly and I are going to work on the menu today."

Aunt Milly nodded in agreement. "We want everything just right for this particular event."

"What's so special about this party?" Kimberly asked unwisely.

Aunt Milly looked at her in amused astonishment. "Why, because you'll be there, of course. Now do as Ariel says and run along, dear."

Kimberly didn't need any urging. She was far enough behind in *Vendetta* as it was.

SHORTLY AFTER TEN O'CLOCK on Saturday evening Cavenaugh glanced across the crowded living room and managed to catch a glimpse of Kimberly. He considered himself lucky. It had been difficult keeping track of her tonight. From the moment the guests had begun arriving she had been the focal point of one after the other.

The fact that some of the people in the crowd had read her books certainly accounted for some of the attention she was receiving, but Cavenaugh was aware there was a lot more involved. The details of the kidnapping had been in the local papers, and Julia had seen to it that everyone knew Kimberly was the woman who had rescued Scott. In addition, everyone in the Cavenaugh household was treating Kim virtually as a member of the family.

That last undeniable fact was being interpreted by the vast majority of the guests to mean that Kim was due shortly to become a member of the family. In the past half hour Cav-

enaugh had overheard at least three clusters of people discussing when the marriage would be announced.

He had done nothing to squelch the speculation. Just as he had done nothing to stem the gossip that had arisen among his employees after he'd taken Kim on a tour of the wine-making facilities earlier this week.

By now Cavenaugh was fairly certain that Kimberly herself had realized just how everyone was viewing her presence. She looked up as he glanced across the room and the wariness was back in her eyes. For an instant their gazes clashed, and then she took a long sip from the glass of Cavenaugh wine she was drinking and went back to her discussion with a group of local wine makers. They seemed enthralled with whatever she was saying.

Cavenaugh retreated to the edge of the crowd and helped himself to another glass of wine. Then he stood quietly and watched Kimberly for a while longer. Other than the familiar wariness in her eyes, she looked good tonight, he thought, wryly aware of a fierce sense of possessiveness.

Kimberly and Julia had gone shopping yesterday under Starke's supervision. They had returned with the turquoise and yellow silk gown Kimberly wore tonight. Tiny, strappy turquoise sandals and a small strand of gold at her throat constituted the remainder of the outfit. Cavenaugh had wanted to pick up the tab for the obviously expensive dress but had prudently refrained from making the offer. Something told him that Kim would be furious. She had a fierce pride that he respected, even if it did annoy him at times.

He studied her amber hair, which was caught high on her head in a deceptively careless cascade of curls. The thought of tearing the concoction apart with his fingers later on elicited a now-familiar, heavy ache in his body. Deliberately he put the image out of his mind. There were matters that had

to be cleared up before he took Kim back to bed. Or so he kept telling himself.

He swallowed some more of his excellent Merlot wine and let himself fantasize about what it would be like to be able to take Kimberly up to bed after everyone left tonight. He had been savagely strict with himself following the one night he had spent with her. There was still too much that lay unsettled between them. The talk with the lawyer in L.A. had made that clear.

Cavenaugh suspected that Kimberly merely assumed he was staying away from her bed out of a sense of gentlemanly behavior. He had allowed her to believe that, because he hadn't yet figured out how to tell her there was much more involved. It was becoming increasingly difficult to keep his hands off her. Soon, he promised himself, he would have it all sorted out and Kimberly would be free of her past. He was letting himself speculate on the future when Starke moved quietly up beside him.

"She's doing all right," Starke observed, his gaze on Kimberly.

"Especially for someone who's accustomed to being a loner," Cavenaugh agreed.

Starke shrugged. "Everyone's alone in some ways."

"Why is it you always get philosophical after a couple of whiskies, Starke?"

"Brings out the intellectual side of my nature."

"I see."

"She's good for you, Dare. I like her."

Cavenaugh's mouth twisted faintly. "Knowing how selective you are about people, that's saying something. As it happens, I agree with you."

Starke's eyes were on Kimberly. "So when are you going to get this other thing out of the way so you'll be free to stop playing games?"

"I've arranged the meeting for the day after tomorrow."

"On neutral grounds?"

Cavenaugh nodded. "The lobby of a San Francisco hotel."

"You're sure this is the right way to go about it?"

"You got a better idea?" Cavenaugh challenged grimly.

Starke sighed. "No."

"I want her free of the past, Starke. The only way to do that is to confront it. Besides, they'll hound her until they get to her. They're desperate. Better to arrange the meeting on our terms rather than theirs."

"You're just going to spring the whole thing on Kim?"

"She'll never agree to a meeting with her grandparents."

"I don't know, Dare. Women don't like surprises."

"Kim will understand why I did it. When it's all over she'll see it was the only way."

Across the room Kim managed to excuse herself from the cluster of people around her and drifted out onto the patio. It was nippy out there, but after the crowded, overheated environment of the party it was a relief to her.

She was experiencing that trapped sensation again. There was no doubt about what people were thinking when they looked at her. They were seeing her as the new Cavenaugh bride, and none of the Cavenaughs was doing anything to discourage the assumption. Not even Darius Cavenaugh.

What was going on in his head tonight, Kimberly wondered as she walked to the edge of the patio. There were times when she thought she could tell exactly what he was thinking. But there were other occasions when he remained unfathomable.

He hadn't been back to her room since that one night they had spent together. For the hundredth time Kimberly considered that fact. Was he truly playing the gentleman or was there more to it? Perhaps he hadn't found her as physically satisfying as she had found him.

Kimberly's fingers closed tightly around an awning pole and she stood looking out in the darkness. Before her was a section of shadowy garden, and beyond that the rock wall she had been forbidden to pass. In the distance the building that held the fermentation tanks loomed in the darkness. The acres of grapes stretched out on all sides, gliding over gentle hills beneath a pale moon. It was a lovely, prosperous, peaceful setting. Kimberly wondered how it differed from the kind of life-style Cavenaugh had lived before he had returned home.

"Isn't it a little cold out here, Kim?"

She whirled at the sound of Starke's familiar, gravelly voice and smiled at him. She had decided she liked this strange, aloof man, even though she couldn't quite figure him out.

"I needed some fresh air. I'll come back inside in a few minutes," she told him. "Having a good time, Starke?"

"I'm not much for cocktail parties," he murmured blandly.

"Neither am I. Is Cavenaugh?"

"There's a lot you don't know about him yet, isn't there?"

Surprised by the question, Kimberly shook her head. "Sometimes I think I know him. Other times..." She let the sentence drift off into the darkness.

"He feels the same way about you, I think. Human nature."

Kimberly slid him an amused glance. "You're a student of human nature?"

Starke held up the glass in his hand. "It's the whiskey. Brings out my intellectual qualities, as I was just explaining to Cavenaugh."

"Fascinating. What other observations have you got on the subject?"

"Of you and Cavenaugh? Just the obvious, I guess."

"Which is?"

"That you're right for each other," Starke explained. "He needs you, Kim."

"I don't know, Starke," she replied gently. "He has so many other things and people in his life—the winery, his duty to his family. So much. Why would he need me?"

"Because you can keep those things from taking over his whole life. You can give him a separate world where he can relax and be alone with someone who puts him first."

She stirred uneasily. "Maybe that's what I want, too, Starke. Someone who can put me first in his life."

"You don't think Cavenaugh can do that?"

"How can any man in his position do that?" she asked helplessly.

"You still don't know him very well. Give him a chance, Kim. And—" Starke hesitated and then finished bluntly "—try not to be too hard on him on the occasions when you don't understand him completely. He's only a man."

Kim's lips lifted in a teasing smile. "So are you. Are you sure you're qualified to explain the species to me?"

Starke took a long swallow of whiskey. "Probably not, but I guess I felt obliged to try."

Instantly Kim softened. "You're very loyal to Cavenaugh, aren't you?"

"He saved my life a long time ago. Later on I was able to return the favor. That sort of thing builds a certain bond between two people."

"How did he save your life?" Kim demanded with a slight frown.

"It's not important now," Starke said, shifting with an uneasiness that told Kim it was a subject he wished he hadn't brought up for discussion. "I had gotten myself into a messy situation in the Middle East. I was trying to make contact with someone and got caught in the middle of a riot. Cavenaugh had also gotten trapped on the street. All hell broke out and, being the nearest Americans in the vicinity, we got mistaken for devils by the local crowd. I found myself up

against a wall, literally. And then Dare arrived. He knew someone in the neighborhood with whom he'd done business. That association gave him enough clout to get me free from the mob. By the time everyone figured out that his connections shouldn't be allowed to stand in the way of a little mob vengeance, we were clear. Dare used his contacts to pull some strings and got us both out of the country about two steps ahead of the full-scale war that broke out a day later."

Kimberly drew a deep breath. "I had no idea the import-export business could be so, uh, volatile."

"It had its moments," Starke reflected, lifting his glass again. He stared into the whiskey for a few seconds, as if seeing something Kimberly couldn't. "Especially the way Dare ran things."

Kimberly couldn't be sure she'd heard those last few words. Her voice sharpened. "When did you save his life, Starke?" It occurred to her that there was more to this man than met the eye. His laconic speech and quiet mannerisms belied the harshness of his appearance.

He looked at her and blinked owlishly. "There was a knife fight in some alley in Hong Kong. Dare was trying to deal with three punks who had waylaid him outside his hotel. I was on my way to see him and found it all going down in the alley a block from the hotel. I'm pretty good with a knife," Starke explained blandly.

Kimberly shivered. "Oh."

Starke's brows bunched together in a heavy line. "Promise me you won't tell Dare I told you all this, okay? He'd have my head if he thought I was out here scaring you to death with those kind of stories."

"Why are you scaring me to death with those tales, Starke?" Kimberly asked perceptively.

"I guess I just want you to understand that there's a lot more to Dare than may seem obvious by looking at Cavenaugh Vineyards."

"I know that, Starke," Kimberly said gently.

Starke looked suddenly relieved. "Sure you do. If you didn't, you wouldn't love him, would you?"

Kimberly recoiled, a protest rising automatically to her lips. Her love was still a private, personal matter at this point. She had not dreamed that others knew of it. But before she could find the words to make Starke understand that it was much too soon to make such statements, he was slipping out of his jacket and handing it to her.

"Here," he said gruffly. "If you're going to stay out here awhile, you'd better put this on." Then he turned and strode back into the house.

With a sigh, Kimberly walked off the patio and into the garden. She really didn't want to go back into the house just yet. The thought of all those people looking at her, speculating on her relationship with Cavenaugh, perhaps coming to the same conclusion Starke had, was suddenly overwhelming. She needed some time alone.

Not that she would be able to stay out here very long. Julia, Aunt Milly, Ariel, Mrs. Lawson or even Cavenaugh or Starke was likely to miss her and start looking for her. So many people who would concern themselves over her. She wasn't accustomed to it. Kimberly glanced up as she wandered into the garden. The light in Scott's room was finally turned off. He had been sent to bed a couple of hours ago, but only under protest. It had been his future father, Mark, who had taken on the task of putting Scott to bed. Kimberly had seen the warmth in Julia's eyes as she watched her fiancé handle the boy.

At the edge of the garden Kimberly came to a halt again and stood staring at the dark winery facility several yards

beyond the rock wall. A few outside lights illuminated the beautiful grounds in front of the building where tourists gathered during the days. The rear of the large structure was shrouded in darkness.

This was as far as she ought to go. In another few feet she would be crossing the low, rambling rock wall. Doing that would set off the alarms, which in turn would certainly put a damper on the Cavenaugh party tonight, she thought humorously. Aunt Milly and Ariel would never forgive her.

That was assuming, of course, that Starke hadn't had a little too much whiskey tonight and was able to realize an alarm had been triggered.

As for Cavenaugh's reaction, he was more likely to turn her over his knee than make love to her if she pulled that stunt again. Once was forgivable. Disobeying orders a second time probably wouldn't go down well with the lord and master of Cavenaugh Vineyards.

With a wry smile at the thought, Kimberly reluctantly turned to walk back up through the garden to the patio and into the noisy, well-lit house.

The statue-still figure in a cowled robe was waiting for her, blocking the path through the garden.

Kimberly was so stunned by the dark apparition that for a timeless moment she couldn't even scream. Frozen in the moonlight the two stared at each other and then the robed figure raised both hands, revealing the ornate silver dagger he held.

Kimberly did scream then but it was the kind of scream one had in a nightmare, a choked soundless cry that reached no one. Fear stifled the first attempt and before she could make another, the cowled creature took a menacing step forward.

Kimberly got the scream past her lips this time but even as it echoed through the night she told herself that no one would

hear it over the noise of the party. She was at the rear of the garden, much too far from the safety of the house.

The dagger flashed in the watery moonlight and the movement freed her. She picked up the skirts of her silk gown and began to run, attempting to dodge around the hooded threat that stood so obscenely in the beautiful garden.

The creature in the robe shifted position, easily blocking her path. He held the advantage. There was no way she could get past him and back to the house. When he moved toward her again, Kimberly did the only thing she could do; she fled out of the garden toward the low rock wall.

Risking a glance over her shoulder she saw the cowled figure pursuing. He seemed to be having some trouble managing the bulky skirts of his robe. Silver from the wicked blade of the dagger flashed in the darkness and memories of Ariel's card reading chilled Kimberly even more than she already was. As she ran Starke's jacket slipped from her shoulders. It landed on the rambling rock wall as Kimberly scrambled over the top.

Her only hope was that the discreet alarms in the house had been triggered and that Starke would not be too deep into his whiskey to know it.

Panicked, Kimberly fled for her life toward the only possible protection she could imagine, the winery building. If she could reach it far enough ahead of her pursuer perhaps she would be able to get inside and lock a door behind her.

The turquoise sandals proved treacherous on the sandy path that led through the vineyards. Several times she stumbled and nearly fell, but sheer blind fear drove her on toward the looming building.

The cowled figure seemed to be having more trouble running than she was in the heavy robes he wore, and that gave Kimberly hope. Perhaps the flowing garment would hinder his movements enough so that she could get inside the build-

ing before he did. Once inside there were phones she could use to call the main house. She had seen them several days earlier when Cavenaugh had taken her on a tour of the production facilities.

Her breath was like fire in her lungs as she fled toward the rear entrance of the building. Behind her she could hear the crunch of pursuing footsteps. For some insane reason the menacing sound came almost as a relief. Surely only a real human being would make such a sound as he ran. At least she was not being pursued by a specter. Out here alone in the darkness it would've been easy to believe she was dealing with a supernatural threat.

Gasping for breath, her heart thudding from fear and exertion, Kimberly slammed to a halt in front of the door at the rear of the building. She didn't even hesitate. She'd decided what she would do while she was still several yards away.

Whipping off one of the turquoise sandals, Kimberly shattered the door's window. She had her hand inside, reaching to unlock it before the glass had even struck the floor.

A lacerating pain sliced into her arm but she ignored it. The door opened and she was inside, slamming it shut behind her.

In the hall all was in darkness. Kimberly was forced to slow to a walk. Behind her she heard the door open and close again. Then there was silence. The utter darkness must be as much a burden to her pursuer as it was to her.

But Kimberly had one advantage. She knew where she was in the building. With any luck the man with the knife would be forced to wander aimlessly, trying to follow her by sound alone.

Taking off her other sandal so that she could move as silently as possible, Kimberly groped her way carefully down

the hall toward the huge, high-ceilinged room that held the fermentation tanks and the rows of casks used to age the wine.

7

THE GENTLE HUM of machinery and the unique, sharp smell of wine in the making greeted Kimberly as she pushed open the door of the huge room. Towering stainless-steel tanks and several rows of wooden vats loomed around her. They made her think of dinosaurs dozing in the muted darkness. At the far end of the room near a short staircase a dull light gleamed. Otherwise all was in shadow.

For an instant Kimberly hesitated. The room that she thought might promise some shelter seemed suddenly to be filled with giant, alien machines that were half alive. No, she thought hysterically, it wasn't the tanks that were alive, it was the wine inside them. Hadn't Cavenaugh explained that to her on the tour? The process of fermentation and aging was a living process, a process of constant evolution and change. The vats and tanks around her were the wombs that nurtured the wine while it developed and matured.

She listened for sounds behind her and heard nothing. Then, slipping into the shadowy room, Kimberly darted to the left. She would weave a path through the tanks, using them for cover while she made her way toward the dimly lit stairs at the far end.

Cavenaugh, help me. Hurry. For God's sake, hurry.

Halfway toward her goal, unable to hear sounds of pursuit above the hum of the tanks, Kimberly's bare foot came down in a puddle of cold liquid. She gasped aloud and then

immediately bit down on her lip, cursing silently. With any luck her pursuer hadn't heard her faint, startled exclamation.

She felt her way along the darkest side of the room, staying behind the last row of tanks. While the sound of working machinery was a cover for her own progress, it also covered the approach of the creature in the robes. The room at the top of the stairs seemed miles away instead of only a few feet. She had to reach it. It was the tasting room, the last stop on a tour. In it lay a telephone. There was also a fire alarm, Kimberly recalled vaguely. She would break the glass cover on it. That should summon help in a hurry.

But first she had to get through the jungle of tanks.

Every soft sound behind her was a new source of terror. Kimberly kept glancing back over her shoulder, expecting to see the silver dagger plunging toward her at any second.

Arriving at the last tank in the row, Kimberly eyed the stairs with trepidation. To reach them she would have to make a dash out into the open and the small light on the wall would illuminate her quite clearly. She had no reason to think that the door at the top would be locked, but if it were she would be trapped at the top of the stairs.

Cavenaugh, where are you? I need you.

There was no point delaying the inevitable. Her only chance was to reach the tasting room and barricade herself inside while she phoned for help. Collecting her skirts in one hand, Kimberly darted out from behind the shelter of the last tank and ran for the door at the top of the stairs.

With the primitive instinct of the hunted, she knew it was too late. There wasn't going to be enough time. The creature was behind her. He must have guessed her goal.

Kimberly's hands were on the doorknob, twisting frantically when she glanced over her shoulder and saw him.

The dagger was in his fist as the man in the robes raced toward her down the center aisle between the tanks. He was

only a few paces behind. No time, she thought wildly as the door obediently opened inward. There was no time.

Kimberly slammed the door behind her but her pursuer struck it with such force that it crashed back against the wall. She whirled and fled behind the ornate bar of the tasting room. The pale glow from the light at the top of the stairs filtered into the dark room, illuminating the rows of glasses and the neatly stored bottles of Cavenaugh wine.

Without even thinking clearly about what she intended to do, Kimberly grabbed the nearest bottle. It didn't seem like much against a silver dagger but it was all that was available. Grasping the neck of the bottle as though it were a club she swung the end against the highly polished edge of the bar. Then she wondered half-hysterically if this sort of thing only worked in vintage westerns.

Glass shattered. Wine gushed to the floor, spilling over her bare feet. Kimberly was left holding a jagged, crystal blade.

At the open end of the bar the hooded figure halted, silver dagger raised. He was only steps away and for the first time Kimberly could see the dark gleam of human eyes beneath the shrouding cowl. The dim light glinted off the broken wine bottle in her hand as she held it in front of her.

"Cavenaugh will kill you if you so much as touch me," she bit out.

"Your friend Cavenaugh can go to hell."

The voice was low and harsh and it had the sound of city streets in it. It didn't sound at all supernatural or sepulchral. She was facing a street punk, not a warlock, Kimberly thought wildly.

"He'll see you there first. I can promise you that much."

"I'll worry about him later. You're my job for tonight."

He rushed her then, holding the dagger now like a fighting blade, not a sacrificial one. Coming in low and fast, the man

in the robe covered the few steps separating him from his victim with a frightening ferocity.

"Cavenaugh!"

Kimberly screamed the name as she tried to sidestep the attacker's rush. There was so little room to maneuver here behind the bar. But the punk must have had some respect for the jagged bottle in her hand because when she instinctively lashed out at him with it, he faded to the side.

Kimberly swept past him, toward the open end of the bar. He whirled, slashing the dagger through the air in a violent arc.

Kimberly picked up another bottle, still holding on to her first weapon. She hurled the full wine bottle toward the man who, in turn, ducked. The glass cracked on the counter behind him and liquid poured onto the floor.

"You bitch!"

Kimberly was throwing every bottle she could get her hands on now and more than one of them found its target. The bulky robes seemed to provide protection, however, and none of the blows proved devastating.

With a roar of rage, her attacker sprang forward, intending to throw himself into one final rush that would plunge the dagger deeply into her body.

Kimberly turned to run and then heard the scream of fury behind her as the robed figure slipped on the wine-slick floor. She heard the thud as he fell to the tile, and without stopping to think, Kimberly picked up one more bottle of wine.

She brought it down on the back of the cowled head with every ounce of force she possessed.

"Kim!"

Cavenaugh came through the door, a dark lethal shadow in his evening clothes. The glint of metal caught Kimberly's eye as she stood over her victim. Cavenaugh held a gun in his

hand. Starke was right behind him, grabbing for the light switch on the wall.

Cavenaugh reached her as the lights came on, yanking her away from her prone attacker. She felt the taut violence in him as his hand closed over her shoulder. Then he was bending down beside her victim, turning him over to feel for a pulse beneath the heavy hood. Starke stood tensely, waiting for the verdict. He, too, was armed. Both men, she thought dazedly, looked very comfortable with a gun in their hands.

Cavenaugh straightened slowly, shoving his weapon out of sight beneath his elegant evening jacket.

"He's out," Cavenaugh growled. His hard, emerald eyes raked Kim from her head to her bare feet. "She knocked him unconscious."

"Smells like it took half a case of wine to do it," Starke commented as he examined the situation. "Looks like it took half a case, too. We've got a regular swimming pool in here."

"I didn't know neatness counted," Kimberly managed, her stunned eyes never leaving Cavenaugh's.

"Lady," Cavenaugh grated harshly, "the only thing that counts in a situation like this is who's still standing when it's all over. My God, woman, you've taken ten years off my life tonight! Are you all right?"

She nodded mutely, unable to move. Still clutching the jagged blade she had created from the first bottle, Kimberly faced him. Then, with a groan of savage relief, Cavenaugh reached for her. She dropped the bottle and fell into his arms.

"You're bleeding! If that bastard..."

"It's all right. I just cut myself a little on the glass in the door. Oh, Cavenaugh, I thought you and Starke would never get here," she whispered from the safety of his hold.

"Doesn't look like you needed us too badly," Starke said. "You seem to have handled things pretty well on your own.

The next time we find ourselves in a barroom brawl, Dare, we'll have to make sure she's along to back us up."

"She'll be there if that's where I happen to be. I'm never going to let her out of my sight—"

"How did you find me?" she interrupted hastily. There was still a fierce tension flowing in him. She could feel it as he held her close.

"Starke's beeper went off when you crossed the wall. We excused ourselves to go check the control panel, thinking the alarm must have been set off by an animal. Somewhere along the line we noticed that you were nowhere to be found," Cavenaugh explained. Very gently he disengaged himself from her tight hold and turned the water on in the small sink. Then he thrust her bleeding arm under the flowing tap.

"I told Dare I'd last seen you on the patio," Starke put in calmly, bending down to yank back the hood of the attacker. Beneath the mysterious cowl was the face of a dark haired young man in his early twenties.

"Neither of us could believe you'd be stupid enough to actually take a midnight stroll over the wall, of course," Cavenaugh went on.

"I didn't exactly go strolling over that damned wall, you know. I was in the garden, about to start back to the house when this turkey got in the way. I knew I couldn't run past him. So I tried to run away from him, hoping that when we went over the wall, the alarm would go off. Ouch. Cavenaugh, that hurts."

He ignored her and slapped a bar napkin over the small wound. "We found Starke's jacket and knew it was you and not some deer who had triggered things. But we couldn't figure out where you'd gone at that point. When you broke into the winery you tripped another alarm, though, which pinpointed your location. We were right behind you. And then we started hearing all those bottles you were throwing around

with such cheerful abandon." Cavenaugh's mouth twisted wryly. "Some of my best Cabernet Sauvignon, by the way. I may send you a bill."

"Of all the nerve!"

"On second thought," Cavenaugh said consideringly, "I think I'll just take it out of your sweet hide." He released her to bend over the young man in the robes. Fumbling beneath the flowing garment he retrieved the silver dagger. "Call the cops, Starke. And see if you can get hold of that Detective Cranston we've been working with."

"Right." Starke picked up the phone and dialed.

IT WAS SEVERAL HOURS LATER, nearly two in the morning, before Kimberly finally got to bed. Julia and Aunt Milly and Ariel had fussed over her while Mrs. Lawson fixed a soothing herbal tea according to Ariel's directions. Aroused by the hubbub, Scott had wandered sleepily downstairs to see what was going on. Cavenaugh and Starke dealt with the police, while concerned neighbors and guests asked countless questions of one another and of Kimberly.

"Maybe you'll be able to work this into one of your plots," Mark Taylor said lightly at one point.

"Mark!" Julia scolded. "Don't joke like that."

But ultimately the guests and the authorities took their leave. The man in the monk's robes was thrust into the back of a patrol car and taken away, too. He had revived by then but to the best of anyone's knowledge he hadn't said a single word.

Alone at last, aware of her own exhaustion but feeling too restless and wound up to sleep, Kimberly slipped into her T-shirt and crawled into bed. She lay in the darkness and reran the entire episode over and over in her mind. It seemed to her that it would be a long time before she could get the image of that raised dagger out of her head. Every time she closed her

eyes it was there, poised and ready to strike. Her body seemed periodically racked by fine shivers. It was just reaction, she knew, but she couldn't seem to control it.

She was lying on her side, staring out the window when her bedroom door opened softly and then closed again. Kimberly knew who had entered the room without having to see his face.

"Cavenaugh?"

"I told you I wasn't going to let you out of my sight again."

She heard him undressing in the darkness and she turned slowly to meet his shadowed gaze. Her amber hair was spilled around her on the pillow, and the sheet was pulled taut across her breasts. Cavenaugh's possessive eyes moved over her as he slipped off his ruffled evening shirt.

"What about the proprieties? What about the, uh, awkwardness of my position as a guest in your household? What about your concern for my potential embarrassment?" She tried to make the words light and teasing, but the truth was she was incredibly glad to have him here and she knew it must have shown in her voice.

"What about moving over?" he countered as he stepped out of the last of his clothes. "I may not have mentioned it the last time I slept here, but I happen to prefer the left side of the bed."

"I'll keep that in mind." Obediently she moved to the opposite side. But the forced lightness in her words ended as he got into bed beside her. With a small cry she went to him, clinging to his reassuring warmth and strength. "Ah, Cavenaugh, I was so scared tonight."

"I know how it feels, sweetheart," he rasped thickly. "Believe me, I know how it feels. God, you were brave." He stroked her hair, twining his legs with hers. "You looked like a warrior queen when I came through the door. I wanted to kill that punk on the floor. If you hadn't already knocked him

out, I probably would have. It was too close, Kim. Much too close for my peace of mind. That's why I couldn't let you stay alone tonight."

"I would have had nightmares," she confessed.

"You think I wouldn't have had them, too? That little scene in the tasting room is going to haunt me for a long time." He continued to stroke her, not with passion but with long, soothing motions.

"I can't seem to calm down," Kimberly whispered tightly. "All my nerves feel as though they've been plugged into an electric outlet."

"It's reaction, honey, just reaction. Takes a while for your system to settle down after something that traumatic."

"You seem to understand."

"I do."

She thought about the way he had come through the door with the gun in his hand. "You've been through this kind of scene before," she said softly.

"No, never quite like this," Cavenaugh denied flatly. "I've never walked into a room and found my woman facing an armed punk."

"You didn't exactly 'walk' into the tasting room. You and Starke came through that door like the U.S. Marines."

His arms tightened around her and Kimberly snuggled gratefully into his embrace. Inside she savored the words "my woman."

"Don't ever do that to me again, Kim," Cavenaugh ordered harshly.

"Believe me, I didn't set out to do it to you tonight! Or to myself."

"You shouldn't have gone out into the garden alone."

Kimberly lifted her head. "Cavenaugh," she protested. "No one ever said anything about not going out onto the patio or

into the garden. That electronically rigged rock wall was the only barrier!"

He groaned, pushing her head back down on his shoulder. "Technically, you're right. What I'm really trying to say is, don't wander out of my sight again. Understand?"

She smiled faintly in the darkness, inhaling the earthy, masculine scent of his skin. "I understand. I'm not sure how practical that will be, but I understand."

"Damn it, Kim, I wasn't going to yell at you tonight."

"No? You were going to wait until morning?"

"Yes, as a matter of fact I was. I still intend to wait until morning. This isn't the time."

"Why not?"

"Because you're in shock. I told you, I know what the reaction feels like."

"How is it you know so much about it?" she asked softly. "Just what sort of import-export company did you run before you returned to Cavenaugh Vineyards?"

"A perfectly legitimate and profitable one."

She sensed him smiling against her hair. "Rugs and trinkets and doodads from all over the world?"

"Something like that," he agreed absently.

"Do you still own the business?"

"No, I sold it two years ago when I came back here."

"Do you miss it?" she pressed. "All the travel and freedom and everything?"

She felt him hesitate. "No. That part of my life is over. I'm content making my wine. It's a very satisfying kind of work, Kim."

"I know what it's like to have a satisfying career. I'm very lucky to have my writing."

Again she sensed a hesitation in him and then Cavenaugh said quietly, "It won't always be enough for you, Kim. I realize that you think it will because right now your life seems

to hold everything you need. But you're a warm, sensitive woman. You weren't cut out to spend your whole life alone."

"I don't intend to spend it completely alone."

His hand moved impatiently on her thigh. "I know. You're looking for your real-life Josh Valerian. The perfect man, unencumbered by family and responsibility. But he's not out there, Kim. He doesn't exist except in your books. And you're far too passionate and real to be content with a fictional lover."

Surprised by the vehemence in his voice, Kimberly didn't argue. "I agree with you," she said simply.

"What?" Green eyes narrowing, Cavenaugh rolled her over onto her back and trapped her beneath him.

"I said, I agree with you." Smiling up at him, she wrapped her arms around his neck. "Make love to me, Cavenaugh. I need you."

"Not half as much as I need you," he groaned huskily, lowering his head to taste the sweet skin of her shoulder. "Oh, God. Not half as much as I need you. But I won't stop trying until you realize you want me more than anything else on this earth!"

He slid his hands up along her sides, pushing the T-shirt out of the way. When her bare breasts were revealed in the shadows he tantalized the tips gently with the palm of his hand until they became firm.

Kimberly felt the hardness of his arousal as he pressed himself strongly against her thigh. When he drew one of her hands away from his neck and guided it down to his manhood, she moaned in soft wonder.

"Such gentle hands," Cavenaugh muttered achingly. "You drive me out of my mind, sweetheart."

He let his fingers glide teasingly along the inside of her thighs until she was arching against his hand. Then he

touched the dampening heart of her and Kimberly gasped aloud.

Cavenaugh lifted his head from her breast to drink in the sight of her parted lips and luminous eyes. She caught at his shoulders, pulling him to her.

"Love me, Cavenaugh. I love you so much!"

"Kim!"

She hard the ravishing hunger in his voice and then he was forging into her, taking her completely. The elemental power of his lovemaking captured her, binding her to him in the most primitive of ways. Kimberly clung, her nails leaving small marks of passion in his shoulders, her legs wrapped tightly around his driving thighs.

And then came the moment when her head tipped back over his arm and her body shuddered delicately beneath him. Kimberly was vaguely aware of Cavenaugh calling out her name and heard his fierce demand.

"Tell me again, Kim. Say you love me."

"I love you, Cavenaugh. I love you—" Then the words were cut off as he poured the essence of himself deeply into her body. The long moment of violent, male release drained both of them.

It was a long while before Cavenaugh stirred and slowly uncoupled himself from her warmth. Kimberly turned into him, seeking shelter and comfort and empathy.

"Did you mean it, Kim?" he asked finally, his hands moving through the tangled mass of her hair.

"I love you, Cavenaugh."

He muttered something she couldn't understand and folded her more tightly against him. "Remember that, sweetheart."

"How could I forget?"

"Kim, I have to be certain you know what you're saying," he said after a moment. "Do you understand? I want to be

sure you know exactly how you feel. I want you to be completely free to love me."

"Don't worry. I'll give up Josh Valerian. It will be hard on the poor man but I expect he'll survive."

"Honey, I'm not joking." Cavenaugh tilted her chin up so that he could study her face. His own was harsh and unreadable. "I don't want there to be any barriers between us."

Kimberly's mouth curved with love. "Stop worrying, Cavenaugh. I know what I'm doing. You're so good at reading my mind occasionally, can't you read it tonight?"

"I'm not sure." His eyes were hooded and brooding in the darkness. "Kim, the day after tomorrow I want to take you into San Francisco with me. We'll spend the night there."

Kimberly glowed. "A little time to ourselves?"

"There's some business we have to handle but then, yes, we'll have the night to ourselves." He hesitated and then asked carefully. "Would you like that?"

"Very much."

A sigh escaped him. "Go to sleep, Kim. You've had a hell of a night."

She nestled closer and allowed herself to drift comfortably off into oblivion. The last thought on her mind before she fell into a surprisingly dreamless sleep was that Cavenaugh hadn't told her he loved her. He was saving that for San Francisco, she decided.

At dawn Kimberly awoke to find herself deeply enmeshed in Cavenaugh's embrace. She lay quietly for a time, thinking about the night.

"Are you awake, sweetheart?" he murmured into her hair.

"Umm. Cavenaugh, I've been thinking about something."

"Not always a good sign in a woman."

She pinched his hip and he growled, nipping her shoulder in sensuous retaliation. "I'm serious. There's something we didn't talk about last night."

It seemed to Kimberly that he stiffened slightly at her words. "What didn't we discuss?"

"Well, the whole point of your alarm system along the rock wall is to keep intruders out."

"True."

"The only alarm you got last night was the one I set off when I ran toward the winery building."

"Uh-huh."

"But the character in the robes who was chasing me was already inside the grounds. In fact, he was inside the garden, near the patio. How did he get there without tripping the alarm when he arrived?"

"That," Cavenaugh muttered, "is a little matter I've been lying awake thinking about for the past hour."

"Did he slip in when the invited guests arrived?"

"I don't see how. Starke was monitoring everyone's arrival through the gates and Julia greeted everyone at the door. After the last guest arrived the gates were locked. Starke is very thorough about these things."

Starke. The strange man who shared Cavenaugh's past. Kimberly shivered. But she was afraid to bring up any possible suspicions. Cavenaugh and Starke apparently went back a long way together. Cavenaugh would not thank her for voicing any doubts about his friend.

Besides, Kimberly thought, dismissing her momentary questions, she had no reason to doubt Starke in the first place. His loyalty to Cavenaugh had been proven in the past.

"What are you thinking about, Kim?"

"Loyalty," she answered truthfully.

"A difficult concept to deal with at five o'clock in the morning."

"Yes."

"Are you sleepy?"

"No."

"Want to get up?"

"No."

He smiled. "Want to tell me you love me again?"

"How about if I show you?"

"I'm at your mercy."

"I've always had this thing for passive, submissive men."

"Witch," he rasped huskily, pulling her down on top of him.

BY NOON THAT DAY Starke had a preliminary report on the man who had attacked Kimberly the previous night. He sat with Kimberly and Cavenaugh and told them what little he knew.

"This is all unofficial at this point. Cranston gave me the information off the record. The guy's name is Nick Garwood. He's got a record that goes back to his kindergarten days. Questioned twice last year during an investigation of a stabbing death in L.A. The police down there think it was a contract killing. Right now Garwood is busy demanding his rights and a lawyer but Cranston thinks they can get him to talk."

"Any word on the source of that dagger?" Cavenaugh asked calmly, as if discussing a business matter. Kimberly was amazed at the matter-of-fact way he and Starke were handling this whole thing. As if they had dealt with such things often in the past.

"Not yet. But Cranston let me take a look at it. It's not a cheap, stamped out knife, Dare. The handle is genuine silver and it's heavily embossed. Looks like some kind of ceremonial thing. A collector's item. Not the kind of knife a punk would use to carry out a neat, tidy contract killing. It's—" he slid an apologetic glance at Kimberly "—it's not exactly an efficient sort of weapon."

"Lucky for me," Kimberly tossed back smoothly.

"Lucky for all of us," Cavenaugh grated. "Any theories on how he got inside the gate without triggering the alarms?"

Starke shifted his gaze to the garden outside the study window. "Dare, the only thing I can think of is that he somehow snuck in with the other guests. I don't see how, but it must have happened that way. I've been so damned careful...!"

Kimberly saw how harsh Starke was being on himself and felt compelled to interject. "Is it possible someone inside, one of the guests, let him in?"

Cavenaugh and Starke both turned to look at her.

"Do you realize what you're saying, Kim?" Cavenaugh finally asked gently.

"That someone you know is behind this? Yes, I realize it. It's just a passing thought." She smiled bleakly. "I guess I've written one too many crime novels."

Cavenaugh shook his head. "Don't apologize. It's something that has to be considered. Starke and I went over that ground this morning. We couldn't come up with anything useful, though. Everyone here last night is a good, solid, substantial citizen of the community."

True, Kimberly reflected. In fact, realistically speaking, the newest people on the scene locally were Cavenaugh and Starke.

It was getting very involved, she decided. "With any luck the authorities will get that Nick Garwood to talk," she offered firmly. "Perhaps he's the only villain."

"Don't forget the woman. The one who held Scott captive."

"True. But if she's a girlfriend of Garwood's, it should be easy to trace her." Starke fell into a musing silence.

"What doesn't fit in all this is the weird part," Cavenaugh put in bluntly. "The rose with the needle in it, the silver dagger, the robe Garwood was wearing. None of that fits a straight kidnap or murder attempt."

"I know," Starke muttered in dark frustration.

Cavenaugh leaned forward in sudden intensity. "Starke, see if you can get Cranston to give you a photograph of that dagger."

"Sure, but why?"

"You and I imported a lot of odd things during our time, pal. We had to get them appraised occasionally. We've got a lot of contacts who know a lot about weird items. I want to show some of them a photo of that dagger."

Starke was on his feet, heading for the door. "I'll get on it right away, Dare." The man was obviously grateful to have something useful to do. At the door he paused for a moment to glance back at Cavenaugh.

"Are you still going to take Kim into San Francisco tomorrow?"

Kimberly wondered at the disapproval in his voice but Cavenaugh ignored it. "We'll be leaving in the afternooon. As soon as I finish that meeting with the marketing people. Any objections?"

"Would they do any good?"

"No," Cavenaugh said harshly. "I know what I'm doing."

"I'll see you later," Starke said and walked out the door.

Startled at the unexpected discord between the two men, Kimberly frowned at Cavenaugh. "What was all that about?"

He switched his emerald-hard gaze to her. "Forget it, Kim. Like I told Starke, I know what I'm doing."

"I never said you didn't, but—" A sudden, bleak thought struck her and she went on in a tight whisper, "Doesn't Starke approve of...of us? Is he trying to warn you not to get too involved with me?"

Cavenaugh's mouth tilted wryly at the corner. "In case you haven't noticed, I already am involved with you. And if it makes you feel any more comfortable about it, yes, Starke

does approve of you. Most emphatically. So does everyone else around here."

"Oh." A sense of relief went through her. "It's just that I know how demanding families can be in a situation such as this," she began gently. "If they don't approve—"

"No," Cavenaugh cut in with cool deliberation. "You do not know how families are in a situation such as this. You only know how one family was and that was twenty-eight years ago. Before you were even born!"

Kimberly got to her feet, astonished and annoyed at his biting attitude. She had gotten very accustomed lately to being cosseted by Darius Cavenaugh. "Occasionally I forget how overbearing you can be when you choose," she told him as she walked to the door. "I'll see you at dinner."

"Kim, wait!" He was on his feet behind his desk, green eyes urgent and compelling.

"What is it, Cavenaugh?" she asked warily, her hand on the doorknob.

"Kim, you do know that whatever I do, it's because I want everything right between us? I know there are times when I seem like a tyrant to you, but you do understand that I only want what's best for you? And for myself," he added dryly. "I can't pretend to be totally altruistic about all this."

She tilted her head to one side. "About all what?"

"Never mind. Just remember what I said. Oh, and Kim, why don't you have Mrs. Lawson set out a bottle of that new Riesling for dinner."

"Of course," she said politely and closed the door behind her. *And while I'm at it,* she decided grimly, *I might as well tell her I'd like to see a bottle of hot sauce on the table. I may not be sure of my status around here, but I must have some rights!*

He came to her room again that night and while he didn't exactly flaunt the relationship to the rest of the household, it

was obvious Cavenaugh had no intention of trying to pretend that he wasn't sleeping with her. No one seemed to mind the obvious intimacy. In fact, everyone seemed quite pleased about it as far as Kimberly could tell.

But it seemed to her that he made love to her with a kind of fierce energy that night, as if he was trying to imprint himself on her senses. He should realize by now, Kimberly thought fleetingly, that he had succeeded completely in wiping out her image of a fictional lover. She would be satisfied now only with the very real love of Darius Cavenaugh.

8

SOME DEEP INSTINCT warned Kimberly of impending disaster as Cavenaugh escorted her into the ornate lounge of the elegant Union Square hotel. If she were honest with herself she would have known that the promised trip to San Francisco was not really destined to be the romantic idyll she had anticipated.

There had been a tension about Cavenaugh since the day before, when he had made a point of telling her that whatever he did would be for her own good. When people, especially men, started telling you that what they did was for your own good, a smart woman ran. As fast and as far as she could.

But she hadn't been a smart woman lately, Kimberly reflected. She had been a woman in love. Quite a difference.

Cavenaugh's tension had communicated itself to Kimberly until she herself bristled with it. He had been almost silent during the drive into the city that afternoon. There had been an implacable, forbidding aura about him that had squelched her attempts at conversation.

When they had checked into the hotel he had taken her upstairs to the room and brusquely suggested she change for the evening. Out of a fleeting wish that the atmosphere between them might be explained and mitigated before the night was over, Kimberly had dressed with hope.

The sophisticated little black knit dress with its piping of gold at the collar and cuffs had been discovered by Julia yes-

terday during a shopping trip. Together with black, high-heeled evening sandals and hair brushed into a chic twist at the back of her head, Kimberly felt as ready as she ever would to face what promised to be an uncertain evening. It had seemed to her that Cavenaugh had dressed as though he were going to war. He looked formidable and aloof, essentially masculine in the dark evening jacket and dazzling white shirt. She felt the distance between them grow more frighteningly intense with every passing second. Her dreams of an evening of love and promises faded.

By the time they were facing the smiling hostess in the lounge, Kimberly knew that something devastating was about to occur. Beside her Cavenaugh spoke with quiet authority.

"We're expected by the Marlands."

Kimberly went absolutely still even as the hostess nodded politely and turned to lead the way.

"Cavenaugh, what have you done?" Kimberly whispered with a bleakness that reached all the way to her heart. She turned vulnerable, stricken eyes up to his unyielding gaze. "What have you done to us?"

His mouth tightened as he looked down at her, and for an instant she thought she read desperation in the depths of his emerald eyes. But it was masked almost immediately by fierce determination.

"It had to be this way, Kim. You would never have agreed to meet them otherwise."

She shook her head, trying to clear it. "I knew from the beginning that you were arrogant, but I never thought you would do this to me."

His hand closed around her wrist. "Let's get it over with, Kim. it's not going to be as bad as you think it will be. Trust me."

She looked up at him uncomprehendingly. "Trust you? But Cavenaugh, after tonight I'll never be able to trust you again, will I?"

Fury hardened his features even more than they already were. "You don't know what you're saying. Don't fight it, Kim. And don't be afraid. I'm with you, remember? I won't let anything happen to you."

"What more could happen?" she asked. "Do you know that I thought you were bringing me to San Francisco so we could spend some time alone? And I thought tonight was going to be a very special one for us. I always thought I kept my fantasy world confined to the pages of my books but apparently I allowed it to slip over into real life."

"I'm no fantasy, damn it!"

"No. But the man I fell in love with is."

"We'll deal with this later, after you've faced the Marlands and found out that there's no need to deny your heritage."

"Cavenaugh. . ." she whispered distantly as he led her through the crowded lounge.

But it was too late. They were confronting a refined looking couple seated at a round table in the corner. Her grandparents must have been in their seventies, Kimberly realized vaguely as Wesley Marland got to his feet and politely extended his hand to Cavenaugh. But even as the older man went through the formalities, neither he nor his expensively dressed, silver-haired wife could take their eyes off their granddaughter.

When she looked into Wesley Marland's face, Kimberly found herself meeting eyes the same amber color as her own. Marland must have been a handsome man in his youth, she reflected as she acknowledged the quiet introductions with the barest inclination of her head. Without a word she took the chair Cavenaugh held for her, refusing to look at him as she did so. He sat beside her, close and protective.

No, not protective. Possessive perhaps, but not protective. A man who cared enough to protect her would never have thrown her into deep water as Cavenaugh had done tonight.

"Oh, my dear Kim," Anne Marland murmured as though she could no longer restrain herself. "You have your father's eyes."

"With any luck," Kimberly said coolly, "that's all I inherited from him."

Mrs. Marland flinched and withdrew the hand she had been extending tentatively toward her granddaughter.

"Kim," Cavenaugh began, softly warning, but Wesley Marland interrupted him.

"No, Mr. Cavenaugh, she has a right to be bitter."

Kimberly lifted her chin. "Let's get one thing straight. I will not be patronized. I'm sure Cavenaugh has explained to you that this whole thing has been sprung on me without any advance notice. I would appreciate it if we could keep everything short and businesslike. Let's get this momentous occasion over with as quickly as possible."

Before anyone could respond the waitress appeared at the table, politely requesting drink orders. When the other three hesitated, as though their minds had been anywhere but on drinks, Kimberly smoothly gave her order.

"I'll have a glass of your house wine as long as it's not from the Cavenaugh Vineyards."

"Uh, no, ma'am, it's not," the waitress said, surprised. "Cavenaugh wines are much too expensive to serve as house wines."

"I'm beginning to realize that."

The Marlands quickly ordered and Cavenaugh asked for a Scotch on the rocks. When the young woman took her leave, Kimberly faced her grandparents.

"Now suppose we get down to business so that we can all be on our way. What do you want from me?"

It was Cavenaugh who responded, green eyes gleaming with faint threat. "Kim, the Marlands only wanted to meet you. There's no reason to be aggressive. Just relax."

Mrs. Marland said hastily, "Your fiancé is right, dear. We only wanted to meet you."

Kimberly's eyes widened in mocking astonishment. "My *fiancé*? Who on earth are you talking about?"

Wesley Marland frowned. "Mr. Cavenaugh here has given us to understand that he intends to marry you."

"Really? First I've heard of it." Kimberly smiled in a brittle fashion as the cocktail waitress returned with the order.

"Marriage is a matter I intend to sort out with Kim after this meeting takes place," Cavenaugh said calmly.

"Another little surprise you were going to spring on me, Cavenaugh?" Kimberly took a deep swallow of her wine. It wasn't nearly as good as a Cavenaugh vintage but it certainly tasted better to her tonight than any of the noble bottles Cavenaugh produced. "Hmm, not bad," she offered dryly, holding it up to the light. "It has a clean, *honest* taste."

"Stop it, Kim," Cavenaugh ordered gently. "You're acting like a child."

"What?" she asked sardonically. "Aren't things going the way you had planned? Did you expect me to throw myself into my grandparents' arms after all these years? How terribly disappointing for you."

It was Wesley Marland who interceded as his wife looked on unhappily. "Kim, we understand this is difficult for you and that it's been something of a surprise. But we honestly didn't think we could get you to agree to meet with us in any other way. The lawyers told me that you categorically refused any overtures."

"Categorically," Kimberly agreed.

"We had to see you, Kim," Anne Marland whispered. "You're all we have left now. It's taken us so long to find you, dear. Years, in fact. We started looking a long time ago but all we found out was that your mother had died. It took the lawyers forever to trace you. It wasn't until your books started appearing in print that they finally got a lead. They contacted your publisher and your agent, neither of whom would give out your address until we convinced them that we really were your only surviving relations."

Kimberly looked into the aging, once-beautiful face and thought of what this woman had done to her mother. "You're twenty-eight years too late, Mrs. Marland."

"Don't you think we know that?" Wesley Marland asked bitterly. "But we can't undo the past, Kim. We can only work with the present and the future." He drew a deep breath and then announced grandly, "We want you to know that, as our only surviving descendant, you will be inheriting everything we own."

Kimberly stared at them, utterly astounded. "My God," she gritted. "Do you really think I'd touch a penny of your money?"

The Marlands stared back at her, obviously not prepared for the vehemence in her words. Cavenaugh quietly sipped his drink and watched Kimberly over the rim of his glass.

Wesley cleared his throat. "Forgive me, my dear. It's just that, well, we understand it takes quite a while to become, uh, financially successful as a mystery writer and we thought that...Kim, our money can be a legacy to your children. Perhaps you should think of them before you allow pride to dictate your answers."

"What children?" she asked politely.

Anne glanced uneasily at Cavenaugh. "Surely when you and Mr. Cavenaugh are married you'll want children?"

"Not only has Cavenaugh failed to discuss marriage with me, he has certainly not brought up the subject of children." Kim flashed a brilliant smile at the man beside her. "Another little example of our failure to communicate, I suppose."

"Kim," he said roughly, "you're making this hard on everyone, including yourself. Why don't you deal with the situation like the warm, sensitive woman you really are?"

"What did everyone expect to accomplish with this dramatic encounter?" she demanded tightly.

"A chance to get to know our only grandchild," Mrs. Marland said softly. "After your father was killed and we realized there was no hope of...of..."

"No hope of ever having a properly bred Marland heir?" Kim offered helpfully.

"You don't understand how it was twenty-eight years ago," her grandfather said quietly. "Your father was so young. We were convinced that what he felt for your mother was only infatuation that would wear off quickly. Frankly, we believe that's exactly what did happen. John didn't put up all that much of a battle in the end. He seemed, well, almost relieved when we arranged the divorce for him. I know that's not what you want to hear, but that's the truth."

"Did it ever occur to either one of you that you had no right to arrange his life for him?" Kimberly demanded.

"John had certain responsibilities," Anne Marland began firmly. "Or so we convinced ourselves at the time."

Kimberly nodded. "I understand completely."

"You do?" Marland looked at her in surprise.

"Certainly. Cavenaugh, here, is a perfect example of how family responsibilities can dictate a man's entire life. I really do understand the kind of pressure my father must have been under." She met Cavenaugh's eyes and the angry aggression in her began to disintegrate. "All of you have been the victims of that inbred sense of responsibility and loyalty. When

I was very young I used to feel I had been denied something important because I had been disowned by my grandparents and by my father. Now I realize that I was very, very lucky. I grew up without the kind of pressure all of you must have endured. I grew up to be independent and self-contained. And I don't need my grandparents now. I don't need anyone." What a joke that was. If only she had never met Cavenaugh. The words might actually have been true before she'd fallen in love with Darius Cavenaugh.

Anne Marland leaned forward urgently. "Kim, my dear, you are on the verge of a very good marriage. The Cavenaughs are a solid, respectable, old California family. By acknowledging your grandfather and myself you can bring something important to that family. You can bring a solid, respectable background of your own.

Kimberly set down her glass with fingers that trembled. "Is that what this is all about?" She looked at Cavenaugh. "Were you hoping to establish a proper background for me before bringing me into the family?"

Grim fury flared in the emerald ice of his eyes. "You know very well that's not why I did this."

And quite suddenly Kim knew she believed him. She believed all of them. Closing her eyes briefly she summoned a small sad smile. "I know," she whispered. "I know. You were only doing what you thought was best for me."

"For all of us, Kim," Wesley Marland said quietly. "Please believe me. Anne and I don't want to hurt you any more than we already have. We want to make up for what happened twenty-eight years ago. You were the one innocent victim in the whole mess."

"There was my mother," Kimberly pointed out wearily.

Anne flicked a quick glance at her husband and then looked directly at Kimberly. "Darling, your mother was very young and very desperate to hold on to John."

"What's that supposed to mean?"

Wesley sighed. "Kim, your mother deliberately got pregnant when the divorce proceedings started. She admitted as much to John. She hoped that a baby would hold the marriage together. We never heard from her after that. In fact, we all assumed. . .well, we assumed she'd probably had an abortion when she realized she wasn't going to receive a large settlement."

Kimberly shook her head. "I'm not going to argue with you. You may be right for all I know. Women have done less intelligent things when they're in love." She was aware of Cavenaugh slanting a cool glance at her but she ignored it. "There's really no point in rehashing the past, is there? No good can come of it now. What's done is done." She smiled wryly at the Marlands. "But I'm afraid you really will have to find something else to do with your money. Give it to a worthy charity. How about starting a fund for impoverished, unpublished writers?"

Wesley looked directly at Cavenaugh. "Don't let her throw away her inheritance, Mr. Cavenaugh."

Cavenaugh shrugged. "I don't care what she does with the inheritance. I only brought her here today to reestablish contact with you. I wanted her to see that her grandparents weren't monsters and that she doesn't have to be afraid of families that are bound by loyalty and responsibility."

"Are we such monsters?" Anne Marland asked sadly. "We did what we thought was best at the time. We were wrong."

Kimberly shook her head. Her grandmother had paid a heavy price for interfering in her son's life so many years ago. "Who am I to punish you now? You've lost everything that really counted, haven't you? Your son and heir, a granddaughter to spoil, the hope of future generations who will acknowledge you on the family tree. No, Mrs. Marland, you're not a monster. I wish you and Mr. Marland all the best.

I truly mean that. I'm not holding a grudge against you any longer. But neither can I give you back everything you threw away twenty-eight years ago."

"You can give us great-grandchildren," Wesley Marland stated gruffly.

"You wouldn't deny us our great-grandchildren, would you, Kim?" Anne asked desperately.

"I don't have any to offer you," Kimberly pointed out simply.

"Yet," Cavenaugh interjected coolly.

She wasn't going to argue with him now. Kimberly was feeling emotionally drained. There wasn't enough energy left over for an argument with Cavenaugh. Besides, there was nothing left to argue about.

An awkward silence descended on the table as the four people sitting around it confronted one another and themselves. Then Wesley asked cautiously, "Would it be too much to hope you and Darius will join us for dinner, Kim?"

Too much to hope? These proud, wealthy, influential, eminently respectable people had reached the far end of their lives and found themselves reduced to begging for some time with their granddaughter. Twenty-eight years ago they could not possibly have dreamed that it would all turn out this way. Twenty-eight years ago they had probably assumed money could buy them anything. They had learned the hard way that it had its limits. It could not buy a meal shared with a granddaughter. They could only hope that the granddaughter would grant it to them.

Cavenaugh waited for her answer along with the Marlands. He made no effort to force her into the next step of the fragile relationship.

"Cavenaugh and I will have dinner with you," Kimberly said quietly.

The relief and gratitude in the proud eyes of her grandparents were eloquent thanks. But it was the satisfaction in Cavenaugh's gaze that roused some of Kimberly's anger and despair.

Who did he think he was to play God with her life like this?

Sitting next to her, Cavenaugh felt the immense effort of will Kimberly was exercising to maintain a cool, polite facade, and his own sense of foreboding increased.

He had been so certain that the way he had chosen to handle the situation was the best, so convinced of the rightness of his instincts in the matter. Now he was not so sure. Starke had warned him that women didn't like surprises.

Cavenaugh watched Kimberly as she carefully chatted with her grandparents. She was behaving very civilly now, although there was not yet any sign of her relaxing. There was even an occasional smile. It was almost painful to see how eagerly the Marlands greeted the faint hints of Kimberly's softened mood.

They couldn't be any more grateful than he was, Cavenaugh thought as he finished his drink. For a while there he thought he'd set a match to a powder keg. Now, although the threat of immediate explosion seemed to have passed, he knew he was still dealing with a woman on a very short fuse.

She wasn't used to having someone else in her life, he assured himself as they all rose to go into dinner in the hotel dining room. Kim was so damned independent, so accustomed to making her own decisions without any input from people who cared, that it was probably difficult for her to adjust to what he had done tonight. But she was an intelligent, sensitive woman and she would understand that he'd handled this the only way he could.

Ultimately, Cavenaugh decided as he ate his trout mousse, Kim would relax and accept the situation. After all, just look how much progress had already been made. Here she was

communicating quite politely, if a little stiffly, with people she had once sworn to never even contact.

But even as he tried to cheer himself with that thought, Cavenaugh couldn't shake his own sense of apprehension. He was both thankful and wary as the evening drew to a close.

"I want both of you to feel free to visit us at the winery soon," Cavenaugh said as he shook Wesley Marland's hand in farewell.

"Thank you," his wife answered gratefully. "We'd like that very much." She looked uncertainly at Kim, obviously not sure how to say good-bye to her newfound granddaughter.

Cavenaugh realized he was holding his breath but he needn't have worried. Kimberly hesitated and then leaned forward to quickly kiss her grandmother's pale cheek. Mrs. Marland patted her awkwardly on the shoulder and then turned away with tears in her eyes.

"You've made her very happy, Kim," Wesley Marland said quietly. "We shall always be grateful for your generosity tonight."

"Don't thank me," Kimberly said. "Thank Cavenaugh. It was all his doing."

Marland shook his head. "He set things up but you're the one who made it work. Good night, Kim." He turned away to take his wife's arm.

Cavenaugh watched them walk through the lobby to a waiting taxi. Two intensely proud people. What it must have cost them to acknowledge the mistake they had made twenty-eight years ago, he thought.

"Well, Cavenaugh, you pulled it off. Congratulations. I never even suspected that you had this little scene up your sleeve when you said we were going to spend an evening in San Francisco." Kimberly collected her small, black evening bag and smiled at him with the same brittle expression he'd already seen on her at various times during the confrontation.

"It's over, Kim," he murmured as he took her arm. "You handled it very well."

"Golly, thanks. You can't imagine how terrific that makes me feel."

Warning signals hummed along his nerve endings. Cavenaugh kept a very tight grip on Kimberly's arm as they made their way out of the dining room. He had the oddest impression that if he didn't physically hang on to her he might lose her tonight.

"You're through the hard part, honey. You've made the contact and found out that, while they may be far from perfect, your grandparents aren't inhuman despots, either. No one is going to make you accept them completely but you needed to face them and understand them."

He didn't like the innocently blank look she gave him. "Why?"

Cavenaugh felt his tension increase. This was going to be more difficult than he had anticipated. "Because I wanted you to get over your fear of a certain kind of...of family relationship. I didn't want you holding the actions of your father's family against me for the rest of your life. I wanted you free of the past. Can't you understand that, Kim?"

"I was free of my past. I had absolutely no contact with it. How much freer can a woman be?" she asked with an unnatural calm.

"The hell you were. It was between us constantly. You were wary of me from the beginning because of it. You constructed your Amy Solitaire character to be as unfettered and emotionally free as *you* wanted to be and then you gave her the perfect mate, Josh Valerian. A man who has no other responsibilities in the world except the ones he has to Amy. Damn it, Kim, I felt I had all these ghosts from your past to deal with before I could have you."

She came to a halt in the middle of the lobby, amber eyes cool and fathomless under her lashes. "You've already had me, remember? The ghosts didn't seem to get in your way."

Cavenaugh gritted his teeth. "How long are you going to punish me for the way I handled this whole thing tonight?"

She turned away. "I'm not going to punish you, Cavenaugh. I don't have that kind of power."

He caught her arm but when she shot him a defiant glance he released her. The last thing he wanted was a major scene here in the lobby. Kimberly was walking swiftly toward the bank of elevators. Lights from the heavy crystal chandeliers dappled the amber of her hair. Her head was high and she carried herself with a pride he had just witnessed in two other people. Cavenaugh strode forward, catching up to her as she paused to punch the elevator call button.

"It wasn't just your grandfather's eyes you inherited, Kim. You've got the Marland pride. Just imagine how they felt tonight."

To his surprise she inclined her head, not looking at him. "I know it must have been difficult for them. Twenty-eight years ago I'll bet they couldn't have managed it. Time changes everyone, I suppose."

"Everyone, Kim," he emphasized meaningfully as one of the bronzed elevator doors slid silently open. "Including you."

She shrugged elegantly in the sleek black dress. "Look me up in twenty-eight years and I'll let you know."

"I'm not going to wait around that long for you to forgive me," Cavenaugh snapped, beginning to feel goaded. "When you've had a chance to think about it you'll realize I handled this the only way I could."

"Will I?" She stepped inside the elevator and he followed quickly.

Cavenaugh drew a deep breath, seeking patience. "I know you're upset, honey, but by morning you'll have calmed down. You're too intelligent not to realize this has all been for the best."

She didn't answer him, her gaze fixed steadfastly on the closed elevator doors. Kimberly maintained her silence all the way up to the room and by the time he unlocked the door Cavenaugh knew he was more than tense. He was getting damned scared. She wasn't coming out of it as fast as he had anticipated. When she slipped past him into the room he shut the door and leaned back against it, watching her through narrowed, brooding eyes. Kimberly went immediately over to the closet and began pulling out her small suitcase.

"What do you think you're doing?" Cavenaugh asked harshly.

"What does it look like I'm doing?"

He came away from the door, moving toward her with such obvious intent that she stepped back a pace. Instantly Cavenaugh halted. "Damn it, Kim, don't look at me like that."

"If you don't want me looking at you like that then I suggest you don't threaten me."

"I am not threatening you. But neither am I going to let you pack up and leave this room," he growled.

"Why would you want me to stay?" she asked too calmly.

"Because you belong here!" His patience was fraying to a dangerous degree, mostly because of his growing fear that he'd done something incredibly stupid tonight. "You belong with me, Kim. Hell, you belong *to* me. You love me, remember?"

"Ah, Cavenaugh," she whispered hopelessly. "I remember. But the problem is that you don't love me. You proved that tonight. I had fooled myself into believing that you did, you see. That was sheer idiocy on my part, of course. You

never gave me any reason to think that you did. When I told you that I loved you, there was no answering response from you, was there? Do you know I had decided that tonight was the night you would tell me how much you loved me? I thought that this trip to San Francisco was planned by you to give us a chance to be alone so that you could tell me your true feelings."

"Kim, now that we've gotten through that confrontation with your grandparents we're both free to talk about the future."

"I don't see much future for myself with a man who doesn't love me," she flung back in a tight voice.

"Give me a chance, Kim. This wasn't the way I wanted everything to go, damn it!" He ran a hand restlessly through his hair. His whole body was seething with frustration and anger. Standing with his feet braced slightly apart, adrenaline pouring through his system, he knew he was poised to reach out and grab her. He wanted to pull her down onto the bed and shut off the flow of her resentment with the kind of lovemaking that would remind her of just whose woman she was.

"A man who really cared for me would never have done what you did tonight. He would never have set me up like that. He would have understood that I had a right to handle my past in any way I saw fit. He would have respected the fact I'm an adult and entitled to make my own decisions. He would have empathized with my feelings about my grandparents, even if he thought I should confront them. He might, conceivably, have tried to talk me into a meeting with them but he would never have arranged one behind my back the way you did."

"Kim, I wanted it over and done, can't you understand? I had to know you were really free to love me. It's because I want you so much that I had to make certain what you felt

was real. I didn't want any barriers between us, and I thought your wariness of families that wielded their power the way your grandparents once did was standing in the way of our relationship."

"So you decided to wield a little power of your own, is that it? Was tonight's act of sheer, unadulterated arrogance supposed to reassure me? My God, do you realize I had actually begun to think that you could almost read my mind? That we were becoming emotionally and intellectually intimate? That you understood me?"

"Kim, I'm a man!" Cavenaugh gritted, his fists clenching in impotent fury. "Men see some things differently than women see them. Sometimes we make mistakes dealing with women because we can't think like them. Maybe I made a mistake tonight. But I didn't intend to set you up. I only wanted you to face your past and deal with it. That's the way I do things, Kim. I face them. I don't pretend they aren't in my life. I don't build a fantasy world for myself as a way of dealing with real life."

"A fantasy world!" she snapped. "You think I live between the pages of my books?"

"Well, haven't you done exactly that?"

She stared at him as though seeing him finally for the first time. "Cavenaugh, you don't know me at all, do you?"

"Kim, wait...!"

She turned her back on him and disappeared into the bathroom. A moment later she was back with her toothbrush and a handful of other items, stuffing them into her small case. Yanking the blouse in the closet off the hanger, she dumped it in on top of the rest and closed the lid.

"Just where do you think you're going tonight?" Cavenaugh was almost afraid to touch her, fearing that once he did he would do something drastic. But he had to stop her. He

knew his fingers closed much too tightly around her fragile wrist but she disdained any protest.

"I'm going to find a place to spend the night," Kimberly told him simply. "Alone."

"You're spending the night here. With me."

"No."

He grappled with that single word. It would have been easier if she'd yelled something along the lines of "not if you were the last man on earth." He could have dealt with that kind of outrage. But Cavenaugh freely admitted to himself that he wasn't at all sure how to handle Kim in her present mood. He released her wrist as he realized that his hand was beginning to shake with the force of his barely restrained emotions.

As soon as he freed her she turned and started toward the door.

"That's far enough, Kim. You've not leaving this hotel. For both our sakes, don't push me." He heard the lethal threat in his own voice and knew she understood it, because at the door she stopped and turned around to face him. Her head was still held with dignity but he could see the uncertainty in her eyes. *Nice going, Cavenaugh. Now you've managed to frighten her. You're really handling this whole thing with finesse.*

"If you're going to threaten me, Cavenaugh, be up front about it. What exactly are you going to do if I exercise my right to leave this room?"

He closed his eyes in exasperation and then glared at her thorugh narrowed lids. *Back off, Cavenaugh, or you're going to blow this completely. Give her time. She needs a little time.* He forced himself to speak calmly.

"If you're absolutely determined to run instead of staying with me tonight, I'll call the front desk and get you another

room in this hotel." Without waiting for her response he picked up the phone on the nearby end table.

Kimberly watched him in utter silence. In fact, Cavenaugh reflected a few minutes later as he escorted her down the hall to another room on the same floor, he got the distinct impression she didn't quite know what to make of his actions. Obviously getting her a room of her own without further protest was not what she had expected him to do. As he opened the door of her new room, he looked down at her.

"This isn't how I wanted it to be between us tonight, Kim. You know that, don't you?"

"It isn't how I wanted it to be, either, Cavenaugh. As you've already taken pains to point out, I live in something of a fantasy world. But the fantasy I was living in was taking place in real life, not in one of my books."

"Damn you," he gritted and reached for her.

He pulled her into his arms, deliberately giving her no opportunity to resist. Frustrated hunger and a large dose of his seething fury combined in the kiss. His mouth closed over hers with a possessiveness he made no attempt to hide. She might choose to sleep alone tonight but she would go to bed with the taste of him on her lips.

Kimberly didn't fight him but that was probably because he didn't allow her to do so. Cavenaugh wasn't interested in a response tonight. He only wanted to imprint himself on her in a way that would last until morning. He wanted her to lie awake thinking of him all night, he realized. The same way he was going to lie awake thinking of her. When he finally released her she stumbled back a step, her fingers lifting to touch her sensually bruised mouth. It seemed to Cavenaugh that he had never seen her golden eyes so wide or so unreadable. For a long moment they looked at each other and then Cavenaugh shook off the spell.

"Good night, witch. Go to sleep. If you can."

Two hours later the uneasiness became so intense that Cavenaugh knew he had to act. He hadn't slept at all but this restless feeling wasn't from lack of sleep. Something was very, very wrong.

Unable to stand it any longer he climbed out of bed, pulled on his slacks and his shoes and went out into the hall.

He was too late. Kimberly had left the hotel.

9

SHE HAD BEEN A FOOL, Kimberly told herself. A fool to think that she had achieved some kind of rare, magical intimacy with Darius Cavenaugh. A fool to let him trick her into that confrontation in San Francisco. A fool to let herself believe that Cavenaugh was somehow different from other men in his position.

Most of all, she decided ruefully as she gripped the wheel of the rental car, she was a fool for making the long drive up the coast at one o'clock in the morning. But when you were running from your own foolishness, home was where you instinctively wanted to hide. And if home lay a hundred and fifty miles away, you just kept going until you got there.

In spite of the lousy weather.

Kimberly struggled with the tension of fighting the steady rain as well as her own inner anxiety. Refusing to spend the night with Cavenaugh hadn't been enough for her high-strung nerves. She'd needed to be alone, really alone. Kimberly didn't have any misconceptions about what would have happened if she'd stayed in the hotel.

Cavenaugh would have been at her door when she opened it in the morning, waiting to see if she had gotten over her snit. And he would have continued to haunt her, arguing his case, condemning her own behavior until she finally admitted that he had been right. It infuriated her to think that she had been so blissfully unsuspecting about that trip to San

Francisco. She should have paid more attention to her instincts. After all, there had been plenty of evidence that the trip wasn't starting out as a romantic jaunt for two! But she had chosen to ignore Cavenaugh's increasing silence and tension.

When you were in love, Kimberly reflected sadly, you saw things the way you wanted to see them, not as they really were.

Cavenaugh had been right about one thing. He was a man and he didn't think like a woman. More importantly, he didn't think the way she, Kimberly Sawyer, did. That was the bottom line. He didn't think the way she did. He might at times be able to almost read her mind, to know what she was thinking, but that didn't mean he shared the same emotions or analyzed those thoughts the same way she did.

He wasn't Josh Valerian. How many times had he told her that, Kimberly asked herself wryly. She supposed it had been his way of trying to warn her that the warm, shared intimacy that she imagined was beginning to take shape between them had its limitations.

The truth was she had never confused him for a moment with her fictional male character. It would have been impossible to mistake Cavenaugh for anyone but himself. He was too real, too dynamic, too solid and far too virile to be a stand-in for Josh Valerian or anyone else.

Everything about him was unique, Kimberly realized as she slowed the car to compensate for the increasing rain. The taste of his mouth, the earthy scent of his body, the feel of him as he crushed her deeply into the bedclothes. She would never forget the physical side of him.

But what she would miss the most were the more intangible aspects of their short-lived affair. Damn it, she thought, there *had* been moments of shared understanding. She hadn't

imagined them all. The night he had held her in his arms and told her he knew what it was like to be wired with tension after a frightening confrontation with violence, for instance. He had comforted and soothed her and she knew he understood exactly what she was going through.

There had been other times, too, Kimberly remembered. He had understood her need to be alone in a busy household. He had been quietly, deeply appreciative of the way she had interceded to establish some rules for his working hours.

How could a man who seemed so in tune with her in so many instances do to her what Cavenaugh had done tonight?

The answer was simple enough, Kimberly thought grimly. He'd given it to her himself. He was a man. More than that, he was *Cavenaugh*. The basic masculine arrogance in him was an intrinsic part of his nature as was his sense of responsibility. It was instinctive of him to take charge of a situation and do what he thought had to be done. That part of him would never change.

Accepting Cavenaugh as her lover meant accepting the total man.

Tonight had been one of the most difficult in her life. It had been traumatic facing the grandparents she had sworn never to meet. But on the whole, the confrontation had not gone the way she would have expected. It was impossible to hate the Marlands.

Kimberly wasn't sure, yet, exactly what she felt toward the elderly couple who had been forced to beg her to acknowledge them. They seemed like strangers to her—people whom she had heard about from her mother and from the lawyers who had written to her explaining the history of the situation. But they were people whom she'd never actually met and on some levels they had remained unreal until now.

Tonight she had learned that they were two very human people who were trying to salvage something they had once foolishly thrown aside. It was impossible to hate them.

Kimberly bit her lip as she reflected on her own pride. Cavenaugh had been right about that aspect of her personality. Just as he'd been right abut the fact that she had nothing to fear in meeting her grandparents. Cavenaugh was no doubt right about a lot of things.

But that didn't mean he was the right man for her to love, she told herself. Unfortunately, telling herself that and learning to unlove him were two entirely different matters. In spite of the turmoil of her emotions tonight, she knew that she loved the man.

The anger and resentment that had driven her from the hotel in search of solitude had faded into a dull, sad ache by the time Kimberly pulled into the drive of her darkened beach house. The storm was really raging at this point on the coast, and she was exhausted from fighting it for the past hundred and fifty miles.

Lightning crackled as she stood on the porch, fumbling in her purse for the key. She had changed into a pair of jeans and the full-sleeved white blouse she had intended to wear on the drive back to the Napa Valley, but she hadn't brought along an umbrella. The rain had almost drenched her just during the short dash from the car.

Her fingers trembled slightly as she finally located the correct key and thrust it into the lock. It seemed that every nerve in her body was being delicately probed with a razor. It was no wonder that she was suddenly so shaky. It was nearly four o'clock in the morning. She had been through a great deal tonight and the drive through the worsening storm had not helped. What she needed was a glass of wine and bed. Tak-

ing a grip on herself, she turned the key in the lock and pushed open the door.

And saw at once that the last things she was fated to get tonight were a glass of wine and the privacy of her own bed. Panic smashed through her, scattering her senses for a timeless instant.

It was the candle burning in the middle of the pentagram that caught her eye first. The ancient, magical symbol had been drawn on her living room floor and the candle glowed evilly in a low, squat metal holder that sat at the center of the design.

The candlelight was the only light in the room but it was enough to illuminate the hooded figure who sat cross-legged on the far side of the pentagram.

"Come in, Kimberly Sawyer. You are expected."

Kimberly flinched at the familiar voice but before she could react two other figures stepped out of the darkness and into the faint light of the candle. They were both hooded and robed but one had his hand extended and in it was a gun.

"Close the door," a man's voice commanded from the depths of the flowing cowl.

Kimberly desperately tried to weigh her chances. He could kill her easily before she could dash back through the door, she realized. She might have been able to outrun a knife but no one could outrun a bullet. Slowly, she closed the door behind her. She felt a distant kind of surprise that her chilled muscles responded to the silent effort. The door seemed very heavy.

"The power is strong tonight, my lady," murmured the second standing figure. "It has brought her here, right into our grasp." There was awed wonder in the tones and also a touch of familiarity. Kimberly knew she had heard that voice sometime in the past, too.

"The power," intoned the woman who remained seated in front of the pentagram, "grows stronger every day. Have I not told you that?" She lifted her head so that her features were illuminated beneath the shadowy hood. "Good evening, Kimberly."

Kimberly stared back at her, calling on a kind of pride that only tonight she had learned was inherited from her grandparents. That pride was all she had to get her through this terrifying encounter. With an effort of will she forced a measure of cool mockery into her response.

"Hello, Ariel. Graduated from tea leaves to the big time, I see." The sardonic comment startled her because it didn't reflect the panic that seemed to have invaded every corner of her mind. She discovered that managing the cool remark gave her a measure of courage, however. Kimberly seized on that spark of strength.

Ariel Llewellyn smiled back at her, but the cheerful, scatterbrained expression of the woman who had been virtually a member of the Cavenaugh household for almost a year was gone. A hint of madness gleamed in her eyes and there was an unnaturally serene smile on Ariel's mouth, as if she could see into the future and found it satisfying.

"You have been incredibly foolish, Kim. And now you will pay."

Kimberly concealed the tremor of fear that went through her. Ariel meant it. "Well, I know a one-hundred-fifty-mile drive through a storm probably isn't the brightest thing someone can do at three in the morning, but what can I say? I was bored."

Ariel shook her head once as if unable to believe such stupidity. "Foolish woman. You had no option but to make that drive tonight. You were summoned. That was not a matter of choice for you. No, you made your mistake two months

ago when you chose to interfere in matters that did not pertain to you."

"The little matter of the kidnapping?" Kimberly swallowed the sickening taste of fear and swung her gaze to the standing woman. "You're the one who was holding Scott in that beach house, aren't you? The one I took him away from so easily that night." She turned her attention back to Ariel. "It seems to me you've got some problems in the personnel section of your organization, Ariel. I know good help is hard to get but you've really picked some blunderers. This idiot didn't even hear me the night I came by to fetch Scott. And then there was that turkey with the knife who kept tripping over his Halloween costume. This guy with the gun probably forgot the ammunition."

There was an ominous growl from the armed man and the nose of the gun lifted menacingly.

"I assure you it is loaded," Ariel said calmly. "But I do hope you won't force him to use it. We have much more interesting plans for you, Kim."

"Wonderful. Are we going to sit around and read cards?"

"I told you the day of the card reading that you should take the omens seriously. Of course, I knew you wouldn't. But you learned a lesson that night, didn't you, Kim?"

"Why did you do things the hard way the other night, Ariel? Why make your hit man use an antique silver dagger, which, I have on the best authority, isn't a particularly efficient weapon? Stylish, yes. Efficient, no."

Ariel's mouth hardened and in the glow of the candle flame her eyes seemed to glitter. "It was important that you die properly. It has been a hundred years since the Dagger has been blooded. You were chosen as its victim."

"Because I interfered in the kidnapping." Kimberly nodded, as though it all made perfect sense. "Why did you take

Scott two months ago? Was he the original choice for the sacrifice?"

"Oh, no. Kidnapping Scott was purely a financial move," Ariel assured her. "We needed the money. It was decreed that Cavenaugh should be the source."

"You mean this magical power of yours can't conjure up something as simple as a credit card?"

That seemed to crack Ariel's unnatural serenity. "It was the power that decided the money should come from the Cavenaughs!"

"But you never got it, did you?"

"We will in time," Ariel declared, calming again. "All will happen as the power said it would happen. In time."

Kimberly glanced at the shadowed faces of the other two people in the room. "Are you guys as crazy as she is? Do you actually believe in all this inane nonsense? Sooner or later, you know, the whole mess is going to cave in on you and you're going to get caught. That turkey who tried to kill me the other night is probably singing his heart out to the cops now!"

"That punk knows nothing," the figure with the gun assured her. "No names, no faces. It was all arranged very carefully. He knew only that he had to do it in the prescribed manner, using the Dagger, because he would not be paid otherwise."

"You're out of your mind if you think he won't be able to provide the authorities with some clues. The knife alone is a very big one."

"No one but the Select know the meaning and purpose of the Dagger," Ariel put in evenly. "There are only a few of us in each generation. The secrets are always guarded most carefully. The authorities will learn nothing from the Dagger."

"Where did you get it, Ariel?" Kimberly couldn't think of anything else to do except keep the conversation going. Ariel seemed willing enough to chat about her "power" and the other two seemed totally under her control.

But before Ariel could answer, the phone rang.

Kimberly wasn't the only one who flinched at the unexpected, shrill command of the instrument. The guy with the gun must have jumped an inch, she decided. And the young woman looked momentarily panicked.

Without even having to think about it, Kimberly knew who was on the other end of the line.

"That will be Cavenaugh," she said quite clearly. "He'll be checking to see that I got home safely."

"No!" The sharp denial was from Ariel.

"Of course it is," Kimberly assured her. "Who else would be calling at four in the morning? Why don't you get out your fortune-telling cards and see if I'm right?" The phone rang again, harshly demanding. "The only problem," Kimberly continued, "is that by the time you've dealt the cards to determine who's calling, Cavenaugh will have given up and decided something must be wrong. Knowing him, I expect his next move will be to call the Highway Patrol. With his name and clout he'll probably get them to come check on me."

The phone rang again and the man with the gun was definitely nervous now. He looked at Ariel for guidance.

"We'd better let her answer it, my lady."

Ariel lifted an admonishing hand. "I will decide, Emlyn." Her once-cheerful eyes were full of threat as she nodded brusquely at Kimberly. "Answer it. And be very, very careful what you say, Kim, or I will have Emlyn kill you where you stand. Tell Cavenaugh you're fine. Then get rid of him."

Aware of the other three watching her with violent intensity, Kimberly moved to answer the phone. She was so cer-

tain it would be Cavenaugh that she wasn't at all surprised at the sound of his voice. What did surprise her was the urgent concern in his words.

"Kim? Are you all right?"

"I'm fine, Cavenaugh. It was a long drive, but I'm home. I told you there wouldn't be any problem, didn't I?"

"You didn't have the courtesy to tell me a thing," he exploded softly. "You just did a midnight flit without bothering to mention the little fact that you were leaving town."

"You know how writers are, darling. They get the oddest compulsions at the oddest hours. I just had to come back here to finish what I started."

Across the room Ariel glowered at her, motioning her to get off the phone.

"You don't work like that. You work regular hours. What the hell are we discussing your writing for, anyway? You know that's not what's wrong between us. Kim, listen to me. We've got to talk about what happened tonight."

Kimberly steadied herself, deliberately dropping her voice to what she hoped would sound like a sensuous purr to the three people watching her so malevolently. "You know I'll look forward to that. I always enjoy our pillow talk. Remember the last chat we had in bed?"

"Kimberly, you're not making a whole lot of sense. But, yes, I do remember the conversation," Cavenaugh said roughly. "You told me you loved me. Are you trying to tell me that you've realized you still do?"

"Actually, I was referring to the other topic we discussed," she murmured lovingly. Emlyn raised the snout of the gun in a gesture of warning. "I remember how you assured me that you understood. Your understanding would mean a great deal to me right now, Cavenaugh."

There was a taut silence on the other end of the phone. Kimberly could almost feel Cavenaugh sorting through her words. When he spoke again there was a new edge in his voice, one she had never heard before.

"You were scared that night."

"Yes, darling," she whispered lightly.

"And tonight?"

"Oh, I still feel the same way, Cavenaugh. Even more so."

He swore with soft violence. "How much time have I got?"

Kimberly swallowed. "I don't know how I'll make it through the rest of the night without you," she said, some of the purring quality draining from her voice.

"How many of them?" The question was as hard and cold as a knife blade.

Kimberly swallowed. "I've got three chapters to get done for that deadline. A lot of work so I really must get to bed. It's been a very long, tiring drive. Take care, darling. I'll look forward to seeing you when I've finished *Vendetta*." She hung up the phone before an obviously nervous Emlyn could get any more restless.

The younger woman looked relieved and glanced at Ariel for direction. Ariel nodded. "Tie her up, Zorah, and put her in the bedroom for now. We have preparations to make." She flung a coldly amused look at Kimberly. "It's a good thing you had the sense to keep Darius out of this. Loving him as much as you do, I'm sure you wouldn't want him hurt. Take her away, Zorah. Emlyn, give her a hand and then come back here. There is much to be done before tonight."

Loving him as much as you do. The words played about in Kimberly's brain as she submitted to having her wrists bound behind her back and her ankles tied. Emlyn supervised the process, his gun never wavering.

Loving him as much as you do. The old witch was right, Kimberly realized as Zorah and Emlyn left the room. Maybe Ariel really did have some power. Kimberly tested her bonds carefully. Her captors had left her trussed up in the middle of her bed.

Loving him as much as you do. There was no point in denying it, Kimberly told herself bleakly as she lay staring at the far wall. Self-honesty seemed appropriate when you found yourself in such dangerous circumstances. She loved Cavenaugh. Perhaps when she had run from the hotel tonight she had only been running from the truth.

She knew she had made him understand that something was wrong but what would he do next, Kimberly wondered. He was probably still back in San Francisco. The only thing he could do was call the local authorities and ask them to check out the situation.

Her fate was in his hands, Kimberly reflected. On the whole, she couldn't imagine trusting anyone other than Cavenaugh with her life.

SEVERAL MILES DOWN THE ROAD Cavenaugh hung up the pay phone in the all-night convenience store and went outside to the waiting Jaguar. So the compelling sense of urgency, which had been governing his actions since the moment he knew he had to go to Kim's room, had been based on something more than the uneasiness left by a lovers' quarrel. He had left the hotel a little more than an hour behind her, but he'd made better time than she had. He was only a half hour from her home.

Cavenaugh yanked open the car door, his mind spinning as he considered the possibilities that lay ahead. Kim had implied there were three people in the house with her. There wasn't much time, but then, there never was in situations like

this. He would go into this as prepared as possible. Before starting the engine he leaned down and removed a couple of items from underneath the front seat. The knife he slipped inside his low boot, strapping it to his ankle. He shoved the small, flat, metal box inside the waistband of his jeans so that it lay snug against his spine. Then he turned the key in the ignition and pulled out onto the rain-slicked road.

Given the driving conditions, it should have been a thirty minute trip to Kimberly's beach house. Cavenaugh decided that with a little effort he could make it in twenty. That was a good deal less time than it would take to try and rouse the local authorities into efficient action.

KIMBERLY WAS INCHING HER WAY across the bed, trying to get close to the glass-based bedside lamp when the door to her room opened. The woman called Zorah stood in the doorway. She was holding a small brazier in her hands.

"I didn't phone for room service," Kimberly managed. She was very scared now.

"You are foolish to mock what you do not understand," Zorah informed her softly. She set the brazier down on the floor and knelt in front of it. "But soon you will pay the price. Your life will be forfeited to the Darkness, Kimberly Sawyer."

Kimberly watched uneasily as the woman applied a match to the small pile of coals in the bottom of the pan.

"Look, Zorah, don't you think this has gone far enough? Why don't you get out of it before you're trapped? You know it's only a matter of time before Ariel is discovered. She's not clever enough to cover her tracks or yours for much longer. And after I disappear you can bet Cavenaugh won't stop until he's uncovered the truth."

"Darius Cavenaugh cannot deal with my lady's power," Zorah said serenely.

"What power? Everything Ariel's arranged so far has been screwed up. The kidnapping went wrong. The attempt to kill me fizzled. What makes you think she'll pull off her next trick successfully?"

Zorah glared at her, some of the assured serenity faltering. "She brought you here tonight with her power, didn't she?"

"Not exactly. I think we can write tonight off as one very large coincidence. A coincidence she was shrewd enough to capitalize on. Did she really tell you that she would make me appear this evening?"

"She said we had to come here to your house in order to discover the best method of dealing with you. The emanations of your essence are strongest here where you live, and the power can be wielded most effectively in such an environment."

"But did she actually promise to produce me?" Kimberly prodded. "Or did she just say you'd do a bit of hocus pocus and decide on your next course of action?"

Zorah sprinkled powder from a small leather packet onto the glowing coals and got to her feet. "You are wasting your time trying to put doubts in my head. I believe in my lady's power. Someday she has promised it will be mine!"

Zorah turned and walked out of the room, closing the door firmly behind her. Kimberly lay eyeing the heated coals in the brazier. A strange scent was beginning to permeate the room.

Kimberly inhaled cautiously, wondering what was happening. The fragrance was curiously tantalizing. An herbal smell that was both acrid and sweet. Perhaps it was some sort of ritual, she decided. Turning back on her side she continued her interrupted worm crawl across the bed.

Kimberly had reached the far edge of the quilted surface and was studying the lamp, looking for a way to break the

glass base without making too much noise when she began to question her actions. She inhaled deeply, absently enjoying the strange fragrance from the brazier and wondered if this project was worth all the effort she was exerting.

It would be so much easier to close her eyes and rest for a few minutes. Perhaps after she'd had a small nap she would be able to think more clearly about the task of breaking the glass lamp base.

In fact, Kimberly thought critically, why should she even want to break such a lovely piece of glass? It had something to do with a vague notion of using the sharp edges to cut her bonds but that seemed highly unrealistic now.

The herbal scent was filling the room, drifting into the corners, hanging lightly over the bed. Kimberly took another, deeper breath and realized she hadn't felt so relaxed in ages.

It had been a hard night, she decided. She needed to unwind. There had been that confrontation with her grandparents, the quarrel with Cavenaugh and then the long drive through the storm.

The storm.

Outside her bedroom window thunder rolled and lightning crackled over the ocean. The momentary brilliance jarred her. There was something she was supposed to be doing, some task that demanded attention. Glass. It had to do with glass.

Once before she had used broken glass, Kimberly remembered dazedly. She had been defending herself. There had been a silver dagger and a man in robes. Glass. She needed a piece of broken glass.

Ridiculous. Who had any use for broken glass? Gazing over the edge of the bed, Kimberly stared at the coals in the brazier. Such beautiful coals. And they gave off such a lovely

fragrance. Too bad Cavenaugh wasn't here so that he could enjoy the aroma with her.

But Cavenaugh was safely in San Francisco. Or was he safe? Her mind drifted around that thought. It wasn't like Cavenaugh to keep himself safe while she was in danger. He was a man who understood responsibility. And he had definite responsibilities toward her.

He was her lover, Kimberly told herself, and he felt it was his job to protect her. So how could he be sitting safely in a hotel room right now? No, he must be coming after her. It was the only logical conclusion.

Danger. Where was the danger? It was so difficult to keep her mind focused on it. Yet when a person was in peril surely her attention should be riveted on it? Somehow it all seemed like such an effort.

Ever since she had begun enjoying the scent of the brazier smoke she had been having a hard time remembering that crazy Ariel Llewellyn was out there in the living room going through who-knew-what nutty rituals. It was even harder to remember that she, Kimberly, was going to play a starring role in the upcoming drama.

Ariel. Ariel and smoke. Ariel knew a lot about herbs. There were those herbal tea concoctions she was always fixing for people. Certain herbs released their power when heated. Kimberly frowned, remembering the packet of powder Zorah had sprinkled on the brazier.

Lightning sparked angrily outside the window, as though demanding Kimberly's attention. For a moment she obeyed, turning her head to gaze out into the darkness. Soon it would be dawn but the storm was raging so wildly it would be a long time before the sky grew light.

Herbs sprinkled on the brazier coals. Cavenaugh making his way through the storm to get to her. Witches and dag-

gers. A ripple of fear pulsed under Kimberly's unnatural relaxation. That smoke was doing this to her, she thought, twisting on the bed. Smoke was dangerous.

Desperately she sought for a new focus of attention. Images of Cavenaugh flashed into her head. Cavenaugh making love to her, holding her, telling her he understood. Cavenaugh forcing her to meet her grandparents. Cavenaugh on the phone tonight, comprehending immediately that she was in real trouble. Cavenaugh, who could almost read her mind at times and who, at other times, infuriated her with his male arrogance. Cavenaugh whom she loved.

He was the reason she had to keep trying to break that glass lamp base, Kimberly realized with sudden clarity. Cavenaugh would expect her to at least try. But that damned smoke was so overpowering. Desperately Kimberly twisted, knocking her shoulder against the end table.

The crash of the lamp as it fell to the floor coincided with the opening of her bedroom door. The destruction of the bulb left only the glow of the brazier coals for light. In the sudden darkness Kimberly heard people moving around.

"What the hell have you done to her?"

It was Cavenaugh's voice, Kimberly realized dreamily. "Ah, Cavenaugh. I knew you'd get here. What took you so long?"

The light from the hall shafted through the haze in the room, providing just enough illumination for Kimberly to see that Cavenaugh was not alone. Emlyn was behind him.

"Oh, dear. They got you, too," she whispered sadly. "I'm so sorry, Cavenaugh. I think I made a mistake tonight."

"You've drugged her with this goddamned smoke," Cavenaugh said somewhere in the haze.

"She'll live until tonight. Just thought we'd give her a little something to keep her quiet. She's the kind who would have

made trouble. Wonder why she pushed that lamp over? Oh, well, if she wants to lie here in the darkness, that's her problem. Get on the bed. Zorah, tie his ankles. And be careful."

"Do you think it's safe to leave both of them here together?" Zorah asked.

"The smoke will keep them under control. Besides, where else can we put him? Ariel won't want him watching her preparation rituals."

Kimberly felt the bed give beside her as Cavenaugh obediently allowed Zorah to finish binding him. A moment later the two had left the room, leaving Kimberly and her companion in smoky darkness.

"Kim, are you all right?"

"The smoke," she tried to explain sleepily.

"Yeah, I know." He was moving, sitting up beside her and shifting around. "Wake up, honey. This will go a lot faster if you help. That smoke will get to me soon."

"Help? How?"

"There's a knife inside my boot. Turn around so you can reach down and pull it out."

Kimberly struggled to concentrate as he urged her onto her side. She felt his leg and then the leather of one boot. Behind her back her fingers fumbled awkwardly.

"Why did you let them get you?" she whispered unhappily. "I didn't want them to get you, Cavenaugh."

"I had to let them take me. I had no way of knowing where you were or what they might have already done to you. So I just walked up to the front door and pretended total ignorance."

"Quite a surprise seeing Ariel, wasn't it?" For some reason that seemed inordinately funny. Kimberly giggled and her fingers slid off the boot.

Cavenaugh swore. "When I think of harboring her under my roof for the past twelve months. . .Kim, stop it," he ordered harshly.

"I'm sorry," she mumbled guiltily. "Didn't mean to laugh. Just seemed funny."

"Get the knife!"

The command in his voice cut through her foggy senses. Another moment of clarity returned and Kimberly managed to get her fingers inside his boot. She felt the handle of the knife and tugged.

"That's it, honey," he said approvingly. Then he coughed. "Now hold it as firmly as you can. And be careful, it's very, very sharp."

"I'm not a little kid. I know about sharp knives," she informed him loftily. But obediently Kimberly held the knife firmly. She was vaguely aware of him turning around so that he could rub his bonds against the sharp blade but her mind was on another matter.

"About the mistake I made this evening, Cavenaugh."

"We both made a few. We'll talk about it later," he gritted. "Damn it, Kim, hold the knife still!"

"You're always telling me what to do," she said with a sigh, but instinctively she responded to his orders and tightened her grip on the knife handle.

"You'll get used to it."

A moment later something gave and Cavenaugh moved away from her. She heard him cough again and through the shadows saw him rip the pillowcase off one pillow. Holding the material over his mouth, he quickly freed his ankles. Seconds later he was kneeling on the bed, opening the window behind it.

The cold, wet air rushed into the room and into Kimberly's brain, clearing it a little. The strange sense of amuse-

ment she had been feeling faded rapidly as the effects of the smoke subsided. Panic returned. Then Cavenaugh was working on her bonds, slicing through them with efficient ease.

"Now what?" she whispered, gulping in the fresh air. Her brain still felt very foggy.

"Now we get out of here."

But even as Cavenaugh pushed her toward the window, the hall door opened. Light poured into the room.

"They're getting away!" Zorah screamed.

10

"LET'S GO, KIM," Cavenaugh ordered. "She's not armed. Hurry!"

Kimberly tried frantically to obey him, scrabbling for the windowsill. But the smoke seemed to have played tricks not only with her brain but with her body. She felt oddly lethargic still, and her muscles refused to coordinate with her mind.

"My lady!" Zorah screamed, "They're escaping!"

"Come on, Kim, *move*." Cavenaugh reached for Kimberly's arm, trying to push her through the open window, but she was unable to cooperate in her own escape. Every movement seemed to require incredible effort.

"Cavenaugh, I can't. . . !"

"Goddamn it, Kim!" Cavenaugh grabbed her, trying to forcibly stuff her through the window. He was interrupted by another voice from the doorway.

"You shall not escape the power this time!" Ariel's shrill screech of fury was backed up a second later by Emlyn's uneasy command.

"Stop where you are, Cavenaugh, or I'll shoot the woman."

"Which woman?" Cavenaugh asked, sounding vastly annoyed. "Right now all three of them are giving me a headache."

But he reluctantly stopped trying to push Kimberly through the window and stepped down off the bed to face Emlyn's gun.

The smoke from the brazier continued to waft through the room. It was diluted now by the effects of the open window and door but it had not completely dissipated.

Kimberly remained on the bed, her legs feeling shaky as she stared at the three people in the doorway. "Aren't these about the poorest excuses for witches you've ever seen, Cavenaugh?" she muttered.

"Yeah," Cavenaugh agreed, his eyes narrowed on Emlyn's gun. "Pretty poor. Kim, stay right where you are."

"You have mocked the power one too many times," Ariel shrieked at Kim. She lifted her hands high above her head. The full sleeves of her robe fell back revealing a variety of odd bracelets on her wrists.

"Uh, my lady," Emlyn began with what Cavenaugh thought was superb diplomacy under the circumstances. "Perhaps we should wait until later?"

"Let her teach the bitch a lesson," Zorah interrupted fiercely. "Call up the power, my lady! Let the darkness rain on her. Let her see what it is she mocks!"

Oh hell, thought Cavenaugh. Looking straight at Emlyn he said coolly, "This whole scene is getting a little out of hand, isn't it? Maybe it's time for you to split. I think you can write off any money you might have been hoping to see."

Emlyn glowered first at Cavenaugh and then at Ariel who was still standing with her hands raised above her head. The older woman had shut her eyes, her face twisted intensely. She was beginning to chant.

"Let the power that dwells in the depths of darkness come forth to answer the challenge of this foolish creature of light," Ariel intoned while Zorah watched in anticipation. "Let that which lives on the fringes of the universe and in the center of the Earth rise to smash the impudent being."

"Cavenaugh..." Kim began uneasily and then closed her mouth. This was nothing but a crazy woman's act. It was

probably just the remnants of the smoke lingering in her head that made Ariel seem so menacing.

Cavenaugh ignored the new fear he heard in Kim's voice. Right now the only one who held any real power was the guy with the gun, and Emlyn was looking distinctly unhappy. That didn't make him any less dangerous.

"My lady," the male witch tried again, "I think it would be better if we saved this bit for another time."

"Shut up!" Zorah hissed.

Ariel's voice was rising in intensity now, filling the room as she chanted.

"All that answers to me; all that I have chained and bound according to the ancient laws, hear me now!" Ariel called.

"Hear her," Zorah echoed fervently, her eyes glittering with excitement. "As her handmaiden I, too, call on that which is raw power!"

Kimberly shuddered and didn't know if the shiver was caused by the cold night air pouring into the room or Ariel's chanting. But she obeyed Cavenaugh and stayed very still on the bed.

Emlyn moved uneasily. "Zorah, stop her, we've got to get these two under control. She can use her witchcraft later!"

Zorah turned on him violently, her eyes wild. "Hush! You are only a man. You will never understand the depths of the power you serve. Leave my lady alone!"

Ariel droned on, oblivious to the conversation. "Out of the bottom of the pit of darkness, gathering the forces of the ancient magic as it rises, lifting up into the surface world, flooding in from the farthest reaches of emptiness..."

Cavenaugh slanted a glance at Kimberly who was still sitting on the bed. At least she was staying put although she appeared half-mesmerized by Ariel's chant. When he made his move he didn't want her getting in the way.

"The time has come," Ariel shrieked. "Fill this space, oh spirits of the great void, fill it with fire and darkness and destruction..."

"Zorah," Emlyn snapped, "this has gone far enough. She's nuttier than a fruitcake. Stop her!"

"You, too, shall suffer for mockery and disobedience!" Zorah promised him. "Only my lady and I will be left alive in this room!"

"*Now*!" Ariel yelled. "Let it be now!"

"*Now*!" Zorah screamed, lifting her own arms high above her head.

Emlyn lost patience and reached out to grab one of Ariel's raised arms. "Stop it, you dumb broad!"

"Don't touch her, you fool!" Zorah shouted. "The power is flowing now!"

It might as well flow now, Cavenaugh decided, agreeing silently with the woman. Emlyn's full attention was on dealing with Ariel and Zorah. There wasn't going to be a better opportunity.

With a quick movement Cavenaugh reached behind his back and withdrew the flat metal case that he had concealed there.

"The moment of power is here!" Ariel cried out.

"Let it be now!" Zorah yelped, trying to fend off Emlyn.

"You've got it, ladies," Cavenaugh muttered and hurled the flat case at the feet of the trio in the doorway.

An instant later brilliant, blinding light flashed through the room. Screams from everyone except Cavenaugh echoed from one end of the house to the other as each sought to cover his or her eyes. Cavenaugh had already prudently covered his own eyes with his hand. He counted to five and then opened them.

The fiery white light produced by the exploding chemical compound in the case was still blazing but the initial brilli-

ance had faded. Cavenaugh was careful to keep from looking directly at the case as he leaped across the room.

Seconds later he reached Emlyn who was shouting idiotically. The gun lay on the floor where it had been dropped during the first shock of the explosion. Zorah was screaming.

"My eyes! My eyes!" Emlyn yelled. "I can't see."

Ariel seemed stunned. She fell back, reeling, holding her hands protectively out in front of her. Temporarily blinded, she stared sightlessly at what she must have been convinced she had just unleashed.

Kimberly was still on the bed, her palms over her eyes. "Cavenaugh!"

"Right here, Kim. It's okay. You'll be able to see in a couple of minutes."

"Oh, my God, Cavenaugh, what happened?" She lowered her hands to her sides, her head turned in the direction of his voice.

Cavenaugh looked at his brave, temporarily blinded witch. "Everything's under control, honey. I've got the gun."

She blinked rapidly a few times. "I can't see!"

"It's just the light. You'll be all right soon," he soothed as he grabbed Emlyn and began tying the man's hands behind his back with the rope belt that Emlyn had worn. Soon the still-stunned Ariel was secured. He was working on Zorah when Kimberly got shakily up off the bed. She was still blinking rapidly.

"That's a hell of an act, Cavenaugh. You should take it on the road," she murmured, still sounding shocked. "You never told me you were into witchcraft, yourself."

He smiled grimly as he finished tying Zorah's wrists. "You learn a lot in the import-export business."

"So I see. I think I've asked this before, but what exactly did you import?"

"I'll tell you later. How are your eyes?"

She shook her head as if to clear it. But when she looked at him Kimberly was focusing almost normally. "Okay, I think. Geez, Cavenaugh, what was that stuff?"

"A chemical powder that reacts with oxygen. When the case is broken the chemical explodes in a bright flash."

"Like a small bomb," she said in awe. "I could use that in a book."

"Be my guest. How are you feeling?"

"Odd."

"Yeah, you look a little odd. Get some water from the bathroom and put out the coals in that brazier."

Kimberly looked at the still-glowing brazier and then nodded obediently. She walked into the bath and returned a moment later with a drinking glass full of water. Very carefully she poured the contents over the coals. There was a hissing sound and a small cloud of steam.

"Now go call the cops," Cavenaugh ordered distinctly.

Kimberly started out of the room and then stopped for a moment in front of Ariel. The older woman's eyes were wet with tears.

"She's crying, Cavenaugh."

"Yes, so she is," Cavenaugh said gently. "Go make the phone call, Kim."

"IT'S ALL SO SAD," Kimberly said several hours later as she reached into her cupboard and pulled out a bottle of Cavenaugh Riesling. "Aunt Milly is going to be crushed when she hears how Ariel was deceiving her."

Cavenaugh took the bottle from her and inserted a corkscrew. With a smooth, thoroughly expert movement, he removed the cork and started pouring the wine. "I don't feel so good about it myself. When I think of how none of us suspected what a fruitcake Ariel really was, I get cold chills." He

swore softly and took a large swallow of wine from one of the two glasses he's just filled. "What a fool I was."

Kimberly watched him from under her lashes. This was the first time they had been alone since the authorities had come to collect Ariel and her pals. There had been endless questions and statements and explanations. But finally everyone had left.

"I know how you must feel," Kimberly said softly as she picked up her own glass of wine. "But no one realized what she was really like."

He looked at her broodingly. "It was my responsibility to protect my family and you. I blew it."

Kimberly picked up a platter of cheese and French bread she had prepared. "Nonsense. You saved us all. And I for one am extremely grateful." She led the way over to the two chairs in front of the fireplace. "You do realize what was on the agenda for me this evening? Ariel was going to make me the star attraction in her first sacrifice ceremony. Nothing like being a guinea pig in some witch's act." She shuddered and flopped back in one of the chairs.

Cavenaugh followed slowly, pausing to stoke up the fire he had started an hour earlier. For a moment he stood staring down into the flames. "Are you sure you feel okay?"

"What? Oh, you mean am I suffering any aftereffects of that herb Ariel used on me. No, I'm fine, really I am. As brilliantly clear-headed as I've ever been."

His mouth crooked faintly in spite of his mood. "I'm not certain that's very reassuring."

Kimberly grinned briefly. "Poor Cavenaugh. You've had a rough time of it lately, haven't you? And all because of me."

"I wasn't the only male who was having trouble with females this morning. I almost felt a twinge of sympathy for poor Emlyn."

"Emlyn!"

"Well, he was only playing at being a witch because he really thought Ariel's plan for kidnapping Scott would work. After it fell apart, I guess she convinced him she had another scheme up her sleeve. It must have been a shock when he realized what a real nut she was."

"I wonder how he and Zorah met Ariel."

"The cops are wondering, too. They promised to let me know the whole story when they've finished dredging it out of those three. The first thing they'll have to do is find out Emlyn and Zorah's real names!"

"I thought they sounded a bit on the theatrical side," Kimberly noted. "How did Ariel become such friends with Aunt Milly?"

Cavenaugh's face hardened. "They met in a garden club." He winced. "I can still remember Milly telling me what a 'magical' touch Ariel had with herbs."

"She does know a lot about them. Probably from studying all sorts of arcane books. Ariel really feels she's this generation's keeper of some sort of witchcraft mysteries. I'll have to work her into a book. . . ."

"Just as long as you don't feel you have to do any hands-on research," Cavenaugh growled forbiddingly.

Kimberly's response was a yawn that she barely managed to cover. "My God, I'm exhausted. You must be, too."

"I am. In spite of what you may be thinking, this really has been a slightly abnormal day, even for members of the Cavenaugh household," Cavenaugh said with real feeling.

Kimberly smiled briefly and then fixed him with a very earnest expression. "But it's all over now. You've more than kept your promise. You've fulfilled the responsibility you felt you had toward me. I want you to know that, Cavenaugh. You don't owe me anything else." It was important to her that he understood he was free in that sense, Kimberly realized. "You've kept your promise."

"My promise to take care of you? Kim, I want to talk to you about that." He walked over to the other overstuffed chair and lowered himself into it.

Kimberly watched him obliquely. She liked watching him, she reflected. There was an easy, masculine grace in his movements, even when he was simply taking a seat.

"What's to talk about?" she tried to ask lightly. "It's over. You've done what you said you'd do. And without a lot of help from me, either," she added wryly.

"You did your part," he interjected.

Kimberly took another sip of wine. "Thank you for coming after me, Cavenaugh. You saved my life." She didn't meet his eyes, her gaze on the fire instead.

"I owed you any protection I could give you," he returned bluntly.

"Why?"

"Why?" He frowned. "For a lot of reasons. Because of what you did for Scott, naturally, and because you're my—"

"No, I mean, why did you follow me from San Francisco?"

"Oh, that." Cavenaugh hesitated. "Well, there are a number of reasons for that, too. I didn't get much sleep last night. None at all, in fact. And somewhere around two in the morning I had the feeling something was really wrong."

"More of your telepathy?" she mused.

"It wasn't telepathy. Just the restless brain of a man who knows he's handled something very badly."

She flicked him a wary glance. "You're referring to the way you set up that meeting with my grandparents?"

"I didn't handle it well, Kim. I admit it. My only excuse is that I honestly thought I was dealing with a difficult situation in the most efficient manner. I thought...I thought that after you got over the shock and had a chance to put it all in perspective you'd realize I'd done the right thing. I see now that I had no business springing it on you like that."

"Was it so very important that I be made to confront my grandparents, Cavenaugh?" she asked quietly.

"Yes," he said flatly. "I saw your relationship with them as the last barrier between us."

"You were really that worried about the fact your current bed partner had a mental block when it came to dealing with powerful families?"

He looked at her until she was compelled to switch her gaze from the fire to his face. The emerald eyes gleamed with a relentlessness that astonished Kimberly.

"I was not concerned about my current bed partner's feelings toward families. I was concerned with how my future *wife* dealt with the issue."

"Your wife!"

"I'm asking you to marry me, Kim. I was only waiting until we'd gotten the meeting with your grandparents out of the way."

She swallowed uncomfortably as her fingers tightened around the stem of her wineglass. Eyes wide, she stared at him. "Cavenaugh, you don't have to go that far out of some misguided sense of responsibility."

"I know you're not much interested in marriage, Kim," he returned softly. "You've gotten along fine for years without anything that really resembles a family. After pushing you into that meeting with your grandparents, you probably haven't changed your mind much. Especially when it comes to overbearing, arrogant males who happen to be heads of families. But I know that if you'll give us a chance we'll be good together in a lot of ways, not just in bed. I also know that I am not in a position to install a live-in lover in my household. Having you for a guest will work for a while, but quite soon everyone's going to want to know when I intend to marry you. Your grandfather will probably be at the head of the line demanding explanations."

Kimberly sat very still, totally unable to read his mind at all now. "I don't particularly care what my grandparents think."

Cavenaugh sighed. "No, I don't suppose you do." There was a long period of silence. "You said once that you loved me. I realize you've had some, uh, second thoughts thanks to the way I forced you into that scene with your grandparents."

"I have done some thinking," Kimberly admitted cautiously. She remembered that under the influence of the herbal smoke she had been trying to tell Cavenaugh that she had made a mistake. He hadn't had time to listen then and so she had not told him that she still loved him, in spite of the scene in San Francisco. Perhaps it was just as well. After all, she had no real idea of how deep his feelings went for her.

Except for the fact that he's asking you to marry him, she reminded herself. That didn't mean he was in love with her, of course. He was attracted to her and he felt a strong sense of responsibility toward her. Cavenaugh might also have found her useful in organizing his household. What was it Starke had said? Something about Cavenaugh needing a woman who could occasionally protect him from his own sense of duty.

"Sitting here now reminds me of that evening I came to get you, after you'd phoned the house a couple of times," Cavenaugh mused. "You were just as wary and cautious then as you are at the moment."

He was right, Kimberly thought. She was wary. But for different reasons. Falling in love with Darius Cavenaugh had been a dangerous thing to do. It left her vulnerable in a way she had never been before. She wished desperately that she really could see into his head. What was he thinking, she wondered. How did he feel? How long would it take him to

fall in love with her? Or would his feelings always be limited to a combination of duty, responsibility and attraction?

"I think," she began hesitantly, choosing her words carefully, "that we need more time."

To her surprise, he nodded and lifted his glass to his mouth. "I agree with you. We need time for you to get to know me well enough to trust me again. Unfortunately, time is not something I have a great deal of to spend as I choose. You've lived in my house for several days. You know what it's like. Someone or something is always needing attention. It would be hard just trying to get away to see you on occasional weekends. And I don't want to limit our time together to just weekends."

"A life full of responsibilities," she said thoughtfully, more to herself than to him.

"It's the life I've chosen, Kim. Or perhaps it chose me. I don't know and it doesn't matter. That's the way it is. That's the way I am." His voice had roughened and it seemed to her that the emerald in his eyes was lit with implacableness.

"And you want me to be a part of that life?"

"I think you can be happy in it if you'll give yourself a chance. I know it will be a change for you and I know there will be adjustments. But you've already proven you can handle the day-to-day hassle. You've taken control of it rather than let it control you. Things are so much more organized at home now and they'll be even calmer when Julia and Scott move out. You can have all the privacy you need for your work. I'll make certain the staff understands that. I'm asking you to make changes, I know, but I think that a woman who is brave enough to taunt a witch and face an attacker with only a broken wine bottle in her hand is brave enough to risk a new life-style."

"Cavenaugh, I think..."

He lifted a hand to silence her. "Let me finish, Kim. I said I understand your need for time, and I'm proposing to give it to you."

"How? You've just said you would find it uncomfortable to install me as your live-in lover," she gritted, thoroughly irritated with the description.

"I'm asking that you marry me. In return I'll give you the time you want."

She looked at him blankly for a second, not comprehending. And then it hit her. "Oh, I see." She was suddenly, inexplicably embarrassed. "We'll, uh, have separate bedrooms after we're married?"

Cavenaugh took a very long swallow of wine. Kimberly had the feeling he was nerving himself up for something. "I thought it would take some of the pressure off you," he explained evenly. "I realize that for you the sex is more than just, well, pleasant."

"Pleasant?" she repeated faintly, wondering how going to bed with Darius Cavenaugh could ever be described by such a mundane word as *pleasant*. "Is that all it is for you?"

"No!" The glass in his hand suddenly appeared very fragile as his knuckles whitened around it. "You know damn well it's not just pleasant. Now let me finish!"

Kimberly arched an eyebrow but kept her peace. It was becoming clear that Cavenaugh was straying near the bounds of his normally excellent self-control. She wondered why. Perhaps it had something to do with the fact that he hadn't had any sleep in the past twenty-four hours.

"As I was trying to say," he went on, "I am aware of the fact that you give a great deal of yourself when you go to bed with me. To be blunt you give yourself completely." His eyes locked with hers as if daring her to deny it. Kimberly again kept her mouth shut and covered the uncomfortable moment with another sip of wine. Cavenaugh continued cau-

tiously. "I feel that asking you to share my bed would be putting an added strain on you while you settle down in my household as my wife. It might make you feel too vulnerable, too committed to something you weren't yet really sure you wanted."

"And you don't think just the existence of the wedding license would put a similar sort of strain on me?" Kimberly inquired far too politely. "Are you trying to tell me that if I decided I don't like being married to you I will be free to walk out the door? That I will feel free to do so because we're not sleeping together?"

Cavenaugh set down his wineglass with an audible snap. "Don't twist my words, Kim!"

"I'm not twisting them. I'm only trying to figure out what they mean!"

He surged to his feet, striding over to stand in front of the hearth. With one hand resting on the mantel he turned to glower at her. "I don't see how I can make the matter much clearer. I'm asking you to marry me. I'm sorry if I'm botching up the job but this is the first time I've tried it."

"You're nearly forty years old and you've never asked a woman to marry you?" she asked disbelievingly.

"Up until two years ago I wasn't particularly interested in marriage. There was no room in my life for a permanent woman. Since then I've been too busy trying to put the winery back on its feet financially," he explained harshly.

"And now you've come to realize that it's time you married," she concluded with a nod of comprehension. "You have, after all, a responsibility to continue the family line, right? People will expect you to marry. You'll need a wife to lend the proper background to your role as an established, prosperous vintner. And, of course, I now have a thoroughly respectable background myself, thanks to your tracking down my grandparents."

He watched her through narrowed eyes, his lean body dangerously poised. "I warned you not to twist my words, Kim."

"I'm just trying to get all the details straight," she flung back, feeling increasingly incensed. "So far I can see what's in it for you, but I'm not sure what's in it for me."

"You need a husband!" he blazed. "You need me!"

"I do?"

He moved toward her with unnerving intent, reaching down to pull her up out of the chair. Cavenaugh's emerald eyes reminded Kim of a bird of prey, and quite suddenly she knew she had goaded him too far.

"Cavenaugh, wait...!"

His hands closed around her waist, holding her securely. "Little witch," he muttered, "you don't know when to stop, do you? Did you think you could just sit there and provoke me indefinitely?"

Before she could respond, his mouth was crushing hers. Kimberly stood trapped in his arms and let the storm of his emotion break over her. The frustration and implacable determination she sensed in him told her more than words could have just how close he was to the end of his tether.

The strange thing was that her instincts were to yield and soothe rather than resist. Kimberly parted her lips obediently when he demanded entrance to the warmth of her mouth and she let her body sway against his. Cavenaugh moved his hands up to cradle her head. His low groan of need and hunger reverberated through his chest, touching her at a deep level of awareness. He wanted her. She knew that with a certainty that went beyond words.

His tongue probed deeply, simulating the primitive rhythm of lovemaking until Kimberly moaned softly in response. Then she felt his teeth nip at her lower lip with passionate care. Keeping one palm wrapped around the nape of her

neck, Cavenaugh ran his other hand down her back to her buttocks, pulling her up and into the heat of his lower body.

"You have a talent for driving me crazy," he rasped against the curve of her throat.

"Cavenaugh, listen to me," Kimberly pleaded with the last remnants of her intelligence. "This is dangerous. Neither of us is in any condition to handle a major discussion about our future right now. I'm sorry if I've provoked you. But the truth is both of us need sleep and. . .and some time to think. We're exhausted and we've been through some very traumatic scenes in the past twenty-four hours."

"I've tried to reason with you," he growled, his fingers on the buttons of her blouse. "And I've tried to set up an unthreatening situation. But you're determined to resist every inch of the way."

"That's not true!"

"Yes, it is. But I know one way you won't fight me. Like I said earlier, when you're in my arms, you give yourself completely. I'm going to make love to you until you can't say anything but 'yes, Cavenaugh,' until you're shivering and hot and completely mine." His hands were moving inside the parted edges of her shirt.

"Is this what I could expect if I agree to your proposal? If I marry you will you immediately forget your promise to give me some time before demanding your conjugal rights?"

There was a moment of lethal stillness. Kimberly realized belatedly that she was holding her breath. And then Cavenaugh slowly raised his head to look down at her with eyes that were dark and dangerously enigmatic.

"Lady, you sure know how to walk a risky line." His hands fell away from her, and he moved slowly back to stand in front of the fire. "You'd better go to bed, Kim," he went on in an unnaturally level voice. "I'll sleep out here on the couch. I know where the blankets are."

Kimberly trembled with love and emotion. She could feel the leashed emotion in him even though she couldn't be certain just what those emotions were. The intensity of his manner ate at her heart and she longed to comfort him. But there was a self-protective wariness in her, too. Cavenaugh had the power to hurt her as no one else could. And she was still uncertain of his underlying feelings for her.

He was asking her to take all the risks, Kimberly told herself as she watched the rigid line of his back. No, that wasn't strictly true. Whatever he felt for her, it was not superficial. She knew that with her deepest instincts. While she couldn't actually read his mind, she did know that the intensity and power of his commitment was genuine. He would be a strong, dependable, honorable husband. And she loved him.

"Cavenaugh," Kimberly whispered, "I'll marry you."

He swung around, his gaze piercing in the soft light. But he made no move toward her. A curious tension hovered between them.

"You're sure? Be sure, Kim, because I won't let you change your mind in the morning."

She shook her head. "I won't change my mind."

He took a deep breath and inclined his head almost formally. "I will do my best to make you happy, Kim."

In spite of her tension, Kimberly found herself smiling. "Yes, I think you will. And I'll try to make you a good wife, Cavenaugh."

They stood quietly for a long moment, absorbing the impact of their simple promises to each other. And then Kimberly turned to walk down the hall to her bedroom.

"Good night," she said, not quite knowing what else to say. It was obvious he didn't intend to follow her.

"Good night, Kim."

She was almost at the door of her bedroom when his voice stopped her once more.

"Kim?"

Her head came up quickly. Had he changed his mind about sleeping with her? She would welcome him, she thought. She would welcome him with all her heart.

"I think you should invite your grandparents to the wedding, Kim."

Kimberly's mouth curved wryly and she lifted silently beseeching eyes heavenward.

"You don't know when to quit, do you, Cavenaugh?" She slammed the door of her bedroom behind her.

STARKE HAD IGNORED the wedding champagne and concentrated on whiskey most of the evening. Kimberly decided he'd had enough to put him in one of his philosophical moods, and when she found herself momentarily alone she decided to talk to him.

Holding her champagne glass in one hand she lifted the skirts of her wedding gown with the other and moved quickly across the crowded room.

"Enjoying yourself, Starke?" She smiled.

His craggy face cracked into a genuine grin. "Would you believe this is only the second wedding I've been to in my entire life?"

"When was the first?"

"My own."

"Oh." Kimberly tilted her head, uncertain about whether or not to pry further. "Somehow, I don't see you married," she ventured.

"Neither did I. But I was only nineteen and the girl claimed she was pregnant." He shrugged his massive shoulders. "I thought I ought to do the right thing."

"But she wasn't pregnant?" Kimberly hazarded.

"No. And my wife quickly decided that marriage wasn't all it was made out to be. Not when you're nineteen and stone broke. We split by mutual agreement within six months."

"I see."

He gave her a sharp glance. "Hey, you're not drawing any parallels here, are you? Believe me, if you're pregnant, Dare's going to be thrilled!"

Kimberly felt the blush stain her cheeks and concentrated determinedly on the cluster of men across the room. Cavenaugh, austerely formal in his conservative wedding jacket and ruffled shirt, was the focus of the laughing, jesting group.

She was married to him now, Kimberly had to remind herself. Tied to him with vows and a band of gold. But she felt more nervously uncertain about his true feelings and thoughts tonight than she had at any point during the entire time she had known him.

It was no wonder she was so apprehensive. For the past six weeks they had seen relatively little of each other. Kimberly had stayed in her beach house working on *Vendetta,* and Cavenaugh had only come to see her on the weekends. When he was there he had slept on the sofa. On the one or two occasions when she had spent a weekend at his home, he had kissed her good night at her bedroom door.

She did not fully understand his restraint or the rather cautious, distant way he treated her. Kimberly knew it probably had something to do with Cavenaugh's determination not to "pressure" her. But she couldn't help wondering if he intended to spend his wedding night in his own bedroom. There was no telling how far Cavenaugh would let his sense of responsibility and duty take him.

"Kim?" Starke's voice held a note of concern. "Don't look so uneasy. Dare won't mind at all."

"Mind what?" She pulled her attention away from her husband's hard-edged profile.

"If you're pregnant."

"That's very reassuring," she said with commendable lightness, "but as it happens, I'm not."

"Oh. Too bad. Dare should have a couple of kids."

"To, uh, carry on the Cavenaugh name?" Kimberly asked dryly.

"No, just because he'd make a good father."

Kimberly peered at her oblivious husband. "Do you think so?"

"Yeah. Your grandparents would love some, too. They're having a good time tonight, aren't they?" Starke glanced with satisfaction to the far edge of the crowd where Wesley Marland and his wife were chatting enthusiastically with Aunt Milly and several of her friends. Starke was right. They were delighted with the wedding, embarrassingly grateful to have been invited. And they would adore a couple of grandchildren.

"Cavenaugh made me invite them, you know," Kimberly confided after another sip of champagne. "Or perhaps I should say he strongly advised it."

"Dare wanted to tie up all the loose ends," Starke said bluntly. "He's like that. How are you getting along with the Marlands?"

"With cautious politeness," Kimberly admitted honestly.

"Well, look at it this way," Starke advised, "some people don't even have a cautiously polite relationship with their relatives!"

"I suppose you're right."

"Do you really hate them?"

Kimberly thought about that for a split second and then shook her head. "No." It was the truth. She still wasn't certain how she felt about her grandparents but she knew she didn't hate them. Perhaps she was simply too much in love with Cavenaugh to have any emotion left over for something as useless as hate.

"I told Dare he was an idiot to force you into meeting them," Starke informed her, sipping his whiskey. "But maybe

he was right. Maybe it was the most efficient way of handling the situation. Dare's instincts are usually pretty solid."

"Uh-huh, well, if he ever springs a surprise like that on me again, I'll probably break his neck."

"I don't think you'll have to worry about Dare doing anything so risky for a long while," Starke said consideringly. "He's been handling you with kid gloves for the past six weeks."

Kimberly bit her lip, knowing Starke was right and knowing, too, that she didn't really want that kind of cautious treatment from Cavenaugh. Determinedly she changed the subject.

"Aunt Milly finally seems recovered from the shock of finding out Ariel was the villain of the piece. I was afraid she was going to go on blaming herself indefinitely for what happened."

"Dare wouldn't let her do that," Starke said with a wryly crooked mouth. "He insisted on taking all the blame himself."

"He's big on assuming responsibility." Kimberly sighed.

"It's in his blood," Starke opined. "Comes naturally to him. Some men are like that."

Kimberly slanted him a sardonic glance. "Is that so?"

"Yeah. But there's a price tag attached."

"What do you mean?"

Starke hesitated, as if trying to find the best way of saying what he had to say. "Men who have the guts to handle a lot of responsibility usually have the, well, uh, the *assertiveness* it takes to make sure things get done right."

"Assertiveness?" Kimberly tasted the word. "You mean the arrogance, the overbearing, domineering, stubborn machismo that it takes to railroad everyone into doing things the way said male wants them done?"

Starke looked pleased at her understanding. "Something like that."

"Forget assertiveness. Tell me about the dagger. What did you ever find out about it?"

Starke shrugged. "Dare was right. Some of our old contacts in the import business finally recognized it. The design dates back a few centuries to a style that was used in Europe at one time by people who called themselves witches."

"How did Ariel get hold of it?" Kimberly asked.

"This particular dagger wasn't really old. It's a copy. Ariel apparently found a drawing in one of her occult books and took it to a knifemaker who made it up for her. We would have eventually found the guy who did it. There aren't that many good custom knifemakers around. But we wouldn't have found him in time."

"Did the authorities ever find out how Zorah and Emlyn came to be involved with Ariel?"

"Zorah's real name is Charlotte Martin. Emlyn's name is Joseph Williams."

Kimberly grimaced. "So much for the exotic names. Ariel's doing, no doubt."

"She ran into them when she was exploring sources for some of the herbs she was always experimenting with. Charlotte ran an herb shop and Joe was her boyfriend. Poor Charlotte really wanted to believe in Ariel's power and the possibility of having it passed on to her. Joe was far more practical about the situation. He's the kind of guy who will always be looking for a fast buck. He thought Ariel's kidnapping plans might work. When they didn't he stuck around because he still thought there was a possibility of getting money out of Dare. When Ariel said they had to kill you he went along with it because you were the only one who could identify Charlotte. You'd seen her face to face at the house the day you rescued Scott."

Kimberly shuddered. "So they hired some street punk to do the job. Ariel was the one who let him onto the grounds that night, I suppose."

Starke nodded. "Luckily Ariel insisted it had to be done in a ceremonial fashion. She's the one who said he wouldn't get paid unless he wore the right outfit and used the proper weapon. The punk is still complaining about the limitations she put on him, according to Cranston."

"All of which probably saved my life that night." Kimberly shook her head ruefully. "What a situation."

"Going to get a book out of it?"

"You bet!"

"I like your books," Starke told her seriously. "That Josh Valerian guy's a little strange, but I like the stories."

"What's wrong with Josh?" Kimberly demanded.

"Well, he's not exactly realistic," Starke said carefully. "I mean, all that business about being able to understand the heroine isn't so weird. But having him always feel the same way about things, see them in the same way she does. That's weird."

"You think so?" Kimberly asked wistfully.

"Yup. Valerian's supposed to be a man. Men don't see things quite the same way women do. Nearly drove Dare crazy trying to figure out how he could compete with a fantasy."

"He managed," Kimberly shot back dryly.

"Does Dare know that?"

Kimberly glanced up at him quizzically. "I think so," she said very seriously.

"Then why's he acting so carefully around you?"

"You noticed?"

"Who hasn't?"

"Your guess is as good as mine," Kimberly said evenly. Then she told herself that now was as good a time as any to

ask a question that had been on her mind. She gauged the amount of whiskey Starke had had to drink and decided to take the plunge. "I've been wondering about something, Starke," she began with deceptive lightness.

"Hmm?"

"What is it exactly that you and Cavenaugh imported and exported?"

Starke blinked owlishly. "Stuff."

"What kind of stuff?"

"Junk. Trinkets, jewelry, odd things from different corners of the world. Cavenaugh bought whatever took his fancy and whatever he thought he could sell."

"Starke, why do I have the feeling you are not being one hundred percent straightforward with me?"

"Uh, I think Cavenaugh is trying to get your attention."

"Starke..." She gave up. "I think I'd like more champagne."

"What a coincidence," Starke said brightly. "Here comes Dare and he's carrying two glasses."

Cavenaugh's emerald eyes seemed to glitter with a curious intensity as he took in the sight of his wife, but his voice was lacking in expression. Instead he was as coolly polite as he had been for the past six weeks.

"More champagne, Kim?"

She smiled equally coolly, setting down her empty glass to accept the full one he handed to her. "You must have read my mind."

"I do my best. Starke, I just saw Ginny Adams. She's looking for you."

To Kimberly's astonishment the normally unflappable Starke suddenly looked slightly nervous. He ran his finger around his collar and then checked his tie. "Was she?" He nodded formally at Kimberly and then muttered, "Excuse me."

Kimberly stared after him as he forged through the crowd toward the attractive, forty-year-old woman near the door.

"Ginny Adams?" Kimberly asked.

"I think they make a good pair. Ginny needs someone solid and dependable like Starke. Her husband left her last year."

"Oh. I hadn't realized Starke had a, uh, romantic interest in her."

"You haven't been here enough during the past six weeks to keep track of what's been going on. Finish *Vendetta*?"

"No, but I made a lot of progress." Kimberly gulped the champagne, feeling uncomfortable and shy around her husband. Most of their conversations lately had been like this, polite but rather distant. Kimberly had told herself everything would be all right once they were married, but now she was beginning to wonder if she'd been deluding herself.

"Something wrong, Kim?"

"As a matter of fact, you can answer a question for me," she began assertively.

"A question Starke wouldn't answer? Is that why he was looking so uncomfortable when I arrived?"

"I only wanted to know what it was you two really imported and exported. A simple enough question. And don't tell me it was junk."

Cavenaugh eyed her speculatively. "A lot of it was."

"But what else was involved?"

He hesitated and then shrugged. "Occasionally Starke and I handled transactions involving information. We were sometimes in a position to acquire useful details that regular government agents couldn't get. Does that satisfy your mystery writer's curiosity?"

"Uh, yes, but tell me—"

He cut off the flow of her questions with a curious half smile. "That's it, Kim. That's all you get from me on the subject. And I hope I never see anything close to it in one of your

books." His expression softened briefly when he saw the disappointment in her eyes. "I really can't talk about it."

"Another responsibility you've assumed?"

The softness in him vanished. "Call it whatever you like. Going to hold my silence on the subject against me along with everything else?"

Kimberly frowned. "Of course not. I'm sure you've given your word not to talk about your former line of work. I wouldn't expect you to break it." Not Darius Cavenaugh. He'd see his responsibilities through to the end of his life. Kimberly drank some champagne and considered her own uncertain future.

What if she'd made a terrible mistake, Kimberly wondered with a touch of panic. Maybe everything wasn't going to be all right now. Maybe everything was going to be a total disaster.

"You must be exhausted," Cavenaugh said gently. "It's been a long day."

"I'll survive," she muttered.

He looked at her through faintly narrowed eyes. "I'm not sure I will."

She wasn't certain she'd heard him. It was the first indication of any emotion other than bland politeness she'd caught in his words for weeks. "I beg your pardon?"

"Nothing," he assured her quickly, taking her arm. "Let's go talk to your grandparents. They want to show you off a bit."

"They're delighted I've made such an excellent marriage," Kimberly said dryly.

"More delighted about it than you are, apparently."

Kimberly blinked. Again she sensed the blade of the knife beneath his words. Cavenaugh's carefully controlled temperament was fraying slightly around the edges. She wondered why.

SHE WAS STILL WONDERING two hours later, when she found herself alone in her bedroom. The last of the guests had left the estate and the various inhabitants of the house had settled down in their own rooms.

Kimberly realized she was pacing the floor in front of the bed and forced herself to stop. This wasn't exactly how she had envisioned spending her wedding night. She was alone and it was clear now that Cavenaugh would not be joining her. He had walked her upstairs, kissed her good night at the door and disappeared into his own room.

Eyes burning with tears of frustration and dismay, Kimberly sank down onto the edge of her bed and desperately tried to decide what to do next.

She was at a loss. There had been no talk of a honeymoon, not even a trip to the coast to spend some time in her beach house.

This was insane, she told herself. Here she was head over heels in love with her husband of only a few hours and he was spending the night in his own bedroom! It was beginning to appear as though he intended to live by the vow he had made the night he asked her to marry him. She would be given all the time she wanted to get to know him.

Somehow Kimberly hadn't really expected him to honor those rash words. Especially since she had never meant him to do so. It was ludicrous to think that they could truly get to know each other as long as they were fencing emotionally like this.

What she wouldn't give for some genuine telepathic talent, Kimberly thought. She would sacrifice a great deal at this moment to know what was going on in Darius Cavenaugh's head.

Slowly she stood up and unbuttoned the delicate fastenings of her wedding dress. Hanging it carefully in the closet,

she pulled out the nightgown she had bought for the occasion of her wedding night.

Grimly she stared at the frilly concoction of satin and lace and then she put it away again. No sense wasting it, Kimberly told herself. She might as well wear her usual T-shirt. There would be no one sharing the bed with her and thus no one to appreciate the horribly expensive nightgown.

Standing barefooted in front of the mirror, she brushed her hair down around her shoulders, studying herself critically in the thigh-length T-shirt. From the beginning she had never doubted the physical attraction between herself and Cavenuagh. He wanted her, or at least he *had* wanted her. She examined the thrust of her breasts against the T-shirt and licked her lower lip uncertainly. What if even that elemental attraction had faded?

No, she concluded, that wasn't the case. She had seen the barely concealed possessiveness in those emerald eyes on more than one occasion during the past six weeks. And she was certain she'd felt him restraining himself when he'd taken her in his arms to kiss her good night.

Kimberly pulled the brush through her hair one last time and threw it down on the dresser. Cavenaugh was sticking by his plan to "give her time." That was the only explanation for his odd behavior. But she couldn't figure out what he expected her to do while she waited patiently for him to signal that enough time had passed between them.

It had all gone far enough, Kimberly decided with sudden resolution. She was a married woman in love with her husband. Her husband might not love her but he wanted her and he needed her. That made for a better foundation than a lot of marriages had, she assured herself.

Without pausing to think, Kimberly whirled and grabbed her old terry cloth robe out of the closet. Flinging it on she let herself out into the hall. The house was dark and quiet. She

looked at the door of Cavenaugh's room and saw that there was no shaft of light under the door. He must have gone to bed.

It took almost as much courage to walk down the hall to Cavenaugh's bedroom as it had to face the punk with the silver dagger. In front of the door Kimberly lifted her hand to knock and then changed her mind. Taking a long, steadying breath she tried the doorknob.

It gave silently and the door swung open with only the smallest of sounds. She stood for a few seconds, letting her eyes adjust to the shadows. If Cavenaugh hadn't moved slightly in the darkness she wouldn't have seen him. He was sitting in a chair by the window, his legs sprawled out in front of him. There was a bottle beside him and the movement she saw was the one he made when he reached for it. She couldn't see his face.

"Cavenaugh?"

"You have a talent for it, Kim." His voice was a low growl of sound.

"A talent for what?" she whispered, daring to close the door behind her.

"For finding trouble, of course. Especially at night. Most of your big adventures lately have taken place at night, haven't they?" He poured the brandy with unnatural care.

Kimberly clung to the doorknob behind her back. "Are you...are you very drunk, Cavenaugh?"

"Not yet, but I'm getting there. Don't rush me, Kim. I'm doing my damnedest not to rush you, the least you can do is return the favor."

She still couldn't see much of him as he sprawled in the chair; only his arm was visible as he raised the brandy glass to his mouth. The arm was bare though, and Kimberly realized that all Cavenaugh was wearing was a pair of jeans.

"Is that why you haven't shown any interest in me for the past six weeks? You're trying not to rush me?" Her voice was a thread of husky sound in the darkness. Her pulse was racing with trepidation and a strange kind of uncertain fear.

"What do you mean I haven't shown any interest in you? I married you, didn't I? A man doesn't generally marry a woman unless he's at least mildly interested in her."

She winced. Cavenaugh was definitely beginning to sound surly. If his temper had been showing signs of fraying earlier in the evening it was ragged now.

"I can't tell you how reassuring that is," Kimberly managed bravely.

"Go back to your room, Kim," he said softly.

"Why?"

"Because if you stay here much longer, you won't be going back at all. Is that plain enough for you?"

She stepped away from the door, clutching the old terry cloth robe tightly around herself. "I'm your wife, Cavenaugh. Maybe I don't want to go back to my bed alone. I...I have a right to be here with you."

"Don't talk to me about rights!"

"Then let's talk about why you're afraid of rushing me," she flung back, goaded. "What are you afraid of rushing me into? Bed? I'm not trying to resist, in case you hadn't noticed!"

He set down the brandy glass with a fierce clatter and came up out of the chair with a lethally graceful movement. Nude from the waist up, his face carved in harsh, rigid lines, Cavenaugh was a formidable opponent to face in the dark. Kimberly almost lost her courage.

Placatingly she held out one hand. "Cavenaugh, how long do you think we can last in separate bedrooms?"

"Until you trust me enough to let yourself love me again," he told her with barely suppressed violence. "I don't want you

in my bed until you can say you love me the way you did before I mishandled that business with your grandparents."

She stared at him. "I don't think you've been doing your usual hot job of reading my mind lately," she finally said weakly. Her hands were trembling, and she clutched at the tie of the robe in an effort to still them.

"Reading your mind has always been a fairly haphazard business," Cavenaugh rasped. "Maybe it's because you've got a rather haphazard way of thinking. A *feminine* way of thinking," he clarified accusingly.

"Is that right? And I suppose your thinking processes are more intelligible? Well, let me tell you something, Cavenaugh, I haven't been able to figure out what's going on in that. . .that male head of yours for weeks! I've been wondering why on earth you even bothered to marry me, for example."

"Because I love you!" he exploded. "Why else would I marry you?"

"Sex, companionship, to acquire someone who can protect you from your oversized sense of responsibility, because you felt grateful to me: all kinds of reasons!"

His eyes glittered and his voice was raw. "I married you because I love you, Kim."

She caught her breath. "Well, that's why I married you. So why are we spending our wedding night in separate bedrooms?" she whispered achingly.

Cavenaugh moved then, gliding across the floor to scoop her up into his arms. He swung her around with a fierce exuberance and tossed her down on the bed. Then he was lying heavily on top of her, pinning her to the bedclothes.

"Kim, are you sure? Are you very, very sure? I was so afraid that I'd ruined everything."

She speared her fingers through his hair, her heart in her eyes. "Cavenaugh, I've never stopped loving you. I was an-

gry and hurt and I was sure you couldn't possibly have loved me or you wouldn't have pulled a stunt like that, but I never stopped loving you."

"I only did it because I thought it was for the best, Kim. I wanted you to be completely free of the past, free to love me. I needed all of you."

"I understand, darling."

"Do you really,?" He was studying her with a burning intensity.

Kimberly's mouth curved gently. "I didn't say I approved. I said I understood. There's a difference, I've learned."

"Tell me about it!" he grated hoarsely, and then he kissed her with rough passion. As she began to respond he lifted his head again. "I know I'm not what you thought you wanted in a man. But I love you so very much, sweetheart. That love is going to get us through the communication problems, I swear it."

"You mean through all the times when you're having trouble comprehending my 'haphazard' thinking processes?" she teased softly. "Actually, I've been meaning to tell you that I'm thinking of changing the character of Josh Valerian slightly."

"Is that so?"

"Umm. I'm going to make him a little more like you. Not quite so comprehensible to the heroine, but maybe a bit more interesting."

"I love the way your mind works," he assured her deeply, bending his head to nibble provocatively behind her ear.

"At the moment I'm having trouble thinking at all," she confided, slipping her hands across his shoulders.

"Don't worry about it. I'll do all the thinking for us." He lifted himself slightly away and undid the tie of her robe. "You look so damn sexy in a T-shirt."

"I would have looked even sexier in my new nightgown. But when I realized you weren't going to come to my room

tonight or invite me into yours, I decided not to waste it," she told him sadly.

"So you just put on your usual T-shirt and this old robe and trotted down the hall to confront me, hmm?" He was toying with the hem of the T-shirt, inching it slowly up to her waist. "Thank God you did. I was going crazy in here telling myself I had to be patient. In fact, I've been going crazy for the past six weeks convincing myself I had to give you time to learn to love me again."

"And I've been going crazy wondering if you would ever learn to love me. Ah, Cavenaugh, we've both been fools, haven't we?"

"No. We've just been having a little trouble communicating. It won't happen again."

"You think not?"

"Well, I suppose we're always going to have to work around the fact that you are a woman.. "

"And you're a man "

"Umm. And in some ways the communication problem will always exist between us." Cavenaugh lost patience with the T-shirt and stripped it off over her head. "But I expect that's why love got invented," he stated confidently.

"To help men and woman communicate? An interesting anthropological theory, Cavenaugh." She laughed up at him with her eyes, her body warming under his. "Do you really love me?" Her hands twined around his neck.

"More than anything else on earth." He was suddenly deadly serious. "Don't ever doubt that, Kim. There will be times when I'll have my hands full with other matters and other people's problems. But there will never be a time when my heart isn't full of love for you. Do you understand?"

"Yes, Cavenaugh. I understand. And there will be times when my haphazard mind will seem full of plots and char-

acters but there will never be a time when I am not completely in love with you."

"Good." With quick, wrenching movements he unsnapped his jeans and kicked them onto the floor. Then he turned back the quilt and tucked Kimberly underneath.

She went into his arms with a new, serene confidence, her body flowing along his. "I love you, Cavenaugh."

"You couldn't love me any more than I love you. You've been mine since the first time I made love to you. But tonight you're finally home. You're finally in my bed, where you've belonged all along."

He caressed her with wonder, his fingers seeking out the hidden places of her body until she twisted gloriously beneath his touch. When he dipped his fingers tantalizingly into the hot, damp warmth between her legs she gasped.

Then, with reverent care he began to trail a line of kisses from the shadows between her breasts to the even darker shadows at the apex of her thighs. Kimberly stirred with faint, embarrassed protest but he ignored it. Gently, with undeniable insistence, he parted her legs and gave her the most intimate of kisses.

Kimberly cried out softly, lifting herself against him as the excitement rippled through her. "Cavenaugh!"

"Sweet witch." He worked his way up her body until her questing fingers found the evidence of his arousal and he groaned aloud.

"Love me, Cavenaugh. Please love me!"

"Always."

It was a vow, and Kimberly knew in the deepest recesses of her mind that she could rely on it. Cavenaugh was that kind of man. She would be able to trust in him and in his love for the rest of her life.

He brought his body into hers, possessing and possessed, and Kimberly clung to him. The witchcraft that swirled in the

darkened room was a very ancient kind, and it wrapped the two lovers in the softest of spells. Kimberly and her beloved Cavenaugh gave themselves up to it with delight, united in a passionate comprehension of each other that went beyond words.

D0058198

FIVE DOLLARS AND A PORK CHOP SANDWICH

FIVE DOLLARS *and a* PORK CHOP SANDWICH

Vote Buying and the Corruption of Democracy

Mary Frances Berry

Beacon Press
Boston

Beacon Press
Boston, Massachusetts
www.beacon.org

Beacon Press books
are published under the auspices of
the Unitarian Universalist Association of Congregations.

Printed in the United States of America

19 18 17 16 8 7 6 5 4 3 2 1

This book is printed on acid-free paper that meets the uncoated paper
ANSI/NISO specifications for permanence as revised in 1992.

Text design by Wilsted & Taylor Publishing Services

Library of Congress Cataloging-in-Publication Data
Berry, Mary Frances.
Five dollars and a pork chop sandwich : vote buying and the corruption of democracy / Mary Frances Berry.
pages cm
Includes bibliographical references and index.
ISBN 978-0-8070-7640-8 (hardcover : acid-free paper) — ISBN 978-0-8070-7641-5 (ebook)
1. Elections—Corrupt practices. 2. Voting. I. Title.
JF1083.B47 2016
364.1'324—dc23 2015025756

To Francis Guess, who understood

CONTENTS

PREFACE

In 1958, when my little brother was in the fifth grade, he went to Carter Lawrence School in South Nashville. One day in October, he saw signs and preparations for an afterschool "White Bean Supper" sponsored by Gene "Little Evil" Jacobs. Little Evil, a bar owner and junk furniture dealer, served as city councilman of our poor, predominantly black district, south of the courthouse along the river. He owed his election to the backing of bootlegger-turned-politician Charlie Riley. Little Evil's duty was to deliver blocs of unquestioning voters on Election Day; "whether the voters were dead or alive was a needless distinction."[1]

People in the "black bottom" of South Nashville came to white bean suppers to eat and drink while Little Evil talked about the upcoming election. He took care of people's needs all year, not just during election season. He also handed out Thanksgiving and Christmas baskets. He made sure he could deliver his voters to himself and the candidates he supported.

Decades later, my fellow civil rights commissioner Francis Guess, whose family has been among those African Americans who have voted Republican since Mr. Lincoln, recalled similar stories about vote gathering in Nashville. Little Evil eventually ran afoul of a reform movement in the 1960s. He was targeted by the local newspaper and jailed for election fraud. "Walking-around money" and other gifts

are still put on the street during campaigns, but they don't have the influence they had in the old days.[2]

My mother's sister, Aunt Serriner, and her husband Uncle Will, were not formally educated people but they always voted. When the Voting Rights Act of 1965 was being debated in Congress, their son Dewitt, an aeronautical engineer, got into an argument with his co-workers in the North. They insisted that anyone who couldn't read and write shouldn't have the right to vote. Dewitt told them that his parents cherished the right to vote. And he said they knew as much or more than he about the issues because all of their children read the newspapers to them.

My mother, the youngest and best-educated of twelve children, having finished the eighth grade, always voted too. She was most proud of casting her first ballot for Senator Albert Gore Sr., first elected to the Congress in 1938 and to the US Senate in 1952. He, of course, was the father of Vice President Albert Gore Jr., who also got her vote.

My mother and my aunts and uncles saw nothing wrong with the attention Little Evil and other ward-heelers paid to them throughout the year. They appreciated the benefits they provided, unlike any public agency. They were pleased that people turned out to vote and understood the importance of the ballot. And they taught their children, by example, to value the franchise. They might have been shocked at some of the voter suppression and manipulation that is discussed in this book. But I am sure they would have liked the ideas for increasing voter turnout and accountability.

FIVE DOLLARS AND A PORK CHOP SANDWICH

CHAPTER I

Voting Rights, Rules, and Suppression
A Brief History

> This is the way it's s'posed to be. . . .
> Besides, we poor people need the money.
>
> —*Anonymous voter*

In 2000, a few weeks into his work as head of Louisiana's new Voter Fraud Division, Greg Malveaux knew he had the most challenging job in his life. After twelve years as a deputy sheriff in Orleans Parish and five years detailed to the city council, he had learned quite a lot about scandals and shenanigans, and had observed firsthand Louisiana's corrupt politicians. However, what people were telling him about the manipulation of the electoral process was more outrageous than he had ever imagined.

All of this came home one day when he was investigating a complaint in Cajun country. He talked to an elderly black woman about a recent local election. When he approached her, she saw a thirty-eight-year-old African American man in a suit and tie who politely explained he was a voter-fraud investigator for the state. Suspicious, she demanded what he wanted with her. He asked, "Did you vote? Did you notice anything unusual?"

Malveaux's respectful manner erased her doubts. She was pleased to see a black man in such a big government job. She told him she

voted and began casually explaining how politicians bought votes on Election Day. She would be driven to the polls with instructions on whom to vote for. When she cast her ballot, the driver gave her five dollars. She didn't know this was illegal. "This is the way it's s'posed to be," she said. That was the way it was always done, and "besides, we poor people need the money."

All over Louisiana, Malveaux found evidence of election corruption by both Democrats and Republicans. Vote buyers in rural areas, acting as middlemen, generally received ten dollars per voter from a candidate who had no personal contact with the voters in the process. Half of the money, five dollars, went to the voter, as the elderly woman had told him. Sometimes the payment was "lagniappe": a pork chop sandwich and a cold drink. In urban areas, the process and payoffs were handled by organizations with benign names like the Alliance for Government and Citizens for Responsible Government. Politicians paid these groups surreptitiously for their endorsement. Vote buying gives "retail politics" an entirely different meaning.

But this was not the only corrupt practice Malveaux confronted. Local prosecutors, because they too were elected, refused to abolish the system by prosecuting the people they themselves sometimes "hired" to win office. Malveaux was disgusted by the way politicians took advantage of poor people by buying their votes and then ignoring their needs. Under his leadership, Louisiana's Voter Fraud Division became an agency that sought to empower voters and end election corruption.

Readers may be surprised to learn that vote buying and vote selling even exists. Some may think this form of election corruption ended a long time ago, or that its effects are negligible. Other issues about voting and elections seem to be more pressing: the influence of corporations and corporate donations on candidates and issues, the ever-declining turnout of voters in elections, and the disfranchisement that may result from requiring voters to present identification. The contemporary focus on voter suppression and the declining po-

litical power of ordinary citizens to "make their voices heard" motivates Tea Party sippers and Coffee Collective drinkers alike.[1]

Paying people to vote for a specific candidate may not seem to fit the definition of "voter suppression," but it is one of several ways that campaign operators manipulate the outcome of elections. Vote buying, misuse of absentee ballots, and other stratagems tend to defraud the very citizens who need government services the most: the poor, the elderly, and minority voters. These are also the people who may not have "proper" government-issued identification to vote. Whether their vote is bought, or not cast at all, their political power is suppressed. Buying votes is another form of suppression: paying eligible citizens to vote for candidates whom they might not otherwise support. And since a single ballot lists candidates for other offices at the local, state, and even federal level, the entire election can be corrupted.[2]

"Who Can Vote?," a study funded by the Carnegie and Knight foundations, compiled data on electoral fraud, documenting 2,068 instances of criminal prosecution between 2000 and 2012. These cases were collected from state officials, though not everyone responded to requests. Forty-six percent of resolved cases resulted in acquittals, dropped charges, or a decision not to bring charges. A search of cases that were appealed in the states' highest courts before 2000 produced about four hundred cases of electoral fraud. This number is not definitive. Most criminal complaints are not prosecuted, and those that go to trial are often unreported. Earlier cases are even more difficult to find because people convicted of criminal offenses before the 1960s had to pay for their own lawyers if they wanted to appeal.

Vote buying in Louisiana is not an anomaly, though many in the state hope the television reality show *Duck Dynasty* is. Across the country, Kentucky, Illinois, and other states have long histories of electoral fraud, primarily in state and local elections. In order to explore the extent of voter fraud beyond Louisiana and efforts to combat it, I researched vote buying and abuse of the ballot laws elsewhere

in the country. I discovered that most states don't have dedicated voting fraud units, so investigations and criminal prosecutions are haphazard if they occur at all.[3] However, newspaper accounts, oral histories, and other source materials reveal numerous violations and prosecutions.

In this book, I have included places with a long and well-documented history of fraud and powerful political machines. Chicago is an obvious example. In some of Kentucky's counties, vote buying has been going on since at least the early 1900s, when coal, timber, and railroad barons used it to destroy unions and local party organizations. In Texas, the widespread use of the buying, hauling, and abuse of absentee ballots in rural areas among Latino *politiqueras* has become entrenched. I also found some states that resorted to rather novel ways to curb vote buying without resorting to threats of prison. There were also examples of incentives given legally to voters to increase election turnout.

The criminal cases of vote buying and selling that were appealed include misbehavior by election officials as well as prosecution of voters and officials. Candidates themselves filed suit to contest elections, and charged their opponents with fraud. These civil cases provide important evidence of the extent of vote buying and selling. Further, in civil cases the court could discard election results, bar a candidate from holding office, or order participants to stay out of political campaigns for a period of time.[4] It appears that judges in civil cases were more likely to find parties guilty of election fraud because perpetrators did not face prison.

Malveaux approached election fraud as a criminal offense; he investigated hundreds of complaints and sent detailed accounts to local prosecutors who could have prosecuted wrongdoers by using the evidence compiled by the Fraud Division. As we will see in the next chapters, these cases almost never went to court. To Malveaux, this was a gross miscarriage of justice, a civil rights violation of the worst order. He didn't think this way just because he was a lawman by

training and profession who thought he should put vote buyers in jail. He thought this because he wanted voters to get power. To him, vote buying debased government of the people and by the people.

Candidates are expected to make promises to voters, which most people interpret as a perfectly legal form of vote "buying." A senator in Alaska can pledge to build a "bridge to nowhere." Another candidate says she will obtain highway construction funds, or federal money to build a hospital, or other jobs and infrastructure projects, offering an economic reward to voters while paying a particular community with public funds. Other rewards may come in the form of patronage for those who support the winner, and these benefits are perfectly routine and permissible according to Supreme Court decisions.[5]

Sometimes vote buying turns into extortion. In Fond du Lac, Wisconsin in 1964, city officials offered voters "free rent for a year" in public housing in exchange for their signatures on an annexation petition. Those who refused the offer of free rent were threatened with eviction. The state supreme court decided that the officials' actions were clearly corrupt; there was nothing for the "public good" in such behavior. The use of "economic pressure . . . to obtain favorable signatures" was "a shocking disregard of the political process of government."[6] In fact, "The city's action was the equivalent of buying votes and improper."

When a candidate or a campaign operator buys a vote outright, the balance of power is disrupted. Once elected, the official has no political motivation to address the economic and social problems citizens face in their daily lives. The city councilman has no reason to ensure that people in their districts have good schools, paved roads, health care, responsive police, or public services, because at reelection time, however poorly he has served his constituents, they won't vote him out of office. It creates the impression that a vote is an individual choice, a civic responsibility, rather than a demonstration of a community's collective power. And in Louisiana, where the money to buy votes appears to come from "big money" campaign donations

made by oil and petrochemical interests, lawmakers are even less responsive to their constituents' interests.[7]

Authentic democracies are based on citizen participation and the delivery of government benefits to constituents by elected officials. Voters may invest their hopes in a candidate who promises to change their situation, believing that this time around, elections actually do matter. But when good jobs at decent wages remain stubbornly difficult to obtain, and other reminders of growing inequality are revealed, pessimism is the mood in barbershops and beauty salons. It leads a cynic to suggest that a pork chop sandwich and a few dollars would at least be some kind of reward in return for supporting President Obama or Chicago mayor Rahm Emanuel.

Cynicism and disbelief in the power of collective political action deeply affects local elections too. The impact of nonparticipation in municipal elections and lack of influence became apparent in Ferguson, Missouri, and in other communities where whites control local government. African Americans make up two-thirds of Ferguson's population, yet the mayor, school board, and city council are all majority white; only two members of a fifty-three-member police force are people of color. White voter turnout in Ferguson was three times that of blacks in the April 2013 municipal election.[8] These disparities and inequalities came to national attention after Michael Brown was killed by police officer Darren Wilson on August 9, 2014.

The primarily white police force of Ferguson raised most of the city's operating funds through traffic fines. US Attorney General Eric Holder called this practice "revenue generation through policing." "Driving while black" means that police targeted African American drivers for mostly minor infractions in numbers that far exceeded their population, according to a report done by Missouri's attorney general. In 2013, African Americans were 86 percent of police stops, 92 percent of vehicle searches, and 93 percent of arrests. Yet police found contraband more often on white drivers (34 percent) than on black drivers (22 percent). The US Department of Justice made a

series of recommendations for reforming the police department, announcing that if Ferguson did not act voluntarily to implement their recommendations quickly, there would be a federal lawsuit forcing compliance.[9]

Political disfranchisement in Ferguson won't be overcome simply by increasing black voter turnout or electing African Americans to political offices. Local citizens who are organizing on the ground know that, even though the outside political commentators who weighed in after the shooting tried to affix blame on low political participation. The township's off-cycle municipal elections—a Progressive-era reform designed to focus voters on local issues—may have contributed to reduced turnout and fewer black officeholders, but it was not the only factor. Local political organizers recognize that Ferguson and adjoining suburban towns are essentially fiefdoms: municipal managers appointed by white elected officials distribute government jobs, award city contracts, and distribute patronage without being held accountable to voters.[10]

Grassroots activists spent the better part of early 2015 organizing and educating Ferguson's voters to use their collective power by voting in the April elections. "In order to be motivated to vote, people have to have something to vote for," said Reginald Rounds of Missourians Organizing for Reform and Empowerment (MORE). "That's why we're so glad to be supporting candidates who really want to fix Ferguson and make our justice system work for all of us."[11] Turnout went up two-and-a-half times from the previous election, to 30 percent of eligible voters, even though only 128 new people registered to vote. Two new black council members, both solid members of the professional middle class, were elected; the candidates supported by the activists did not win. The city council now has three black members and three white members including Mayor James Knowles, who has a vote. Political accountability remains the priority of Ferguson activists, who want not just reform of the police department but also revisions in municipal financing.[12] In other communities where protests

against police killings of African American men and women have occurred since Michael Brown's death, similar organizing campaigns by local activists have begun to confront entrenched political and police power.

The massacre of nine African American worshippers by a Confederate sympathizer at Emanuel African Methodist Episcopal Church in Charleston, South Carolina, led to a successful movement to remove the Confederate flag from the capitol grounds, but not political reform. Calls for the legislature to overturn South Carolina's photo identification law have not gained sufficient support. Even the invocation of Reverend Clementa Pinckney, one of those murdered in the June 17 massacre, church pastor and a South Carolina state senator, who had made voting one of his principal goals, was insufficient.[13]

Martin Luther King Jr. asked in 1967, after the legislative victories of the Civil Rights Act and the Voting Rights Act, "Where do we go from here?" Voter registration, citizen education programs, economic development programs, and greater educational opportunities should have made "things different now."[14] Yet almost forty years later, Ferguson and events in other cities make it seem that ordinary American citizens possess very little political power. The expansion of voting rights since the colonial period has, in theory, enfranchised everyone over the age of eighteen born in the United States or its territories. We're at a peak—yet we have achieved a new low.

VOTING RIGHTS FROM COLONIAL TIMES TO WORLD WAR II

The history of voting rights in the United States is not the story of steady progress toward the inclusion of (nearly) every citizen. It is better described as a push-pull phenomenon. Each expansion of the franchise has led to efforts to suppress the vote. For example, after ratification of the Fifteenth Amendment in 1869, almost one million formerly enslaved African American men registered to vote.[15]

Southern states responded with violent repression and a host of laws containing devices, such as literacy requirements and grandfather clauses, to keep those same men from voting. Structural oppression negated formal rights. Changes in the late twentieth and early twenty-first century, intended to increase voter participation by relaxing registration requirements, have been accompanied by the influence of corporations and wealthy contributors that discourage voters. What looks like reform is often in reality a decline in the power of individual citizens and the collective power of the vote.

Voter suppression, not surprisingly, is not a new phenomenon and can be found the world over. It has existed since the colonial period in America and seems to come naturally in any system in which voters choose their political leadership. Democracy requires the expression of voter choice but, ironically, it is "choice" that opens the way for the manipulation of rules in pursuit of elected office.[16]

Voting has historically been a raucous affair. In the election for the Virginia House of Burgesses in 1758, George Washington spent a considerable sum for gallons of liquor and beer to treat prospective voters, a necessary part of winning. One rationale for national prohibition was to remove the influence of "Demon Rum" on elections. After the Twenty-First Amendment repealed prohibition in 1933, alcohol began to flow again. South Carolina, the last state to have a total statewide ban in alcohol sales on Election Day, repealed that law in 2014. Bans in Alaska and Massachusetts permit local governments to remain exempt.[17]

When the framers wrote the Constitution, they created a system of limited democracy that enfranchised only some citizens. They believed that imposing national electoral rules on the states would violate the principles of local autonomy, principles for which they had just fought the War of Independence. The framers consciously supported both federalism and states' rights by making voting in national elections dependent on state laws. The national government has the power to define who is a citizen, but the states determine who

is a voter. Since the 1920s, all states have required voters to be US citizens in order to cast a ballot in state or federal elections. Those who wish there were uniform federal rules for voting must contend with the Constitution's federalism.

During the Jacksonian period, from roughly 1824 to 1840, states abolished property ownership and tax paying as qualifications for voting. Some states barred men who received public charity from voting until the late nineteenth century. Political participation, at least by free white men over the age of twenty-one, did indeed increase. Only 27 percent of the eligible electorate voted in 1824; when Jackson ran a second time, in 1828, 58 percent of eligible voters turned out. By 1840, almost 80 percent cast ballots in the election of William Henry Harrison, who won in a campaign featuring torchlight parades, coonskin caps, and the slogan "Tippecanoe and Tyler too." However, conflict and anxiety over the right to vote followed with westward expansion, divisive conflicts over slavery, and the arrival of new waves of Irish, German, and other immigrants.

Before the Constitution was in force, only a few states expressly disfranchised free African Americans; some blacks and even a few women apparently voted in New York and elsewhere prior to 1789. Exclusion then became the rule until the Civil War. In the 1857 *Dred Scott* decision, the Supreme Court ruled that blacks, free or slave, could not be citizens of the United States. If voters must be citizens, then black men could be neither voters nor potential voters.[18]

Congress passed the Reconstruction Act after the Civil War, permitting black men throughout the South to vote in the 1868 presidential election. In return, the Republican Party of Lincoln rewarded black voters with patronage posts in local communities as well as national government. Frederick Douglass's appointment as president of the Freedman's Savings and Trust Company, a bank chartered by Congress in 1865 to safeguard the savings of African American Civil War veterans and former slaves, made him one of the black Republicans who benefited from this practice. Radical Republicans in the

Fortieth Congress also acted to secure black votes for their party by drafting a constitutional amendment for equal manhood suffrage.

The Fifteenth Amendment to the Constitution, ratified in February 1870, forbids federal and state governments from denying the vote to citizens based on "race, or color, or previous condition of servitude." For the first time, the Constitution actually included the words "right to vote," and the amendment's second section gave Congress the "power to enforce this article by appropriate legislation." White violence and intimidation all over the South, however, frightened blacks away from the polls. Even state Republican Party conventions had difficulty meeting because new racial segregation laws prohibited blacks and whites from sitting together.

A push-pull phenomenon expanded voting rights to include black men while imposing tighter restrictions on all voters. Congress passed campaign reform laws after the Civil War that restricted the benefits that officeholders could dispense to party loyalists and their family members. Federal officials were prohibited from soliciting donations from workers in the Washington Navy Yard. Though such reform seems logical, workers had come to expect raises and promotions in exchange for their contributions. The widows and daughters of Civil War veterans were also affected; though they could not vote, through political donations they too secured clerical jobs in the federal government.[19]

The assassination of President Garfield by a disappointed government job seeker made civil service reform a national issue, inspiring the passage of the first federal Civil Service measure, the Pendleton Act, in 1883. Elected officials could no longer demand that office seekers help in campaigns, contribute funds, or otherwise pay for civil service posts. Though Congress eliminated this form of political patronage, cities and states were much slower to adopt similar reforms. As a result, though national elections were not as rewarding to voters as they once had been, candidates for local and state offices could still whip up "enthusiasm" for their campaigns.

Elections, of course, determine who has power in the coming term. Elections also allow voters to determine other government matters, such as the issuance of bonds to build roads and public buildings, proposals to amend the state constitution, and voter-initiated propositions. In the late nineteenth century, the "county seat wars" in Kansas led to several famously corrupt elections. The 1889 contest to determine which town would become the seat of Gray County forced the judges in the state supreme court to "[wade] through the scum, filth, and mercenary degradation of this record, and find but little to commend in the action of either party."

In Kansas, the founders of the towns of Cimarron and Ingalls vied to be the county seat. The town that won would be rewarded by having a railroad routed through it. The prize was so great that leaders in both towns resorted to corruption in their determination to win. When Cimarron won, Ingalls contested the results. Chief Justice Horton found Cimarron's victory fraudulent. "The testimony in the case discloses so much fraud, corruption, and bribery that the election was a travesty upon justice, and therefore wholly void." Among the irregularities unearthed in three thousand printed pages of testimony was the existence of a secret, oath-bound society of six dozen men who promised to vote for "the town that would pay them the largest amount of money for their votes." The society had received a ten-thousand-dollar bond, signed by prominent citizens of Cimarron, to pay the money. They voted for Cimarron. The board of elections permitted the ballot box to be stuffed with a total of seven or eight hundred fraudulent ballots.

The conflict did not end there. Cimarron demanded a rehearing. While acknowledging that "gross frauds and irregularities occurred," this time the court decided that Ingalls probably received the majority of votes cast "and of those cast by what appeared to be legal voters." As for "the principal frauds and irregularities," these "were committed by the friends of [Cimarron]." Yet "there were some honest votes cast at that election. There is nothing left for us to do but to

endeavor to give expression to the declarations of an honest majority. We hope and trust that we have found it rightfully."[20]

Westward expansion, the building of railroads, and the admission of new states to the Union meant an increasingly mobile population. Yet rather than forcing states to be more flexible in registering new voters, legislatures responded by instituting residency requirements. These were another means to suppress the vote. Poor people were and still are especially affected because these laws assume a fixed address. Merely living in a community for a period of time was not enough to establish residency. States excluded people who lived in custodial institutions, and college and university students could not vote where they attended school, though some exceptions were made based on their intention to remain in the community after graduation. In 1904, the US Supreme Court, in a Maryland case, *Pope v. Williams*, upheld the constitutionality of residency qualifications. An off-campus address plus demonstrable intent to remain indefinitely were required.

Yet the mobility of certain citizens was recognized by the creation of the absentee ballot. They were first offered to soldiers during the Civil War and later legalized in all states by 1918, at least for members of the armed forces during wartime. By 1920, over twenty states had absentee voting for anyone whose absence from home during an election was required. As we will see, absentee ballots have proven particularly susceptible to vote buying because campaign workers collaborate with county clerks and voting registrars to accept ballots signed and submitted in bulk.

At the same time that absentee ballots were created, two dozen states disfranchised convicted felons. By 1920, most states sentenced felons to "civil death" even after they had completed prison sentences and parole.[21] Few people objected to these suppression measures, even for people who had completed their sentences; the courts turned down challenges. A consensus had developed that "criminals" were immoral and did not deserve to vote.[22]

Some states did not consider Native Americans "white" and therefore they were automatically disfranchised in federal and state elections. The Supreme Court in *Cherokee Nation v. Georgia* (1831) and other decisions expressly declared that indigenous people were not US citizens and thus could not vote. It was not until 1924 that Congress passed the Indian Citizenship Act recognizing all indigenous people born in the United States as full citizens. But states still had the power to determine voting qualifications. The right to vote for Native Americans grew gradually in the twentieth century, and the last state to legalize it, New Mexico, did so in 1962. Notably, indigenous people were a sizable portion of the state's population.[23]

As women, poor people, people of color, and naturalized immigrants secured voting rights, states enacted literacy and education tests to suppress their political power. After the First World War, participation in elections declined greatly, despite the ratification of the Nineteenth Amendment, which granted women the right to vote. Progressive Era reformers were quite concerned about the lack of civil participation and began discussing whether voting should be compulsory, as it was in some other nations. "Get Out the Vote" campaigns began in 1924, as advocates of good government urged citizens to do their duty. But when elites discovered that most nonvoters were poor people, their campaign talk quickly ended.

Many of the reforms advocated by progressives actually contributed to the decline in voting. Policies to end the influence of the corporate interests on candidates, to abolish machine politics and patronage, to elect city officials using at-large elections, and to hire professional city managers who oversaw a reformed civil service system, all undermined the reward system that had encouraged the participation of working class and poor people. The "new broom that swept clean"—as women suffragists had promised—made politics uninteresting to the men who had once dominated it. By the late 1960s, almost half of the nation's cities and towns were governed by city managers and at-large commissioners. As a result, voting seemed to

be far removed from decisions about law enforcement policies, public transportation, and the provision of other municipal services.

In Kentucky, politics remained mostly untouched by such reforms. The state had earned its reputation for corruption as coal miners fought coalmine owners for political control. For those who wanted out of the mines, securing a government job was one of the few options, and candidates leveraged voters' desires to win. In the 1930s, the state supreme court decided candidates should be allowed to promise voters taxpayer-funded jobs and public building repairs. Handing out "ginger cakes" to prospective voters was also permissible, and it did not violate the Corrupt Practices Act. After all, "Ginger cakes are good if made right—and there is no evidence that the [cakes offered in this election] were not made right—and it is not a corrupt practice to buy them. It is not claimed that the voters who ate them were either corrupted or painfully affected. The making of these tips or donations is one of the pleasures of running for office—or penalties, as one may look at it." Based on the judges' own experiences of running for election, candidates were "an easy mark by everyone who seeks a willing donor for many things," and once elected, "such donations often constitute a serious drain upon their meager income."[24]

UNIVERSAL SUFFRAGE

The geopolitics of World War II brought demands for universal suffrage to the center stage of American politics. The "Double-V Campaign" launched by the African American press in 1942 called for a double victory: democracy abroad and democracy at home. For blacks, the Supreme Court decision *Smith v. Allwright* (1944) was the first of three crucial steps toward realizing the voting rights guaranteed in the Fourteenth and Fifteenth Amendments. The decision abolished the segregated "white primary," in which parties nominated candidates for the general election. In the South's de facto one-party system controlled by the Democratic Party, the nominee always won.

Excluding African Americans from those conventions was racially discriminatory.

The "war for democracy" eventually forced the federal government to recognize the military service of African Americans, Mexican Americans, and Asian Americans and extend voting rights and civil rights to racial minorities. Yet the xenophobia whipped up during the war also led to the internment of most Japanese Americans and the loss of civil liberties. Restrictions against Filipinos—who had long served in the US Navy—were eased; the federal government also pressured states to ease restrictions against immigrants from China and India, nations that were strategic allies. After Congress eased quotas on Asian immigration, a series of federal court cases overturned state laws that prohibited naturalized citizens from voting and holding political office. In Texas, Mexican American veterans established the American G.I. Forum to press for civil rights nationally.

During the war, just when union membership was skyrocketing as a result of war production and New Deal–era laws affirming the right of workers to organize, Congress curtailed union political power. Unions in the Congress of Industrial Organizations (CIO) formed the first Political Action Committee (PAC), using members' dues so that they could contribute to political campaigns. The Smith-Connally Act of 1943 abolished union donations to federal candidates, rationalizing that since corporations and banks could not contribute to these races, then neither should workers' organizations. The Taft-Hartley Act of 1947, among many of its union-busting provisions, prohibited both corporations and unions from spending money independently in federal political campaigns.

Fair and free elections are a democratic ideal, a value that the US State Department has insisted upon in international affairs since the close of World War II. But stateside, even as the coldest of Cold War warriors pounded podiums at the United Nations, entire groups of citizens remained disfranchised. African Americans who attempted to vote in the South after the war faced intimidation, harassment,

economic reprisals, and even death. Whites violently attacked black military veterans in uniform. In February 1946, US Army sergeant Isaac Woodard was brutally attacked and permanently blinded by police near Aiken, South Carolina, less than one day after his honorable discharge. As national outrage mounted over the attack against Woodard and news spread of violence against ex-servicemen and women, members of Congress called for federal legislation criminalizing such assaults.[25]

Racial violence threatened to upset President Harry S. Truman's pledge of "Freedom from Fear." In response to Woodard's blinding—and his own Justice Department's flubbing of the case—he appointed a diverse national President's Committee on Civil Rights in late 1946. Its mandate was to make recommendations for "more adequate and effective means and procedures for the protection of the civil rights of the people of the United States."[26]

The committee's report, *To Secure These Rights*, emphasized: "We cannot escape the fact that our civil rights record has been an issue in world politics. . . . [Foreign news reports] have tried to prove our democracy an empty fraud, and our nation a consistent oppressor of underprivileged people." Acting secretary of state Dean Acheson had testified that "the existence of discrimination against minority groups in this country has an adverse effect upon our relations with other countries."[27] The committee's thirty-five detailed recommendations established an ambitious civil rights agenda, some of whose demands and provisions have yet to be achieved almost seventy years later.[28]

Access to the polls and the protection of voters were the focus of the committee's recommendations "to strengthen the right to citizenship and its privileges." It prioritized the abolition of poll taxes, the second crucial step to voting rights. Congress approved a joint resolution for a constitutional amendment in March 1962, which was ratified by thirty-eight states in just twenty-three months.[29] The committee called on the federal government to protect the rights of all qualified persons to participate in federal elections, and to bar

discrimination based on race, color, or "any other unreasonable classification" in state and federal elections. The committee insisted that the national government should take the lead in enforcing civil rights, including the right to vote, rather than relying on the states.

The Truman committee was part of the long slog toward universal suffrage. The president issued executive orders to desegregate the armed forces and promote fair employment practices by the federal government, but he did not move on the voting recommendations. His efforts, as well as the efforts of future presidents, were hampered by the intransigence of powerful Senate chairmen from the South, who refused even to hold hearings on proposed civil rights bills.[30]

Contrary to the perception that African Americans in the South could not vote, in major cities such as Atlanta, Nashville, and New Orleans, as well as some smaller towns, the black vote was an important factor in municipal elections. The Atlanta Negro Voters League (ANVL) was formed by the city's black leaders in 1949 after the abolition of the state's white primary. ANVL sought to maximize the political strength of the African American community through bipartisan action; within a year, its leaders boasted that 25 percent of Atlanta's registered voters had joined. Throughout the 1950s, ANVL brokered black votes, providing the margin of victory for Mayor William B. Hartsfield in three elections, and serving as a clearinghouse for race issues.[31] In New Orleans, sociologist Nathan Glazer predicted in 1960 that soon "it may not be possible for candidates *not* to campaign for Negro votes."[32]

In Nashville, candidates relied on Henry Anderson Jones, known as "Good Jelly," to deliver black voters. A local legend, he was the subject of remembrances, newspaper accounts, and local court records. "A dark stocky man" nicknamed for his love of jelly donuts, he was a flamboyant ward-heeler in a poor black neighborhood just west of the Capitol on Jefferson Street in the 1940s and '50s. Good Jelly reportedly controlled three hundred votes, and he tended to voters' needs all year-round, not just at election time. He fed, clothed, and

housed voters, got them medical treatment, and attended to their basic needs, which many of them could not afford to meet. When he thought a candidate was a "good man," he simply asked his wards to vote for him. Rumor had it that candidates paid for his support, which underwrote his financial "help" for voters.[33]

Good Jelly cooked, bootlegged, and politicked out of his Jones Barbecue café nestled on an alley corner right smack in the middle of his ward. The police raided his café and arrested him repeatedly, especially during political campaigns when the opposing candidate wanted to negate his influence. During a single week in 1958 when the mayor's race was especially hot, the police raided his café three times, arresting twenty-three people. City judge Andrew J. Doyle dismissed every case of disorderly conduct but one, upholding charges against the last person, the police chief. He was accused of "maliciously threatening" Good Jelly. Judge Doyle declared from the bench that he didn't understand all of these "raids on little Negro operators and not swankier clubs and mixing bars," and released the chief on bond.[34]

The civil rights movement eventually forced Congress to pass legislation protecting the right to vote. President Dwight D. Eisenhower signed the first two laws. The Civil Rights Act of 1957, the first such law since Reconstruction, was primarily a voting rights act, empowering federal officials in the newly established Civil Rights Division of the Justice Department to prosecute individuals who conspired to deny or abridge another citizen's right to vote. The 1960 Civil Rights Act gave federal officials the right to inspect local voter registration polls and set criminal sentences and fines for anyone who obstructed a citizen's attempt to register to vote. Title I of the landmark Civil Rights Act of 1964 barred registrars from applying different qualifications for white and black citizens, such as requiring potential voters to "interpret" the state constitution to the registrar's satisfaction.

The Voting Rights Act of 1965 was the third and final step that guaranteed African American suffrage. It abolished the notion that

US citizens needed to "qualify" to vote in federal elections, moving the nation closer to universal suffrage. Many tricks that registrars in the South and elsewhere had used to manipulate elections were outlawed, including literacy tests, which until then were still in effect in the State of New York. By 1970, the federal government was fully responsible for protecting voting rights. However, states retained the right to determine voting qualifications using residency, valid government-issued identification, and other means, so long as such measures were not racially discriminatory.

The Constitution does not require voters to be citizens. However, states can demand proof of citizenship as a requirement to vote, a requirement that the Supreme Court does not view as racially discriminatory. The first purges of "aliens" from the voting rolls were carried out at the beginning of the nineteenth century by Progressive reformers. Asians were barred from becoming citizens at all under the Chinese Exclusion Act of 1882, and laws passed in the 1920s excluded Japanese immigrants and most Filipinos. The McCarran-Walter Act of 1952 removed all barriers to citizenship against people of Asian ancestry. Beginning in the late 1960s, some cities began to grant limited suffrage to immigrant voters in school board elections and other local functions.

Until ratification of the Twenty-Sixth Amendment in 1971, citizens had to be twenty-one years of age to vote, though younger citizens could drink alcohol, buy cigarettes, marry, work in dangerous jobs, and be drafted. The amendment lowered the age to vote in both federal and state elections to eighteen years. It received wide support as a means to recognize the military sacrifices of young men and women who volunteered and served in the Vietnam conflict, following the pattern of expanded suffrage for racial minorities after World War II.

Political candidates rarely considered the "women's vote" in the early half of the twentieth century. After World War II, black women's participation in elections increased exponentially, though they

had exerted a critical influence in municipal elections since 1920.[35] Until the 1980s, the participation rate for all women lagged behind that of men by at least 10 percent. Female turnout increased in the 1984 presidential election when Democratic presidential candidate Walter Mondale put New York congresswoman Geraldine Ferraro on the ticket as the vice presidential nominee. In fact, the percentage of women voting exceeded that of men for the first time and has continued at high levels. Since 1984, campaign managers who ignored the "women's vote" did so at their own peril.

NEW TRICKS TO MANIPULATE ELECTIONS

Despite—or perhaps because of—the (near) universal suffrage attained in the 1960s, lawmakers responded with new tricks to restrict access to the polls and diminish the political power of ordinary people. In the states, laws governing elections, like most areas of law, increasingly focused on protecting the rights of individuals. This may seem fine, but it ignores the ways that structural discrimination operates to disfranchise citizens. Starting in the late 1960s, the federal courts redefined political representation and electoral districts in ways that diluted the strength of minority communities. African Americans, Latinos, and the poor were not prevented from voting, but segregated neighborhoods were lumped into districts that diminished residents' influence on political affairs. In other places, the statutory powers of elected representatives were reduced or transferred to other officials. As a result, policy matters such as the location of toxic waste disposal sites, participation in federal housing programs, and approval of a new supervisor of public schools are no longer decided by city council members but instead by county supervisors elected at large, or even state agencies with little local input.[36]

Persuading the courts to recognize structural barriers to political power has been a major priority of civil rights organizations for decades. Court decisions and the Civil Rights Division of the US

Department of Justice approved electoral districts that gave minority voters the opportunity to elect minority representatives of their choice. Activists would eventually realize, however, that such districts actually diluted the power of blacks. "What often gets lost and overlooked in the debate about this is that an African-American's candidate of choice is not always an African-American candidate," North Carolina NAACP president William Barber observed.[37] Holding white officials accountable to their black constituents is just as important as electing minorities to office.

The creation of the first black majority district in the Mississippi Delta came about only after the Supreme Court invalidated the legislature's 1980 redistricting plan. Penda Hair, a civil rights litigator with the Advancement Project, explained:

> Whites in Mississippi, as well as many other places in the United States, tend not to vote for African-American candidates. This "racial-bloc voting" can operate to allow a white majority to cancel out all political power of a racial minority. To address this problem, the Voting Rights Act can require that districts be created in which racially marginalized groups have a fair chance to elect representatives of their choice. Mississippi's African-American voting population is poorer, less well-educated and subject to intimidation in voting—all factors that tend to suppress voting numbers. In these circumstances, voting-rights districts typically have required an African-American population in the vicinity of 65 percent to be "electable."[38]

Southern Echo, a grassroots organization born from the civil rights movement, successfully challenged the tradition of county supervisors and state legislatures drawing districts in 1990. In coalition with other groups, members decided to create as many "electable" local,

state, and congressional districts as possible. In the early 1990s, with the assistance of the Civil Rights Division of the US Department of Justice, blacks and Latinos were elected to Congress and state legislatures all over the South. The number of African American members of the Mississippi state legislature doubled from twenty-one to forty-two, giving the Legislative Black Caucus a substantial voting bloc in the state senate and house.[39]

But what had appeared to be a victory turned into a loss. Redistricting became a partisan issue with strong support from Republicans. Party strategists realized they could minimize Democratic voting strength by "packing" African American and Latino voters into "electable" districts. As a result, Democrats found it difficult to win statewide elections and congressional seats reflective of the state's overall population. The most infamous of these bizarrely gerrymandered districts, North Carolina's Twelfth Congressional District, stretches from Greensboro in the north and meanders southwest through five counties to Pineville, just south of Charlotte. Since the 1990s, the district has been the subject of at least a dozen lawsuits challenging the dilution of black political power. As William Barber described the redistricting plan, "What the North Carolina legislature did was stack, pack and bleach African-American votes out of certain districts."[40]

Democrats tended to see voter turnout as the answer to winning more political power. In the 1990s, they worked to make voter registration more streamlined and accessible, focusing on individuals rather than addressing structural barriers to voting. Attention-grabbing media stunts like Rock the Vote were organized, which relied on celebrities to register and turn out young voters aged eighteen to twenty-four. Calls for election reforms led eventually to "Motor Voter," signed into law by President Bill Clinton. Motor Voter, the National Voter Registration Act of 1993, required states to permit applicants for driver's licenses to simultaneously register to vote. States were also required to allow registration by mail for federal elections,

and to provide voter registration services at designated public agencies, including social service agencies that provided public assistance, housing vouchers, food stamps, and aid to the disabled.

Supporters of Motor Voter believed states would adopt a single registration system for federal and state elections, since operating two separate systems would be costly and inefficient. In some states, people apply for a driver's license and/or register to vote using the same form. Other states still use two separate forms, and the department of motor vehicles automatically sends the registration form to the registrar of voters. By signing, applicants acknowledge they are US citizens. Since documented immigrants (and in some states, undocumented immigrants) are encouraged to have a state-issued driver's license, the inclusion of voter registration on the same form led inadvertently to the addition of immigrants to voting rolls. In addition, people who had lost their right to vote because of a criminal conviction were enrolled.

Nationally, the new registrants were mostly young members of racial minorities who were high school–educated Democrats. In the South, Motor Voter expanded election rolls with white Republicans. But like earlier Progressive era efforts to get out the vote through greater efficiency, turnout was unaffected. The peak of Rock the Vote's effectiveness was in 1992, before Motor Voter became law.[41] Motor Voter did not create motivated voters.

Democratic presidential nominee Albert Gore Jr. thought that the uptick in voters—some eleven million new voters, according to one report—would help to secure his bid for the White House in November 2000.[42] But Democratic strategists apparently did not count on the impact of Republican-controlled statehouses on election procedures. Republicans even worked against their own candidates in state and local elections. Earlier, in February during South Carolina's open primary, many polling places suddenly closed in Greenville County, despite court orders to keep open as many polls as possible. These were precisely the same districts where presidential hope-

ful Senator John McCain, coming off a win in the New Hampshire primary, expected strong support from independent and Democratic voters. Instead, former Texas governor George W. Bush, assisted by Karl Rove—famous for pulling dirty tricks—won by huge margins.[43]

Florida provided the clearest evidence of election corruption. Both campaigns knew they needed Florida's Electoral College votes to win the presidency. Jeb Bush, George's brother, was Florida's governor at the time, and Katherine Harris, who had campaigned for Bush in New Hampshire, was the secretary of state and official certifier of elections. Complaints about voters being turned away on Election Day, of confusingly designed "butterfly ballots," of polling places that were inaccessible for the handicapped—located in gated communities—or simply not open at all, were the topic of hundreds of press reports. The chaos led to an inability to accurately determine the winner from the 5,963,110 votes considered valid.[44] Ultimately, a singular Supreme Court decision gave the election to Bush in January 2001.

That spring, the United States Commission on Civil Rights held hearings in Florida on allegations of discrimination in the election process. The commission subpoenaed witnesses who included Governor Bush, Katherine Harris, and election supervisors in several counties, as well as individuals who described their experiences attempting to vote. In addition to the "hanging chads" and confusing ballot designs, the commission found widespread violations of state and federal law. State officials had purged legal voters from the polls, established inaccessible polling places, and issued confusing information and ballots—all of which kept many disabled (including elderly people), African Americans, and Latinos in areas having a majority of Democratic districts from voting. Some registered voters were wrongfully purged from the rolls as convicted felons, making them ineligible under state law. Other prospective voters found that their usual polling places had been moved without notice or were inaccessible. The registrations of many voters, especially those of students (using Motor Voter), were inexplicably lost. Not only did this make

Bush's win suspect, it also meant that state and local elections may have been unfairly determined. The commission recommended congressional legislation to institute provisional voting and other measures to end the problems.[45]

Former president Jimmy Carter cochaired two separate commissions on voting and election procedures. The first, cochaired by former president Gerald Ford, had convened in 2001. Once more, the primary focus was on registration procedures, more reliable technology, and a federal oversight commission that would develop voting machine standards and give grants to states to purchase up-to-date equipment. Recommendations for eliminating structural barriers, such as holding elections on national holidays and the automatic restoration of voting rights to ex-felons, were ignored. The Help America Vote Act (HAVA) passed in 2002 created the Election Assistance Commission and set aside $3 billion for new voting machines. To appease Republicans, HAVA required first-time voters and mail-in voters to present identification. Florida was the first state to purchase new machines. But the machines proved unreliable, and after more failures in 2007, Florida bought new machines—now with optical scanners—to replace them. But the technology was merely a panacea. Computer specialists have repeatedly warned that electronic voting machines can be hacked as easily as cell phones and computers, and even paper receipts can be miscounted and manipulated.

A second bipartisan commission, cochaired by former secretary of state James A. Baker III, met in 2005. It was created after more questions about election corruption arose in the 2004 presidential election. John Kerry lost in Ohio counties with big Democratic populations and as a result lost the state, though polls had shown him winning. Carter-Baker acknowledged that HAVA was not enough. Intent to restore voters' faith in a haphazardly managed system that treated voters differently not only from state to state but from county to county, the commission's eighty-seven recommendations fixated on ballot integrity.[46]

Carter-Baker's most controversial recommendation expanded the requirement of photo identification cards. In the wake of national security concerns after 9/11, states were to adopt Real IDs by 2010. For the one-eighth of eligible voters without driver's licenses, states were to provide voters with identification cards at no cost. Commission member Senator Tom Daschle (D-SD) and others dissented, calling ID cards a "modern day poll tax." They argued that requiring identification from all voters would decrease turnout for people of color, the elderly, and youth.

When Congress reauthorized the Voting Rights Act in 2006, it ignored the issues raised by Carter-Baker. Republicans claimed they weren't necessary because there were so few voting rights cases. Under Attorneys General John Ashcroft and Alberto Gonzales, the Voting Rights Division of the US Justice Department reported that it had not pursued any voting discrimination cases on behalf of voters of color between 2001 and 2006.[47]

Republican officials in the states embraced the recommendation for voter identification. At polling stations in South Dakota in 2006, indigenous people were forced to show identification, even though state election rules didn't require them. After the Supreme Court, in *Crawford v. Marion County* (2008), upheld Indiana's law requiring IDs in all elections, lawmakers elsewhere stepped up these provisions, claiming their goal was to reduce the potential for voter fraud. Other provisions in these laws contradict that claim. Legislators cut back early voting, ended same-day registration, placed new barriers on the restoration of voting rights to ex-felons, heightened scrutiny of voter registration drives, demanded proof-of-citizenship documents at registration, and limited the types of acceptable forms of photo identification at the polls. Public opinion showed support for requiring identification, but the socioeconomic class of people who tend to answer such polls is accustomed to showing IDs. People who can't enter government buildings because they lack proper identification are rarely polled for their opinion.

Though Democratic pundits and civil rights activists strongly condemned the Court's decision supporting ID laws, their predictions of another "Florida 2000" debacle did not occur. Motor Voter and the abolition of some of the other barriers to registration encouraged a new generation of young, poor blacks and Latinos to become voters. But the enthusiasm and participation of 5 million more voters in the November 2008 election cannot be attributed merely to better electoral procedures.[48] The candidacy of US senator Barack Obama for president on the Democratic ticket offered them someone to vote for. Though African American turnout declined somewhat when Obama ran for reelection in 2012, African American and Latino citizens' participation in federal elections has continued to grow. Some commentators, including myself, have speculated that increased turnout by voters of color can be viewed as an act of defiance against Republican efforts to curb participation.

The impact of identification laws on voter turnout is negligible, according to a 2014 report by the Government Accountability Office (GAO). Democratic leaders imply that such laws disproportionately affect African American voters, citing the problems of expense, record keeping, and access to government agencies. Provisional ballots, a measure first recommended by the Civil Rights Commission in 2001, allow voters without proper identification to vote and return later with necessary documents. The burden of proof, though, remains on voters rather than on government officials.

Fifteen states, mostly under Republican control, have added new restrictions on voting that took effect in November 2014. In Kansas, the Republican secretary of state, Kris Kolbach, alleged that "illegal immigrants" with driver's licenses had voted through Motor Voter. "We have so many aliens on our voter rolls who check that box—either because they're trying to break the law or because they didn't know exactly what they were doing." The claims led Republicans legislators in Kansas, Arizona, Georgia, and Alabama to require applicants to provide proof of citizenship before registering to vote.

But while Republicans focus on tightening restrictions in the name of ballot integrity, sixteen states have made voting easier. More than a dozen states have liberalized felon disfranchisement laws, and in fourteen states, all in the North and West, former prisoners now automatically regain their civil rights upon completion of their sentences.[49]

Both parties manipulate elections, using legal and illegal methods; sometimes they employ merely unethical but legitimate means to win. Figuring out appropriate responses demands bipartisan solutions.

Obtaining the right to vote, as we have seen, does not automatically result in power if the process is not utilized with all of its potential and if suppression occurs. Acknowledging the impotency of traditional vote buying makes it even more urgent to ease the effect of Supreme Court decisions that have gutted the spirit of the Voting Rights Act of 1965.

Large infusions of money, in the form of contributions to campaigns, are another means of manipulating elections. After Obama's election, this reality, like voter restrictions, increased in importance. Money in politics also dampened voter turnout. In 2002, a bipartisan Campaign Reform Act passed, sponsored by Senators John McCain and Russell Feingold, limiting the use of "soft money," which had continued to grow. In 2008, Barack Obama became the first major presidential candidate to decline public financing for the general election. He did this despite promising otherwise during the primary season. He explained that the system was so broken that just taking public financing was unsustainable. John McCain, who took public financing, was heavily outspent.

After the Supreme Court 2010 decision *Citizens United v. FEC* rejected McCain-Feingold's ban on independent expenditures by corporations and labor, the money flow became a tidal wave. The Court extended the doctrine that corporations as people have First Amendment rights—including money as a form of speech—that the law must not constrain. In 2010, neither Romney nor Obama took public

financing. In 2014, the Supreme Court in *McCutcheon v. FEC* found that capping the amount any single donor can give to candidates and party committees is a violation of the First Amendment. The decision encourages elected officials to cater to their largest donors. The influence and power of ordinary voters was further weakened, and campaigns now have more funds to buy votes and engage in other corruption. Some states have never had campaign contribution restrictions.[50]

By the twenty-first century, voting in state and federal elections had become a right belonging to nearly all American citizens, but it is a right hemmed in by restrictions, felony disfranchisement, onerous identification requirements, and the influence of money. As head of the Louisiana Fraud Division, Greg Malveaux tried to ensure that people in his state could vote in fair elections that were free of fraud.

CHAPTER 2

The Voter Fraud Division and Louisiana's Culture of Corruption

Where do I get my money?

—*Anonymous voter in St. Helena Parish*

"THE SISTER-IN-LAW DEAL"

The Louisiana State Fraud Division grew out of the modern history of political corruption in the state. Suzanne Haik Terrell, a Republican, took advantage of her popularity after serving two terms as a member of the overwhelmingly Democratic-controlled New Orleans City Council to run successfully for state commissioner of elections. Success in the post could position her for higher office. Terrell appointed thirty-eight-year-old Greg Malveaux, who had been on her security team in New Orleans, as director. Malveaux knew he would be confronting Louisiana's history of political corruption, but he did not reckon with the power of elected local judges and the district attorney, who would refuse to prosecute despite overwhelming evidence of law breaking.

Elected officials in Louisiana have long been known for their pro-family positions, meaning that when they need someone to fill a government position, they appoint a family member. And that, in short, is how Governor Earl K. Long's sister-in-law became "custodian of

voting machines," a predecessor office of the elections commissioner, in 1957.[1]

The longer story is how the corruption became a pattern. In 1956, Governor Long won his third nonconsecutive term as governor of Louisiana, while Wade O. Martin Jr. won a third consecutive term as secretary of state. "Little Wade" had been a "Long-ite" because his daddy, Wade Sr., supported the administration of Governor Huey Long (Earl's big brother). But that relationship had soured. As secretary of state, Martin instituted several ballot reforms. To speed voting, candidates were numbered (rather than marked with their party symbols), which also ensured secrecy for illiterate voters, almost all of whom were white in those days.

Once back in the governor's office, Long pushed through new legislation that took away most of the secretary of state's powers, removing the insurance commission and the custody of voting machines from that office and creating two new patronage positions to oversee them. Long endorsed Wiley Douglas Fowler Sr. as elections commissioner on the ballot in 1959; when Fowler retired in 1979, his son, Jerry Marston Fowler, was appointed as interim commissioner, and then was elected in 1980. The name "Fowler" became synonymous with the job, whose primary responsibilities were buying and repairing machinery and delivering the machines to polling places. Father and son won election ten times.

Unlike his father, young Fowler had never held political office. His primary qualifications, such as they were, were his filial relationship and a degree in education from Northwestern State College in 1958. Until appointed to office to fill the remaining year of his father's term, he had been an offensive lineman for the Houston Oilers and then characterized himself as a "businessman" in Natchitoches. In the 1980 election, he ran on the Democratic ticket against a Republican reformer, John Henry Baker, who campaigned to abolish the "useless" office and return election responsibilities to the secretary of state. Baker won endorsements from several "good government" groups and

the support of the major newspapers. But even in the national Reagan landslide of 1980, Democrats maintained control of Louisiana. Fowler would go on to win, with only nominal opposition, in four more elections, with more than 75 percent of the votes.

Fowler's large margins were attributed to name recognition, but some may have wondered whether the commissioner of elections perhaps rigged his voting machines to ensure victory. That rumor was never proven, but there was bribery, corruption, and malfeasance of office. The investigations of the state's legislative auditor, Daniel Kyle, whose office sign boasted "In God We Trust, All Others We Audit," would lead to the indictment of nearly 250 state officials and employees for various forms of embezzlement, cronyism, and political kickbacks. Jerry Fowler was one of the crooks indicted.[2]

The commissioner of elections had a rather generous budget given its decidedly limited responsibilities. During Fowler's last term (fiscal years 1997–1998 and 1998–1999), the legislature appropriated $29,411,421 for maintenance of machines, support services to hold elections, election expenses, maintenance of a statewide voter registration system, and monitoring compliance with state laws regarding voter registration. Kyle's audit showed that the department bought mechanical voting machines, counters, and their installation from Elections Services, Inc., spending $8 million more than necessary because the commission did not buy directly or pay market rates for suppliers and installation.[3]

Fowler had received $900,000 in kickbacks (though some claimed it was more than $3 million), practically chump change given his two decades in office. His acts of cronyism were, likewise, rather trifling: he occasionally paid his friends to haul the machines around the state, even when no election was scheduled. He was indicted on eight counts of malfeasance in office, entered a guilty plea in 2000, and served a five-year prison sentence. Kyle himself ran on the Republican ticket for insurance commissioner in 2003 (another office known for its corrupt officials) but lost.[4]

Revelations of Fowler's misdeeds made him an easy target in the 1999 election. Suzanne Terrell ran against him and Woody Jenkins, another Republican, in the open primary; Jenkins won a plurality and Fowler dropped out. The runoff was the first (and only) time two Republicans ran against each other for a statewide office; both candidates pledged to clean up Louisiana elections and create a Voter Fraud Unit.[5]

The forty-five-year-old Terrell was a native New Orleanian, educated at Tulane University, and held a law degree from Loyola. During her time on the city council, she represented the uptown neighborhoods west of Audubon Park toward Lakeview, bordering the suburb of Metairie. Known as a reformer, she earned her popularity with both Democrats and Republicans.

Terrell would be the first Republican woman to win a statewide office, running on the ticket with Murphy James "Mike" Foster, who was seeking reelection as governor; Foster's grandfather, Murphy James Sr., had served as governor from 1892 to 1900. When Mike Foster ran for a second term in 1988, the Democratic candidate was William Jefferson, who lost in a landslide. In the best Louisiana political tradition, both Foster and Jefferson would have ethical troubles. In the 1995 race, Foster failed to report paying former Ku Klux Klansman and gubernatorial candidate David Duke $150,000 for his mailing list. (Duke's notoriety remains embedded in the state's political psyche. A few years later, Steve Scalise campaigned as "David Duke without the baggage," a slogan that would later haunt him when, in 2015, he became Republican majority whip.) Foster was forced to pay a fine for violating the state's ethics code. "Dollar Bill" Jefferson, the state's first African American congressman since Reconstruction, was later convicted of accepting bribes, including thousands of dollars found in his refrigerator freezer.[6]

When she took office as commissioner of elections, Terrell promised to enforce laws already on the books that made bribery of a voter

a felony. The penalty for a first offense was a two-thousand-dollar fine and two years in prison, and fines were to be awarded to whoever reported a vote-buying scheme that led to a successful prosecution. Terrell appointed Malveaux as director of the Fraud Division.

GREG MALVEAUX AND THE VOTER FRAUD DIVISION

Malveaux, like Terrell, was a native Louisianan. His father was a mechanic who, in his 70s, was still working; his mother had been disabled for a number of years. A West Jefferson High School graduate, he earned an associate degree in criminal justice at local Delgado Community College, attending part-time while working. He and his wife, Deidre, had a son and daughter.

Malveaux had an exemplary public service record. He had been an Orleans Parish sheriff's deputy since 1983. For twelve years, he had served in executive protection and had been detailed to Terrell as her staff assistant and bodyguard. She knew he had impeccable investigative experience and was loyal and trustworthy. As an African American and a Democrat, Malveaux also challenged the business as usual template of patronage appointments. He enthusiastically accepted the new opportunity at an increased salary with broad responsibilities. It's not clear whether Terrell thought he would pursue his duties as actively as he did. Terrell may have also anticipated that the fraud complaints would largely involve local Democratic officials, not Republican fat cats. Her primary goal was to burnish her credentials and then run for higher office. So long as Republicans remained largely unscathed, Terrell would achieve her objectives. She would soon find out whether her strategy worked.

The hotline of the Voter Fraud Division received hundreds of mostly anonymous complaints from all over the state soon after Terrell announced its formation. People seemed eager to report corruption, even without the promise of a future reward. Some appeared to

be do-gooders and others were candidates for local office who had lost in the 1999 election that had put Terrell in office. The complaints went directly to Malveaux's office.

Malveaux quickly hired a staff. Stephen Watts, a Democrat turned Republican who had ties to former Secretary of State W. Fox McKeithen (whose father, John Julian McKeithen, was the state's forty-ninth governor), was appointed assistant director. The Division had thirty-five investigators working under contract. The Louisiana state police commissioner authorized Malveaux and Watts to make arrests statewide.[7]

Malveaux's office would confront every type of electoral fraud known to man during the four years he headed the Fraud Division. Their investigations frequently elicited anger and violence. Few of their cases involved voter impersonation, the familiar target of Republican voter identification laws. Instead, they would see hundreds of complaints of vote buying or unlawful voter registration and other violations of the state's election law. Registrars routinely reported vote buyers, who submitted registration forms from convicted felons who were disfranchised under state law. There were also reports of vote haulers who brought out-of-parish residents to register and vote, and payroll padding with precinct workers who were paid to work and didn't appear. Malveaux discovered that Democrats, Republicans, and political independents engaged in voter fraud. Distressingly, poor people were often the targets of vote buyers. Though the poor are with us everywhere, tenants in public housing developments were especially targeted, sometimes with an implied threat of eviction if they failed to sell their votes. In some communities, vote buyers—some of them wearing law enforcement uniforms—made paid calls on the neighborhoods where poor and working-class people lived.

As the complaints came in over the hotline, the Division established an Election Integrity Task Force composed of state troopers and contract investigators to monitor activity during absentee ballot week and on Election Day for the primary and general elections of

2000. In September, training sessions were held in Baton Rouge and Alexandria. Trainers emphasized that troopers couldn't be stationed at polling places on Election Day so as to avoid the appearance of intimidation. Task force members could enter only to vote. They could, however, respond to requests from registrars or clerks of court to keep order or prevent violations. The task force would monitor each registrar's office during absentee voting.

From all of the complaints received, the division investigated about two hundred cases during its first year. Malveaux was astounded by the embedded culture of corruption he encountered in town after town, parish after parish. By the September 1, 2000, the first arrests had been made, seven involving convicted felons on probation or parole registering to vote in the 1999 elections. Terrell told the Monroe, Louisiana, *News Star*, "Elections have to be above board. . . . For years with what we've allowed to go on people have lost faith in the election process."[8]

RED RIVER

The first case Malveaux investigated came from Red River, a thinly populated parish in northwestern Louisiana. The Fowlers—yes, Jerry Junior's extended family—had ruled local politics for decades. Hendrix Marion "Mutt" Fowler was the former mayor and state representative. Like much of northern Louisiana, Red River was a land of cotton plantations, slavery, and "slavery by another name." Solomon Northrup spent most of his twelve years enslaved in the area. In 1874 in the parish seat, Coushatta, six elected white Republicans, and six freedmen were murdered by the White League, which was bent on ending Reconstruction. In the early twentieth century, thousands of African Americans in the parish and the rest of the state began to migrate north and then west, seeking escape from the oppression of segregation, underfunded education, and electoral disfranchisement. As President Lyndon B. Johnson predicted, political realignment of

whites began after the Voting Rights Act of 1965. A conservative white majority in Red River Parish voted to reelect George W. Bush in 2004, yet at the state and local level, white and black parish voters continue to support homegrown Democratic candidates.[9]

Lester Shields "Buddy" Huckabay III, the sheriff of Red River, claimed to have beaten his opponent, David Adkins, by three absentee votes in the 1999 runoff election. Adkins, who had a clear majority of in-person votes, filed suit claiming the election was rigged. Huckabay's wife was the parish clerk and chief of the Election Board that oversaw voting. Adkins charged that the board had accepted specious absentee ballots, some of which the registrar of voters had obtained by visiting voters.

The local judge, who was also an elected official, recused himself because he had a conflict of interest. As a result, a retired judge, appointed by the state supreme court, heard Adkins's case and decided in his favor. The Court of Appeals overruled, finding that challenged absentee ballots should be liberally evaluated without too much concern with strict voter qualification requirements (anticipating the "hanging chads" controversy the following year in Dade County, Florida). The state supreme court reversed, finding there was not even minimal compliance with the absentee ballot law, and ordered a new election. Somehow, and even with extended newspaper coverage about the conflict, Huckabay won again in April 2000 with an impressive number of absentee ballots. This was when the Fraud Division entered the case.[10]

Malveaux and his investigators tried to nail down the facts. The new parish clerk reported that his office had requests for 121 absentee ballots, which seemed quite high. Especially suspicious was that the requests came from a housing project assistant manager who had later turned in completed ballots for the "absentee" residents. The parish clerk said he didn't know if this was illegal, but that before the election, he warned everyone that if they were in town on Election Day, they should vote in person.

Malveaux was learning how difficult, and frustrating, it was to enforce election laws. There were judges who didn't want to decide cases and law enforcement officials who refused to uphold the law. Hotline complaints reported that Sheriff Huckabay and some campaign workers set up a roadblock on a railroad crossing, stopping people on their way to the polls. Witnesses said the sheriff turned back anyone who didn't plan to vote for him. A state trooper stationed in the parish declined to act when Malveaux asked him to stop Huckabay, objecting on the grounds that he had to "work with" the sheriff. Malveaux himself went to the roadblock, identified himself to Huckabay, and told him he must be at least six hundred feet away from any polling place. The sheriff asked him whether he had the authority to arrest him. When he answered yes, the sheriff and his deputies backed away. Huckabay, who had served as sheriff since 1984, remained in office until his retirement in 2004.[11]

TENSAS

One early investigation focused on an election in Tensas, named for the decimated Taensa Indians. It is the least populous parish, located in the northeastern corner of the state in the Delta, and though the small towns of Belzoni and Ruleville, Mississippi, across the river are better known for their murderous civil rights battles, Tensas has had its own clashes. While the FBI searched for the bodies of James Chaney, Andrew Goodman, and Michael Schwerner, Louisiana CORE (Congress of Racial Equality) field secretary Ronnie Moore reported in November 1964 that "the mutilated bodies of two Negroes were found floating in a Louisiana river in the parishes of Tensas and Madison."[12] No African Americans were registered to vote in the parish until 1964, when the registrar accepted applications from fifteen residents. On January 12, 1964, twelve African Americans voted in the parish primaries, the first time since 1902.[13] But it was not until long after the enactment of the Voting Rights Act that large numbers

of Tensas Parish blacks registered to vote. The white power structure remains firmly in control today.

A few complaints of forgery and of convicted felons attempting to register for the 1999 election began the Fraud Division's investigations in Tensas. For example, some witnesses on absentee ballots knew that a voter's signature was, in fact, false. Also, some convicted felons filled out applications to register, even though they knew they were not allowed to vote. These violations were just the kinds of "voter fraud" that Republicans were complaining about, and prosecutors had no difficulty prosecuting the culprits.[14]

In the town of Waterproof (population eight hundred), native son Bobby Higginbotham ran unsuccessfully for sheriff in 1999. According to the complaint, Higginbotham "solicited four felons to vote and gave them cards." He told Assistant Director Watts, who was investigating the complaint, that the Fraud Division appeared to be selectively enforcing the election laws. Why were only black felons who attempted to vote arrested while white felons were not, Higginbotham asked. Even if it was illegal for any felon, regardless of race, to vote, Higginbotham said that the law hadn't been enforced before. Rather than digging deeper into the fraudulent methods that whites used to maintain their political power, Watts lectured Higginbotham: "This was a new administration that believed in the integrity of the election system and wanted to restore the confidence of the citizens of Louisiana in the process." Nonetheless, the exchange reinforced for Malveaux that his division had to be evenhanded in its investigation of election fraud.[15]

TANGIPAHOA, OUACHITA, AND ST. HELENA PARISHES

In Tangipahoa Parish on the Mississippi border, Mike Muscarello, the losing mayoral candidate in the town of Independence, complained of votes cast by nonresidents. The parish's population of about 1,600 had a number of voters with homestead exemptions elsewhere. A "spokes-

person for concerned citizens of Tickfaw," a village of about 600 people, sent the Fraud Division a list of nonresidents who he claimed had voted. According to his complaint, the chief of police brought people into the clerk's office where they were permitted to vote. Investigators found that of the thirty-eight names on the list, eight had local homestead exemptions and the rest lived outside the parish.[16]

Monroe, in Ouachita Parish on the Arkansas border, is the birthplace of Black Panther founder Huey P. Newton, whose father named his seventh son for the governor who had done so much for Louisiana's poor people. The Newtons, like thousands of others in the state, migrated to California in the 1940s and '50s. Yet many of those who stayed, like Ronnie Moore of CORE and Monroe's Dr. John Reddix, fought against African American political disfranchisement. In 1957, Reddix filed a lawsuit against the local registrar of voters, Mrs. Mae Lucky, when she purged almost six thousand black voters from the parish registration lists.

Lucky colluded with white voters to strip African Americans of the franchise. Using a nineteenth-century Louisiana law that permitted registered voters to challenge anyone's registration, she sent challenge notices out, demanding the registrant appear before her, where they would be required to reregister. Reddix pointed out that Lucky "mailed more challenges than her office could accommodate and hundreds of Negroes never got into her office to answer the challenge." The court found nothing wrong with this scheme. Lucky, the judges ruled, was only carrying out her duties under the law. But the landmark case eventually led to the Voting Rights Act, which excluded the use of such devices to prevent blacks from voting. Since that time blacks have voted and held office regularly in the parish, though voting irregularities have still surfaced.[17]

In 2000, Rodney Pierre, a black Monroe City prosecutor, ran a voter registration drive on behalf of Kappa Alpha Pi, a prelaw professional coed fraternity, at Neville High school prior to the March 14 election. Twenty-five white students complained that although the

registration cards of eligible black students were sent to the registrar on time, their cards were turned in after the deadline. Because of the delay, they were turned away when they went to the polls. Pierre insisted that he "carried the forms directly to the registrar's office and turned them all in on time."[18] The FBI, local police, and Malveaux's office all opened investigations but found insufficient evidence to support prosecution. Pierre left office when his political mentor lost in the mayoral election.

St. Helena has a scandalous political record. In 1997, Sheriff Eugene Holland pleaded guilty to misuse of government funds and resigned. Five prominent residents were accused of paying people twenty dollars to vote absentee in the special election to replace him. State troopers who made the arrests said this was nothing new. "This is not the first time we've arrested people for this kind of thing in St. Helena Parish," said Trooper Kevin Allen. There were seven hundred absentee ballots filed for the special election, whereas in any previous election there were usually only four hundred.[19]

Chaney L. Phillips, who had been the parish tax assessor, replaced Holland. But only a year later, a federal court found Phillips guilty of financial fraud while he was tax assessor. His partner was Emerson Newman, the owner of a local hardware store, who had been arrested in the 1997 vote-buying case. Phillips and Newman received short federal sentences and restitution orders.

Ronald "Gun" Ficklin, who took over the sheriff's office after Phillips's conviction, pleaded guilty in 2007 to multiple counts of malfeasance, including using prisoners to resell stolen automobiles and machine parts, and also for serving on the pit crew for his race car.[20]

By the time Malveaux and the Division's full-time investigator Jared Labue got to St. Helena Parish, vote buying and hauling was so entrenched that an unknown man had come into the registrar's office and demanded, "Where do I get my money?"[21] Malveaux and Labue were following up on an anonymous complaint of a vote-buying scheme that involved several family members.[22]

WINN PARISH

Similar difficulties in prosecuting vote buying and fraud challenged Malveaux's investigators in Winn Parish, the home of the Long family dynasty, founded by Huey Long. Winn is the birthplace of three governors of Louisiana. Governor Earl Long is buried in Winnfield in a public square known as the Earl K. Long State Park. Winn parishioners followed the Longs' lessons in their own attempts to win office, and like their political godfathers, were too slick to be convicted, as the Fraud Division discovered in the April 2002 election.

Winnfield police chief Gleason Nugent complained that voter irregularities led to his defeat and sued the winner, Benji Phelps, the mayor Deano Thornton, and the secretary of state and the commissioner of elections Susie Terrell, who had approved the election outcomes. "During the election," when he heard of the vote buying, Nugent reported his concerns to the Fraud Division and began collecting evidence. The tragic case would eventually ensnare the Winn Parish assistant district attorney, Terry Reeves; the Winnfield Housing Authority executive director Sheila White; and Police Chief Nugent.

White and two other Nugent supporters told the Fraud Division that they were prevented from voting because Reeves had conspired to put them in jail right before the election and on through Election Day. Their three votes, they contended, would have been enough to reelect Nugent, and coincidentally, defeat Reeves and Mayor Thornton.

Reeves and Thornton had once supported White. Indeed, they helped her to become executive director of the Winnfield Housing Authority (WHA). Trouble came, though, when the mayor demanded that White use housing funds to build a community center. She believed, rightly, that doing so would be a violation of the law and refused to write the $100,000 check. Thereafter, she said, Mayor Thornton and Reeves began a campaign that "terrorized" her, which was intended to "break her" and extract the "donation."

Reeves impaneled a grand jury to investigate White's financial operation of the WHA. He subpoenaed her repeatedly to appear and to submit WHA records for several months, while he continued to misuse public funds. Three days before the election, the grand jury indicted White and two Gleason supporters. Judge James Wiley, a former assistant to Reeves, signed the arrest warrants. The "Winnfield Three" found themselves in the parish prison on April 4, 2002. The judge refused to set bail without a hearing and would not set a hearing prior to the election.

When the votes were counted two days later, Phelps received 911 votes, while Nugent received 907. Mayor Thornton won reelection by a much larger margin.

Nugent's evidence against Phelps shows how vote buying and vote hauling is done in small rural towns. Phelps gave each of his voters a numbered ballot and told them how to vote. After they voted, they were taken to the Winni-Mart or to the Corner Store. According to Nugent, Phelps had opened an account at the Winni-Mart where people could use the code word "Lip" to pay for purchases up to five dollars. Lip was the nickname of Robert Hall Jr., a driver for Phelps. Nugent identified seven voters who admitted they received liquor and cigarettes in exchange for voting for Phelps.[23] The voters likely knew this was illegal, but Nugent said they weren't afraid of prosecution because they also knew that Reeves wanted his buddy Phelps to be elected sheriff.

Just as in the case in Red River, the Winn Parish judge recused himself. The case was heard by John Joyce, a retired judge appointed by the Louisiana Supreme Court. Called to testify, Benji Phelps denied or explained away the charges. True, he had set up the account at Winni-Mart, but it was only to give the people who were helping his campaign "something to eat and drink." Of course he knew Lip, but denied that his job was to haul people to the polls.

A clerk at the Winni-Mart said people came in and told him to put their cold drinks, candy, beer, and cigarettes on "Benji's account."

A voter said Lip gave him a paper with ballot numbers marked for the police chief (Phelps) and mayor (Thornton), took him to cast an absentee ballot, and then drove him to the Corner Store, where he bought beer and a pack of cigarettes. Another voter said Lip got him a "40 ounce Magnum" to drink after he voted. One witness said he received a hundred dollars from Phelps to get people to vote for him. Everyone admitted they took the snacks and cigarettes, but insisted they voted for Phelps because they "wanted to."

District Attorney Terry Reeves was also called to testify. He explained that he had impaneled the grand jury to investigate White and the WHA because he thought the agency's finances needed scrutiny. He denied that he had manipulated the grand jury, and accused the prosecution of spreading a "specious lie." Judge Joyce refused to allow Sheila White to testify about Reeves and Thompson's efforts to extort $100,000 from the WHA.

Nugent lost his case. The judge dismissed the suit on the grounds that the irregularities did not prove the election would have gone another way, even though it was decided by only four votes. Nugent also lost on appeal. The court ruled that Nugent needed to show "that because of fraud or irregularities, the outcome of the election is impossible to determine." As for the fraud and irregularities that Nugent discovered, the court said that "a vote should not be rejected because a voter was offered a bribe, or even because a voter accepted something of value for the vote, provided that voter still voted the way he originally intended." Besides, though the judges believed there was "evidence of irregularities and/or fraud," that was a criminal matter, not a civil one. The Court of Appeals concluded that only two votes could be subtracted from the final tally, "a difference that would be insufficient to change the election result or make it impossible to determine."

Susie Terrell, in her capacity as commissioner of elections, was one of the defendants named in Nugent's lawsuit. In reviewing the case, the Court of Appeals noted that the commissioner's attorney

"often objected to evidence" relevant to "charges of fraud and vote buying." This was "most curious," they said, since her office was currently investigating the criminal case. The Fraud Division's Stephen Watts, who had observed the trial, noted these objections too, and told Malveaux about his concerns. Watts thought that Terrell's attorney was trying to help Phelps win the case, even though, ethically, he should have been a neutral party.

The Winn Parish case underscores one of the primary problems with challenging election corruption. The district attorney is supposed to prosecute violations, but that office is an elected one, and candidates themselves may be engaged in vote buying and vote hauling; at the very least they are part of the local political establishment and need to stay on good terms with other elected officials. Additionally, prosecutors are members of the bar, and other lawyers know they need to remain on good terms with the DA's office, which, under state law, has the power to decide whether to indict, prosecute, plea bargain, or ignore every criminal case in its jurisdiction. Finally, the voters who elect the district attorney and local judges form the pool from which juries are drawn. In small parishes where everyone knows everyone else and is married to someone's second cousin, this can be a problem.[24]

As district attorney, Reeves used his office not as a bully pulpit to benefit the people of Winn Parish, but for his own benefit. He had no interest in prosecuting the vote-buying offenses that Malveaux discovered. He was also a bully who punished anyone who crossed him. Before Nugent sued him, Reeves had indicted and prosecuted Gary R. Connors, the chief criminal deputy, for malfeasance in carrying out his duties. The judge dismissed the case for lack of evidence. Connors then sued Reeves for malicious prosecution, presenting evidence that the charges were false, that Reeves knew they were false, and that he was therefore guilty of malice. Reeves did not deny his actions. But since the DA could claim prosecutorial immunity, Connors lost.

Reeves successfully offered the same defense again when Nugent's supporters filed a civil claim of prosecutorial malice against the DA for impaneling a grand jury that prevented them from campaigning in the 2002 election.[25]

That, however, is not the end of the story. It turned out that Reeves was not only a bully but a crook. In July 2004, the Winn Parish Police Jury (in other states, the county council) asked the legislative auditor's office to review the DA's finances. Their report, issued in April 2005, found that Reeves had failed to keep proper records for $169,000 that he said was expenses to attend conferences and seminars. His office also illegally or unnecessarily spent public funds for alcoholic beverages and expensive dinners whose guests included state employees. Reeves spent at least $49,000 on trips that were either personal or unjustified.

Reeves had been warned in 1999 that his office's finances were problematic, which he promised to correct at that time. According to the report, the Winn Parish DA inexplicably spent much more than other parishes. And the office's finances were increasingly precarious. By June 2005, its $275,000 annual budget allocation was spent, and it had a $400,000 deficit from the prior fiscal year. The Internal Revenue Service filed a tax lien against his office—an extraordinary action—and was investigating Reeves for not paying payroll taxes in 2004 and 2005, even though he had taken the money from his employees' paychecks.[26]

Gleason Nugent, depressed by his failure to oust Reeves and his political cronies, was reported to have committed suicide in March 2005, just one month before the devastating audit became public. Five months afterward, when news of the audit and the IRS charges was the talk of Winnfield, it was reported that Reeves too had committed suicide, killing himself with a single shot in the chest while sitting on his back porch.[27]

ASCENSION PARISH

Ascension Parish, in Cajun country, had long been a Democratic bastion. That changed in 2000, when fourteen thousand new voters registered, only a thousand of them as Democrats. Though national and statewide Republican candidates always win the parish in November, candidates for local office are almost all Democrats who run against each other in local open elections. Under Louisiana law, voters may also register as "No Party" and are permitted to vote in the open primaries. Robert Poche, the parish voter registrar, told the *Baton Rouge Advocate* in 2007, "History tells us that those with no party affiliation have been voting conservatively." He predicted the parish's results in the 2008 presidential contest in which Republican candidates John McCain and Sarah Palin received 67 percent (31,239) of the vote, while Barack Obama and Joseph Biden won 31 percent (14,625).[28]

The Fraud Division's hotline received a number of complaints from Ascension Parish in its first year of operation, but these too failed to result in prosecution of those involved. Poche reported to Malveaux that one person had sent in absentee ballots for twelve unqualified voters, which Poche had rejected. In Donaldsonville, the parish seat, some voters cast ballots in the wrong district. The Council on Aging had engaged in "vote hauling" when it transported seniors to the polls in its taxpayer-supported bus.[29]

HOUMA

Houma, the seat of Terrebonne Parish, is fifty-seven miles southwest of New Orleans and is one of the fastest-growing cities in America. There, Malveaux would learn that helpful political officials could be just as conniving as recalcitrant ones. His would-be "helper" was Norval Rhodes, who, in 1984, had been accused of dropping cocaine possession charges against the son of a wealthy contributor to Mike

Foster's gubernatorial campaign in exchange for an appointment to head the state's Fisheries and Wildlife Bureau. According to John Magannis, the dean of the Baton Rouge press corps, "that balloon [was] shot down immediately by angry Terrebonne hunters and fishermen, who disliked Norval Rhodes enough as DA to fear what he could have done in Wildlife and Fisheries."[30]

Rhodes's reputation as a bully, feared even by the good old boys, came from the decades that he had used his position as the parish district attorney to punish anyone who crossed him. It seemed unfortunate that the reality show, *Cajun Justice*, wouldn't be filmed in Terrebonne until a decade later; given his bad behavior, Rhodes could have been a star. When Columbus "Chris" Williams testified against Rhodes in 1997, the district attorney's office went out of its way to punish him.[31]

One of Rhodes's early victims was Cheryle Beridon, a twenty-two-year-old African American woman with whom he had a brief affair. When she broke it off and refused to renew the relationship, Rhodes turned into the psycho ex-boyfriend in a lawyer's striped suit. With cool calculation, he used the power of his position to punish her. He threatened her with prison, knowing that Beridon used drugs and engaged in sex work to support herself. He set her up with a police informant, and then had his office prosecute her for the unlawful sale of $125 worth of heroin. The case came to trial in August 1977, and the "black, drug-addicted prostitute" stood no chance against the successful white district attorney who took the stand against her. The judge sentenced Beridon to life in prison.

But "God Don't Like Ugly," as they say in the South, and Rhodes was "ugly." Rhodes finally was ensnared by his pattern of misbehavior. In 1983, when Edwin Edwards was elected governor for the first time, a federal grand jury in New Orleans was looking into why cocaine charges against a law client of Mr. Edwards were dropped. Terrebonne District Attorney Norval Rhodes dismissed the charges. Rhodes was indicted on four counts of perjury after testifying falsely that he had

not discussed the subject with anyone in Mr. Edwards's law firm and did not expect a state job in return for the dismissals. The new governor distanced himself, saying the public could rest assured that he personally would not be indicted.[32]

Back then, Chris Williams worked as an investigator in Rhodes's office and witnessed the way he railroaded Beridon into prison. He didn't forget the case, but he also didn't do anything at the time to help her.

Beridon's imprisonment took a great toll on her mother, Ella Townsend, who was left to raise Cheryle's children as well as her own. Her younger brother Steven Hayes didn't forget the injustice, and others in Houma's black community didn't either. When he ran into Jerome Boykin, president of the Terrebonne chapter of the NAACP, several years later, Williams told his old friend about his sister and how she had been wrongly convicted. Boykin resolved that he would fight for Beridon's release. Boykin told Hayes, "Give me your mother's phone number. The NAACP is going to take up Cheryle's fight. I'm making a promise to you right now: We're going to get her out of prison and bring her home."

Boykin and the Innocence Project of New Orleans persuaded the Pardon Board to commute Beridon's sentence to forty-five years, making her eligible for parole. Chris Williams corroborated her story about Rhodes. Governor Foster granted her a full pardon in 1999.

The district attorney's office was infuriated that Williams had testified against Rhodes, and Williams had nothing but trouble thereafter. In the years following Beridon's pardon, he was arrested for allegedly threatening the employees of a daiquiri drive-through and threatening the police who tried to arrest him; he had four counts of writing bad checks, and another for filing false public records. These charges, however, didn't stop him from running as one of three Republican candidates for the Louisiana state senate.[33]

Malveaux became involved before the February 2001 parish election when Linda Rodrigue, the local registrar of voters, reported sus-

picious activity. Given the arrest record Williams had compiled by then, Malveaux initially thought Williams could conceivably be engaged in election fraud.

Rodrigue complained that Williams had brought several voters into her office, four of whom listed Williams's campaign office as their home address. While Houma is the only incorporated town in this bayou parish where "Beasts of the Southern Wild" roam, people nonetheless have home addresses. Malveaux quickly discovered the newly registered voters still living in La Fourche, confirming that they didn't live in Williams's office.[34]

Placed in jail for the third time, Williams refused to cooperate with the Fraud Division. But after Malveaux learned the back story about his having stood up against Rhodes, he realized Williams was again being set up. Williams refused to a plea bargain and was convicted in a few minutes. The judge sentenced him to five years in prison. Williams was the only person who served time for violating the state's election fraud law that year.[35]

VERMILION PARISH

In Vermilion Parish, Malveaux tried a different tactic to prevent the vote hauling and vote buying conducted through absentee voting. Working with a reporter of the parish seat newspaper, the *Abbeville Meridional*, he gave an interview about voting irregularities and his division's efforts to prevent unfair elections. The editors added an opinion piece, "How Much Is a Vote Worth Today?" The editorial advised voters to accept the money and then "vote for whomever you want." Anyone who called the paper could have their names published along with the name of the candidate who paid them. After the story ran, local candidates met with the editors and agreed to encourage each other not to buy votes. Candidates who did not show up were listed in the paper. Malveaux worked with a community awareness group on the issue and also engaged the state police. The tactic

worked. After the election, he and the newspaper agreed that the voting "had gone well."[36]

That paying and hauling voters was illegal was news to the citizens and mayoral candidates of Marksville, the Avoyelles Parish seat. The mayor, Dr. Richard Michel, told a local reporter that he planned to pay drivers to haul black voters to the polls. The reporter told Malveaux, who told Michel that it was illegal for candidates to pay vote haulers and to buy votes. However, a candidate could use volunteer drivers or hire a commercial transportation company to encourage turnout.[37]

Malveaux and his staff monitored the election in which Michel beat John Ed Laborde by 103 votes; 111 of these were absentee ballots cast for Michel. Malveaux's investigators amassed overwhelming evidence of vote buying by Michel's campaign. As the publicity mounted, Eddie Knoll, the district attorney who had served five consecutive terms since 1972, took two local law enforcement officers, Lincoln J. Carmouche and Larry Dauzat, before a grand jury, which indicted them.

Carmouche was found guilty of bribing a voter in a mayoral election. He appealed the decision but lost. But unlike Chris Williams, he did not go to prison. Judge Billy Bennett gave him a suspended, two-year prison sentence and two years of supervised probation. He was also fined $1,050 and ordered to perform sixty-four hours of community service. But as a condition of probation, he had to remain under house arrest, beginning three days before any election, including absentee voting, until the voting ended.[38]

Dauzat was charged with bribery, offering five dollars per vote to influence a mayoral election. Though he denied everything, he too was convicted and sentenced to a suspended two-year prison sentence and two years of supervised probation. He was also fined $1,050 and ordered to perform forty hours of community service.

In sentencing the two convicted law enforcement officials, Judge Bennett warned them from the bench that he would change their suspended sentences to prison time if he heard of any threats against

Michel's opponent John Laborde or against Laborde's family. The judge pointed out that they had no prior felonies and were both law enforcement officers. Acknowledging that vote buying and hauling had been tolerated for years in the parish, he said he intended to make examples of Carmouche and Dauzat for their illegal politicking. "Vote buying for the most part, has been readily accepted in our society for many years. In one manner, this court considers Larry Dauzat and Lincoln Carmouche to be guinea pigs for those vote buyers who went before and those vote buyers who will come after."[39]

Dauzat's sentence was overturned on appeal because the court determined that the state had not proven its case. At his trial, Eve Normand testified that she was on the porch with her great grandson when Dauzat took down her Laborde sign and put up a Michel sign. She told Dauzat to put her sign back up. When asked if he offered her any money she said he told her, "Dr. Michel will pay five dollars." Dauzat said that, on Election Day, "I will pick you up and after you vote, I'll give you your five dollars." Normand told him, "No, sir, I ain't going. I don't want your money. . . . Just keep on going . . . with the signs." But since Normand also testified that she decided not to vote in the mayoral election, Dauzat could not be convicted of actually bribing a voter. The court overlooked the question of voter suppression. Dauzat and Carmouche were law enforcement officers, and a voter like Normand might avoid being seen as opposing the candidate they recommended by simply not voting.[40]

PLAQUEMINE

In Plaquemine, where Malveaux was first schooled about how vote buying took place, Howard Oubre Jr., a black council member, was identified by witnesses as the "bag man" who collected and distributed the money for vote buying and hauling. Robin Rills said she saw Oubre offer two people working in her front yard ten dollars each to vote for him. A local police official tried to downplay the incident in his press comments. "We're surprised in the fact that it's going as far

as its going and we're really happy about that because if these things are going on they need to be stopped."

Six people swore they were paid by Oubre to vote for him in the October 2003 elections. According to the affidavits Malveaux collected, Oubre approached these individuals, took them to the polls, and had the driver give each of them numbered ballots with which to cast their votes.[41] Then the driver took them home. One voter described how he later "met up with Howard [Oubre] when I was going to the store and he said, 'Here you go and thank you.' He gave me five bucks, a five dollar bill. Howard has paid me to go and vote in past elections."[42]

Another witness said he saw Oubre after he voted and "he gave me my little few dollars (six or seven dollars)." Malveaux wrote to District Attorney Richard "Ricky" Ward Jr., enclosing affidavits of vote buying and vote hauling and requesting prosecution of Oubre and the voters. Ward did nothing. Oubre has won reelection four times, most recently in 2012. His current term expires in 2016.[43]

The Fraud Division also sent the district attorney evidence regarding the illegal actions of Victoria McKnight. Witnesses said she approached, bribed, and transported several black voters to the polls to vote for Richard "Ricky" Ward and a district judge candidate. McKnight allegedly paid each voter ten dollars. Witnesses Michael Riley and Geraldine Mitchell said a hauler told them to vote for Ward and Alvin Baptiste, who were running for city council. Terry Wayne Baker was accused of helping Mitchell. Despite the state's evidence, Ward did not file charges against himself or against anyone else. Ward won reelection in October 2002 with 57.4 percent of the votes cast.[44]

ACADIA PARISH

An anonymous caller to Malveaux's hot line complained that the commissioner in charge of the Rayne Housing Authority in Acadia Parish and others conspired to take unregistered people to the polls

to vote. The voters were all rewarded with "cheap liquor" afterwards. It was alleged that the Housing Authority commissioner was buying the votes of her tenants so that Russel Benoit would remain in office as the parish tax assessor; he had held the position continuously since 1991. Benoit's opponent was Debra Grimmer, who had run against Benoit in the previous election in 1999.[45]

Thelma Jones was one of the voters who had filed an absentee ballot. Malveaux and a staff member, Benny Broussard, went to her home in October 2003. She admitted she signed the completed ballot given to her by Helen Francis, a vote buyer. She invited Malveaux and Broussard into her home, where, it happened, Jones's daughter was also visiting. During the conversation that followed, the daughter bragged that she had made tape recordings of vote-buying conversations. When Malveaux questioned her further, she said she didn't have them anymore because her house had mysteriously burned to the ground.[46]

Then Helen Francis showed up at Jones's house carrying a black police baton. When Broussard asked who she was, she answered: "You know who the fuck I am. Who the fuck are you?" Francis was unimpressed when Broussard showed his state police badge and commission. She threatened the investigators in an angry exchange and ordered them out of Jones's house.

Malveaux and Broussard left, but as they got into their state vehicle, Francis slammed the door on Malveaux's leg. He told her she was under arrest. When she swung the baton he cuffed her and took her to jail, charging her with public intimidation, resisting arrest, and aggravated assault.

Investigations of election irregularities in Acadia Parish continued. One identified violator agreed to become a confidential informant and to secretly record conversations with the principal culprits. In various talks, they agreed to "put out" money for Russel Benoit, the tax assessor, in order to buy and haul the votes in his favor. One participant described how they would just "go to register's office and

tell them that there's a lot of people who can't come to the polls and need absentee ballots."[47]

The confidential informant pretended to support Grimmer in order to elicit more talk about the money changing hands. She argued her candidate would serve Acadia better: "Benoit didn't retire because his favorite couldn't beat Debbie Grimmer. The poor people worried because companies were leaving town that couldn't get tax breaks." She went on: "You know this whole area won't be nothing but a ghost town. That's why a lot of our people are locked up. That's why a lot of our people are living paycheck to paycheck. 'Cause these people don't want these companies to come in if they won't pay good for a job. That's why I'm campaigning for this lady."

"Hercule" said she might be right but his grandmother had relied on Benoit. "He was responsible for her getting medical treatment, sent her to Washington. Everybody can't just do that." The confidential informant countered, "Benoit is not doing what he needs to do to bring in and create jobs." Hercule was unpersuaded. "He's done more for my grandma than Grimmer could do in a lifetime." Further, "Russel [Benoit] also paid for food" at any function they had.

When "Joe" arrived, the group discussed how much money they needed to buy and haul votes. One person suggested they just needed to pay more than Grimmer's vote buyers, perhaps six or seven dollars per voter. Joe said maybe they could instead "pay [for] a couple bottles of cheap whiskey." After more talk, the informant reminded everyone that that was how "Russel [Benoit] beat Debra bad last time by buying those votes." "John" commented, "He gonna do it again, if you don't watch it." Benoit was reelected time and time again until he resigned for health reasons in 2010.[48]

The Fraud Division arrested some of the Rayne vote buyers, but that was about all Malveaux's office could do. The cases were turned over to local prosecutors but then stalled. Cases were either not prosecuted or dismissed. Press coverage occasionally made a difference as in Abbeville in 2002, where absentee voting declined in the election

that year. Council member John Win told the press that he hoped the days of buying votes with a six-pack of beer and a pork chop sandwich were over in that town.[49]

The 2002 imprisonment of Governor Edwin Edwards for racketeering was a reminder, however. As the Opelousas newspaper said, "For too many years, elections in Louisiana were decided in 'dark, smoky rooms.' Throughout the state's history of vote buying, bribery and blackmail were all tools at a politician's disposal. Corruption was accepted as the way things were, and in some places that remains true today. But an era may be passing."[50]

Malveaux thought that was a rather optimistic view. Prosecutors wouldn't pursue cases. Local judges were also politicians, and they preferred to admonish violators, hand out suspended or probationary sentences, and later clear their records for good behavior. Successful prosecution and punishment were elusive. Corruption—and history—stymied the division's efforts.

CHAPTER 3

"Rat Infestation, Rotten Wood, and Rusty Metal"
Electoral Fraud in St. Martinville

> We do feel that some of our witnesses,
> for lack of a better word, crawfished on us.
>
> —*Attorney Jermaine Williams*

Driving west from New Orleans, Interstate I-10 passes over Maurepas Swamp until the miasma of noxious fumes from the smokestacks around Baton Rouge appears. Crossing the Mississippi, after another hour of driving—maybe less because Louisianans view speed limits as a federal conspiracy in this state of oil rigs and petrochemical by-product factories—one arrives at Bayou Teche. St. Martinville is the "Birthplace of Acadiana," with the ancient Evangeline Oak and Longfellow Evangeline historic site in a town of a few more than seven thousand people. For African Americans, the double execution of seventeen-year-old Willie Francis in 1947 was a haunting reminder of modern racial injustice. It is the seat of St. Martin Parish, known as the "Crawfish Capital of the World." With a population of 49,000 people, the parish harvests 22 million pounds of crawfish annually om the Atchafalaya Basin and local production ponds; that's almost e tons per parish resident. It was here that Greg Malveaux found ost frustrating case of election corruption.[1]

isn't a historian, so he can be forgiven for not knowing the

long history of electoral fraud in St. Martin Parish. "An Honest Election Officer Removed by the Governor," reported the *New York Times* in April 1884, where "every known appliance [has been] brought to bear to defeat the will of the people." The registrar "refused to tabulate the returns of one precinct which were a notorious forgery in the interest of the judicial district candidate." The removal of the official was one of Governor Samuel D. McEnery's smaller offenses. State Treasurer Edward A. Burke, who administered the notorious Louisiana Lottery Company, essentially controlled the state government, along with Samuel Jones, who controlled the leasing of convict labor from the state penitentiary. McEnery's successor in 1888 was Murphy James Foster Sr., the grandfather of Murphy "Mike" Foster, the state's fifty-third governor, whose years in office were clouded with ethics violations.[2]

The Martin-Champagne and Thibodeaux families had controlled St. Martinville politics since the early twentieth century. (The Bulliard and Melancon families, who own the town's hot sauce factories and sugar mills, are involved in state and national politics.) In St. Martin Parish, Martins and Thibodeauxes, with their abundant relatives, were so intermarried that trying to explain who was related to whom was not unlike untangling a couple of wrestling alligators. Up in Arnaudville on Bayou Teche, there was a "Big Wade" Martin, who was the father of Wade Jr., Louisiana's long-serving secretary of state, and his other son, Dr. Murphy Martin, who spent his career as public health director of St. Martin, Iberia, and Lafayette parishes. The Thibodeauxes could trace their family history further back: Gaston, born in 1885, served on the St. Martin Parish Police Jury, the equivalent of a county board of supervisors in Louisiana; as a member of the state legislature, he chaired several powerful committees. In local politics, the Martin-Thibodeaux families controlled almost every elected and appointed position in St. Martinville, and had done so for as lor as most everyone could remember. Whoever challenged their pc risked their integrity, their livelihood, even their freedom. Th the fate of Eddy Grieg, Mary Francois, and Greg Malveaux.[3]

Eddy Grieg's brother Errol had ribbed him publicly for years about the corrupt politics in his town. Errol thought it was hilarious that St. Martinville had not held a local election in recent memory—since 1988, in fact. The Grieg brothers were two local white guys, born and raised in Acadiana. Eddy was the owner-operator of a furniture and machinery repair shop in St. Martinville; Errol lived in a neighborhood down by Bayou Teche and was a house builder until he retired. His jokes increasingly irritated Eddy. He spent much of his free time observing the local courts and St. Martinville City Council and by the year 2000, he'd had enough with the city's failure to hold local elections, especially since they managed to hold regular elections for state and federal offices.[4]

On his own, though, Eddy Grieg couldn't do much. Though everyone in St. Martinville, black and white, was effectively disfranchised by the town's failure to hold elections, there is no Louisiana or federal law requiring municipalities to conduct local elections on a regular basis. His only recourse was to sue under the Voting Rights Act of 1965, which gave the US Justice Department the authority to oversee elections to ensure racial fairness. Under the law, African Americans, long disfranchised under the South's Jim Crow laws, are considered a protected class. As a white citizen, Grieg's disfranchisement in local elections was unjust but not illegal. Grieg reached out to the town's NAACP chapter, offering to fund a case if they would find African Americans who were willing to be plaintiffs.

It was not that the civil rights movement had never come to St. Martinville. It had passed through in the 1960s, though its passage was not very noticeable. When the 1973 senior class of St. Martinville High School announced plans for its fortieth reunion in 2012, a "whites only" post–homecoming game party was part of the plan[5]—this in a town where African Americans represent over 60 percent of the population and students of color make up 58 percent of the town's only public high school.[6] Like most towns south and north, St. Mar[illegible]nville had residential segregation. Districts 4 and 5 were primarily [illegible]ican American and voted along racial lines. As a result they had

elected two black members to the city council. District 3 had a majority of black residents too, though around 30 percent of the ward was white. Except for a brief four-year period in the 1970s, Zerben Champagne had represented the district since 1966.[7] His daughter Pamela had married into the Thibodeaux family.

Champagne's hold on the city council seat was only one reason the US Justice Department was concerned about elections in St. Martinville. Under the Voting Rights Act of 1965, Louisiana and other states with a history of de jure racial discrimination must obtain permission from the federal government to change an election process. This means that either the Justice Department or the federal Court of Appeals in the District of Columbia has the discretionary authority to accept ("preclear") or to reject (deny preclearance of) any changes proposed in election district lines, polling places, election rules, or procedures that would affect voter registration and voting in local, state, and national elections. Preclearance assures that black citizens as well as other protected classes continue to have effective representation as their populations shift over time.

The racial composition of District 3 meant that a fair redistricting would threaten the hold that the Martin-Thibodeauxes had over the five-member city council. If they lost control over the District 3 seat through the election of another black council member, the three African American representatives would have control of city finances. White control over patronage jobs, city contracts, appointed positions in the city agencies, and all the fruits of political power would be in jeopardy. Mayor Eric Martin; his father, Police Chief Dickie Martin; and their Thibodeaux in-laws and cronies were determined to stay in power. And that led to the shenanigans that brought Greg Malveaux and Mary Francois into the fray.

Political redistricting occurs after every decennial census in order to ensure "one person, one vote." In theory, every political jurisdiction should have approximately the same number of citizens. After the 1990 census was tabulated, St. Martinville submitted its red

tricting plan to the Justice Department for preclearance. Mayor Eric Martin sent in the town's first plan in 1991, but despite subsequent additions and negotiations with Assistant Attorney General John Dunne through October 1992, the Bush administration refused to preclear any of the proposals. Just before President Bill Clinton took office in January 1993, Dunne again wrote to Martin, rejecting the city's plan.

From the record, it seems rather obvious that officials in St. Martinville had been manipulating council district lines for years in order to keep three seats under white control. According to the 1990 census, the city's population of less than six thousand was 59 percent African American; black households were almost entirely in three of the five council districts. Recognizing the long history of racially polarized voting in the South, AAG Dunne informed Mayor Martin that African Americans could possibly elect a third council member of their choice. For that reason, the Justice Department was concerned that the new districting plan packed black households into District 4, making it virtually all black. District 5 under the plan would become 84 percent black. District 3 was subjected to illegal "retrogression." In Dunne's opinion, St. Martinville's plan would diminish African American representation in District 3 from 73 percent to 61 percent, which would impermissibly reduce the voting power of black citizens. Moreover, the redistricting plan failed to provide evidence that the proposed changes would not be racially discriminatory in intent or effect. The electoral districts, as laid out in the submitted plan, did not receive preclearance and were therefore unenforceable. The city could submit additional information, or it might appeal the decision through the appropriate channels.

It appears that Mayor Martin interpreted this impasse differently than officials in Washington expected. Instead of trying to work out an agreement with the Justice Department or providing the Civil Rights Division (CRD) with the requested information, the city simply withdrew the plan. In the absence of preclearance, in 1993 the

St. Martinville City Council decided to simply remain in office without holding new elections.[8]

Four years after the Justice Department had requested it, the city submitted a new redistricting plan and supplemental information. The new plan still packed African American households into District 4 (99 percent) and District 5 (84 percent) the racial composition of the redrawn District 3 remained questionable because it reduced the African American population by 13 percent. This time, rather than relying on the 1990 federal data, St. Martinville had created election maps based on a recount it had commissioned independently in 1996. CRD questioned the reliability of the city's numbers and its methodology, particularly the fact that canvassers conducted their household counts between 9 a.m. and 6 p.m. when many people are not at home. To counter Mayor Martin's claim that the city's population had declined, the Justice Department examined utility customer rolls in 1990 and 1996. These showed no significant population declines over six years. The city wasted taxpayers' money trying to fool the Justice Department with its absurd census; once more they were directed to redraw election district maps based on the 1990 census.

Isabelle Katz Pinzler, the acting assistant attorney general for civil rights, rejected St. Martinville's redistricting plan, just as John Dunne, Bush's AAG, had done. She thought the new plan appeared to be a devious effort to obscure the facts and subvert the legal requirements of the Voting Rights Act. Indeed, though the district lines were slightly different from those in earlier submissions, they were not substantially different. Pinzler also took note of the fact that "the city has not conducted elections for city council since 1990." She demanded that the mayor and the city's legal counsel inform the DOJ "what you plan to do."[9]

In fact, the city apparently planned to do nothing. The only change in the city council happened in June 1997, when Mayor Martin appointed Pamela Thibodeaux, who is white, as the District 3 council member, replacing her father when he passed away. As far as

the mayor was concerned, no outsiders were going to upset the political power of the Martin-Thibodeauxes.

The stubborn resistance of the St. Martinville mayor and city council to comply with Sections 4 and 5 of the Voting Rights Act was an actionable offense. The Department of Justice should have demanded a third districting plan, and sent their lawyers to work out something that met federal guidelines. CRD could have asked the Federal Appeals Court in the District of Columbia to order and approve a plan. But none of this happened. Pinzler was only the acting assistant attorney general; President Clinton had nominated Bill Lann Lee for the position early that year. However, the US Senate judiciary chairman, Orrin Hatch (R-UT), refused to hold a confirmation hearing because he represented officials who opposed Lee's civil rights views (Lee had spent the first two decades of his law career working for the NAACP Legal Defense and Educational Fund, the law firm founded by Thurgood Marshall). As a result, oversight of cases in the civil rights division fell into some disarray. Down in St. Martinville, it seemed that federal officials had dropped their case, so Mayor Martin and his cronies figured they could leave everything as it had been for the last decade.

The Martin-Thibodeaux clans had reasons to keep a low profile. In 1997, St. Martin Parish was at the center of a vote-buying and vote-hauling case that led to a grand jury indictment of sixty-four people, the largest case in contemporary Louisiana history. The case began when two losing candidates for St. Martin sheriff filed complaints about a "votes-for-cash scheme" nine days before the 1995 primary. Two of the candidates, Vincent Alexander (who was also a local NAACP official) and his friend Donald Thibodeaux, both of Beaux Bridge, filmed vans that they claimed transported voters to the polls, and recorded voters arriving at the parish courthouse to cast absentee ballots. The complaint was initially investigated by the Louisiana State Police and St. Martinville Assistant District Attorney Phil Haney, but because of its scope and notoriety, Bernie Boudreaux,

the judicial district attorney for the tri-parish area, requested that his office handle the case.

The investigation took eighteen months, and hundreds of witnesses were interviewed. The grand jury apparently only heard evidence related to the sheriff's election, though the ballot included races for the clerk of court, the assessor, and the parish police jury. Alexander and Thibodeaux told the press they'd been subpoenaed, but the grand jury never saw their videos of vote hauling. The indictments finally came down in April 1997. Forty-two people pleaded guilty to felony counts of selling their votes; another eight pleaded guilty to vote hauling. They were sentenced to two years of unsupervised probation, were prohibited from being involved in or participating in any political campaign during that time, and lost their right to vote.[10]

Alexander found it curious that "just a lot of little fish" had been caught up in Boudreaux's net. Of the sixty-four indicted, sixty-two were African Americans, raising questions about selective prosecution. The money used for vote buying, which was sometimes five dollars and as much as twenty-five dollars, "didn't fall out of the sky." In a press conference with state NAACP officials in April 1998, Alexander and Thibodeaux wanted to know, "Who were the money providers?" Those who had pleaded guilty didn't have that kind of money to spread in the parish. The NAACP wanted the state attorney general to release the 776-page report compiled by the state police; they believed state officials wanted to protect some "powerful people."

Perhaps they did. This was one of the few cases in Louisiana in which allegations of vote buying and vote hauling were sent up the line to the judicial district attorney. Speculations focused on Sheriff Mike Fuselier of St. Martinville, reelected to his fifth term, but who was never called to testify to the grand jury. But while Boudreaux had no reason to hold back on his investigation into local election fraud, he may have felt a need to go lightly on his peers and superiors. Moreover, the 1996 election for the US Senate, in which Mary Landrieu

beat her Republican opponent Louis "Woody" Jenkins by 5,788 votes, was the subject of acrimonious ethics and rules committee hearings in Washington.[11]

Meanwhile, the absence of elections in St. Martinville continued to concern some people, including Eddy Grieg and black residents of District 3. Pam Thibodeaux's appointment to her father's council seat was especially galling, since blacks in District 3 wanted to elect their own representative. If another African American held that seat, blacks would finally have the power to offer city jobs and award contracts to members of their community. The Senate confirmation fights over the assistant attorney for civil rights meant their case was getting lost in a big pile of voting rights cases.

Fed up, Eddy Grieg hired a private attorney, Richard Spears, to file a lawsuit against the city to force an election. Spears, whose practice was usually outside St. Martin Parish, agreed to take the case, provided that Grieg could find plaintiffs who qualified as victims under the federal Voting Rights Act. Local NAACP members, already aware of election fraud in parish elections, were primed to fight the city's entrenched white power structure. They agreed to join Grieg's complaint, despite the risks they were taking in defying the Martin-Thibodeauxes.[12]

In 2000, Spears filed suit against the US government and the State of Louisiana government for denying African American citizens their right to vote under the Fourteenth Amendment. The lawsuit embarrassed the Justice Department and the Clinton administration because it looked as though CRD was disorganized and had failed to carry out its enforcement responsibilities. Belatedly, Bill Lann Lee, whom Clinton had appointed as the assistant attorney general for civil rights during a Senate recess, recognized that his office needed to go on the offensive. By this time there hadn't been a council election in twelve years.[13]

Lee went to Louisiana to work the case himself. On June 2, 2000, the Department of Justice filed its own suit against the City

of St. Martinville for violating Section 2 of the Voting Rights Act, which prohibits discrimination on the basis of race, color, or membership in a language minority group. The suit claimed that the city's refusal to create acceptable electoral districts throughout the 1990s, and council members' seemingly permanent terms of office, denied African Americans the right to vote on account of race. Because the federal government suit made essentially the same claims as the suit filed by Spears, Grieg and the NAACP dropped their suit.[14]

New district maps that met the "one person, one vote" rule were prepared by a special master appointed by federal judge Rebecca F. Doherty. After approving the redrawn electoral maps, the judge ordered St. Martinville to hold an election in April 2002. Pam Thibodeaux's District 3 seat along with the rest of the city council position, and the mayor's position, were up for election.[15]

Local blacks mobilized to nominate Mary L. Francois, an African American businesswoman and a distant relative of city council member Douglas Francois, to run against Thibodeaux. Despite the massive vote-buying case in the parish five years earlier, and despite the twelve-year election hiatus in St. Martinville, it appeared that no one had forgotten how to buy votes, or how their votes could be bought. If the Martin-Thibodeauxes couldn't stay in office by ignoring the Justice Department, they would hold on through election corruption. Greg Malveaux's office was about to spend two years trying to stop two very determined political clans.

Soon after the campaign began, Francois complained to the Louisiana Fraud Division and to reporters that Mayor Martin and Pam Thibodeaux were "putting money on the street." The press reported at least one person was "soliciting the poor and elderly" for votes with "beer and cigarettes." Another pair had registered to vote listing their address as a vacant lot. Malveaux and his staff reviewed and investigated voter registration cards and absentee ballots, and chased down leads throughout the April primary season. Speaking to reporters, Malveaux wasn't unwilling to undermine the worthiness of some citi-

zens as probable "drug addicts and alcoholics" whom he suspected of selling their votes for cigarettes and beer. More troubling were voters identified by Malveaux and his staff who received promises of Section Eight housing assistance, set aside for low-income families, if they agreed to register and vote for Pam Thibodeaux.

At the close of voter registration in March 2002, there were 936 registered voters in St. Martinville. Of these, 359 were white (38.5 percent), 576 black (61.5 percent), and one person whose race was unknown. Fraud investigators were alert to the ruses used elsewhere in Louisiana. Several people who registered to vote in St. Martinville claimed homestead exemptions in other parishes. Either they were breaking state election law by claiming to live where they did not (which was Greg's concern), or they were defrauding the state on their income taxes by claiming an illegal homestead benefit. Indeed, the state attorney general had issued a ruling on exactly this matter in 1998: "If any person claims a homestead exemption, he shall register and vote in the precinct in which the residence is located." It was the voter's responsibility to follow the law, though officials could warn registrants on voter application forms.[16]

Mayor Martin was unimpressed when told of the illegal registration forms. He brushed this off as part of local "les-bon-temps-roulez" culture, telling the press that lots of Acadians didn't change their official addresses when they moved. When it happened, it was just "human error that requires education."[17]

The mayor himself required education to correct his own human error. Nine voters had registered their home address as Police Chief Dickie Martin's house. All nine had legal residences elsewhere; some were family members and others were in-laws.[18] Chief Martin sounded like an absent-minded patriarch who couldn't keep track of his children, saying they "all have lived there [in my house] and in many ways are still living there from time to time." Two other "residents" were city employees, who Martin also claimed had lived with him at one time. The chief said his son the mayor wasn't concerned about the

matter. "If you went through every house in Acadiana you're going to find one two three people who don't live there every day but are registered [to vote] there . . . I don't think nine votes are going to make a difference."[19]

"What's the point of having rules about residency and such if they're not going to be enforced better than it appears they are in this situation?" wrote the publisher of the *Iberian* in an editorial. "No laws may have been broken by the many people registered at the same address in St. Martinville. But clearly the spirit of residency is not being followed. . . . More needs to be done to clean up voter rolls."[20]

The Martin-Thibodeaux clan was equally adept at redirecting the attention of the Fraud Division investigator to their political rivals. Malveaux sent Jared Labue to St. Martinville, where local officials told him the only problems in town were caused by Mary Francois. With exaggerated claims of innocence, they told Labue that any claims of vote buying could never be traced to the Martins or the Thibodeauxes because they did not believe in such illegal behavior. Ignoring his director's orders, Labue began investigating Francois, even though the division had received no evidence against her campaign. He set up surveillance outside Francois's home, leaving both the Martin and Thibodeaux homes unwatched. When Labue reported to Malveaux, he was told to refocus his investigation on the mayor, the chief, and Pam Thibodeaux.

Chief Martin then tried another ruse to divert Malveaux and Labue's investigation. Martin claimed the NAACP had illegally engaged in "vote hauling" on Election Day. What was the Fraud Division doing investigating his family, while ignoring this huge violation by the civil rights organization? Martin claimed that by endorsing Mary Francois and driving voters to the polls, the NAACP should be criminally prosecuted. Ernest Johnson, the St. Martinville NAACP official, responded that because they were a nonprofit organization, "we may take people to the polls." The NAACP did not instruct people how to vote, or reward voters with anything of financial value

for voting, Malveaux told the press. Their activities were permissible "get-out-the-vote" undertakings, even when the nonprofit paid drivers to take voters to polling places.

The results of the April 2002 primary gave Mayor Martin 6 percent of the vote for a "fourth" election victory, though his "third" term had lasted twelve years. Pam Thibodeaux won a plurality of votes in District 3, but not 50 percent, requiring a run-off election the first Tuesday in May. Francois won 30 percent of the vote, and two other contenders together received the remainder. Anticipating more tricks from the Martins and Thibodeauxes, Malveaux and his staff stayed on to monitor the run-off campaign.[21]

The Fraud Division documented many "irregularities" that had occurred during the primary, but because it could only investigate and not charge anyone, its hands were tied. At the end of April, Malveaux turned over his investigative file to St. Martinville's assistant district attorney Chester Cedars, recommending prosecution of those who had falsely registered to vote, those engaged in buying or selling votes, and vote haulers who had turned in forged absentee ballots. Cedars told the *Teche News* he would proceed if there was any legal basis to do so, but on the day before the run-off election, announced that there wasn't enough evidence to warrant prosecution.[22]

Francois feared for her own safety and did not want people in St. Martinville to see her meeting with fraud investigators. When she had information to share, Malveaux met her at the Waffle House in Lafayette fifteen miles away. Her paranoia was not unfounded: a spurious arrest warrant had been issued by St. Martin Parish district attorney Phil Haney, charging her with falsely claiming a homestead exemption. The mysterious warrant, which was never served, was later discovered in the investigation files reviewed by the commissioner of elections. In addition, Francois avoided talking to the press and refused to answer questions raised by her opponent Pam Thibodeaux or by Mayor Martin. It was hardly the best way to campaign for office. She lost the runoff by thirteen votes.

Francois challenged the election results, filing suit in state court claiming the same irregularities that the Fraud Division had documented. At trial, Francois's lawyer attempted to "paint a portrait of wrongdoing and incompetence in St. Martinville's election system." Francois said she witnessed "campaign workers for Thibodeaux going door to door on [Election Day] and 'intimidating' people to vote for the incumbent, including Mayor Eric Martin's father, [former police chief] Dickie Martin."[23] Malveaux testified under oath that he could not trust the honesty of officials in St. Martinville. His office's efforts to investigate had been met with flagrant lies and deliberate efforts to mislead his staff. Indeed, the parish registrar of voters was Pam Thibodeaux's cousin, Sue Thibodeaux.

Sue Thibodeaux was asked to explain why her office ignored Louisiana's voter identification law, and allowed her election commissioners to improperly complete the affidavits of voters who failed to bring picture identification to polling stations. Francois's attorney submitted several affidavits on which commissioners had written their own names, which the voter was supposed to sign. Clarence Porter, a resident in District 3, had tried to vote in the run-off election, only to be told someone had already voted absentee using his name.[24] He was not permitted to cast a provisional ballot.

State District Judge Gerard Wattigny threw out twelve contested ballots, which left Pam Thibodeaux with a one-vote margin of victory. Because she lost her case, Francois had to pay the legal fees and costs of the litigation. (As a side note, when Judge Wattigny retired in 2014, Anthony Thibodeaux was elected to his seat.) When the city council of St. Martinville met on July 2, 2002, it was the first time they'd been sworn in since 1990. Two newly elected members joined Pam Thibodeaux, Pat Martin, and Mike Fuselier, who was the son of parish sheriff Mike Fuselier and also related to Mayor Eric Martin. Outside the building, about twenty-five people marched to protest the irregular election.[25]

Eddy Grieg was furious at the turn of events. He started a recall

petition against Pam Thibodeaux, which went well until several supporters "including his own mother" began removing their names from the petition. Grieg found that some supporters had been the targets of threats and intimidation such as pointing out that a relative in jail would be sent too far away to visit if people did not withdraw their names. Grieg's attorney for the recall petition, Jermaine Williams, told the *New Iberian*, "We do feel that some of our witnesses, for lack of a better word, crawfished on us," after a judge threw out their case.[26]

City inspectors, possibly sent by Mayor Martin, harassed Grieg's business. They cited his woodworking and welding shop for "rat infestation, rotten wood and rusty metal." Grieg told a reporter, "I had no rats in here, no rotten wood. You can't build outdoor furniture with rotten wood. Rusty iron, I plead guilty to that because anywhere you've got iron there's going to be rust." After the recall effort died, the citations were dropped.[27]

Meanwhile, Francois tried to appeal Judge Wattigny's decision to award the seat to Thibodeaux, rather than to order a recount or weigh the preponderance of evidence of election fraud. But a curious series of events prevented her from filing the appeal bond on time. On the day it was due, as Francois was hurrying into the Parish Courthouse with the funds she had finally collected, the clerk of court gave her employees the rest of the day off. By the time Francois arrived at the office, the doors were closed, so she could not post the bond.[28]

At that point, Francois decided to fight, not for the lost seat on the city council, but to protest the entire election process in St. Martinville. With supporters from the NAACP and other concerned citizens, she joined in a federal class action suit that sought to prevent future violations of the Voting Rights Act.[29]

The federal suit forced Commissioner of Elections Terrell to pay attention to events in St. Martinville, because they jeopardized her campaign promise to clean up election corruption. Terrell directed her outside counsel, Michael Walsh, to review Malveaux's report and

Mary Francois's case, and to advise her whether her office should take further action. Walsh noted numerous errors made by Judge Wattigny: during the trial, he refused to permit Francois to submit evidence regarding some illegal voters; he rejected her complaints about officials who had permitted voters without identification to vote, because Francois had poll watchers who could have challenged any issues as they arose. Walsh found Wattigny's decision "legally suspect and politically dangerous, including his misinterpretation of the state law regarding residency." Given the one-vote margin, Walsh thought Wattigny should have ordered a recount, especially given the many allegations of corruption.[30]

Walsh advised Terrell that, as the commissioner of elections, she should press for the prosecution of Mayor Eric Martin and his father, Dickie Martin. Both men had publicly acknowledged wrongdoing when they told the press there were people who had fraudulently registered to vote using Dickie Martin's house as their address; they had also voted. Failing to request their prosecution would raise charges of selective prosecution in other cases. Not pursuing a case, not even one for misdemeanor charges for filing false public documents, could "prove damaging to [Terrell], the parish, and all other parties involved in the election and subsequent court action." Walsh reminded Terrell that given the recent (and older) history of St. Martinville, and the closeness of the election, such irregularities practically invited a federal lawsuit under the Voting Rights Act.

Commissioner Terrell followed Walsh's advice. She turned Malveaux's files documenting voting fraud in the Francois-Thibodeaux election over to the parish's District Attorney Haney. She apparently agreed with Walsh's view that it was best (for her own political career) that Haney sort out the matter, allowing local authorities to benefit from the "diligence of [her] department in investigating elections problems, without appearing overbearing." Haney could determine who needed punishment and who was simply negli-

gent, since he was in a better situation to know local "feelings" on the matter.[31]

None of this was shared with Greg Malveaux at the time, however. He only knew that, once again, no one would be prosecuted despite the evidence his division uncovered. He was as frustrated as Eddy Grieg about Pam Thibodeaux's election, but despite feeling worn down by the forces conspiring against him, Malveaux soldiered on.

CHAPTER 4

Making a Federal Case

I've been hearing about election fraud my whole life.

—*Eddy Grieg*

The situation in St. Martinville did not dissipate after Mary Francois lost her case against Pam Thibodeaux. The decision of the commissioner of elections to turn Greg Malveaux's investigative files over to the local prosecutor allowed Suzanne Terrell to distance herself from the discoveries made by her subordinates. Phil Haney, the St. Martinville district attorney, understood that Malveaux was now fair game: in order to protect his political patrons, the Martin and Thibodeaux clans, Haney set out to destroy Malveaux's reputation.

Greg didn't seem to understand the Machiavellian machinations at work. He is, at heart, a cop who believes that vote sellers and vote buyers should be prosecuted for breaking the law. He brushed off suggestions made by some local officials that he was overly zealous in his pursuit of justice. Like many cases in the South, the St. Martinville case had implications of racism, intimidation, and discrimination, but in pushing for fair elections, Greg thought he was wearing the white hat: he was defending an African American woman's election over a member of a historically powerful white family. If he won, the

case would give hope to poor black voters throughout the parish and perhaps Louisiana.

Haney and his assistant Chester Cedars had extensive relationships with the local press, which regularly covered their cases in the criminal courts. Working the phones, they provided background to reporters about Malveaux, giving unflattering accounts of his work and telling lies about his career. Haney complained in the press that Malveaux had produced incomplete data; Ricky Ward, the prosecutor in Iberville, himself accused of election fraud in a Plaquemine Parish case, said Malveaux's affidavits were improperly executed. Cedars diminished and distorted Greg's previous experience by describing his previous job for Terrell as being her "driver" when she was on the New Orleans city council, though he was in fact a deputy sheriff in Orleans Parish who had been detailed for her security. The *Teche News* was not pleased when, at Greg's insistence, it had to correct the record.

Investigating Malveaux's experience more thoroughly, the *Teche News* reported that everyone in the Orleans Parish sheriff's office spoke highly of his experience and ability; prosecutors in other parishes vouched for the quality of the evidence he delivered even when they chose not to prosecute. The Houma district attorney's office said the Fraud Division's investigation there "was good and a conviction was secured." Haney and Cedars realized they had lost the trust of the local press and backed off, but warned Malveaux personally that they would fight him every step of the way.[1]

Cedars met with Greg and Commissioner Terrell's staff attorney Julie Thompson to discuss the case. Thompson was already on quite friendly terms with St. Martinville officials, and had blocked some of Malveaux's earlier inquiries. When Cedars repeated the DA's intention not to proceed, following procedure, Malveaux asked if he had a right to appeal to state officials since there was no interest in the DA's office. Cedars was perhaps negligent when he failed to ask Greg which "state officials" he planned to appeal to; maybe Malveaux de-

liberately misled Cedars with his vague query. But Cedars told him to go ahead, assuming the appeal would go to the state attorney general.

Haney, in the meantime, announced he would meet with Terrell in Baton Rouge to discuss "deficiencies" in the record that were delaying his prosecution. That meeting, which Greg did not attend, turned into a strategy session in which Haney, Terrell, and Cedars apparently agreed not to bring a case against Mayor Eric Martin and others who had acknowledged breaking the law. In that meeting, Haney agreed to pursue eleven cases, with Terrell's consent. Reframing Mayor Martin's description of Acadian voters, Haney suggested that his inquiry would decide whether the alleged perpetrators were simply negligent or had deliberately falsified their voter registrations. He effectively dismissed a dozen more instances of possible fraud, rationalizing that there was insufficient evidence to prosecute and questionable technical violations; one alleged perpetrator was "pardoned" because he had a disability. Haney argued that the best solution was not prosecution but more voter education. Yet he further delayed filing charges, setting aside six cases for further investigation by his office, and forwarding only five for prosecution.[2]

Malveaux was upset that his white hat had been slapped into the mud by Haney and his own boss. But Malveaux didn't work with lawyers, he worked with law enforcement. In June 2002, he appealed to Colonel Terry Landry, superintendent of the Louisiana State Police, for assistance. Landry, an African American from New Iberia, had spent twenty-seven years working his way up the ranks, and had earned his appointment from Governor Mike Foster in 2000. He asked a federal judge to issue twenty-four arrest warrants against the perpetrators in St. Martinville, and formally requested Terrell to send a memo to Superintendent Landry, asking the state police to execute the warrants since the Elections Commission did not have the manpower. Landry instructed the Lafayette commander to make arrests the following Monday.

Haney was in a quandary. He did not want to offend his political

base, but if the warrants were served he would be expected to act; he would be forced to waive the charges, or worse, be forced to prosecute people who helped elect him. He appealed to Governor Foster's office to prevent their execution. Bernie Boudreaux, the governor's legal counsel, saved him. Boudreaux, the former judicial district attorney who had prosecuted the "little fish" engaged in vote buying and selling in St. Martin Parish in 1997, was acutely aware of the delicacy of Haney's situation. Boudreaux warned Colonel Landry that it would be illegal for the State Police to make the arrests. But Landry heard the warning as a challenge to his authority and jurisdiction; he did not pass it on to the commandant in Lafayette, who was geared up and ready to go on Monday. But Malveaux, wishing to prevent trouble for a fellow African American officer, told the commandant he could forget the warrants. He recognized that Haney was simply too volatile: if the warrants were executed Haney would dismiss the charges, and lay blame on the Fraud Division and the commissioner of elections.

This was exactly the situation that Michael Walsh had tried to prevent in advising Terrell earlier. As her outside counsel, he had recommended that the commissioner emphasize to reporters and legislators the "law and order" division of responsibilities between her office and local prosecutors. The Fraud Division was tasked with investigating complaints, but it was primarily the decision of local district attorneys to determine which cases to prosecute. Renewed scrutiny over the investigation in the St. Martinville situation forced Terrell's hand. She explained publicly that her agency would not try to displace authorities in St. Martin Parish by attempting to obtain arrest warrants. Her staff would simply deliver materials to the district attorney to use at his discretion.[3]

Haney ultimately charged only five people with breaking state laws regarding residency and voting fraud. Pam Thibodeaux's brother, Burton James Champagne, was charged with voting illegally in the primary and the runoff. Albert Anthony DeCuir had also falsified

his voter registration card and engaged in voter fraud. Notably, Haney still chose not to pursue charges against Pam Thibodeaux, Mayor Martin, or his father, Dickie Martin.[4]

But Malveaux would not back off. He resented the fact that political considerations allowed lawbreakers to go free and perpetuate the Martin-Thibodeaux fiefdom in St. Martinville. He also believed strongly that the criminal behavior corrupted the electoral system and perpetuated economic injustice. Having Haney check him through the governor's office, Malveaux realized that an appeal to the Louisiana attorney general was also futile. But Eddy Grieg's lawsuit pointed to another option: electoral fraud that resulted in the disfranchisement of African American citizens. This was a violation of their constitutional rights under the Fourteenth and Fifteenth Amendments, as well as the federal Voting Rights Act. The Thibodeauxes at least, and perhaps the Martins, had potentially committed federal crimes as a result.

Malveaux decided to make a federal case out of the St. Martinville situation. He met with Donald Washington, the US attorney in Lafayette who had been appointed by President George W. Bush. At first, Washington and his staff refused to get involved, viewing the problem as a local matter, not a federal violation. On its face, that much was true. Malveaux argued back that a federal judge had ordered the election in 2000, and the case had begun under the Voting Rights Act. Therefore voting fraud that disfranchised African Americans in a federally ordered election obligated the US attorney to refer the case to the Justice Department in Washington. Given the public distrust of Attorney General John Ashcroft and of the Bush administration, especially on electoral fraud issues in the aftermath of *Bush* v. *Gore*, the Civil Rights Division could not refuse the case, however much they were loath to be involved.[5]

The FBI assigned a local agent in charge, a former Louisiana State University football player who knew the landscape. He oversaw a raid of Registrar Sue Thibodeaux's office by half a dozen FBI agents, which

turned up more copies of the documents Malveaux had collected, independently confirming the evidence. They confiscated twenty-four signed voter registration cards, including those of Pam Thibodeaux, her brother Burton Champagne, and Dickie Martin. This time, the federal grand jury subpoenas could not be circumvented by Governor Foster's office.[6]

With so much press coverage of the FBI raid, Haney was forced to move forward. He was still trying to protect the Martins and other local political officials from federal prosecution, Malveaux realized. When the deal was announced it was typical but hardly justice. The US attorney would pursue only the case against Pam Thibodeaux, their chief target, and leave the remaining "little fish" cases for Haney to handle. He could deal with them however he wished.

Greg knew this was a bad deal. He watched as Haney ignored most of the cases he kept and took a few to trial, all of which were heard by a local judge. The convictions that followed levied less punishment than a parking violation. There were no fines and no jail time, and the judge expressed reluctance to punish the convicted from the bench.[7]

Meanwhile, the federal case against Pam Thibodeaux proceeded, presided over by US District Court judge Richard Haik. Appointed by President George W. Bush in 1991, Haik had practiced in New Iberia before serving on the Louisiana District Court; he was not related to Suzanne Haik Terrell. The trial commenced in January 2006, and brought to light the schemes Thibodeaux used to ensure she won the city council election. Cards were distributed to friends, family members, and supporters who signed them without including a valid address. Thibodeaux then supplied a false address within her district, which her relative, Registrar Sue Thibodeaux, did not verify. On one count of conspiracy to submit false information in order to register to vote, Judge Haik concluded that she had won an "extremely tight race, only as a result of the fraudulent votes." For this, Pam Thibodeaux was permitted to plea bargain. The govern-

ment dismissed all charges except one. She pleaded guilty to one count of conspiracy to submit false information in order to register to vote.[8]

Adjudged guilty in federal court, Thibodeaux resigned from her council seat before sentencing. In her statement to other council members, she claimed "[she] wanted to show her child personal responsibility." That last-minute declaration, as well as her statement that she had "learned from the experience" that "ignorance does not make you innocent," greatly irritated Judge Haik. He called for a brief recess after her statement. When she came back into the courtroom she was crying and apologized profusely for what she'd said. She acknowledged to Judge Haik, "What I did was illegal and wrong."

Thibodeaux received three years' probation and six months of home confinement with electronic monitoring. Judge Haik also imposed a fine of $2,000 and $1,500 in restitution for conspiracy to falsely register others to vote. Because these were felonies, Thibodeaux lost her license to sell insurance and also lost her voting rights. In the aftermath, her husband, Conrad, also resigned his civil service job as an electrical foreman for the City of St. Martinville. She herself left town after he committed suicide.[9]

The conviction of Pam Thibodeaux, and the trivial punishments meted out to her coconspirators, did not address the persistent disfranchisement experienced by the African American citizens of St. Martinville. In their view, electoral fraud was the means by which a small, tight-knit group of white politicians suppressed the city's black majority. Haney's taps on the pinkie fingers of the other conspirators further aggravated the black voters.

Mary Francois would have won election to city council for District 3 had the runoff been carried out fairly. Locals wanted her to fill the vacancy created by Pam Thibodeaux's resignation; even Eddy Grieg, who had stirred up the situation in the first place, would have been a better choice. But Mayor Martin, whose participation in the fraud was never put on trial, was still in charge. He chose to appoint Dennis

Paul Williams, an artist and musician in his brother's well-known and respected band, Nathan & The Zydeco Cha-Chas.

Williams had never held office before, nor shown the slightest interest in local government. "I don't know anything about politics," he said when Mayor Martin announced his six-month interim appointment. "I haven't been at any meetings or anything. The whole idea is for me to come in as a neutral person."[10]

Grieg opposed Williams's appointment to the city council from the outset. "Why didn't they put in Mary Francois, who ran for the seat and people voted for?" he asked. "It looks like to me that they just put somebody in there who they thought they could get to do what they want or vote the way they want." Years later, when I talked to Grieg at his shop, he said he'd been hearing about election fraud "my whole life." The 2002 election "was business as usual."[11]

It's not that Williams was unknown around town; indeed "everyone" knew him and liked him. But they felt cheated out of choosing their own representative. "I thought it was a slap in the face to the black community," said Paulma Johnson, who had served on the St. Martin Parish school board for thirty-three years. "Mary Francois won the election. The election was stolen. It's just that simple. It doesn't take a Philadelphia lawyer to figure that out. How can you win something and then have to give up the seat? This city better re-examine itself and try and set an example for our children and the generations to come. The city council ought to be embarrassed."[12]

Mayor Martin insisted he had acted fairly. "Mary [Francois] hadn't shown interest in the city." That was not quite accurate: Francois's work as an insurance broker—in the years when Hurricane Katrina (August 2005) and Hurricane Rita (September 2005) had tossed hundreds of thousands of Louisianans' lives into disarray—had taken her all over the state at that time. Francois also had supporters on the city council: Murphy Simon spoke in favor of her appointment to the vacant seat. After all, she had actually run for the seat, while Williams, who had been Simon's student in St. Martinville High School, had "never been interested in politics."[13]

Mayor Martin dismissed black voters' discontent, saying too many people had adopted "racist conspiracy theories" about his motives. Some people, he claimed, put Francois "on a pedestal." Williams would help heal the community's wounds. "It's typical to see Dennis out on the sidewalk with his broom waving at cars as they go by," Martin told the press. "About the only thing you can say about Dennis is he goes to church a lot. He's just a good fella." Williams said that his own religious-spiritual philosophy is to heal and find a way to resolve differences rather than to fight. The mayor showed the voters of District 3: they had said they wanted an African American representative on the council, so he gave them one.[14]

White members of the city council approved Williams's interim appointment. The two African American representatives from Districts Four and Five had both endorsed Francois in the 2000 election, and they again voted for her to fill the District 3 vacancy. Council members Mike Fuselier (the parish sheriff's son) and Pat Martin (the mayor's cousin) voted for Williams. The 2–2 tie was broken by Mayor Martin. A special election for District 3 was scheduled for April 2006.[15]

Benefiting from his incumbency, Williams was elected by thirty-three votes, a smaller margin than in any other council race. He won reelection four years later and continues to serve today. When I visited him at his home in St. Martinville in February 2012, he had the open, sunny demeanor everyone had described, and was eager to tell me how he got along with everyone and avoided controversy, and about how spirituality motivated him.[16]

Meanwhile, Terrell made good on her political promise to abolish the office of commissioner of elections. In 2004, the legislature merged it back into the secretary of state's office. In doing so, it reduced the Fraud Division's authority to oversee compliance with state law without an investigative function. Secretary of State W. Fox McKeithen, for whom Malveaux's deputy Stephen Watts had worked, wasn't interested in retaining the staff. In fact, he went after the commission's work, criticizing Terrell's administration.

Malveaux was also targeted, in comeuppance, perhaps, for his dogged pursuit of lawbreakers.[17]

McKeithen thought Terrell had established a "dangerous precedent" by approving so much overtime for voting fraud investigators. He claimed that "Malveaux got $50,000, including $37,655 for overtime," and received "pay for 75.5 hours of annual leave." Though these payments were legal and accurately documented, McKeithen said it "looks like they were trying to get everything they could get." That was a horrible example of state service, especially when "the majority of it developed when they were leaving" the division. McKeithen highlighted the community college courses Malveaux had taken while working for the state, unable to believe that anyone could carry such a heavy work load.[18]

Apparently the secretary of state thought Fraud Division workers should work like other state employees: show up at their offices in Baton Rouge at 9 a.m. and leave at 5 p.m. But Malveaux and his staff put a tremendous number of hours into their investigations, intensively working in the run-up to Election Day. In some years there was an election every month, so the staff had to work long hours. Terrell herself said she was proud that her office had, as promised, investigated so many cases of election fraud. Further, because the complaints came from all over the state requiring long hours on the road, the staff deserved reimbursement, especially since they drove their own cars rather than using state vehicles.[19]

The Louisiana inspector general cleared Malveaux of wrongdoing; his expense vouchers had been approved by Terrell's chief of staff, Charles Patrick Bergeron. However, Bergeron "did not verify or question any information or lack of presented on Mr. Malveaux's travel voucher."[20] To prevent technical problems in the future, the inspector general recommended tweaking accounting rules for payments and oversight, especially for compensatory leave for unclassified employees.

Terrell defended her actions, telling the press, "It's about paying

people for earned overtime." Though the inspector general had implicated her, Terrell herself was never interviewed during the review. Her chief of staff had adhered to the policies of Governor Foster's executive branch. Her record as commissioner of elections was exemplary. Previous commissioners (all of them Democrats) had received 20 percent annual budget increases, though they did not use the money. Terrell had never requested an increase, but instead, after reviewing the budget she had returned $25 million to the state treasury.[21]

But Democratic politicians seemed to view her small-government efficiency as a threat. And it is true that under Terrell's administration, the people the commission had ensnared and prosecuted were mostly Democrats. In St. Martinville, all but one of the false registrations and other irregularities discovered by Malveaux's staff had been perpetrated by white conservative "Blue Dog" Democrats. At the end of her term, Terrell's political career was at a nadir. Once a rising star in the state as a (white) Republican woman, she had lost two high-profile elections. While still holding the office of commissioner, she ran and lost in 2002 against Mary Landrieu for the US Senate; in 2003, she ran for attorney general of Louisiana against Charles C. Foti Jr., the former Orleans Parish criminal sheriff. Democrats had defeated her twice—perhaps having President Bush II tour the state in support of an "honest" commissioner of elections was not the best political decision to sway voters to her side—and now they wanted to ensure she couldn't make a comeback.

As for the people in St. Martinville, and for Greg Malveaux and Terry Landry, their stories explain why an entirely different approach is needed to address electoral fraud. Greg himself returned to the Orleans Parish Sheriff's office in 2006, again detailed to providing security for city council members.

After securing Dennis Williams's city council seat, Mayor Martin stepped down in 2006 to represent the Pfizer Company's interests in Louisiana. He's still popular in St. Martinville, where he reigned as the Rotary Club's Mardi Gras king in 2010.[22] But that was just the

start of his attempt at a political comeback. When the Louisiana legislature created a new "black" legislative seat that included much of St. Martin Parish after the 2010 census, Martin ran as an independent in the open primary. Reflecting the needs of corporations such as his employer, Martin's platform said taxes were too high, and that Louisiana was "not the friendliest" for attracting outside companies. He promised to fight for job creation and to make Acadia a "southern leader in small business, agriculture, oil and gas, healthcare and tourism." He won enough votes to force a runoff. His opponent was Terry Landry, the State Police superintendent who agreed to help Greg Malveaux with the vote-buying warrants, who ran as a Democrat. Landry defeated Martin by four votes and is still in office.[23]

Mary Francois dropped out of politics after her defeat in 2006. She continued to visit her son, a student at the prestigious St. Augustine High School in New Orleans, while the city began to rebuild from the devastation caused by the levee breaks. She had left her job as an insurance broker in 2005 to start a new business, America's Best Mortgage and Creative Solutions in St. Martinville. But when the housing and bank financing scandals crashed the economy in 2008, she was one of the "little fish" caught up in the net. In 2011, she pleaded guilty in federal court to wire fraud in a mortgage-lending scheme. She assisted numerous clients without the income or necessary credit rating to obtain mortgages totaling $2.3 million by falsifying their loan applications. Francois admitted that she had made agreements with sellers that allowed her to pocket the difference between loans and purchase prices as part of her "payment" for obtaining a loan.[24]

Judge Haik, who had also handled Thibodeaux's electoral fraud case, was the trial judge. Francois faced a potential twenty-year federal prison sentence and fines as high as $500,000 for the two counts of wire fraud. However, Judge Haik was reluctant to punish her. He granted bail and delayed her sentencing twice while he heard evidence on whether she had profited from the illegal activity. The evidence showed she had pocketed about $150,000, not the extraordi-

nary amounts prosecutors had claimed. Francois received a fourteen-month prison sentence with three years of supervised probation.[25]

At the time of this writing, her father Leonard Francois, who still lives in St. Martinville, said Mary was managing quite well and living in Houston. He remains proud of the stand she took for fair elections.[26]

Dennis Williams's desire to get along with everyone has not helped his reputation with black voters in District 3; he just narrowly won reelection in 2015. Voters criticized him for representing the interests of the mayor and other council members in patronage allocations. Williams stood up for merit hiring, which, in a perfect world, might have put more African Americans in city jobs. But officials used "merit" to beat back black applicants while making sure their friends were hired instead. Williams still seems oblivious to the possibility that in awarding him the District 3 seat, whites in St. Martinville had gotten exactly what they needed to perpetuate their power.[27]

CHAPTER 5

Electoral Fraud Chicago Style

> He went to "every hotel and flophouse in the West Side ward to pay for votes and obtain lists of people who had died or moved and would not be voting."
>
> —*Raymond Hicks*

Democrats in Illinois were deeply concerned about voter turnout in the November 2014 elections. Political strategists had declared incumbent governor Pat Quinn the most vulnerable candidate in the nation, with razor-thin margins against the Republican candidate, wealthy venture capitalist Bruce Rauner. Rauner put $6 million from his own pocket into his campaign, making Chicago's overwhelmingly Democratic voters a potentially deciding factor in the race.

Alderwoman Leslie Hairston, whose Fifth Ward covered Chicago's South Shore and Hyde Park neighborhoods, was a good machine politician. Though she herself was not up for reelection, she too worried about turnout. To encourage voters, she offered residents in her ward a chance to participate in a raffle for gift cards from Walgreens, Starbucks, Potbelly, and other places. Raffle "tickets" would be given out free to anyone who voted in November. Hairston posted the raffle offer on Facebook and other social media.[1]

Hairston's former opponent, Anne Marie Miles, complained to the Cook County state's attorney election hotline that giving out prizes

for voting was prohibited under Illinois election law. Questioned by the news media about the legality of the raffle, Hairston defended the offer: "I'm owning it, yeah. I'm owning it. Absolutely." The election office said they were "looking into the matter." Like most states, Illinois doesn't have a special agency to investigate election fraud. As in almost every other state, voters in Illinois elect their state attorneys and their judges. But when editorials in the local press accused Hairston of vote buying, she backed off and canceled the raffle. In the heat of the Quinn-Rauner election, the raffle story disappeared.

Hairston's raffle was made in good faith, a rather benign gesture compared to the vote buying and election fraud that occurs in Louisiana and some other states. Illinois law prohibits giving benefits to encourage voting, even if not directed at influencing a vote for a particular candidate. Federal law prohibits paying a voter. Yet states as different as Louisiana and Massachusetts permit giving incentives to vote for nonpartisan purposes; the incentive cannot be intended to influence the voter's choice. The vote buying and electoral fraud that occurs in Chicago is not so different from the cases Greg Malveaux investigated in Louisiana. But Illinois and Chicago have different approaches to election corruption, offering an opportunity to weigh the effectiveness of other responses.[2]

Illinois's tight laws don't seem to reduce reports of fraud any more than in Louisiana, New York, and other states where elected officials face jail time for abusing the public trust. Quinn, who lost his reelection bid, became the fourth consecutive governor to face a federal investigation for corruption.[3]

A political scientist at the University of Illinois at Chicago concluded, "The Chicago metropolitan region has been the most corrupt area in the country since 1976," in an obdurate race to the bottom with Louisiana's record. According to that 2012 study, Illinois is the third-most corrupt state in the union, after New York and California. In addition, four consecutive corrupt governors and nearly one-third of Chicago's one hundred alderpersons since 1973 have been con

victed of corruption, mostly involving bribes to influence government decisions or for personal financial benefit. Yet corruption is not a one-party party: the Republicans dominating the states of North Dakota, South Dakota, and Mississippi have had the highest number of corruption cases in the country in the last four decades, when states are ranked by convictions of public officials per capita. In contrast, Oregon, Washington State, and Utah are the least corrupt.[4]

Taking money or gifts for a politician's own benefit is a widely agreed upon form of corruption. But are politicians and political parties who give out small amounts of money or small gifts to voters necessarily corrupt? Get-out-the-vote efforts coordinated by churches, nonprofit organizations, corporations, and political parties are permissible election activities, provided they don't demand voters cast their ballots for a specific candidate. But giving gifts, as in the case of Hairston's raffle idea, is considered suspicious activity. Though state legislatures and Congress have passed numerous laws against political corruption, it is up to prosecutors to decide whom they will charge with corruption. As the previous chapters on Louisiana exposed, the intractable problem of electoral fraud is that prosecutors themselves are elected and dependent on voters (and political money) to remain in power. This is one of the primary reasons why cases of election fraud almost never hook the sharks, but instead scoop up the little fish.

The raffle set up by Alderwoman Hairston didn't seek to exploit donors seeking favorable votes or even steer voters into supporting Governor Quinn. But it turns out that the raffle was nonetheless illegal under Illinois election law, which does not account for nuance or purpose. Illinois legislators wanted to prevent candidates from offering inducements to voters. Yet in Kentucky and elsewhere, "ginger cakes" and other door prizes as rewards for voting might be given out by local governments as rewards to citizens exercising the privilege of democracy. The key factor is to not use such incentives to influence the vote for a particular candidate.

Do campaign promises and special programs constitute inducements to voters? In Illinois, Governor Quinn was charged with corruption not because he *promised* to establish community-based programs to prevent gun violence but because he actually *created* one. His antiviolence initiative, "The Neighborhood Recovery Initiative," launched before his first full-term governor's race, did not have the usual features of an illegal incentive. The initiative gave money to community groups on Chicago's South Side and south suburbs to establish antiviolence programs, and to stop the shootings of innocent bystanders, many of whom were children.

After Quinn won the 2010 election, his critics began calling the Neighborhood Recovery Initiative a political slush fund to influence the largely Democratic voters in South Chicago. They demanded that the FBI and the state investigate. The withering criticism forced Quinn to drop a program his constituents wanted and needed.[5] Despite this, the investigations continued. The state auditor found the Initiative hastily implemented and sloppily organized, though he did not find any wrongdoing on the part of the governor. However, the charges helped to undermine Quinn's 2014 bid for reelection.[6]

Illinois's decades-old notoriety for election corruption is legendary. Many people still remember stories about the first Mayor Richard A. Daley rigging the presidential election of John F. Kennedy in 1960, for example, but even in those times, electoral fraud was probably common in local elections. In fact, the bigger news in the 1960 election was that State's Attorney Benjamin Adamowski, a Republican running for reelection, was posed to run against Richard J. Daley in the next mayoral race. Common knowledge attributed his loss most definitely to fraud.[7]

To counter political corruption in Chicago, attorney Michael Shakman coordinated a series of lawsuits beginning in 1969 that protected city employees from the whims and wrath of elected officials. Patronage jobs, which award government jobs to party loyalists for turning out votes and support in favor of a candidate, are not neces-

sarily corrupt and were long perfectly legal; among other examples, President Lincoln created the office of postmaster general precisely so someone else would take over the onerous task of appointing Republican loyalists to local post office jobs. But Democratic pols in Chicago did the Grand Old Party one better: they expected appointees to pay up at election time, shaking down civil servants for campaign "donations" so they could keep their jobs. Shakman won judicial decrees ending the practice. "Shakman decrees" did not abolish patronage hiring, nor did they address the "work around" that later Chicago mayors created. During his five terms in office (1989–2011), Mayor Richard M. Daley initiated the practice of contracting government services out to companies who could hire whomever they wished, including an elected official's supporters, friends, and family.

Election officials knew about and permitted some patronage to continue, even when it bordered on fraud—at least until they themselves were caught. In the Chicago and Illinois general election of November 1982, twenty-six people, a majority of them election officials, were indicted for election fraud in federal court. The case was brought by Dan Webb, the Republican US attorney, who had federal jurisdiction since the ballot included a congressional race in addition to local and state offices. People accused Webb of targeting Democrats, but officials of both parties used illegal practices to maintain their hold on office. Democrats were especially concerned about Republican vote fraud outside of Chicago, which they claimed was the reason why their gubernatorial candidate Adlai Stevenson lost the election.[8]

Conviction for violating federal election law carries a potential fine of not more than ten thousand dollars or imprisonment for up to five years, or both. This was a high-stakes indictment. The Chicago Board of Election Commissioners appoints election judges, choosing among nominees submitted by the Democratic and Republican parties, with confirmation by the Cook County Circuit Court.

Witnesses accused the defendants of forging signatures, imper-

sonating voters, registering ineligible voters, "assisting" older or disabled voters, bribing voters, illegally dispensing and voting absentee ballots, and using weapons and force to persuade voters and campaign workers. One official was accused of running a ballot through the tabulator two hundred times in order to increase his candidate's margin of victory.

Joe Novak, a longtime Chicago political operative who knew the intimate details of the election system, explained in 2002 that election fraud still worked the way it had for years. "Precinct captains still like to control the vote by pushing absentees." The captain goes to a retirement center or other places where the elderly gather and gets a signed statement from a voter that they can't make it to the polls on Election Day. The captain can tell the voter how to vote. The idea is "Captains like to be ranked No. 1" in their ward organization.[9] Alderman Joseph Moore from the Forty-Ninth Ward added, "The captain will offer to take (a completed absentee ballot) downtown for you."[10] "Until they tightened the rules a few years ago," Moore said, "it was common to see captains bringing in buckets full of ballots."[11]

A *Chicago Tribune* investigation of massive fraud, published in January 1983, led Webb to announce that his investigators would "use a computer" (which was at the time an innovative crime-fighting technology) to determine how many dead people were registered to vote or registered in more than one location throughout the city's 2,910 precincts.[12] Overall, 10 percent of Chicago's one million votes for governor, mayor, city council, and other public officials were alleged to be fraudulent. "The fraud we uncovered in these indictments is so great, the scheme so intense, that the exact number of votes stolen in the November elections is unknown," Webb announced at a press conference revealing the arrest of ten officials on the city's West Side.[13]

"Electoral fraud Chicago style" was highly coordinated among Democrats, with a few Republican facilitators thrown in as nonparti-

san accessories. Webb's case focused on activities in the Seventeenth Precinct in the Twenty-Seventh Ward, where votes were bought and sold for a cup of cocoa, two dollars, a glass of wine, or a cigarette. The ringleader was Democratic precinct captain Raymond Hicks, who coordinated ballot box stuffing with the assistance of precinct election judges. At a meeting at the L & B Chicken Restaurant, Hicks told precinct officials that all the elderly and mentally disabled people in a residential care home were "crazy." He said to simply "punch 10" on the computerized absentee ballot for every resident, which were all votes for Democratic candidates.[14] When Webb examined the voters' ballot signatures against other records, his team discovered one resident whose full name appeared signed on his application, even though he had "no fingers or thumbs and can write only an 'X' by holding a pen between the stumps of his hands."[15]

Elsewhere in the precinct, the "standard operating procedure" for stealing votes was similar. Hicks, who pleaded guilty in exchange for testifying against others, recounted "visiting every hotel and flophouse in the West Side ward to pay for votes and obtain lists of people who had died or moved and would not be voting." One hotel clerk demanded a case of wine, which Hicks supplied in exchange for a list of residents.[16]

Throughout press coverage of the trials, newspaper reporters stressed that Hicks and his codefendants faced up to fifteen years in federal prison for defrauding voters.[17] When the sentences were announced in December 1983, however, federal judge James Moran punished the conspirators lightly. Hicks received the longest sentence, nine months on work-release at the Metropolitan Correctional Center, with an additional five years on probation. He kept his day job as a laborer in the Chicago sewer system (where, perhaps not incidentally, his boss was one of the Ward 27 Democratic Party leaders). The others also received work-release sentences ranging from six month to ten days. One person, Francis Olinger, a Republican election judge, was also ordered to enter an alcoholic rehabilitation program.[18] The

light sentences by the federal court for electoral fraud in Chicago show the reluctance to punish people under the current system.[19]

In another Chicago case involving election fraud, city jobs, and Democratic ward bosses, US Attorney Webb brought indictments against Edward "Captain Eddie" Howard and Thomas Cusack, who he contended were loyalists to Thirty-Ninth Ward alderman Anthony Laurino. The key witness had been promised a city job by Howard if he helped cast absentee ballots for fictional, nonexistent, or deceased ward residents. In addition, a Democratic election judge and her daughter, a Republican election judge in the same precinct, permitted Howard to cast a ballot for another family member, a marine stationed at Camp Lejeune in North Carolina.[20] A jury ultimately convicted Howard on twenty-three counts; he received nine months of work-release and five years' probation. Cusack, convicted on fourteen counts, received six months' work-release and five years' probation.[21]

Testifying before Congress later that year, Webb was asked to explain why the vast majority of cases he prosecuted were against campaign workers, election officials, and precinct captains. It's "very simple," he said. "We have discovered that those [officials] are the most culpable people in connection with the vote fraud that occurs on Election Day." The system encouraged deceit because "there [was] an unmistakable link between the patronage system and vote fraud." Chicago's patronage system created incentives for precinct captains to steal votes to reap rewards and benefits, including city jobs, no-bid contracts, orders for public works projects in their wards, and even preferential snowplowing during the city's blasted snowstorms. Patronage is the carrot held by a precinct captain to obtain cooperation from election judges to continue their illegal activities.[22]

Despite the most highly publicized trials and convictions for election fraud in city history, the cases are reminiscent of the consequences that came with reversing the course of the Chicago River, the state's celebrated public works project of 1900. Then, the city's

sewer and water workers built a giant shipping canal to prevent human, meatpacking, and other industrial wastes from contaminating Lake Michigan. But by sending the effluvia downstate, the "great wonder" also created an opportunity for invasive Asian carp to move freely through the Sanitary and Ship Canal into the Mississippi River to Louisiana.[23] Reversing the river also meant sending huge amounts of pollutants toward St. Louis rather than into Lake Michigan. (This may be why the Cubs vs. Cardinals rivalry endures.) Webb may have exposed many of the tricks used to commit election fraud, but political operatives and patronage-dependent city workers created new channels to keep their bosses in office.

Webb left the US attorney's office for private practice and founded a watchdog group, Election Watch '87, to monitor the next round of Chicago elections. The group collected evidence of violations in the February 1987 primary elections for mayor, clerk, and treasurer, and aldermen, in which Harold Washington prevailed over former mayor Jane Byrne, who was attempting a political comeback. Now an outsider, Webb demanded that the current US attorney convene a grand jury to look into the violations that his watchdogs had discovered. He insisted the amount of fraud and irregularities was even greater than when he brought the 1982 cases. During the 1987 election, Webb said, votes were cast by people registered to nonexistent addresses and vacant lots. Other votes were cast by people registered more than once or people who had moved.[24] But the US attorney was busy prosecuting judges and attorneys from the Cook County Circuit Court accused of corruption.

Richard M. Daley, then the Cook County state's attorney, was interested in the evidence Webb had collected. In addition, Michael Lavelle, chair of the Chicago Board of Election Commissioners, joined in, announcing he had information on election fraud that he thought the US attorney should investigate.[25] Lavelle acknowledged that the election board had difficulty removing dead people from voter rolls. He blamed the Cook County Bureau of Vital Statistics,

saying that the agency was three to four months behind schedule in providing death notices. He blamed the election judges, whom he regarded as unqualified political hacks. "Most of the fraud and irregularity problems being brought to my attention could be stopped or curbed if we had professional judges," Lavelle said. "The way it stands now, the door is open to allow these abuses to continue." Yet neither Daley nor Lavelle pursued criminal election fraud investigations.

Board of Elections officials bragged during the 2004 elections that only about 5 percent of the city votes were cast using absentee ballots and that most absentee voters seemed perfectly legal. That seemed true everywhere except the Fourteenth Ward, where Edward Burke followed in the footsteps of his father as Democratic committeeman and then as an alderman for over three decades. There, about 10 percent of ward residents voted absentee. "Maybe a lot of traveling salesmen live in the ward," suggested one observer. Board of Elections chairman Langdon Neal claimed, "We've been able to isolate this problem to a few areas." Without resources to fully look into the situation, the Board's investigation method consists of calling about one in twenty absentee applicants to confirm their status.[26]

Also in 2004, three women who participated in a drive to register more Puerto Rican voters in Cook County ran afoul of the law. Rather than going door-to-door to meet potential voters or setting up voter registration tables in public places, the three copied names and addresses from city phone books. The Chicago Board of Elections officials discovered their ruse while checking some of the names and addresses they had submitted. The three were eventually convicted for theft and mutilation of election materials, and sentenced to two years' probation.[27]

Patronage posts and the "Shakman decrees" designed to rid Chicago politics of the jobs-for-votes schemes that encouraged election fraud, created problems for politicians elected outside the Democratic machine. Mayor Jane Byrne, elected as a reformer in 1979, couldn't get city workers to plow the streets during blizzards, in part because

the sanitation workers weren't enlisted to participate in her campaign. Mayor Harold Washington, elected in 1983 as the city's first black mayor, won the predominantly African American South Side largely on his promise to end patronage. Washington wanted to open up city jobs to blacks and Hispanics who had historically been shut out. But he quickly discovered that a Shakman decree prohibited him from removing some high-ranking city officials who controlled those jobs and were determined to create chaos during his administration, especially in his battles against the city council.

Richard M. Daley, the son of Richard A. Daley, became mayor in 1989, profiting from his father's Democratic Party machine. His administration quickly found ways to get around the Shakman decrees, building on President Ronald Reagan's neoliberal policies to shrink government services through privatization. Daley awarded public contracts to his cronies in business who did their own hiring, sometimes simply ignoring the law. But in 2004, after he won his fifth term with 79 percent of the vote, scandal after scandal erupted, eventually forcing him not to seek reelection.

The FBI and US Attorney Patrick J. Fitzgerald ran multiple investigations during Daley's final term. Among the scandals the Daley administration was accused of were that truckers were caught paying bribes for city contracts and that white businessmen were found to be setting up front companies to win minority contracts. Noelle Brennan, who was hired to monitor enforcement of the Shakman decrees, acknowledged that the system was easily corrupted. She herself was "concerned about the fact that the Department of Human Resources had no authority, no ability to enforce the rules."

Plain old vote buying was also rampant, though the payoffs for rounding up votes were jobs and promotions. At the Chicago water department, where Edward "Captain Eddie" Howard had worked in 1982, it was alleged that employees received raises for working on political campaigns.

Fitzgerald ultimately ensnared the leaders of Daley's city hall

patronage operation. Robert Sorich and his aide in the mayor's Office of Intergovernmental Affairs, Timothy McCarthy, were Daley's postmasters general. At trial, witnesses testified that on orders from Sorich, blue-collar jobs and promotions for being loyal and effective were distributed to political workers.[28] The jury convicted both men, agreeing that Chicago's historic "corrupt clout machine" was unlawful. Machine candidates who gave out jobs and promotions to campaign workers were corrupt; they had committed election fraud. "I think what we saw in this case was the revealing of the Chicago machine, the inner workings of the Chicago machine," said S. Jay Olshansky, the jury foreman. "There clearly is one. It has been in existence for quite some time."[29]

Olshansky knew Chi-town's political history well. Mayor Anton Cermak, the founding father of the Chicago machine, liked to say, sure there is criminality, but "only lazy precinct captains steal votes."[30]

For political observers and operatives alike in Chicago, "corruption" is a relative term. Likewise, modern-day politicians and good-government types call for "reform" when they want power to shift from the other party to their own party. Calls for "reform" are also heard as the city's many ethnic groups jockey for political power. This was well understood by Progressive Era municipal reformer Colonel Robert McCormick, the longtime editor and publisher of the *Chicago Tribune*. The newspaper remained a forum for debating the "complicated ballet" of corruption and reform. The trials of Mayor Daley provided ample fodder for Ron Grossman, a former history professor turned reporter on Chicago's ethnic neighborhoods, and David Axelrod, a former reporter turned political operative for the Daley campaign.[31]

Not surprisingly, Axelrod defended his boss, expressing doubt about the charges leveled by US Attorney Fitzgerald. Though he said he had always believed in ending political influence over civil service jobs, using the "criminal code to enforce that vision" seemed too harsh

a means for removing "politics from government." Elected officials are expected to use their political influence to help their constituents. Sometimes this can mean "the exchange of favors—consideration for jobs being just one." Or an alderman or a US senator might agree to support a judicial appointment in exchange for a program in their district. Axelrod, a future advisor to President Barack Obama, suggested that "if deals couldn't be made" without being accused of a crime, our democratic government would be worse.

Further, if hiring a qualified worker who comes recommended by a politician is treated as evidence of a criminal act, then "only applicants without political involvement are considered," whatever their qualifications or lack of them. Any political ties a potential servant might have would disqualify him or her from government service. The city would not be assured the benefit of a "better and more responsive" bureaucracy. It certainly would not improve basic services like trash and snow removal. "After a lifetime of observing government and participating in politics," Axelrod wondered if Fitzgerald's threat of prison to force reforms "is really desirable."[32]

Ron Grossman had watched the city's dance with reform twirl its skirts for decades. Historically, he observed, "The more sagacious reformers realize it's better to be allied with the cigar-chomping ward heelers than to advertise a good-government campaign as a punch in their faces." Basic services like garbage pickup and road repairs came through the ward bosses, and voters continue to support their aldermen, pretending "not to notice when office holders and their friends dip into the public trough." They don't call this election fraud; indeed it was (literally) "more concrete help than an abstract program of civic reform."

The good-government types, who back in the old days were Protestants and prohibitionists, were subjected to "a curious kind of name-calling. Along some streets lined with bungalows and two-flats, 'reformer' is pronounced with a hint of skepticism and scorn." The old

pols, like Edward Burke, the Fourteenth Ward alderman, noted Chicagoans' suspicions about reformers. There is "an ethnic bias against people who would dictate how other people should lead their lives." The ethnic lines that divided city voters could be traced to earlier battles over "reform." It was one thing for a Republican to demand reform, but for a Democrat "to give the impression that you've gone over to the silk-hatters after you've been raised under a fedora is fatal in politics in Chicago." But the fedoras were quite accustomed to holding out their hats to elites without fatality. "Land deals and cushy contracts are the common denominator of Chicago's past and present. That lucrative reality is usually enough to stifle cries for reform from business leaders."[33]

The truth of that observation was made clear in 2011, when Rahm Emanuel became mayor, and then won again in a run-off campaign in 2015. Both an "ethnic" and a "reformer," Emanuel figured out how to change city operations to benefit the business leaders who funded his election. Echoing his former boss, President Obama, the mayor proclaimed his administration "a new day in Chicago, wherein hiring at City Hall is all about what you know rather than who you know." His speechwriter took a few liberties in writing those words.

In fact, Emanuel persuaded city hall's venerable nemesis, the unimpeachable reformer Michael Shakman, who had sued to eliminate political influence in city hiring practices, to endorse the end of federal monitoring.[34] Federal monitor Noelle Brennan agreed with Shakman that there were enough policies and procedures now in place to end patronage jobs, at least for the greatly reduced number of blue-collar workers the city still employed. Shakman didn't think patronage was dead and buried, "but it is in a position where it can be controlled, limited and reduced to zero. We are headed in that direction." Patrick McDonough, a city worker, was less optimistic. "There is still retaliation for people who blow the whistle on corruption." He didn't believe it would "ever end."

A longtime Chicago political campaign operative, "WB," ex-

plained to me in February 2015 that lifting the Shakman decrees wouldn't affect the ways that political connections influenced the election process. Nor was he convinced that influence was always bad for politics. Shakman and other good-government types are politically naïve, in WB's opinion. Before the Shakman decrees, a low-skilled person or a "knuckle-headed nephew" could get a union job in the water department through a political patron and work his way into the middle class through promotions and seniority. Now patronage is distributed through outsourced entities and government contractors, who are usually the cronies of the politicians and unaffected by the "reforms."

Opportunities for corruption may have shrunk for the fedora-wearing civil servants, but not for silk hat–wearing business leaders. Emanuel's ethnic voting base split during his reelection campaign, forcing him into a runoff in 2015. Corporate funders from in and outside of Chicago, frightened by the support from progressives for Mayor Harold Washington's protégé Jesus "Chuy" Garcia, poured at least $20.5 million into Emanuel's coffers. In addition to buying weeks of television and radio ads, the campaign spread "walking-around money" throughout needy neighborhoods, as well as rumors that electing a Latino would be bad for African Americans. Emanuel's twelve-point margin over Garcia was clearly a matter of money; Chuy didn't have big money, but with only five million dollars he still won 44 percent of the votes.[35]

Chicago's experience is much like that of Louisiana in important ways. From Greg Malveaux's perspective, vote buying and manipulation violates the law and should be punished. Local campaigns and officials see it as just routine and not that harmful, and the voters involved see it as a way to get some economic benefit. Only when stealing taxpayers' money for personal benefit occurred did the public show real concern, or when, as in St. Martinville, elections disappeared for years. Chicago has exhibited the same pattern. A Republican prosecutor attacked the Democratic political machine, but the violations

were punished lightly if at all. The Shakman decrees limited patronage but did not stamp it out; they just redirected it. The people who were targeted by street money wanted and used the money to improve their economic situation in the short run, and the money stimulated turnout optimally. Some electoral fraud is, apparently, a concomitant of democracy.

CHAPTER 6

"A Saturnalia of Corruption and Crime"

He's no bigger a crook than every other politician.

—*Karen Joy Jones*

Political campaigns may rely on electoral fraud and other forms of corruption to win. It's impossible to call such corruption exclusively Democratic or exclusively Republican "dirty tricks"; both parties have used it to varying degrees, at different times, and in multiple locations. Its legality or illegality differs across states. Sometimes the scheme is simply unethical but perfectly legal. Politicians—or in bigger races, their strategists operating without the candidate's explicit knowledge—will resort to all sorts of tactics to get out the vote. But vote buying, vote hauling, the misuse of absentee ballots, patronage jobs for votes, and contributions for contracts, as we've seen in Chicago and Louisiana, are just some of the ruses employed by campaign operatives. Discouraging people from voting has been just as efficient in ensuring a candidate's victory. The point is that voter turnout is routinely manipulated by both parties in an effort to elect their candidates. That is why vote buying remains common in some places.

Vote buying is also common because many people don't think it's a crime. Will Ramsey, the longtime editor of the Gadsden County,

Florida newspaper, observed in 1979, "There are all kinds of vote buying, but as far as I can tell the only illegal type is when you give a person a buck to vote for you." He thought it was hypocritical to designate one type of vote buying as criminal while letting other kinds of campaign promises go by. "It's OK to promise roads, jobs, fish fries, rides to polls and a chicken in every pot. It's all vote buying."[1] Juries tend to agree, and rarely convict people for buying or selling votes, unless the evidence is overwhelming. Even then, tough sentences are unusual.

Vote buying in Kentucky became widespread in the era of robber barons. During the early 1900s, a group of coal, timber, and railroad operatives bought votes to end the influence and power of local party machines. According to Gordon McKinney, director of the Appalachian Center at Berea College, "They wanted control at the county level because that's where their business was. . . . They began directly to buy votes. And they won." The system was the means to destroy the power of the union movement and it persisted, made possible in large part because Kentucky lawmakers were now obligated to the companies who financed their elections. For example, the state legislature legalized vote hauling, claiming it would assist getting the elderly and the poor to the polls from the rural countryside. But the haulers routinely became brokers who did the buying.[2]

"A saturnalia of corruption and crime," the 1941 Republican primary election in Harlan County, Kentucky, reeked of "confessions of ballot box stuffing and confessions of buying and selling votes for money and whiskey." This chapter in the state's long history of fraud arose in "Bloody Harlan," the center of the United Mine Workers of America's struggle to unionize against the coal mine owners of Appalachia. Political corruption, bombings, private militias, manslaughter, robberies, grand larceny, and assassinations were some of the terrorist tactics used against coal miners for more than a decade. In that light, the massive election fraud committed by Republican candidates in the August 1941 primary appears rather pacific. One of the contend

ers for county judge, Theodore R. Middleton, was a well-known thug. The integrity of his primary opponent, Lonnie M. Davisworth, was, by comparison, almost stellar.[3]

Middleton had ruled as high sheriff of Harlan County since his election in 1934. Then he ran on a "reform" ticket. He "promised to put an end to collusion between county officials and coal operators, and to extend equal protection of the law to miners as well as to their employers," a campaign promise that resonated with workers, who had witnessed the collusion between law enforcement and mine owners. To prevent ballot box stuffing during the "bitterly contested" election, Middleton and his supporters "engaged in a series of gun battles with members of the opposing faction which resulted in the death of at least one man and the wounding of several others," which ended only when the National Guard arrived.

Middleton was also a crafty liar. Under state law, Kentucky requires county sheriffs to post surety bonds in performance of their official duties. Going back on his pledge to reform the system, Middleton received backing from the mine owners, who underwrote $160,000 in assurances—the same operators who had guaranteed the previous sheriff's bonds. Middleton was an army veteran who, after serving federal time for selling moonshine, got a job on the Harlan town police force through his uncle, the police chief. The only "reforms" under his regime as county sheriff were to his bank account. When later called before US senator Robert La Follette's Civil Liberties Committee to explain how his personal assets had grown from less than ten thousand dollars in 1933 to more than a hundred thousand dollars in 1937, Middleton submitted, "I guess there have been a lot of campaign promises that have not been fulfilled."[4]

Five candidates had their names on the Republican primary ballot for county judge in August 1941. Middleton received 2,990 votes and Davisworth 3,512 votes; the other three candidates did not contest the election. However, the former sheriff contended that Davisworth had tried to bribe voters and was therefore ineligible to receive

the nomination. Most of the vote buying had occurred in a sheriff's race, in which "Mrs. Herbert Cawood," the wife of the current sheriff, was running. The UMWA had endorsed Mrs. Cawood "and most, if not all of the local unions, by resolutions, endorsed Davisworth." The contest was, then, yet another battle to "reform" Harlan County politics.

Both judicial candidates, of course, categorically denied any knowledge of election fraud. The UMWA's agents organized voters across the county drumming up support for their slate, their activities "so great and brazen" that Davisworth (and Mrs. Cawood) must have known about their illegal deeds. At trial, witnesses "testified to having received money from Davisworth . . . [though they] had actually done that very thing for his opponent Middleton, on whose behalf they were testifying." For his part, Davisworth claimed he couldn't have participated in Cawood's scheme to bribe voters because Sheriff Cawood turned down his $800 promissory note.

The Kentucky Court of Appeals said, "Middleton is too experienced a politician and participant in election contests and too shrewd to have so publicly operated" a vote-buying scheme. Instead, Middleton's slate was accused of a "chain voting" scheme. Chain voting allows vote buyers to ensure that votes are actually cast for their candidate(s). When the polls open, the first voter obtains his ballot but instead of depositing it in the box, takes the blank ballot outside to the buyer, who marks it for his candidate. The next voter takes the marked ballot in, gets a fresh ballot, and gives the previously marked ballot to election officials. "By 'chain voting' [a] certain candidate may be voted for at the exclusion of all others."[5]

In the town of Lynch, Middleton exploited the fierce loyalty of African Americans to the party of Lincoln, where a very active "colored women's organization" headed by Mrs. Holmes, a preacher's wife, organized a get-out-the-vote party. The gathering, which offered "much beer, soft drinks, sandwiches and hilarity" and perhaps "a liberal quantity of whiskey," was paid for by Middleton. The candidate

claimed participants engaged in "spiritual song and prayer" to which he gave his "blessing" and "benediction," though other attendees described "anything but a religious service."[6]

The Kentucky appeals court, ruling in the case of *Davisworth v. Middleton*, decided that both candidates had violated the state Corrupt Practices Act and threw out the results, declaring that neither man could run on the Republican ticket in the November election. Because this was a civil case, rather than a criminal one brought by a prosecutor, neither candidate faced imprisonment or a fine. Instead, the judges could only deprive Middleton and Davisworth of running as official party candidates in the general election.

To add further folly to the farce, Mrs. Cawood contested her loss in the general election. There were so many fraudulent votes that it took officials almost two weeks to announce the results.[7]

Vote buying continued to be widespread in Kentucky, especially in the six eastern coal counties where, not coincidentally, poverty and quality of life measures are bleak. One grocery store owner said that vote buying was so "common in Breathitt County [that] people came to the store offering to sell their votes." It's said that votes sold for as much as twenty dollars to twenty-five dollars, five times the going price in Louisiana. But it would be incorrect to assume that only people in poor counties were disfranchised by vote buying; this type of fraud is so endemic that it seems part of the state's electoral landscape.[8]

The penalty for vote buying in other states, however, is prison, a fine, and the loss of full citizenship. Mississippi's election laws caught a white Republican politician and his campaign workers in a vote buying and absentee-ballot scheme in 2007, but because the candidate had ties to the governor, he was later pardoned. Political motives obviously tinged the case against Clint Moffitt from beginning to end. State election officials colluded with Arnie McMullen, the Democratic sheriff of Benton County, in a sting operation against Moffitt, who was running for sheriff on the Republican ticket. A key player in

the scheme was McMullen's good friend, former chief deputy sheriff Willie Ed Thompson, who depended on the sheriff for his wrecker business.[9]

McMullen and Thompson had reason to believe the Republican candidate would attempt to buy votes in the upcoming sheriff's race, and asked the state attorney general's office to open an investigation into Moffitt's campaign. Criminal investigator Roger Cribb used Catina Taylor, Willie Ed's daughter, as bait in the case. Catina arranged meetings with Moffitt's supporters they thought might engage in vote buying. Wired with a hidden camera, she enticed Ada Tucker into giving her money, which Taylor characterized as buying her vote. Tucker herself insisted the money was a loan. The evidence of meetings, of money changing hands, supported by video and audio, gave the attorney general's staff enough to bring charges. At trial, one of Moffitt's campaign workers testified that she had taken voters to the polls to cast absentee ballots and gave them twenty dollars for "gas money," as she was instructed to do.[10]

Convicted of vote buying and hauling, Moffitt received a five-year sentence, with two years suspended; he spent two years in prison and one year under house arrest, and was ordered to pay a five-thousand-dollar fine. Tucker also received a five-year sentence, but served one year in prison and one year under house arrest. She too paid five thousand dollars in fines. But the prison terms were not the end of the story. After the *Southern Sentinel* published a "perp walk" photo of Moffitt in handcuffs, he appealed to Governor Haley Barbour, the former head of the Republican National Committee, for a full pardon.[11]

Moffitt's pardon application apparently impressed Governor Barbour. Letters attested to his background from "an extremely fine and acknowledged family in Benton County." Moffitt was the son of lawmen: both his father and mother served as sheriffs. Most humiliating for Moffitt, however, was "the perp walk and media coverage from

Memphis to Tupelo," which greatly embarrassed him and his family. The infamy, he argued, meant he couldn't find a job. Moreover, as a consequence of his sentence, he couldn't work his "outfitter job hands-on because I cannot cross over state lines." Because of his house arrest, he had to observe a curfew that kept him from participating in his children's church, school, and social events. He was a convicted felon, so he could no longer work in criminal justice nor carry firearms. But worst of all, he could not go hunting. He complained,

> My daddy took me on my first gun hunt at the age of 8. My son has a bee-bee gun that I am trying to teach him the concepts of gun safety with. I had always been a law-abiding person and tried to set examples for the young people in our community. I had never had an arrest, never used tobacco, alcohol or drugs and my friends and young people knew that. This pardon would allow our family to get back to our normal way of life.[12]

Compared to vote-buying cases elsewhere, Moffitt's punishment does appear excessive. Rather than deterring vote buying, a very severe sentence likely discourages prosecutors from bringing new cases to jury trial.

Governor Barbour's pardon of Moffitt and 207 others in his last days in office attracted widespread public criticism. Media coverage focused on four murderers who had worked at the governor's mansion as part of a trusty program for inmates, which earned them special privileges. But Barbour did not pardon Ada Tucker, who was convicted as Moffitt's broker. Nor did he grant full pardons to Jamie and Gladys Scott, two African American sisters who were the subject of a national NAACP campaign against the overcriminalization of black citizens. None of the discussion about Barbour's pardon of Moffitt even commented on his crime of vote buying.[13]

TEXAS *POLITIQUERAS*

Texas vote buyers did things somewhat differently than in other states. The campaign operators who hire vote buyers are called *politiqueras*; like brokers and bagmen elsewhere, they can have significant influence in close races. Texas lawmakers who have tried to end corruption must play whack-a-mole. Revisions to election laws never seem to abolish fraud once and for all because vote buyers just figure out new ways to get around the recently enacted restrictions. Though federal prosecutors have had more success, their jurisdiction is limited. And electoral fraud cases, whether they are tried in state or federal courts, are decided by locally drawn juries, citizens who may not think the "crime" was worth all the legal fuss and prison sentences.

Duval County, a sparsely populated county in the most southern part of the state, has a history of corrupt politics and a family dynasty of officeholders, the Parrs, whose patriarchs are "called *El Patrón* or the 'Duke of Duval.' "[14] The Parrs ruled the county for decades; it was their work in 1948, some say, that gave Lyndon Baines Johnson the edge to win his first campaign for the US Senate.[15]

El Patrón, father and son, were long gone in 1982 when county commissioner Fidencio Saenz and county judge Gilberto Uresti devised a novel means to buy votes. They sent campaign workers door-to-door, telling likely voters that they should visit the Duval County public assistance office. There, they would be given vouchers that could be exchanged for food, clothing, or medical services. Campaign worker Domitilla Garza showed a voter a marked sample ballot, telling her that if she voted as the ballot indicated, "they would help [her]." The voter went to the welfare office, where a staffer gave her a voucher worth forty-five dollars. On Election Day, Garza and Norma Solis took the woman to her polling place and gave her a sample ballot to follow when casting her vote. Driven home in Garza's car, the voter asked for payment. Solis bought her a six-pack of beer.

Reformers had attempted to stop such outright vote buying in ear-

lier decades, and particularly in Duval County. Yet local prosecutors were reluctant to punish vote buyers and sellers. This time the fraud involved federal welfare funds, and federal candidates were on the ballot, making it a federal case. Solis, Garza, and Genoveva Garcia were each convicted of vote buying. Garza and Garcia, along with Saenz, were convicted of conspiracy.[16]

Politiqueras assisted communities in their quests for political resources and power. South of Duval County, the Rio Grande Valley border town of Donna, Texas, was rocked by the suicide of the school board president Alfredo Lugo. An investigation into the work of *politiqueras* in the 2012 election revealed another criminal case of election fraud. Three women in the overwhelmingly Democratic town were arrested in January 2014.[17]

Rebecca Gonzalez and Guadalupe Escamilla were accused of paying some voters as little as three dollars for each ballot. Other voters received cigarettes or were taken to buy illegal drugs after receiving cash payments. Because the election in which school board president Lugo ran included candidates for federal and state offices, the FBI took over the investigation. Reporters wondered why the county district attorney, René Guerra, had failed to act when the allegations of Lugo's vote buying arose. Guerra, an elected official, said his office "lacked the manpower." Questioning Mayor David S. Simmons's hiring of *politiqueras* to get out the vote, he responded that the practice was traditional and necessary.[18]

Houston has also been the site of election fraud. Right after the legislature enacted new rules regarding the distribution and collection of absentee ballots, Dwayne Bohac, a Republican candidate from Harris County for the state legislature in 1998, distributed preprinted absentee-ballot application forms with his post office box as the return address. When they were returned, his office got in touch with the absentee voters before they voted. Bohac nonetheless lost in a close election. His opponent, state representative Ken Yarbrough, amended the new law to outlaw the trick.

Consultants, campaign workers, and editorial pundits continue to debate how best to control absentee voting in Texas. Tony Sirvello, chief elections officer for Harris County, observed, "In our primary election, as much as 60 percent to 70 percent of our incoming mail was absentee applications provided by political parties, candidates and campaigns."[19] However, the failure by reformers in the Texas legislature to overhaul absentee ballot rules indicates that despite evidence of fraud, the public is satisfied with the system as it stands. For example, in 1986, there were three hundred more absentee ballots than voter signatures, and evidence of ballot box stuffing by election officials. But when the district attorney seated a grand jury, it refused to indict anyone. The defendants were friends and relatives who refused to testify against each other. Ten years later, a second grand jury seated in 1996 refused to indict fourteen people who had voted twice.

The rules for voting by mail were tightened in 1997 by then secretary of state Tony Garza, a close ally of Governor George W. Bush. "Scams designed to manipulate the voting process by gaining access to mail-in ballots are becoming a widespread problem in Texas," Garza's office warned. Under the new laws, mail-in ballots could be requested by voters who are infirm, or are over 65, or who plan to travel on Election Day. The names of citizens who wished to vote by absentee ballot would not be released publicly for two days after they applied. In addition, ballots were sent directly to voters' residences rather than to a candidate's campaign offices (as is done in some other states), and had to be mailed back. The rationale was to prevent campaign workers from interfering with elections by collecting ballots themselves and turning them in en masse to the county clerk's office. Violations for absentee ballot fraud could result in one-year prison sentences.

Nonetheless, the old routines continued. Public disinterest in prosecuting violators remains common, and most people think paying people for their votes is relatively harmless, especially when me-

dia coverage of "big money" donations to political action committees (PACs) appears more sinister. There's some consensus among policy makers and citizens that giving money or other benefits to voters could increase turnout and thus create real competition among political candidates.

In rural west Texas, absentee ballots were popular for vote-buying schemes. In Fort Stockton, Candida Rangel, a seventy-two-year-old grandmother, collected absentee ballots from senior citizens, who were mostly naturalized Mexican immigrants who didn't speak fluent English. Candidates paid her for collecting ballots, like vote buyers in other states. In Rangel's case, she earned about six dollars an hour.[20]

None of the legislative reforms abolished vote buying in Texas. When a local prosecutor began investigating Rangel, Latinos cried racism, pointing out that poor Latinos had only recently gained some political power locally and across the state. About 60 percent of Fort Stockton's 8,644 residents are Hispanic, while 35 percent are Anglo and 5 percent are black. Rangel's work as a *politiquera* mobilized Latino voters, giving Latinos a majority for the first time on the Fort Stockton City Council. Steve Spurgin, a candidate for district attorney, noted that "wealthy Anglos do the same thing": they mobilize their friends and neighbors. Unsurprisingly, a local grand jury refused to indict Rangel or other *politiqueras*. They rejected the prosecutor's argument that Rangel had victimized the elderly by buying their votes. To them, it was just politics as usual: one community's campaign to win power and access to government resources.[21]

FLORIDA

Anyone who watched the hearings I held as chairperson of the US Commission on Civil Rights in the wake of the 2000 presidential election debacle should not be surprised to hear about election fraud in Florida. The testimony of then governor Jeb Bush and then

secretary of state Katherine Harris—given only after they were subpoenaed and forced to answer our questions—hinted at a long history of election corruption in the state. The commission was unable to investigate that sorry legacy at that time, but the testimony of Reverend Willie Whiting is a reminder that election corruption and racial discrimination are intertwined. Reverend Whiting told us he felt "sling-shotted back to slavery" when he was denied a ballot after being wrongly struck from the rolls of registered voters.[22]

Liberty County, Florida, just west of Tallahassee in the panhandle, has long been singled out by the commission and others for voting rights violations.[23] The disfranchisement of African Americans seems to go hand in hand with other forms of election corruption. And deep-rooted election corruption also seems to be linked to political dynasties that have controlled a city or a county for generations. When both law and order are controlled by one extended family, as we saw in St. Martinville, Louisiana, citizens must appeal to federal prosecutors and the FBI for justice.

The Shulers and their extended clan have run Liberty County for decades. Laquita Shuler, known to her friends as "Skeet," was the county school superintendent and refused to give up the job. In 1978, a local group of activists challenged her regime by running an opposition slate for the school board. They were joyous when it appeared they had succeeded—until a pile of absentee ballots showed up that gave the election to Shuler.

The story about Liberty County intrigued Dudley Clendenin, a reporter for the *St. Petersburg Times*, whose own father, the editorial page editor of the *Tampa Tribune*, had told him stories of Tampa elections "so corrupt that men with machine guns guarded the polling places."[24] Clendenin interviewed many local people who told him of promises made and how they were told to vote. They spoke of being "pressured into selling their votes by the powerful Shuler family." The press attention and the reports from losing opponents put pressure

on the state's law enforcement division to investigate Liberty County. They would conduct approximately 150 interviews on the election.[25]

"Skeet" retaliated, taking aim at those who spoke to officials or the press. People who refused to be pressured into voting for the Shuler slate found themselves jobless. But she was sly: she simply wrote letters informing them they were not being "nominated" for jobs in the school system for the next year. The letters were sent to a high school coach, a teacher, and several teacher's aides. Also not retained was Larry Dawson, a twenty-two-year-old black man who drove a school bus and cleaned at a preschool.

Dawson and his grandmother, Roberta Donar, who worked for a federally financed program for the aged, spoke to Clendenin about the pressure they received from Shuler's supporters to vote for them. Shuler's father, "Colonel Fairchild," and a cousin visited their home, reminding the two that they owed their jobs to the Shuler family. They owed their allegiance to the Shulers. Mrs. Donar added that they had offered a college education and job for her daughter Angela. But those offers were good only if the entire extended family voted for the Shuler ticket. Dawson, unlike the other people Clendenin interviewed, was the most vulnerable informant, since he worked directly under the control of the school board superintendent. Clendenin recognized his precarious situation, and asked if Dawson would fight for his job. "No, probably it's better to just let it go."[26]

Eloise and Clayton Dean, a white couple who ran a hog farm, also talked publicly about the situation in Liberty County. They told Clendenin they had been offered forty dollars apiece for their votes. After they were quoted in the paper, a fire broke out behind their house. Then another fire—apparently set by parties unknown—broke out a few days later along their fence line. They understood the warning, which threatened their investment in hogs and piglets.[27]

County residents—as well as the state press—were surprised when the local prosecutor refused to prosecute the Shulers for vote

buying. But the extensive media coverage, and the fact that Liberty is but forty miles from the state capital, forced Governor Bob Graham to issue an executive order authorizing a special prosecutor. Given the power to convene a grand jury, if necessary, the prosecutor had more than a year to investigate allegations of election fraud. When he sought indictments, the local trial judge recused himself and was replaced by a judge from another county.[28]

The special prosecutor indicted seventeen people for vote buying. George Thomas Brown was convicted in 1979. "It was virtually an open and shut case," AP reported, "because Lacy Morgan Burke, his wife, Monta Della Burke, and another relative, Warren Burke, Jr., all testified that George Brown paid them each $15 for their votes."[29] But the carpetbagger trial judge said it was "sheer luck" that the prosecutor had won.

The trial of the second defendant ended in a mistrial. During recesses, one of the jurors had repeated testimony to the accused, and then denied he had done so. As the appeals court noted, during the trial "direct and subtle efforts to influence jurors and witnesses occurred; where friends and families of the defendant smiled and winked at each other when the second jury was sworn to try the case." There were "chuckles and looks of satisfaction when two witnesses suddenly forgot the facts about which they were to testify." And when opposing witnesses took the stand, there were "look[s] of despise and disgust on the face of the spectators when some incriminating testimony was given."

The special prosecutor filed for a change of venue to take the remaining fifteen defendants to trial. He argued that it was virtually impossible to assemble an unbiased and qualified jury in Liberty County. There was a "complex relationship among families" with almost "everyone having familiarity with almost everyone else and pervasive discussion of vote buying and these charges." (Bristol, the county seat, had a population of less than eight hundred, and the Apalachicola National Forest occupies half the county.) The ap-

peals court recognized the difficulty of seating an impartial jury given "the alliances, allegiances, and antipathies which color the county's politics, public education system, and public employment; the feeling among some in the community that the buyers of votes should not be prosecuted if the sellers are not." But it denied the motion, citing a rule that allowed the defendant to oppose a change of venue. Certainly, the court reasoned six unbiased citizens could be found, since that was all that Florida law requires.

The appeals court opined that juries represent "the conscience and mores of the community in which the crimes were committed." Vote buying "besmirches the community where it occurs; and nothing can be as cleansing as a verdict of the defendant's peers in the community condemning the deed. Certainly no verdict announced from another county, by a jury of strangers, can have comparable effect." It is of course perfectly reasonable to reiterate the lofty lessons of high school civics classes in a legal opinion. But it is naïve to do so without also acknowledging that the conscience of some community leaders is unconcerned with breaking the law if it allows them to maintain their political power.

In the interim, the candidates who lost to Skeet and the Shuler slate filed complaints with the FBI. They also filed a suit in the Florida state court requesting that the absentee ballots, which they alleged were fraudulent, be thrown out. After years of trials and appeals, the Florida Supreme Court decided in 1984 that only votes cast at the polls should be counted when there was widespread abuse of absentee ballots. One county clerk thought the decision a good one. He thought most of the questionable activity during any election involved absentee ballots. In his opinion, absentee voting should be abolished except for servicemen, since they couldn't come home to vote.[30]

Skeet Shuler did eventually step down as superintendent and endorsed Jerry Johnson as her replacement. He was part of the Shuler network, and just as bigoted. A native of Alabama, Johnson had moved to Liberty County to teach and worked his way up to a

principalship. After he had served several terms as head of the county school system, his daughter, Gloria Gay Ouzel, replaced him.[31]

Liberty County, as noted earlier, had attracted federal attention as early as 1956 for denying the franchise to African Americans. The county schools were also under federal investigation for race discrimination; the system did not begin to desegregate until 1968, more than a dozen years after *Brown v. Board*. Black teachers and administrators in the formerly dual system suffered the most from desegregation. The "colored" schools were shut down, and the staff fired or demoted; the African American principal was assigned to teach special education and driver's ed. Since that time, no black person had held a supervisory or countywide administrative position. New positions were never advertised to the public, and the school system did not have a formal application procedure. Teachers and staff were hired, fired, and paid according to who knew whom.

Richard W. Stallworth started teaching in Liberty County in 1963 and saw all of this unfold. Even before the allegations of vote buying arose in 1978, Stallworth complained about illegal race discrimination. He saw the school system hire several white people instead of him, people who possessed less experience and far fewer educational qualifications than he. For example, Stallworth had earned a special master's degree in education administration in 1974 through a state program to train qualified administrators in the Florida panhandle. Another school superintendent, at trial, admitted that race influenced hiring decisions for administrative positions because the elected superintendents wanted to please the county's majority white voters. Stallworth won his case, and the court ordered the school system to pay him almost $150,000 in back pay and punitive damages.

One paltry case was hardly enough for the Liberty County school system to suffer a sudden attack of conscience about race matters. After Jerry Johnson replaced Skeet Shuler as superintendent, the minimum requirements for administrative positions were lowered so that he could hire more white people. In 1981, Stallworth was again passed

over, this time for a principalship, because Johnson had already chosen someone from another Florida county. When forced to explain why Stallworth was not considered for the job at Liberty High, Shuler and Johnson claimed that white teachers would not accept his leadership. Yet those same teachers as well as other white teachers in the system elected Stallworth as their union president and member of the bargaining team for a new contract. Again, the court found the system guilty of race discrimination and ordered an additional one thousand dollars in punitive damages for its malicious behavior.

The legal precedent set by the appeals court awarding the office of school superintendent to Skeet Shuler reverberated far beyond the Florida panhandle. Almost twenty years later, a judge gave the Miami mayoral race to Joe Carollo despite well-documented election fraud. Carollo successfully challenged sitting mayor Xavier L. Suárez, and many Floridians thought the court should have ordered a new election in 1997. Instead the court decided the election based solely on the forty thousand votes cast on Election Day by citizens who had "exercised their constitutionally guaranteed right to vote in the polling places of Miami."

The Florida legislature tightened absentee ballot rules after the Miami decision. The new law prohibits one person from witnessing more than five absentee ballots, unless she or he is a state official. In addition, the secretary of state is now supposed to send an official to supervise voting in nursing homes to prevent vote buying or other coercive practices. However, the new law does not assure enforcement. Though the Florida regulations are considered model legislation, many states have not adopted similar laws.[32]

BALLOT INTEGRITY AFTER *BUSH V. GORE*

In the November 2000 election, Florida and the United States in general learned just how variable and unpredictable election laws were across the nation. The media coverage of hanging chads, but-

terfly ballots, the counting and challenging of absentee ballots, and the plausible possibility that parties unknown had tampered with ballot boxes, led to fierce debates about election fairness. Not a few people asserted that George W. Bush had stolen the presidency with his brother's help.

During Bush's first term, Attorney General John Ashcroft launched his Ballot Access and Voting Integrity Initiative to insure honest elections, he claimed. Kentucky was one of the first states targeted for investigation. In three successive election years, 2002, 2004, and 2006, the US Department of Justice trotted out a spectacle of more than a dozen one-time public officials or election officers—Republicans and Democrats alike—who ultimately pleaded guilty to various charges of conspiracy, racketeering, money laundering, and voter fraud in Clay County. Their numbers included a long-time mayor, an assistant police chief, several city council members, a one-time city administrator, and county magistrates. Because both federal funds and candidates for national office were involved, Assistant US Attorney Jason Parman did not have to overcome the vested interests of locally elected judges. Most of the defendants served time in federal prison, though on appeal, a few were able to reduce their sentences.[33]

The conspiracy involved contracts awarded to an excavation company and a waste-disposal company that enabled officials to maintain their political power as well as enrich themselves. William Bart Morris and his wife, Debra Morris, agreed to assist elected officials in vote buying in exchange for a multiyear contract. "Several thousand" votes were bought, and witnesses also testified that one vote buyer beat up another vote buyer in a dispute over a woman who sold her vote. The jury found conspirators liable for misappropriating $3.2 million "based on the jobs and contracts they received as a result of taking part in illegal acts."[34]

In Knott County, Kentucky, Donnie Newsome's election as the

county judge/executive came under scrutiny through the Ballot Integrity investigation. The judge/executive is the county chief executive.[35] During his first run for office in 1998, Newsome won the Democratic primary only after he and his supporters bought votes; he won again in November. The general election that year between Republican Jim Bunning and Democrat Scotty Baesler was "one of the hottest contests in the nation."[36] Bunning won by only 6,766 votes of 1,145,414 ballots cast; according to FEC records, the candidates raised a record $7.5 million, much of it from soft-money political action committees.[37] If there were votes to buy in the Senate race—an ancient tradition in the state—there was money to buy them. But it was because of the Senate race that the federal government had jurisdiction in Knott County. They had reason to suspect fraud because in a county with an adult population of 13,330, the county clerk received 1,000 absentee ballots even before the election was held.

Newsome came under scrutiny by the Department of Justice in 2002, which again involved a federal election. Convicted and sentenced to twenty-six months in prison in 2003, he stayed out on appeal and continued to serve as county judge/executive. He tried to get his sentence reduced by testifying against Ross Harris, a coalmine operator and one of eastern Kentucky's most prominent political fundraisers, who he said gave him twenty thousand dollars to use in the vote buying. Though convicted felons are not permitted to vote in Kentucky, they may still hold office, unless removed by the state attorney general.[38]

The people of Knott County didn't seem bothered by routine vote buying. Some blamed the whole thing on "imported US attorneys from Lexington." "He's no bigger a crook than every other politician," wrote Karen Joy Jones, editor of the *Troublesome Creek Times*.[39] As for Newsome, one citizen agreed that "What he did was wrong, and he needs to pay for it. But c'mon, every May there are people buying and selling votes here. That's just how it's done. You hand out a little

money or cases of beer." For another, it wasn't the vote-buying charge ("Everyone buys votes around here") but Newsome's misuse of public funds, using a county-owned vehicle for frequent casino trips during work hours, and issuing no-bid county contracts worth hundreds of thousands of dollars to family and friends.[40]

Newsome continued to carry out his duties as county judge/executive while he was in prison, but resigned in 2005 when he lost his case on appeal. His successor was Randall "Randy" Thompson, a Republican appointed by Governor Ernie Fletcher. Thompson and his cronies didn't just hand out a little money or cases of beer in exchange for votes. They "kick[ed] it up a notch," providing voters with blacktopping and gravel-laying for their private roads, at the cost of $1.5 million. Law enforcement described this new scam as "Donnie Newsome on steroids," even though "Newsome had handed out gravel like it was pizza."

High-profile media exposés of Thompson, as well as a whistleblower's complaint filed with the Kentucky attorney general's office, didn't bring Thompson down. Instead, under the Ballot Integrity Initiative, federal prosecutors convicted Thompson in 2006 of misusing federal public works funds to bribe voters. The judge agreed that "political corruption was cultural and pervasive" in the state, yet perversely that made him reluctant to punish Thompson. He and his contractor friends had not enriched themselves by paving and repairing their constituents' roads and driveways. The scheme more closely resembled a campaign promise, a quid pro quo to citizens who needed county services, rather than fraud. Thompson followed Newsome's example, and continued to serve as county judge/executive while on appeal.

After completing his sentence, Governor Steve Beshear restored Newsome's civil rights, making him eligible to run again for county judge/executive. In 2010, the two felons ran against each other. Thompson won.[41]

The Ballot Access and Voting Integrity Initiative came under at-

tack after Alberto Gonzales became US attorney general in 2005. Remarking on the fortieth anniversary of the Voting Rights Act that "our goal is to make voting easier and cheating harder," he infamously fired some US attorneys for not pursuing voter fraud aggressively enough, especially cases of fabricating or falsifying voter registration applications.[42] In fact, "between October 2002 and September 2005, just 38 cases were brought nationally, and of those, 14 ended in dismissals or acquittals, 11 in guilty pleas, and 13 in convictions," according to a study done by political scientist Lorraine Minnite.[43] Contrary to the wishes of President Bush's campaign strategist Karl Rove, the DOJ had failed to find sufficient cases of "voter fraud" designed to scare poor and minority voters away from the polls, though federal prosecutors had identified dozens of vote-buying cases.[44] Under President Obama's attorney general, Eric Holder, the initiative shifted focus slightly. Democrats were particularly concerned with voter intimidation and harassment. As so many of the cases discussed in this book demonstrate, vote buying and voter suppression can include threats of violence.[45]

VOTER TURNOUT AND VOTER SUPPRESSION

The focus on "big money" from corporations and PACs tends to obscure the little money that campaigns use to turn out voters on Election Day. In Maryland, it's called "walk around money," in Chicago it's known as "street money," and in St. Martinville, Louisiana, Mary Francois and Pam Thibodeaux said they were "putting money on the street." The money doesn't go directly into voters' pockets but pays for meals, for people to telephone registered voters on Election Day, to transport voters to polling places, and for media advertising, yard signs, and other political swag. Because some believe the money can be used to get people to vote for a specific candidate surreptitiously, efforts to prevent abuse of this type of soft money have led Georgia, New Jersey, South Carolina, and Louisiana to consider legislation

regulating it, but nothing has been enacted. Only Maryland banned campaign funding of services outright.[46]

The Maryland law specifically outlawed paying voters even when there was no effort to influence how they voted. In Annapolis, lawmakers held up newspaper clippings about long-standing "rampant corruption and vote buying in the electoral process" when the law was first enacted in 1957. The state justified the law as a means to protect the "integrity" of the election process. The law as codified went into effect for the 2002 election.

In 2002, Republican gubernatorial candidate Robert Ehrlich and candidate for lieutenant governor Michael Steele, in violation of the Maryland election law, hired contractors to organize walk-around services. One contractor was a temporary employment agency that paid approximately two hundred residents of homeless shelters in the District of Columbia to pass out campaign literature at the polls. The other two contractors hired students from Maryland high schools and colleges, paying them from $80 to $110 on Election Day to distribute literature and perform other walk-around services. The state attorney general, J. Joseph Curran Jr., a Democrat, filed charges against newly elected Governor Ehrlich and Lieutenant Governor Steele.[47]

The ACLU of Maryland filed a brief in support of Ehrlich and Steele, objecting to the law on the grounds that it violated First Amendment freedom of expression. They argued that electoral integrity was already protected by outlawing "vote buying, endorsement buying or their appearance." Maryland's highest court agreed, finding no evidence that the contractors or the people they hired had voted for the Ehrlich-Steele ticket. Neither were they made more likely to vote for them because they were paid for walk-around services on Election Day. There was also no evidence that voters knew the workers were being paid or anything about their voter preferences. The court declined to interfere with "core political speech" on the basis of speculation and reaction to news stories about "vote buying and selling."[48]

Paying people to distribute leaflets may mislead voters into thinking candidates have more support than they do; since the contractors had focused on hiring young people and poor black people, voters in predominantly black Prince George County might have thought the Republican ticket had more support from African Americans than it in fact did. However, the court decided it could not discern the "subjective intent of each campaigner." "Leaflet circulators" is nothing like the "corruption inherent in the assumption of quid pro quo that arises when individuals make large campaign contributions to a candidate." Chief Justice Bell concluded that the minor expenditures complained about were valid ways of disseminating a candidate's message. Left open, then, is the possibility of recommending legalization of walk-around money in campaigns generally as a way to counteract buying votes.[49]

Chief Justice Bell, since the age of fifteen when he was arrested for violating the state segregation law in a sit-in campaign to integrate Baltimore businesses, had been forced to make his decision based on the established facts. He therefore could not address the other "dirty tricks" played by the Maryland Republican Party and its supporters during the 2002 election. Baltimore's Democratic mayor, Martin O'Malley, warned that the GOP's use of the Baltimore Fraternal Order of Police to serve as Republican poll workers would intimidate voters. Most notoriously, an unsigned flyer appeared on doors in predominantly black neighborhoods that read: "URGENT NOTICE. Come out to vote on November 6th. Before you come to vote make sure you pay your parking tickets, motor vehicle tickets, overdue rent and most important any warrants." The date stated for voting was Wednesday, the day after the election on November 5, and of course, not paying an outstanding parking ticket or rent does NOT prohibit any citizen from voting.[50]

Public disinterest in punishing illegal vote buying means that local prosecutors rarely pursue charges against their fellow elected colleagues. Vote buying and selling has had an influence on the

outcome of close elections, perpetuating the power of political dynasties that do little or nothing for the people whose votes they buy. Federal prosecutors and federal judges are more protected, and have had slightly more success in obtaining convictions. But not every case can become federal, and since many states and local jurisdictions hold elections in "off years," they may be beyond the reach of federal officials unless there are violations of the Voting Rights Act or the Fourteenth Amendment. Abuses of the electoral process are likely to continue, especially when local culture doesn't think it's a criminal offense.

Conclusion

What Greg Malveaux told me about electoral fraud in Louisiana was disturbing. He explained how campaign operatives paid the poor small amounts of money for their votes while making policy contrary to their needs. He talked about the family fiefdoms that perpetuated their power illegally. He described how election officials cavalierly accepted payments to let buyers view the ballots to make sure the bought stayed bought. He related how poor voters didn't mind saying they got paid small amounts of money and treats for their votes, perhaps a pork chop sandwich and a cold drink.

Greg had been a deputy sheriff for twelve years in Orleans Parish. He was not naïve. But he soon realized that his new job of punishing election fraud was very complicated. The manipulation and vote buying seemed accepted by the public as just a routine part of the process. Politics is a game and parties do whatever it takes to win.

Malveaux focused on his job as an enforcer of the fraud law. But after thorough investigations he found he couldn't get help from local officials. Elected local prosecutors and judges recoiled from the

very idea of prosecuting the people who voted for them. Party principle and solidarity also play a role. Elected officials have important connections and relationships with each other and the candidates for other offices. Jobs, contracts, and other matters of patronage are at risk. Put simply, judges and other officials aren't eager to upset the system, because they benefit from it.

Greg had some successes but it was hard, often demoralizing, work. His boss, Suzanne Haik Terrell, had campaigned on an "end the fraud" platform. Ending fraud is certainly great rhetoric and a good campaign slogan. Greg believed Terrell wanted him to succeed, hoping success would propel her to higher office. Success seemed to mean convicting a few low-level brokers and haulers and not the donors or candidates themselves. Basically, the law was hard to enforce because hardly anyone who could enforce it wanted it to be enforced.

The extraordinary effort it took for Malveaux to win his biggest case attests to the difficulty. To penetrate the Martin-Champagne-Thibodeaux network in St. Martinville, he had to overcome intimidation and deliberate undermining by fellow staff members. He did have the helping hand of a few courageous ordinary citizens. He also found an occasional reporter willing to stand up to his or her editors in pursuit of the story. But only when he was able to persuade federal officials to respond did he have some measure of success.

The research his experience inspired shows that electoral fraud, consisting mainly of vote buying and abuse of absentee ballots, does indeed exist in state and local elections. Such fraud is routine in some locales. Family dynasties that perpetuate their own power seem tempted to buy votes with money or influence as a rite of passage. The Martin-Champagne-Thibodeauxes in Louisiana, the Shulers in Florida, the Daleys in Chicago, and others are examples. At the national level we have also seen the good and bad effects of politics as the family business. The role Jeb Bush played in the manipulation of the Florida election in 2000 for his brother George is one recent example of such influence. While in the twenty-first century working to end

voter suppression through identification laws and other mechanisms is necessary and a priority, the influence of often hidden or just plain ignored fraud harms the same group of vulnerable citizens. In fact the very existence of their democratic participation tempts abuse of the election process.

Yet the inclination, no matter how small, to blame the most vulnerable citizens for fraud is misdirected. The prosecution of poor people who get a few dollars for their votes is like making an arrest for selling single cigarettes. In 1904, Indiana tried punishing voter fraud by giving rewards to buyers who would persuade someone to sell them a vote. They soon recognized that all they did was to entrap the needy along with the greedy.[1]

Any outrage over fraud should be reserved for the candidates who buy their votes, neglect the issues that concern the poor, and studiously refuse to implement policies that could help them. Good examples of the latter include the refusal to adequately fund the schools their children attend, fund the medical facilities they utilize, or promote more racially equitable policing.

Candidates who engage in electoral fraud should suffer prosecution, even though it's challenging. Looking for legal ways to give citizens practical incentives to vote may be a way to reduce the attractiveness of vote selling, while increasing turnout. But incentives must be combined with appealing issues and candidates, and organizing needs to assist the marginalized to achieve beneficial policy objectives. Otherwise the increased election totals will serve only to validate the system.

Taking care of voters and potential voters in poor and working-class neighborhoods such as those manipulated by Nashville's Little Evil and Good Jelly, and Chicago's mayors and aldermen, motivates turnout and loyalty to candidates. Street money or walk-around money, designed to increase turnout among people who see no reason to vote, also acts as a short-term jobs program for the unemployed or low-wage workers needing additional income. There are stipends

for putting up yard signs, distributing literature, and circulating petitions. There are payments for hauling voters back and forth to the polls. There are expenses for feeding election judges and other officials and campaign workers. There are also media buys for ethnic and black radio stations and ad consultants. Campaign operatives and the community dependent on the short-term jobs hope for competitive primaries and run-off elections to increase the money flow. Turnout may increase, but whether it is increased legally or though illegal vote buying, the same structural problems of unemployment and inequity remain in the targeted communities once the election is done.

Federal enforcement would be the most certain way to provide more effective oversight, the adjudication of violations, and control of the relationship between money and politics in state and local elections. But unless there are federal candidates on the same ballot, or a federal discrimination issue is raised as in Pam Thibodeaux's case, this is the most unlikely approach. Unlikely, because under the Constitution, the framers deliberately did not include control of state and local elections among the powers delegated to the national government. Therefore, the power is left to the states. The only way to change this responsibility is to adopt a constitutional amendment. The amendment would need to make voting and election protection a federal responsibility instead of a primary responsibility of the states. In 2001, stirred by investigations of irregularities in the 2000 presidential election in Florida, including from the US Civil Rights Commission, Illinois congressman Jesse Jackson Jr. introduced such a Right to Vote Amendment in the Congress. The bill, reintroduced in successive Congresses, would place voting under the direct control of Congress, which would have the power to administer standards and enforce election protection in both state and federal elections. Since Jackson's resignation from Congress, Wisconsin Democratic congressman Mark Pocan and Minnesota Democratic congressman

Keith Ellison have pushed the amendment. It has not yet made it out of committee.

The Right to Vote and any other amendment proposal confronts the reality that though the framers made amending the Constitution possible, they also made it quite hard to achieve. A constitutional amendment requires approval either by a two-thirds vote of both houses of Congress or by a national convention called by Congress at the request of two-thirds of the state legislatures. No convention has ever been called. Even if Congress or a national convention approved an amendment, it would not become valid until ratified by three-fourths of the state legislatures or by ratifying conventions in three-fourths of the states. Congress decides which method to use. The difficulty of negotiating this process is why there have been so many proposals to amend the Constitution but so few amendments. In the more than two hundred years since the first ten amendments constituting the Bill of Rights, there have been only seventeen successful amendments.

Put differently, out of the hundreds of proposals introduced by Congress during each session, only thirty-three have been enacted by the Congress. Of those enacted, only twenty-seven have been ratified. An amendment abolishing child labor passed by Congress and pending since 1924 without a deadline still lacks a sufficient number of states for ratification. This is also the case with the Corwin Amendment, still pending since 1861, at the beginning of the Civil War. It seeks to make slavery permanent and immune to constitutional amendment or law. Other amendments passed by Congress, but not ratified, are obsolete because their congressionally imposed time limits have expired. Ratification, therefore, is no longer possible. Congress extended the time for ratification of the Equal Rights Amendment but the extension also expired.

Amendments covering controversial issues that deeply divide the public such as school prayer, a balanced budget, and "human life"

amendments each have failed to gain congressional passage. The experience suggests that a voting rights amendment that interferes with state's rights, giving control of state and local elections to Congress, will have at least as much difficulty gaining enactment.

But whether adopted or not, amendment proposals do serve a purpose. They help to organize supporters and to keep interest in an issue alive. There is also always the possibility that a proposal may lead to positive action toward achieving the policy goals of the proponents. This was the case with the advocacy of a child labor amendment. It eventually influenced the enactment of a law outlawing child labor, when it affects interstate commerce, in 1938.

If, by a miracle, the Jackson-Pocan-Ellison Right to Vote Amendment, or something similar, gained adoption, it could change the odds against punishing election fraud. Federal executive branch officials and federal judges removed from the local scene have to worry less about party politics and don't need to get reelected. However, when those charged do not plea bargain or plead guilty as in Pam Thibodeaux's case, they might still evade punishment. Defendants can exploit their due process rights to corrupt juries and keep the verdict in the hands of the locals whom they have intimidated or bought, as happened in the Liberty County vote buying case.

Under a Right to Vote Amendment, the Election Assistance Commission (EAC), established after the Bush vs. Gore 2000 election debacle in Florida, could have been given a stronger role. Created under the 2002 Help America Vote Act, the agency distributes federal funds to the states and information to help them improve their electoral process. The Act requires states to comply by having uniform and nondiscriminatory election technology and administration requirements based on their acceptance of the funds. With an amendment that federalizes the electoral process, Congress could authorize EAC to set required instead of voluntary standards for all of the states to follow in the voting process. The agency could also be given the power to negotiate compliance under threat of withhold-

ing funds when there are violations. This is true even though other agencies that have long had such powers have found it politically difficult to actually use the fund termination threat. The Office for Civil Rights in each cabinet department and the Office of Federal Contract Compliance are examples of agencies with such powers.

Shifting the responsibility for voting would also require increased staffing for the Department of Justice Voting Rights Section to litigate court cases for the EAC. Also, the DOJ could pursue fraud and suppression cases in the states without the involvement of a federal election or a discrimination issue.

Along with federal oversight and responsibility, another big area for reform must be large campaign contributions that influence candidates' voting records and political allegiances. But campaign contributions also fund vote buying and other electoral fraud along with legal expenditures. That is one reason why the proposed constitutional amendment to overturn the Supreme Court's 2010 *Citizens United* decision is so important. The Court decided that political spending is a form of protected speech under the First Amendment, and the government, therefore, may not keep corporations or unions from spending money to support or denounce individual candidates in elections. Since the First Amendment applies to the states by virtue of the Supreme Court's long-standing interpretation of the Fourteenth Amendment, the *Citizens United* ruling also affects state campaign laws.

The 2014 Supreme Court decision in the *McCutcheon* case also applies to the states by the same reasoning. The court declared unconstitutional, under the First Amendment, limits on the aggregate amount of political contributions an individual might make to federal candidates, parties, and political action committees in a two-year period. The ruling further extended the "corporations are people" doctrine used in *Citizens United*.[2]

Citizens United and *McCutcheon* further eroded any hope that the Federal Election Commission, established under the Federal Elec-

tion Campaign Act of 1974, would effectively reduce the flow of big money in politics. The FEC is technically responsible for regulating contributions to federal elections. Intentional violations of federal campaign finance laws are federal crimes. But given the equal political balance requirement for commission appointments, the agency has generally been unable to function effectively. With the Supreme Court's loosening of the ability to make contributions and the withdrawal of candidates from receiving public funding, the commission is practically moribund.

Some states in which vote buying takes place have no campaign finance laws, and others like Louisiana have weak ones. That is why "Louisiana Purchased," a joint investigation of Louisiana's campaign finance by NOLA.com, the *Times-Picayune*, and WVUE Fox 8 News, which began in 2013, attracts public interest. It is a comprehensive, interactive database on how politicians used campaign contributions to pay for questionable expenses. The database lists all reported contributions, disclosing networks and relationships and making it possible to track who gets rewarded. The businesses gaining repeated public works contracts and other large donors paying essentially for access lead the lists of donations to parties and candidates.[3]

Groups interested in increasing turnout and getting rid of the influence of large donations in elections have mobilized to overturn *Citizens United* and its progeny. In 2011, Congressman Bernie Sanders of Vermont and others introduced the Saving American Democracy Amendment. It has gathered cosigners but still not sufficient supporters to move toward enactment. Sanders, running for president, made the amendment part of his campaign agenda.

Right after Sanders announced in 2015, Hillary Clinton endorsed campaign finance reform, making it one of four pillars of her 2016 presidential campaign. She ranked the issue as important as help for families and communities; a stronger, more balanced economy; and a strong national defense.[4]

Organizations working to overcome the difficulty in gaining a

constitutional amendment have asked President Obama to act more aggressively on the campaign finance issue. They note that he has used his power to issue executive orders to achieve policy objectives when the Congress won't enact legislation. He did so on immigration and on prohibiting federal contractors from engaging in LGBTQ discrimination. These organizations seek action on the campaign finance issue. They want the president to issue an executive order requiring public disclosure by those corporations that are government contractors of their campaign contributions. The Supreme Court has not ruled out this possibility. They argue that "Right now, corporations with government contracts are able to funnel unlimited sums of dark money to influence the elections of those who can put pressure on the officials deciding who is awarded future contracts."[5]

In the absence of a right to vote and a campaign finance enforcement constitutional amendment, the next best option for punishing election suppression and fraud would be for states to enact legislation making prosecutors career employees instead of elected officials. Or the states could provide for special prosecutors in cases involving vote buying, abuse of absentee ballots generally, and other voter suppression. Special nonelected prosecutors, courts, and investigators could end the practice. This would require the public in the communities where it occurs to see it as a significant reality worth spending lots of taxpayers' money to eradicate. It also would require juries to take the issue seriously despite jobs or bribes distributed by officials and candidates.

If neither of these options is attractive, then developing an approach based on understanding why people do not vote might erode the seduction of vote buying and other fraud. These abuses grow out of the candidates' interest in turning out their voters. Some pundits, good-government advocates, and scholars don't worry about voter turnout. They take the view that people who aren't interested in voting probably don't know the issues and shouldn't vote anyway, leaving it to those who are more informed. Leaving aside the fact that some

well-educated people don't care to vote for any of the choices they're offered, this stance is reminiscent of nineteenth- and early twentieth-century advocates of literacy tests. They remind me of those who assumed my Aunt Serriner and Uncle Will didn't know enough to vote because of their lack of formal years of education. It apparently does not occur to them that large numbers of people who don't vote are aware of the issues, but based on experience, they don't believe voting will change anything. Their apathy or disgust is with the political choices, the promises made and broken, and the policies that don't seem to help people like them. Some of these individuals are willing to vote if they are given something—a few dollars and a cold drink or a job, or getting a driveway paved as a gift—even though they recognize it's illegal. The people whose votes are bought see themselves as merely gaining a little something concrete for their ballots; they also know it's unlikely that any punishment will result.

It's worth emphasizing that the citizens whose votes are bought don't believe the political system is responsive or accountable and generally find voting pointless. We may argue that showing up at the polls is the best way to counter the oversized influence of wealthy special interests. We can also argue the harm of selling their votes. Scholars argue that vote buying lets the buyers gain power to receive reimbursement through the public treasury, thus diminishing overall social wealth. Therefore, the argument goes, individual voters owe the civic duty of opposing this exploitation. But that's not the reality many nonvoters perceive. They are often unenthusiastic about the candidates. Democratic-leaning voters, including single women, young people, blacks, Latinos, and some Asian Americans—and the poor and low-income working class are less likely to vote in elections where there is neither a candidate they would choose, nor issues they think are crucial. They have voted, they know people who have voted, and they don't see their material circumstances improving no matter who wins. Their focus is not on abstract principles but practical objectives.[6]

Some developments have created enough interest to increase turnout, at least temporarily. The possibility of electing someone like Obama, or some other similarly unusual candidate at the state and local level, attracts more voters. In the 2010 California campaign, Jerry Brown, running against Meg Whitman, with the presence of several controversial propositions on the ballot, drew the highest number of people to the polls in five gubernatorial elections. But such campaigns and candidates are rare. For the most part, voter turnout is low, especially in local and state elections.

At the level of city councils, school boards, state legislatures, and other offices, routinely, fewer than 40 percent of eligible adults vote. National election voter turnout was 54.2 percent in 2000, the year of the Bush vs. Gore contest, and 60.4 percent for the 2004 Bush reelection. When Obama was elected in 2008, turnout was 62.3 percent of eligible voters, but it was only 57.5 percent in 2012. More people simply do not vote than vote for either candidate.

Fewer voters have turned out in elections when Obama was not on the ticket than when he was elected in 2008 and reelected in 2012. In the 2014 midterm elections, 36.6 percent voted, compared with 40.9 percent in the 2010 midterm elections. Turnout in Washington, Delaware, Missouri, South Dakota, California, and Indiana all fell by more than ten points. Only twelve states turned out a higher percentage of eligible voters in 2014 than in the 2010 midterms. The 36.6 percent of the voting-eligible population that cast ballots in 2014 was the lowest in any election cycle since World War II.[7]

In 2015, Democrats, led by John Lewis, on the anniversary of the Voting Rights Act of 1965, reintroduced a Voter Empowerment proposal in Congress. First proposed in 2012, the bill, directed at the voter participation issue, would permit registration and voting online and by telephone. It would also make it "unlawful to hinder, interfere or prevent another person from either registering to vote or from aiding another person in registering to vote." Though unlikely to pass, it has a high-minded purpose. Lewis said, "the goal of this bill is to

make voting access equal, fair, and simple for every American. Democracy is not a state; it is an act. The vigilant action of every member of Congress and every citizen is necessary to ensure that liberty, equality and justice remain the guiding principles of our democracy."[8]

It may seem obvious that if politicians make the process of voting as easy as possible, then participation in elections will increase. However, some people will still be too disinterested in the candidates to bother voting. Republicans claim that some reforms may actually facilitate electoral fraud. They argue that organized vote buyers could probably use hackers to breach the security of online or telephone registration or voting. But the best and easiest way to engage in fraud still is low-tech: through the use of absentee ballots. Absentee balloting is perfect for vote buyers and sellers. It is not policed, and vote sellers can make sure the ballot is marked correctly. Yet the public likes absentee ballots and favors extending their unfettered use.

In the fifteen states that offered online registration by 2015, a Pew Foundation report says they experienced less fraud than before their use. The League of Women Voters points out that online voting's requirement of a government-issued ID interferes with the purpose of registering young voters and others who are unregistered. In 2015, Oregon approved automatically registering people to vote. Any adult citizen who has had contact with the Department of Motor vehicles since 2013 and is not registered will get a ballot in the mail twenty days before the next statewide election. It remains to be seen whether this process will result in incidents of fraud.[9]

The desire to increase voter turnout has numerous advocates, including the president of the United States. In March 2015, President Obama created a brief less-than-one-day flap when he suggested public consideration of mandatory voting. Although he seemed to focus on federal elections, the idea and much of the immediate reaction applies equally to state and local elections. The discussion included arguments that held possibilities for increasing turnout.

At the Cleveland town hall event, President Obama described

compulsory voting as "a better strategy" in the short term than trying to achieve the seemingly impossible—to remove the influence of money in politics through a constitutional amendment. "It would be transformative if everybody voted," the president said. "That would counteract [campaign] money more than anything. If everybody voted, then it would completely change the political map in this country." He noted, "The people who tend not to vote are young, they're lower income, they're skewed more heavily towards immigrant groups and minority groups. There's a reason why some folks try to keep them away from the polls." He is correct that if this constituency voted and was organized to hold politicians accountable, it might actually invigorate the electorate. Otherwise disgust might set in and the targeted groups might simply stop voting. The reduced turnout for Obama's reelection expressed that reality.

Obama's suggestion of compulsory voting was not new political fare. At least twenty-six countries have compulsory voting, according to the International Institute for Democracy and Electoral Assistance. Failure to vote is punishable by a fine in countries such as Australia and Belgium; if you fail to pay your fine in Belgium, you could go to prison. In Australia, one of the places Obama cited, 90 percent of eligible voters go to the polls despite minimal enforcement. Registered voters who fail to vote get a form letter asking why; almost any excuse will do to get someone off the hook. Those with no valid excuse face a fine of about twenty dollars, which can escalate if someone refuses to pay, though that is rare.[10]

Senator Marco Rubio, Florida Republican, in the run-up to his candidacy for president, criticized President Obama's suggestion of compulsory voting. Rubio insisted that deciding not to vote is a form of free speech protected by the First Amendment. The president's press secretary Josh Earnest quickly backtracked, arguing that the president had merely offered "a pretty open-ended answer" to a question about how to control money in elections.

While compulsory voting exists elsewhere, as the president noted,

some critics believe it has resulted in new, unintended problems. Haydon Manning, associate professor at Flinders University in Australia, argued that while mandatory voting cured the turnout problem, it did not cure citizen disinterest or disgust with politics. Instead, Manning wrote, "wooing disengaged citizens now requires banal sloganeering and crass misleading negative advertising." This result, lamentably, in his view "can diminish the democratic experience for those who take the time to think through the issues." He must have never observed American elections. They are not governed by mandatory voting, and yet they are usually filled with "banal sloganeering and crass misleading negative advertising" limited only by available funds.[11]

Typical reactions from opponents of compulsory voting tracked Rubio's response. They insisted we are a nation based on individual freedom, and only paying taxes, serving on juries, being subject to the draft, and buying health insurance should be mandatory. Low turnout is not a problem, and instead of forcing people to vote we should educate them about its importance. Of course what this view ignores is voter disinterest based on past election results. Ignorance is not the culprit, but frustration. Acknowledging the frustration and suggesting ways to abate it seems a more effective approach.[12]

Perhaps, therefore, the most important way to increase turnout legally is to have candidates stand for something important to the voters so they won't get disgusted. That, combined with an easy recall process, could excite the electorate. The Obama effect increased turnout but not a sense of accountability. When it produced hope but not the change many were seeking, it was not a permanent turnout game changer. Voters discovered again that campaign promises are one thing and delivery another.

Moreover, Australia actually has had something beyond compulsory voting laws and fines that make voting likely and attractive, if sometimes troublesome. Campaign funds treat voters to alcoholic beverages at polling places. They make the polling place a venue where neighbors meet and socialize and enjoy beer, while engaged

in voting, instead of just a location where they exercise the formality of casting a ballot as quickly as possible. Voting, sausage sizzles, cake stalls, and accompanying community-based fund-raising activities take place together on Election Day. They call it celebrating democracy.[13]

Elections in the United States were once accompanied by treats, including alcoholic beverages, for years beginning in the colonial period. One argument for Prohibition was the need to prevent imbibing from influencing voters' choices. Alcohol continued to flow visibly at voting booths after Prohibition ended. South Carolina, the last state to have a total statewide ban, repealed it in 2014. Bans in Alaska and Massachusetts permit local options to remain exempt.[14]

In this country, a number of private businesses have given prizes to those who vote, including Starbucks, Krispy Kreme, and Chick-fil-A in 2008. Starbucks gave a free tall coffee; Chick-fil-A, a chicken sandwich; and California Tortilla, a free taco at all locations. McCormick & Schmick's extended Happy Hour from 3 p.m. to closing time with $1.95 bar food, and Krispy Kreme stores in some locations offered a free star-shaped doughnut with "patriotic sprinkles."

In 2013, some San Francisco bars offered fifty-cent drinks just for voting as part of the "Straight Up: Vote" campaign. MJR Digital Cinemas, a Michigan movie theater chain, gave those who had voted free popcorn of any size with the purchase of a movie ticket. There was some controversy over whether offering free items to people who voted is considered "buying a vote." But companies required an "I voted" sticker or some other proof of already having voted as a requirement to get a treat.[15]

If we really think it's important to increase turnout of voters no matter whom they might choose, or what issues are on the ballot, we could use such incentives as a modern day version of "ginger cakes." There is no reason why taxpayers or contributors can't fund treats, a lottery, or some other incentives given after voting, without regard to the voter's pick.

The thin line between incentives and potential vote buying ensnared Florida lawyer Theodore Trushin in 1978, when he tried what he believed was an acceptable way to reward voters who promised to vote for his choices. Trushin circulated a letter throughout an apartment complex in Miami Beach in which he promised that for "every resident of the Rooney Plaza Apartments who comes to my office to pledge their vote" for two judges he favored in the upcoming runoff election, he would "prepare a Last Will and Testament for that person without charge." He was charged and convicted for offering something of value to influence the election. He objected that the law excluded some things that anyone would regard as vote buying such as distributing meals and other treats during campaigns. But the court responded that many laws have exclusions and exceptions. Further, "There is an historical basis for the exception of serving food at political rallies—since the early formation of this republic people have gathered together on the grounds, eating fried mullet, chicken pilau, or the like, while candidates extol their virtues and try to persuade the voters to elect them." The legislature could permit an offer of free professional services in the same category as campaign contributions so long as there is no recommendation to vote for the person providing the services. Trushin's offer went beyond getting out the vote.[16]

Before the recent devastating collapse of oil prices, Alaskans adopted some promising incentives for voters who lacked resources to gain ready access to polling places. Perhaps focusing on their needs inspired them to engage, increased turnout, and may have discouraged absentee ballot abuse and vote buying.[17]

Alaska's North Slope Borough began providing a transportation subsidy for its almost six thousand people over a large area where the distances and absence of roads make it difficult for residents in remote areas to reach voting facilities. In some cases, snowmobiles or all-terrain vehicles are the only available transportation. At the time the law was passed, fuel was especially expensive, and because many

residents did not participate fully in the cash economy, paying for it was particularly a problem.

Individual voters could use their own transportation to the polls and then collect reimbursement for the cost of fuel, up to ten gallons of gasoline for each voter who requested it. The indigenous people traveled to town from their hunting, fishing, or whaling sites. The mayor sought and got a positive review of the program from the Election Crimes Unit of the Justice Department before it began.

Opponents, unsuccessfully, objected that the program actually was a subterfuge for paying voters. They noted that it allowed many people to claim more gas than they actually used, since fewer than ten voters signed for less than ten gallons. Further, most Borough residents lived in communities no farther than twelve miles from the polls, so they should not have needed ten gallons of gas.

Another Alaska program offered incentives to turn out for the 1994 election. A private travel agent in Fairbanks gave forty dollars in airfare discounts to 120 to 125 customers who presented a 1994 ballot stub. The Anchorage Chamber of Commerce offered a drawing for various prizes, including two round-trip tickets, to persons submitting their ballot stubs; approximately 4,415 people entered that drawing. The Anchorage People Mover bus system accepted an unknown number of riders' ballot stubs the day after the election in exchange for trips of any length, all day. None of the programs recommended a candidate.[18]

These programs were perfectly legal according to the Alaska Supreme Court. Unlike Illinois law, which conflicted with Alderman Hairston's 2014 proposal in Chicago and federal law, Alaska does not preclude paying a voter, unless there is an inducement to vote a particular way. The state supreme court, in reviewing the incentive programs, concluded that Alaska had debated the issues and decided to permit voter incentive programs that give compensation for voting. This is true, said the court, even if the sponsor of a program intends and expects that it will benefit a particular candidate. Further,

"payment" explicitly does not include rides to the polls or time off from work, which are regarded as "facilitation." This is "part of the costs of our civilization," removing "a practical obstacle to getting out the vote." The public welfare, the domain of the police power, includes "the political well-being of the community" and this proposal fits that definition. Arguably, with low prices and the need for government subsidies to keep refineries from closing, the gas subsidy program is less viable, but the principle remains important. Alaska's experience is a good example of how legal incentives for voting could be developed in other states where they are not prohibited, perhaps undermining the attractiveness of vote buying.[19]

The good news is that all of us who want clean elections with better candidates and accountability can effect change by taking concrete steps. We can work against voter suppression and help citizens who do not have government IDs get them. Such IDs are necessary for a variety of important purposes beyond voting, including traveling, and entering some offices, government buildings, and health facilities. Ending the disfranchisement of felons who have served their time, and joining in the mobilization against the influence of large donations in politics, are also crucial. And certainly, supporting officials like Greg Malveaux who try to punish vote buyers who exploit the poor is a worthwhile cause.

Developing legal incentives just for actually voting along with organizing voters to use their votes to demand accountability could erode illegal vote buying. Combined with voter education and organization, and accountability devices such as a recall, incentives could make the disaffected see that voting matters and beats five dollars and a pork chop sandwich. And casting a ballot might become a real, rather than rhetorical, civic virtue.

ACKNOWLEDGMENTS

Greg Malveaux shared with me the trove of materials from his time as head of the Louisiana Voter Fraud Division. He really believed these stories needed to be told. I hope I have met his expectations.

Greg and I also went to St. Martinville, where I met some of the participants in his biggest case. Eddy Grieg and Dennis Williams were quite receptive to phone conversations, answering my many questions as I followed up. I also had the pleasure of talking with Dennis and listening to him play with his brother's band, Nathan and the Zydeco Cha Chas, at the Jazz Fest in New Orleans.

Ben Johnson, a consummate political organizer who served as assistant to the president in the Clinton administration also helped enormously. He was a repository of detail on the election landscape in local communities around the country. An anonymous longtime local operative gave me the details about turnout tactics in Chicago. Emily Tynes, longtime political communications strategist, was a good sounding board. Melinda Chateauvert brought her research skills and deep knowledge of community organizing and political strategy to bear.

Ruth Greenwood, Voting Rights Project coordinator at the Lawyers' Committee for Civil Rights Under Law, in Chicago, gave me helpful information on compulsory voting and incentives that set my thinking in new directions. Irene Wainwright and Greg Osborne at the Louisiana Division of the New Orleans Public Library helped

me access essential materials. T. J. Davis, V. P. Franklin, and Melinda Chateauvert read all or portions of the manuscript at different stages of development and provided insightful commentary.

The audience and fellow panelists at a plenary session of the 2013 American Historical Association convention offered helpful commentary on the paper I gave on vote buying.

The students in my seminar at the University of Pennsylvania read drafts and raised important points as the project proceeded. My graduate students Anthony Pratcher, Rasul Miller, Camille Suarez, and others in the Thursday afternoon drop-in sessions in my office challenged my interpretations and helped refine my conclusions. Justin Simard provided some research assistance on the project.

Working with staff at Beacon and in particular my editor, Gayatri Patnaik, who understood that voter fraud is yet another means of voter suppression, was a great joy.

NOTES

PREFACE

1. Jim Ridley, "The People vs. Jimmy Hoffa (Part 1)," *Nashville Scene*, March 28, 2002, http://www.nashvillescene.com/nashville/the-people-vs-jimmy-hoffa-part-1/Content?oid=1186830.
2. Ibid.

CHAPTER 1: VOTING RIGHTS, RULES, AND SUPPRESSION

1. Dan Zak, "Coffee Party Activists Say Their Civic Brew's a Tastier Choice Than Tea Party's," *Washington Post*, February 26, 2010.
2. Justin Levitt, *The Truth About Voter Fraud* (New York: Brennan Center for Justice, New York University, 2007).
3. Only Alabama, California, Florida, Georgia, Kansas, Louisiana, Pennsylvania, and Texas have dedicated agencies to report voter-fraud suspicions. Other states have electoral fraud units located in the state attorney general's office, but they are well hidden from public access.
4. Cases can be retrieved on Westlaw or Lexis by searching "vote buying." They include cases involving candidates contesting elections and election officials' misbehavior, not just criminal cases; see "Who Can Vote? A News21 National Project," http://votingrights.news21.com/interactive/election-fraud-database/. See also "Comprehensive Database of US Voter Fraud Uncovers No Evidence That Photo ID Is Needed," http://votingrights.news21.com/article/election-fraud/. These are criminal prosecutions carried out from 2000 to 2012 only.
5. Pamela S. Karlan, "Not by Money but by Virtue Won? Vote Trafficking and the Voting Rights System," *Virginia Law Review* 80 (1994): 1455; Brown v. Hartlage 456 US 45 (1982).

6. Town of Fond Du Lac v. City of Fond Du Lac 22 Wis.2d 533 (1964).
7. "Louisiana Purchased," investigative reports from the *New Orleans Times-Picayune*.
8. Ferguson's demographics shifted rapidly. In 1990, the town was 74 percent white and 25 percent black; in 2000, it was 52 percent black and 45 percent white; in 2010, it was 67 percent black and 29 percent white. Black voters were only 7 percent of the electorate in the off-cycle municipal elections. In Ferguson, turnout in the most recent election was an abysmal 12 percent.
9. "Investigation of the Ferguson Police Department," US Department of Justice, Civil Rights Division, March 4, 2015.
10. We know that in off-year national elections, turnout is lower than in presidential election years, in which, recently, only 40 percent of the eligible voters cast ballots. As of 2012, twenty-one states required all of their municipal elections to be held off-cycle, and almost all of the remaining states had at least some cities with off-cycle elections. Only five states required the scheduling of municipal elections on the same day as national elections. Turnout is higher in California and Minnesota when the elections are held on the same day.
11. Carimah Townes, "What to Expect from the Ferguson Election," *ThinkProgress*, April 2, 2015, http://thinkprogress.org/justice/2015/04/02/3641654/ferguson-elections-2015/.
12. Carey Gillam, "Surge in Voter Turnout Gives Blacks New Voice in Ferguson, Missouri," Reuters, April 8, 2015, http://www.reuters.com/article/2015/04/08/us-usa-election-ferguson-idUSKBN0MZ23520150408.
13. Transcript of South Carolina governor Nikki Haley's *Meet the Press* interview with Chuck Todd, July 12, 2015, http://www.nbcnews.com/meet-the-press/meet-press-transcript-july-12-2015-n390781; Alan Binder and Richard Fausset, "Confederate Flag Down but South Carolina Blacks See Bigger Fights," *New York Times*, July 20, 2015.
14. Martin Luther King, "Where Do We Go from Here: Chaos or Community?," delivered at the 11th Annual SCLC (Southern Christian Leadership Conference) Convention, Atlanta, August 16, 1967, http://mlk-kpp01.stanford.edu/index.php/encyclopedia/documentsentry/where_do_we_go_from_here_delivered_at_the_11th_annual_sclc_convention/.
15. "Introduction To Federal Voting Rights Laws, Before the Voting Rights Act, Reconstruction and the Civil War Amendments," US Department of Justice website, updated August 6, 2015, http://www.justice.gov/crt/about/vot/intro/intro_a.php.

16. Crawford v. Marion County 552 US 1086 (2008), required an unexpired government-issued identification card or a provisional ballot and an appearance within ten days to the county clerk's office with a government-issued identification card. Unless otherwise noted, the history that follows is based on Karen McGill Arrington and William L. Taylor, eds., *Voting Rights in America: Continuing the Quest for Full Participation* (Washington, DC: Leadership Conference Education Fund and Joint Center for Political and Economic Studies, 1992); Mary Frances Berry, *And Justice for All: The United States Commission on Civil Rights and the Continuing Quest for Freedom in America* (New York: Knopf, 2009); and Alexander Keyssar, *The Right to Vote: The Contested History of Democracy in the United States* (New York: Basic Books, 2001; 2009).
17. Tracy Campbell, *Deliver the Vote: A History of Election Fraud, an American Political Tradition—1742–2004* (New York: Carroll & Graf, 2005), 5.
18. By the time of the Supreme Court's decision in Dred Scott v. Sandford 60 US 393 (1856), only five states (Massachusetts, Vermont, New Hampshire, Maine, and Rhode Island) did not exclude blacks from voting. However, only 4 percent of the nation's free black population lived in these states.
19. Cindy S. Aron, "'To Barter Their Souls for Gold': Female Federal Clerical Workers in Late Nineteenth-Century America," PhD diss., University of Maryland, 1981.
20. Supreme Court of Kansas State ex rel. Bradford, Atty. Gen., v. Malo, Sheriff, et al., 42 Kan. 54 (1889); Henry F. Mason, "County Seat Controversies in Southwestern Kansas," *Kansas Historical Quarterly* 2, no. 1 (February 1933): 45–65, http://kshs.org/p/county-seat-controversies-in-southwestern-kansas/12569.
21. Gabriel J. Chin, "The New Civil Death: Rethinking Punishment in the Era of Mass Conviction," *University of Pennsylvania Law Review* 160 (2011–12): 1789.
22. In almost all states, felons were disfranchised while they remained in prison; in many, disfranchisement was permanent, though some states made provisions for restoration of civil rights upon appeal to the governor.
23. Cherokee Nation v. Georgia 30 US 1 (1831); Roxanne Dunbar-Ortiz, *An Indigenous Peoples' History of the United States* (Boston: Beacon, 2014).
24. Lewis et al. v. Sizemore et al.; Sizemore et al. v. Huff 274 Ky. 58 (1938), appeal from Circuit Court, Leslie County.
25. Herman Lee and Booker T. Spicely, "Subject: Racial Incident, Shooting of Negro Soldier, Durham, N.C. on 8 July 1944," War Department investigation, http://nuweb9.neu.edu/civilrights/north-carolina/booker-t-spicely/.
26. Berry, *And Justice for All*; *To Secure These Rights: The Report of the President's*

Committee on Civil Rights, http://www.trumanlibrary.org/civilrights/srights1.htm.

27. *To Secure These Rights*, http://www.trumanlibrary.org/civilrights/srights4.htm, chap. 4, p. 147 in original report.
28. For example, the committee recommended legislation that would eliminate the requirement that public officers, including law enforcement, "had willfully deprived victims of a 'specific constitutional right'[;] the Civil Rights Division has found it very difficult to prove that the accused acted in a 'willful' manner" (157).
29. Virginia ratified the amendment in 1977, North Carolina in 1989; Mississippi has never ratified the Abolition of Poll Taxes amendment.
30. Fielding v. South Carolina Election Commission 305 SC 313 (1991).
31. Ronald H. Bayor, *Race and the Shaping of Twentieth-Century Atlanta* (Chapel Hill: University of North Carolina Press, 1996).
32. Nathan Glazer and Davis McEntire, *Studies in Housing and Minority Groups: Special Research Report to the Commission on Race and Housing* (Berkeley: University of California Press, 1960), 130.
33. "Good Jelly" got into politics when he returned to Nashville after doing blackface comedy, working with Mandy Green from the New Orleans Minstrel Show on the "Chitlin' circuit." He learned the ward-heeler ropes from William "Pie" Hardison, a custodian and the only high black official at the Nashville Courthouse. Hardison had the power to reward black fixers with government city jobs as maids and janitors. Good Jelly became Hardison's chauffeur, found him to be a "good talker" as well as a "good driver," and taught him the political game. When Pie moved on, Good Jelly took over the territory. David Halberstam, "The Bugle Blows for Good Jelly," *Reporter*, 1961, reprinted in *Negro Digest*, February 1962, 16–21; "Good Jelly Jones Makes Page One," *Sarasota Journal*, March 24, 1958, reprinted in *Pittsburgh Courier*, April 16, 1960; conversation with Francis Guess, December 15, 2014.
34. In the 1960s, "Little Evil" Jacobs took the wrong side: he was against the Nashville *Tennessean*'s successful campaign to consolidate Nashville and surrounding towns into a metropolitan government. The campaign was successful, and Jacobs's prediction that the black vote would be diluted as a result was in fact correct. After that, a number of stories appeared in the *Tennessean* shedding light on his political activities. The result was that Little Evil actually went to jail for election fraud. Local attorney and first black councilman Robert Lilliard predicted that with the sit-ins and changes as a result of the civil rights movement, politicians would shift their interest to vying for the black middle class; helping

the poor through ward-heeling was no longer relevant or important. Halberstam, "The Bugle Blows for Good Jelly"; Halberstam, "Good Jelly Jones Makes Page One"; conversation with Troy Merritt, January 21, 2015.

35. Rosalyn Terborg-Penn, *African American Women in the Struggle for the Vote, 1850–1920* (Bloomington: Indiana University Press, 1998).
36. Morgan Kousser, another leading scholar in the voting rights field, in *Colorblind Injustice: Minority Voting Rights and the Undoing of the Second Reconstruction* (Chapel Hill: University of North Carolina Press, 1999), describes the evolution of voting rights through the efforts since Reagan-Bush judicial appointees took over the Supreme Court and other federal courts and diluted the power of voting. He traces the successful efforts of white politicians to reduce or deny minority representation in different locales across the country since passage of the Voting Rights Act of 1965.
37. Alabama Legislative Black Caucus v. Alabama 575 US (2015); Dickson v. Rucho 135 S.Ct. 1843 (2015); Anne Blythe, "US Supreme Court Sends Voting District Case Back to State Supreme Court," *Charlotte News Observer*, April 21, 2015.
38. Penda Hair, "Seizing a Voice in a Democracy: The Mississippi Redistricting Campaign," in *Louder Than Words: Lawyers, Communities and the Struggle for Justice, a Report to the Rockefeller Foundation* (New York: Rockefeller Foundation, March 2001), 60–81, http://b.3cdn.net/advancement/3c05747f6d2c6cb749_ml brgfwlo.pdf.
39. Ibid., 76.
40. *Alabama Legislative Black Caucus v. Alabama*; *Dickson v. Rucho*; Blythe, "US Supreme Court Sends Voting District Case Back to State Supreme Court."
41. Rock the Vote/Center for Information and Research on Civic Learning and Engagement, *Young Voter Registration and Turnout Trends* (Washington, DC: February 2008), http://www.civicyouth.org/PopUps/CIRCLE_RtV_Young_Voter _Trends.pdf.
42. Marshall Ganz, "Motor Voter or Motivated Voter?," *American Prospect*, December 19, 2001, http://prospect.org/article/motor-voter-or-motivated-voter.
43. Ann Banks, "Dirty Tricks, South Carolina and John McCain," *Nation*, January 14, 2008, http://www.thenation.com/article/dirty-tricks-south-carolina-and-john -mccain.
44. Federal Elections Commission, "2000 Presidential General Election Results," http://www.fec.gov/pubrec/fe2000/2000presge.htm#FL.

Florida

Bush, George W.	R	2,912,790	48.85%
Gore, Al	D	2,912,253	48.84
Nader, Ralph	GPF	97,488	1.63
Buchanan, Pat	REF	17,484	0.29
Browne, Harry	LBF	16,415	0.28
Hagelin, John	NLF	2,281	0.04
Moorehead, Monica	WW	1,804	0.03
Phillips, Howard	CPF	1,371	0.02
McReynolds, David	SFL	622	0.01
Harris, James	FSW	562	0.01
Chote, May	W	34	0.00
McCarthy, Ken. C.	W	6	0.00
Total State Votes		5,963,110	

45. US Commission on Civil Rights, *Voting Irregularities in Florida During the 2000 Presidential Election* (Washington, DC: US Commission on Civil Rights, 2001), http://www.usccr.gov/pubs/vote2000/report/main.htm.
46. Dan Balz, "Carter-Baker Panel to Call for Voting Fixes," *Washington Post*, September 19, 2005, http://www.washingtonpost.com/wp-dyn/content/article/2005/09/18/AR2005091801364.html.
47. Commission on Federal Election Reform, *Building Confidence in US Elections* (Washington, DC: Center for Democracy and Election Management, September 2005).
48. US Census Bureau, "Voter Turnout Increases by 5 Million in 2008 Presidential Election, US Census Bureau Reports: Data Show Significant Increases Among Hispanic, Black and Young Voters," press release, July 20, 2009, https://www.census.gov/newsroom/releases/archives/voting/cb09–110.html.
49. Wendy R. Weiser and Erik Opsal, *The State of Voting in 2014* (New York: Brennan Center for Justice, New York University, 2014); "Where Voting Is Now Easier," *New York Times*, editorial, August 11, 2014.
50. The Court removed aggregate spending caps on political action group contributions. There is no limit to the number of PACs that can exist, so big donors can give to a large number of PACs supporting their candidates without caps.

Meanwhile, the base limits for campaign contributions—$2,600 for individuals and $5,000 for PACs—remain. Jaime Fuller, "From George Washington to Shaun McCutcheon: A Brief-ish History of Campaign Finance Reform," *Washington Post*, April 3, 2014.

CHAPTER 2: THE VOTER FRAUD DIVISION AND LOUISIANA'S CULTURE OF CORRUPTION

1. Jack Wardlaw, "Election Law May Finally Be Ditched," *New Orleans Times-Picayune*, May 6, 2001.
2. Louisiana Legislative Auditor, Department of Elections and Registration Commissioner of Elections, March 17, 1999 Investigative Audit, http://www.lla.state.la.us/PublicReports.nsf/86256EA9004C005986256F19007DC1EC/$FILE/40cf5f2e.pdf; August 5, 1999, Compliance Audit, Historical Notes on Elections, http://www.sos.la.gov.
3. Jerry Fowler was serving his fifth term in office. The commissioner's budget for FY 1997–98 and 1998–99 totaled $29,411,421 for maintenance of machines, support services to hold elections, election expenses, maintenance of a statewide voter registration system, and administration of laws regarding registration. An audit by state legislative auditor Daniel Kyle showed the department spent $15,445.23 on mechanical voting machines, counters, and their installation, bought from Election Services, Inc., from 1992 to 1998. If the department had made its purchases directly from suppliers and paid market rates for supplies and installation, they could have saved approximately $8,565,510. From 1991 to 1998, the department spent $10,043,071 to companies associated with Fowler. Fowler received kickbacks for making these deals. The department stored machines in sixty-five warehouses available for distribution among 3,900 voting precincts. Employees of the department did work for which one company was paid, and another employee of the Department was paid for work he supposedly did for which a contractor had billed. Twenty-three people were charged in the probe; eleven, including Fowler, pleaded guilty. He went to prison February 14, 2001. August 5, 1999, Compliance Audit, Historical Notes on Elections, http://www.sos.la.gov.
4. Louisiana Secretary of State Election Results, http://www.sos.la.gov/ElectionsAndVoting/GetElectionInformation/FindResultsAndStatistics/Pages/default.aspx.
5. Ibid.
6. La. Campaign Finance Opinion No. 99–360, Louisiana Board of Ethics, http://domino.ethics.state.la.us/campopn.nsf/999d109733135c25862567f8006847bf/8f58d9e4d672366e86256848006b83df?OpenDocument.

7. Watts served when McKeithen took over the office and changed it into a compliance unit. He was still there in 2014.
8. Ken Stickney, "Voter Fraud Investigation Leads to Arrests," *News Star* (Monroe, LA), September 1, 2000.
9. Ricky Sherrod, "Beyond Coushatta: The 1874 Exodus Out of Red River Parish," *Louisiana History* 52 (2011): 440; "The Southern Terror: Massacre of Northern Men in Louisiana," *New York Times*, September 2, 1874; Louisiana Secretary of State Election Results, http://www.sos.la.gov/ElectionsAndVoting/GetElection Information/FindResultsAndStatistics/Pages/default.aspx.
10. Adkins v. Huckabay 749 So.2d 900 (1999); Adkins v. Huckabay 755 So.2d 206 (2000).
11. Curiously, Huckabay "got 646 more, including 335 absentee votes while Adkins only had 85." The division surmised that the absentee process was where "voter fraud is most prominent." Vickie Welborn, "Investigator Assigned to Red River Election Fraud Case," *Shreveport Times*, April 19, 2000.
12. Ronnie Moore, *Louisiana Summer Project, Summer 1964* (director, CORE Louisiana Project), CORE pamphlet, November 1964, http://www.crmvet.org/docs/64_core1.htm.
13. "Negroes Vote for First Time Since 1902," *CORE-lator* 104 (February 1964), http://www.crmvet.org/docs/core/core6402.pdf.
14. Malveaux's files.
15. Ibid.; Watts conversation on October 12, 2000.
16. Malveaux's files.
17. Reddix v. Lucky 148 F. Supp. 108 (W.D. La. 1957).
18. Chuck Cannon, "Polls Turn Away Voters: Fraud Case Pending," *News Star*, June 22, 2000. Monroe's population of 49,000 was about 69 percent black, with 36.7 percent living below the poverty line. Johnny Gunter, "Neville Opens Look Into Late Voter Sign Ups," *News Star*, March 17, 2000; "Registration Drive Is a Mystery Worth Solving," *News Star*, editorial, March 27, 2000.
19. "Four Charged in St. Helena Parish Voter Fraud Case," *Hammond (AK) Daily Star*, April 2, 1997.
20. US v. Phillips 219 F3d 404 5th Cir. Court of Appeals (2000).
21. Malveaux's files.
22. Ibid.
23. The judge dropped White and the other Nugent supporters from the case because the law permitted only the candidate to sue for a new election, but they testified for Nugent.
24. Steve Bannister, "Chief Loses Challenge," *Town Talk* (Alexandria/Pineville,

LA), April 16, 2002 (Gleason Nugent was in office 1992–2002 and died in 2005); Nugent v. Phelps 816 So.2d 349 (2002).

25. Connors v. Reeves 649 So.2d 804 (1995); Spikes v. Reeves, April 28, 2005, 04–30224 (5th Cir. 2005), unpublished opinion.

26. District Attorney of the Eighth Judicial District, Compliance Audit (April 20, 2005), Louisiana Legislative Auditor, https://app.lla.state.la.us/PublicReports.nsf/22149B004508996486256FE90058BBF5/$FILE/0000088E.pdf.

27. The press coverage of Gleason Nugent's son, police officer Scott Nugent—who was charged in 2008 with homicide in a taser assault on a black man, Baron Pikes—read as if Nugent was corrupt instead of Reeves. Howard Witt, "Taser Death in Troubled Town," *Chicago Tribune*, July 20, 2008; Mandy M. Goodnight, "Winn DA Dies of Apparent Self-Inflicted Gunshot Wound," *Town Talk*, July 24, 2005, http://lapoliticalnews.blogspot.com/2005/07/winn-da-dies-of-apparent-self.html.

28. John McMillan, "Ascension Turns Conservative," *Baton Rouge Advocate*, April 29, 2007; Elections Results, Louisiana State Government, Ascension Parish, http://electionresultsmobile.sos.la.gov/results.html?gaelectiondate=20081104&gaparish=ascension.

29. Cajuns are the descendants of eighteenth-century Acadian exiles from the maritime provinces in Canada. They were expelled by the British and New Englanders during the French and Indian War. See "Registrar Detects Fraudulent Voter Forms," *Baton Rouge Advocate*, November 15, 2000. Ascension Parish has a total population of 114,000, of whom 74 percent are white, and 11 percent of the entire population lives below the poverty line. However, Donaldsonville, with a population of 7,500, is 74 percent African American, with 28 percent living below the poverty line.

30. John Maginnis, *The Last Hayride* (New Orleans: Pelican, 2011), 283.

31. Dee Dee Thurston, "Freedom for Beridon," *Houma (LA) Courier*, November 20, 2000; "Local Woman Seeks Pardon," *Houma Courier*, May 4, 2003; "Foster Grants Pardon to Local Woman," *Houma Courier*, July 30, 2003; Innocence Project New Orleans, http://www.ip-no.org/exonoree-profile/cheryle-beridon.

32. "Governor-Elect Edwards Pledges Higher Taxes and Teachers' Salaries in Louisiana," *New York Times*, October 24, 1983; Maginnis, *The Last Hayride*, 282–83.

33. Charles Lussier and Dee Dee Thurston, "Voter Registration Changes Result in Williams' Charges," *Houma Courier*, February 1, 2001.

34. Malveaux's files.

35. Ibid.

36. The parish also had one convicted felon complaint, among the many complaints

of vote hauling and buying, usually carried out through absentee voting. Wayne Rayo, aka Wayne Briggs, signed a registration card on January 14, 2002, while he was on probation for a felony offense. Investigators found that Rayo, a forty-six-year-old black male, had indeed plea bargained for a sentence of two years' hard labor and a suspended three-year sentence of supervised probation. Chris Rosa, in the Abbeville newspaper, reported on a meeting with John Win, the president of the group. Malveaux and the state police assigned to the area were at the meeting. Chris Rosa, "Candidates Being Asked Not to Buy Votes," *Abbeville (LA) Meridional*, March 21, 2002; Chris Rosa, "First Day of Absentee Voting Clean," *Abbeville Meridional*, March 26, 2002.

37. Bribery of voters as governed by La. R.S. 14:119 includes "giving or offering to give, directly or indirectly, any money, or anything of apparent present or prospective value to any voter at any general, primary, or special election, or at any convention of a recognized political party, with the intent to influence the voter in the casting of his ballot. The acceptance of, or the offer to accept is also bribery."
38. Steve Bannister, "Marksville, LA, Men Given Probation in Voter-Fraud Case," *Town Talk*, September 24, 2002, http://www.freerepublic.com/focus/f-news/756926/posts.
39. Ibid.; "House Arrest During Elections Part of Voting-Fraud Sentence," *Baton Rouge Advocate*, September 26, 2002; State v. Dauzat, 843 So.2d 526 (2003).
40. "House Arrest During Elections"; *State v. Dauzat.*
41. Affidavits, October 20–22, 2002, in Malveaux's files.
42. Malveaux's files.
43. Ibid.; https://voterportal.sos.la.gov/ElectedOfficials.
44. Malveaux's files; https://voterportal.sos.la.gov/ElectedOfficials.
45. Malveaux to Michael Harson, 15th Judicial District Attorney, October 23, 2003, with attached statements and affidavits from voters for whom the culprits filed absentee ballots, and the absentee ballots themselves.
46. Malveaux's files, transcript from January 2002 Acadia and Lafayette Parish investigations, with digital recording from Joseph K. Scott III, a confidential informant at the Lee and Walsh firm.
47. Ibid.; "Russel Benoit Begins Seventh Term as Assessor," *Crowley (LA) Post Signal*, January 8, 2009, http://www.crowleypostsignal.com/russel-benoit-begins-seventh-term-assessrp.
48. "Acadia Assessor to Resign," AcadiaParishToday.com, June 1, 2010, http://www.crowleypostsignal.com/acadia-assessor-resign; Crowley, LA, Acadia Parish Police Jury minutes, June 9, 2010, http://www.appj.org/PJMinutes/PJM_2010/June_9

_2010.htm; Russel Benoit Sr., obituary, *Advertiser* (LA), December 1, 2011, http://www.legacy.com/obituaries/theadvertiser/obituary.aspx?n=russel-benoit&pid=154833044.

49. See note 36.
50. "Promise Not to Lie," *Opelousas (LA) Daily World*, April 4, 2002.

CHAPTER 3: "RAT INFESTATION, ROTTEN WOOD, AND RUSTY METAL"

1. The population of St. Martinville in the 2010 census was about 6,100, of which 62 percent was African American, and St. Martin Parish had a population of about 53,000, of which 31 percent was African American. Gilbert King, *The Execution of Willie Francis: Race, Murder, and the Search for Justice in the American South* (New York: Basic Books, 2008).
2. Richard Burgess, "St. Martinville Elections Troubled for Many Years," *Advocate*, Acadiana Bureau, February 28, 2006; "The Louisiana Election Frauds: An Honest Election Officer Removed by the Governor," *New York Times*, April 29, 1884; Walter Greaves Cowan and Jack B. McGuire, *Louisiana Governors Rulers, Rascals, and Reformers* (Oxford: University Press of Mississippi, 2008), 123–29, 270–78; Sidney J. Romero Jr., "The Political Career of Murphy James Foster, Governor of Louisiana, 1892–1900," *Louisiana Historical Quarterly* 28 (1945): 1129; Mark T. Carleton, "The Politics of the Convict Lease System in Louisiana: 1868–1901," *Louisiana History* 8 (1967): 5; William Ivy Hair, *Bourbonism and Agrarian Protest in Louisiana Politics, 1877–1900* (Baton Rouge: Louisiana State University Press, 1969).
3. Leo Joseph Bulliard, Wade O. Martin, and Gaston Thibodeaux, *Dictionary of Louisiana Biography*, Louisiana Historical Association, http://www.lahistory.org/site30.php; "Gaston Thibodeaux," FamilySearch.org, https://familysearch.org/ark:/61903/1:1:XMT7-WW7; "Obituaries for September 20, 1998: Dr. Murphy Martin Sr.," *Daily Iberian* (LA), September 20, 1998, http://www.iberianet.com/obituaries-for-september-dr-murphy-martin-sr/article_b5421f94-c7e2-5ddd-a4f5-a7d8c239b0c7.html.
4. Conversations with Eddy Grieg in St. Martinville, February 2, 2012, and by phone, April 7, 2015.
5. Alyssa Newcomb, "Class Reunion Letter Lists 'White Graduates Only' Party," ABC News, September 1, 2012, http://abcnews.go.com/blogs/headlines/2012/09/class-reunion-letter-lists-white-graduates-only-party/.
6. "St. Martinville Senior High School," USA.com, http://www.usa.com/public

-school/st-martinville-senior-high-school-saint-martinville-la-220159001229 .html?nv=school-district-2201590. There is only one private high school, Evangel House Christian Academy, with eleven girls enrolled, in St. Martinville. "St. Martin Parish Private Schools," PrivateSchoolReview.com, http://www.privateschoolreview.com/county_private_schools/stateid/LA/county/22099#!high_school.

7. Christine Payton, "St. Martinville's Council Wrestles with Remap Plan," *Daily Iberian*, December 29, 1997, http://www.iberianet.com/st-martinville-s-cuuncil-wrestles-with-remap-plan-by-christine/article_c2a2827a-473d-5b13-bc08-c010a47922f4.html.
8. Dunne cited Beer v. US 425 US 130 (1976); Department of Justice, "§5 Objection Determinations: Louisiana," http://www.justice.gov/crt/voting-determination-letters-louisiana.
9. Isabelle Katz Pinzler, Acting Assistant Attorney General for Civil Rights, to George W. McHugh, 102 E. Berard St., St. Martinville, October 6, 1997. She also cited *Beer*; Department of Justice, Section 5 Objection Determinations: Louisiana, http://www.justice.gov/crt/voting-determination-letters-louisiana.
10. Carissa Hebert, "50 Plead Guilty in Voter Fraud," *Daily Iberian*, July 9, 1997, http://www.iberianet.com/plead-guilty-in-voter-fraudcarissa-hebert-the-daily-iberian-july/article_7b3cd786–4436–5a56–9fde-97bae5e8e78d.html.
11. Ed Anderson, "Jenkins Told to Present Fraud Proof by Sunday," *New Orleans Times Picayune*, November 16, 1996; Stuart Rothenberg, "Louisiana Senate, 1996: It Ain't Over 'Til It's Over," CNN.com, http://www.cnn.com/ALLPOLITICS/1997/05/05/spotlight/; Blaine Harden, "Disputed Election Stirs Memories of Louisiana's Shady Past," *Washington Post*, December 20, 1996.
12. Phone conversation with Spears, September 2011. In his view, people in St. Martinville probably thought that if the Department of Justice didn't do anything, they could just stay in office. He assured me it was not a "black/white thing"; they had "Cajuns and Catholics all mixed up." He viewed whatever they were doing as just "a way of life."
13. Ibid.; Grieg v. City of St. Martinville (W.D. La. 2000).
14. Lee came to Louisiana from time to time on the case. Phone conversation with Spears, September 2011; US Department of Justice, Civil Rights Division, Cases Raising Claims Under Section 2 of the Voting Rights Act, http://www.justice.gov/crt/about/vot/litigation/recent_sec2.php.
15. The case was resolved when the city adopted a new redistricting plan prepared by the court's special master, which received §5 preclearance, and scheduled elections pursuant to the precleared plan. On July 19, 2001, the suit was voluntarily

dismissed. US Department of Justice Civil Rights Division, Cases Raising Claims Under Section 2 of the Voting Rights Act, http://www.justice.gov/crt/about/vot/litigation/recent_sec2.php.

16. Angie Rogers Laplace, assistant attorney general, to Jerry Fowler, commissioner of elections, answering his query about Act 139 (1997), February 17, 1998.
17. Jennifer Boquet, "Martin Remains Mayor," *Daily Iberian*, April 7, 2002.
18. Jennifer Boquet, "Vote Fraud Probe Continues in St. Martinville," *Daily Iberian*, April 11, 2002, http://www.iberianet.com/vote-fraud-probe-continues-in-st-martinville/article_0a4fe598–8d78–580c-ab0f-8d91726148d6.html.
19. Jennifer Boquet, "Father Holds Full House," *Daily Iberian*, April 4, 2002.
20. "Clean Up Voter Rolls," editorial, *Daily Iberian*, April 7, 2002.
21. Steve Landry, "Fraud Investigators Look to File Charges," *Teche News*, April 26, 2002; "Martin Won 3rd Term, 2 Council Seats Filled," *Teche News*, April 10, 2002.
22. Ken Grissom, "Election-Fraud Case Clouded by Prejudices: The DA Balking or the Investigator Inept," *Teche News*, May 1, 2002; see also Jennifer Boquet, "S. M. Vote Probe Complete," *Daily Iberian*, April 25, 2002.
23. Nathan Sampey, "Attorneys Grill Election Witnesses," *Daily Iberian*, May 21, 2002, http://www.iberianet.com/attorneys-grill-election-witnesses/article_9f986ea8–7e56–55a5-aa5a-f0c53845dd85.html.
24. Ibid.
25. News clipping, July 12, 2002, Malveaux's files.
26. Jennifer Boquet, "Judge's Ruling Likely Brings Recall Effort to a Close," *Daily Iberian*, May 9, 2003.
27. In the same election, Mary Francois's distant relative, Douglas Francois, who represented District 5, lost by four votes. Nathan Stubbs, "Council Controversy," *Independent Weekly* (LA), April 13, 2005, http://www.theind.com/lead-news/830-Independent Weekly.
28. "La. High Court Won't Hear Election Case," *Baton Rouge Advocate*, June 14, 2002.
29. Grieg v. City of St. Martinville and US, US District Court Western District, Louisiana, Lafayette Division, dismissed December 14, 2006, by Judge Doherty. "Plaintiffs clearly established a *prima facie* case of voter fraud and/or irregularity under the Voting Rights Act. This court denied defendants' motion to dismiss for failure to state a claim on May 16, 2003." Defendants Thibodeaux, Martin et al. couldn't collect attorney's fees and costs because the claim was not frivolous. However, the lawyer for Grieg et al. did not pursue the case in a timely manner.
30. Michael Walsh to Suzanne Terrell, January 2, 2003; copy in Malveaux's files.

31. Ibid. See also letter drafted for Terrell to send to press and Joe Le Blanc, vice president of the Civil Rights League, who had made inquiries. Joseph Scott III to Pat Bergeron, chief of staff to Terrell, February 18, 2003; copy in Malveaux's files.

CHAPTER 4: MAKING A FEDERAL CASE

1. Grissom, "Election-Fraud Case Clouded"; "Prosecutor Given Voter-Fraud List," *Baton Rouge Advocate*, April 25, 2003.
2. Steve Landry, "12 of 23 Voter Fraud Cases Dropped," *Baton Rouge Advocate*, May 22, 2003.
3. Michael Walsh to Suzanne Terrell, March 14, 2003; Joseph Scott III on behalf of Walsh's firm, to Pat Bergeron, chief of staff to Terrell, copies in Malveaux's files.
4. Marsha Sills, "Five Charged," *Daily Advertiser* (Acadiana), June 6, 2003. Malveaux's files contain warrants and transcripts of their testimony. Bruce Schultz, "Six Face Charges Related to Voting, St. Martinville Councilwoman Indicted on Federal Counts," *Baton Rouge Advocate*, December 17, 2003.
5. Bush v. Gore 531 US 98 (2000), disputed 2000 presidential election.
6. Steve Landry, "FBI Visits St. Martinville in Investigation of 2000 Election," *Baton Rouge Advocate*, June 6, 2003.
7. "Mary Francois Asks Judge to Let Her Continue Her Work with the Poor," *Baton Rouge Advocate*, August 30, 2011.
8. See discussion in Grieg v. Thibodeaux 2006 WL 3873105 (2006).
9. "Former Councilwoman's Husband Dead of a Gunshot Wound," *Teche Today* (LA), April 4, 2010.
10. "April 6, 2002, Council Election," *Independent Weekly*, http://www.theind.com/lead-news/830.
11. Ibid.
12. Ibid.
13. Ibid.
14. Ibid.
15. Ibid.
16. Louisiana Secretary of State, "Official Election Results," St. Martinville, 2006, 2010, staticresults.sos.la.gov/04012006/04012006_50.html.
17. Malveaux to Secretary of State Fox McKeithen, November 18, 2003.
18. Marsha Shuler, "Terrell Rapped for Paying Lots of Overtime Before Exit," *Baton Rouge Advocate*, February 18, 2004.
19. Ibid.

20. Louisiana State Inspector General report on Department of Elections, March 2005, Bill Lynch, Inspector General, approved by Governor Kathleen Babineaux Blanco, February 2005, file no. 1–04–0038.
21. Ibid. "The Department of Elections and Registration prior to its January 12, 2004 merger with the Department of State failed to establish policies procedures and practices which ensured more than $84,000 of payments for employee overtime and $12,000 of travel expenses paid to one employee were adequately supported by documentation."
22. "St. Martinville's Big Mardi Gras Ball," *Teche Today*, February 2, 2010.
23. Christi Landry, "Year One of Change for St. Martinville," *Daily Iberian*, December 29, 2006; Ken Grissom, "Former St. Martinville Mayor Eric Martin Running for State Representative," *Teche Today*, May 3, 2011; Louisiana Secretary of State, "Official Election Results," State Representative, 2011, http://staticresults.sos.la.gov/11192011/11192011_50.html.
24. Jason Brown, "Sentencing Delayed on Wire Fraud Charges," *Baton Rouge Advocate*, Acadiana Bureau, September 2, 2011; "Mary Francois Gets 14 Months for Wire Fraud," *Teche News*, April 4, 2012.
25. Ibid.
26. Conversation with Leonard Francois, April 7, 2015.
27. Conversation with Dennis Williams, April 6, 2015.

CHAPTER 5: ELECTORAL FRAUD CHICAGO STYLE

1. Hal Dardick, "Chicago Alderman Probed in Raffle-for-Vote Offer," *Chicago Tribune*, October 29, 2014.
2. "Authorities Investigate Chicago Alderwoman for Offering Prizes to Those Who Vote," Associated Press, October 29, 2014; "Chicago Dem Alderman Attempted to Buy Votes," *Washington Free Beacon*, October 29, 2014; Dardick, "Chicago Alderman Probed in Raffle-for-Vote Offer." Hairston won reelection with 52 percent of the vote, with all precincts reporting. Anne Marie Miles, the next closest candidate, had 19.5 percent of the votes cast. Private companies such as Starbucks had given free cups of coffee and some meals to those with an "I Voted" sticker in the 2008 and 2010 elections in some locations. Also see Illinois Compiled Statutes, Prohibitions, and Penalties 10, Section 29–1, Public Acts 78-887, which defines "vote buying" as follows: "Any person who knowingly gives, lends or promises to give or lend any money or other valuable consideration to any other person to influence such other person to vote or to register to vote or to influence such other person to vote for or against any candidate or public question to

be voted upon at any election shall be guilty of a Class 4 felony." According to Louisiana Revised Statutes, Chapter 10, Section 1461: "(1) Bribery of voters is the giving or offering to give, directly or indirectly, any money, or anything of apparent present or prospective value to any voter at any general, primary, or special election, or at any convention of a recognized political party, with the intent to influence the voter in the casting of his ballot. The acceptance of, or the offer to accept, directly or indirectly, any money, or anything of apparent present or prospective value, by any such voters under such circumstances shall also constitute bribery of voters. (2) Bribery of voters is also the giving or offering to give, directly or indirectly, any money or anything of apparent present or prospective value to secure or influence registration of a person or to secure or influence a person to sign or not sign a recall or other election petition." Massachusetts Laws, Title 8, Chapter 56, Section 32, says: "No person shall, directly or indirectly, pay, give or promise to a voter, any gift or reward to influence his vote or to induce him to withhold his vote."

3. The FBI's investigation of Quinn came on the heels of the conviction of his former running mate Rod Blagojevich, imprisoned for corruption; the conviction of Republican George Ryan in the licenses-for-bribes scandal; and a trial in which Republican Jim Edgar twice had to testify about a contracting scandal in his administration.
4. Dick Simpson, Jim Nowlan et al., *Chicago and Illinois, Leading the Pack in Corruption*, Anti-Corruption Report Number 5 (Chicago: University of Illinois at Chicago/Illinois Integrity Initiative, February 15, 2012).
5. Rick Pearson and Monique Garcia, "Federal Probe Threatens Quinn's Reelection," *Chicago Tribune*, May 4, 2014.
6. Ibid.; Dave McKinney, "State Auditor Slams Quinn's $54.5 Million Anti-Violence Program; Brady Calls It Gov.'s 2010 Political Slush Fund," *Chicago Sun-Times*, February 25, 2014. Brady was Quinn's 2010 gubernatorial opponent.
7. Campbell, *Deliver the Vote*, 246, 253–54.
8. William B. Crawford Jr. and Jerry Crimmins, "Huge Vote-Fraud Probe: FBI to Check Every Voter, All Precincts," *Chicago Tribune*, January 20, 1983.
9. Greg Hinz, "Already Voted? In Some Chicago Wards, Absentee Ballots Are Still a Show of Precinct Muscle," *Crain's Chicago Business* 27, no. 44 (2004).
10. Ibid.
11. Ibid.
12. Crawford and Crimmins, "Huge Vote-Fraud Probe."
13. William B. Crawford Jr. and Tim Franklin, "US Grand Jury Indicts 10 in Chicago Vote Fraud Probe," *Chicago Tribune*, April 8, 1983.

14. US v. Olinger, 759 F.2d 1293 (1985).
15. Crawford and Franklin, "US Grand Jury Indicts 10."
16. Douglas Frantz, "Democratic Vote Stealer Tells How Wine, Cash Bought Votes," *Chicago Tribune*, October 21, 1983.
17. See, for example, Douglas Frantz, "4 Convicted of 'Vote Fraud Chicago-Style,'" *Chicago Tribune*, October 28, 1983.
18. Rudolph Unger, "8 Sentenced for Roles in 1982 Election Fraud," *Chicago Tribune*, December 9, 1983.
19. 42 US Code § 1973i Prohibited Acts. Three other men were arrested for voting illegally because they were not US citizens, and may not have been in the United States legally. See Crawford and Franklin, "US Grand Jury Indicts 10."
20. Jack Houston and Jerry Crimmins, "'Family Secret' Provides Key Election Fraud Link," *Chicago Tribune*, January 23, 1983.
21. US v. Howard, 774 F2d 838 (1985).
22. 1983 field hearing conducted by the Senate Judiciary Committee, testimony of US attorney Daniel Webb of Chicago; *Voting Rights Act: Criminal Violations: Hearings Before the Subcommittee on the Constitution of the Senate Judiciary Comm.*, 98th Cong., 1st Sess. 6 (1984); "Unsuccessful Candidates May Bring Suit." See Roberts v. Wamser, "In re: Report of the Special January 1982 Grand Jury 1," No. 82 GJ 1909 (N.D. Ill. Dec. 14, 1984) (hereinafter Grand Jury Report); US v. Howard, 774 F.2d 838 (7th Cir. 1985); US v. Olinger, 759 F.2d 1293 (7th Cir. 1985); Crawford and Franklin, "U.S. Grand Jury Indicts 10," *Chicago Tribune*, April 8, 1983.
23. "The Reversal of the Chicago River," American Public Works Association, http://www2.apwa.net/about/awards/toptencentury/chica.htm.
24. Mark Eissman, "Reviews Bare Up to 100,000 Irregularities," *Chicago Tribune*, March 8, 1987; Mark Eissman, "US to Probe Primary Vote Fraud," *Chicago Tribune*, March 11, 1987.
25. Ibid.
26. Hinz, "Already Voted?"
27. "A Cook County judge imposed two years of probation Tuesday for three Chicago women involved in a voter fraud scam. Jalissa Santiago, 21, Migdalia Echevarria, 37, and Windaliz Santiago, 21, each pleaded guilty to theft and mutilation of election materials charges in Judge Dennis Dernbach's courtroom, said Assistant Cook County State's Attorney Lynn McCarthy. Prosecutors say the three women worked between June 2003 and February 2004 as part of an effort to register more Puerto Rican voters in Cook County. Instead, the women simply copied names out of phone books, prosecutors said. The fraud came to light when workers with

the Chicago Board of Elections were checking some of the names and addresses the women submitted." "Probation in Voter Fraud," *Chicago Sun-Times*, August 30, 2006.

28. Rudolph Bush and Dan Mihalopoulos, "Daley Jobs Chief Guilty; Jury Convicts 4 in City Hiring Fraud; Feds Say, 'Stay Tuned,'" *Chicago Tribune*, July 6, 2006.
29. Ibid.
30. Ron Grossman, "A Well-Oiled Machine: A System That Works? Graft and Enterprise Go Hand in Hand in Chicago," *Chicago Tribune*, August 21, 2005.
31. Ibid.; David Axelrod, "A Well-Oiled Machine: A System That Works? Political Debts Contribute to Better City Services," *Chicago Tribune*, August 21, 2005.
32. Axelrod, "Political Debts Contribute to Better City Services."
33. Grossman, "Graft and Enterprise Go Hand in Hand."
34. "Judge Lifts Shakman Decree Federal Oversight on Chicago Hiring," ABC Channel 7 News, Chicago, June 16, 2014, http://abc7chicago.com/politics/judge-lifts-shakman-decree-oversight-on-chicago-hiring/116359/.
35. Fran Spielman, Natasha Korecki, and Rummana Hussain, "Victorious Emanuel Thanks Voters for a Second Term and a Second Chance," *Chicago Sun-Times*, April 7, 2015.

CHAPTER 6: "A SATURNALIA OF CORRUPTION AND CRIME"

1. "Panhandle Vote-Buying No Longer a Bargain," *Lakeland (FL) Ledger*, December 22, 1979.
2. James Dao, "Where Prosecutors Say Votes Are Sold," *New York Times*, August 29, 2004.
3. Ibid.
4. George J. Titler, *Hell in Harlan* (Beckley, WV: BJW, 1972), 53–57; Roger Biles, *The South and the New Deal* (Lexington: University Press of Kentucky, 2015), 98–100.
5. Davisworth v. Middleton 288 Ky. 77 (1941); "Chain Voting Prevented by New Ballots, New Law Makes Fraud Harder," *Gettysburg (PA) Times*, August 27, 1931.
6. *Davisworth v. Middleton.*
7. Ibid.
8. The coal counties are Clay, Breathitt, Lee, Jackson, Leslie, and Magoffin. US v. Johnson, Criminal Action No. 5:11-CR-143 (E.D. Ky. August 21, 2012), Memorandum and Order.
9. Tucker v. Mississippi 62 So.3d 397 (2010).
10. Ibid. Catina handed the envelope to the deputy clerk. The deputy clerk noticed

that Catina had failed to sign her name properly across the flap of the envelope. The deputy clerk instructed Catina to go back into the room where she had voted, remove the marked ballot, place it in another envelope, and sign it correctly.

11. Moffitt was sentenced to five years with the first two years in prison, the third year under house arrest, and then two years of post-release supervision. Both Moffitt and Ada Tucker were fined $5,000. "Jury Convicts Two in Benton Vote Fraud Cases," *Southern Advocate/Southern Sentinel*, July 15, 2009; R. L. Nave, "In Their Words: Jason Moffitt," *Jackson Free Press*, February 8, 2012; Brief of Appellants, NO.2009-CA-01265-COA, Tucker v. Mississippi.
12. Nave, "In Their Words."
13. The Scott sisters had no prior criminal records but had been sentenced to double-life sentences for allegedly "masterminding" an armed robbery with three teenage boys, which netted the group eleven dollars. Barbour commuted their sentences, after they had served sixteen years, to parole for the rest of their lives, with the "bizarre condition that one sister donate a kidney to the other, who needed a transplant because of diabetes." Jay Newton-Small, "Haley Barbour's Pardons: Why No One in Mississippi Is in a Forgiving Mood," *Time*, January 13, 2012; see also "Free the Scott Sisters," http://freethescottsisters.blogspot.com/; "List of Criminals Governor Barbour Pardoned in Mississippi," *USA Today*, January 12, 2102.
14. Murphy Givens, "Cowboy from Matagorda Founded Political Dynasty," *Corpus Christi Caller Times*, August 31, 2011.
15. Murphy Givens, "George Parr Inherited His Father's Political Dynasty," *Corpus Christi Caller Times*, September 7, 2011; see also Judith Ann Sutherland, "W. E. Pope Fought Parr Machine, Vote Fraud," *Corpus Christi Caller Times*, September 13, 2011.
16. US v. Saenz, 747 F.2d 930, 934–35 (5th Cir. 1984). Fidencio Saenz, Domitilla Garza, and Genoveva Garcia were convicted of conspiracy in violation of 42 U.S.C. § 1973i(c) and 18 U.S.C. §§ 371 and 372.1. In addition, appellants Norma Solis, Garza, and Garcia were each convicted on one substantive count of vote buying in violation of 42 U.S.C. § 1973i(c). Appellant Garza was convicted of one substantive count of paying and offering to pay Elizabeth Yarberry for her vote. Appellant Solis was convicted of one substantive count of paying and offering to pay Mercedes Gonzales for her vote.
17. Manny Fernandez, "Texas Vote-Buying Case Casts Glare on Tradition of Election Day Goads," *New York Times*, January 13, 2014.
18. Ildefonso Ortiz, "Donna Campaign Worker Pleads Guilty in Vote-Buying Scheme," *Monitor South Texas*, May 6, 2014.
19. Glenn R. Simpson and Evan Perez, "Brokers Exploit Absentee Ballots; Elderly Are Top Targets for Fraud," *Wall Street Journal*, December 19, 2000.

20. Ibid.
21. Ibid.
22. Berry, *And Justice for All*, 10.
23. Erika L. Wood, "Florida: How Soon We Forget," *New York Times*, April 5, 2012, quoting the US Commission on Civil Rights (USCCR) report *Voting* (1961): "Throughout the Jim Crow era, African-Americans who tried to register and vote in Florida were harassed and intimidated, resulting in extremely low voter registration rates. In 1961, the United States Commission on Civil Rights documented several of these incidents. In Liberty County, according to the Commission's report: 'Some Negroes registered in 1956, but thereafter they were subjected to harassment. Crosses were burned and fire bombs hurled upon their property, and abusive and threatening telephone calls were made late at night. Two white men advised one of the registrants that if the Negroes would remove their names from the books all the trouble would stop. All but one did remove their names, and their troubles ended; the one who did not was forced to leave the county.'" See also Jonel Newman, *Voting Rights in Florida, 1982–2006: A Report*, Renew the VRA.org (March 2006), http://www.protectcivilrights.org/pdf/voting/FloridaVRA.pdf.
24. Colette Bancroft, "Author Dudley Clendinen: Herald of a New Age," *Tampa Bay Tribune*, Sunday, May 11, 2008.
25. *St. Petersburg Times*, July 18, 1979; *Times* staff and wire reports.
26. Dudley Clendenin, "Firing and Fires: The Axe Has Apparently Started to Fall," *St. Petersburg Times*, April 16, 1979.
27. Ibid.
28. *St. Petersburg Times*, July 18, 1979; *Times* staff and wire reports.
29. "Panhandle Vote-Buying No Longer a Bargain," *Lakeland Ledger*, December 22, 1979, and *Sarasota Herald-Tribune*, December 26, 1979.
30. "Panhandle Vote Buying," *Sarasota Herald Tribune*, December 26, 1979.
31. Beckwith v. Florida 386 So.2d 836 (1980). Gloria Uzzell resigned under a deferred prosecution agreement, being charged with grand theft, after investigators say she had opened a credit card in the name of the Liberty County School Board without its approval or knowledge. "Jerry Mack Johnson Sr. (1935–2014): Obituary," http://www.legacy.com/obituaries/tallahassee/obituary.aspx?pid=172396935; "Former Liberty County School Superintendent will be Cleared of All Charges," update, WTXL-TV, November 4, 2013, http://www.wtxl.com/news/state/update-former-liberty-county-school-superintendent-will-be-cleared-of/article_96aaeff0-ef37-11e2-aa45-001a4bcf6878.html.
32. In re: the Matter of the Protest of Election Returns and Absentee Ballots in the

November 4, 1997, Election for the City of Miami, Florida, 707 So.2d 1170 (1998). Simpson and Perez, "Brokers Exploit Absentee Voters."

33. US v. Maricle, CRIM. 6:09–16-KKC (E.D. Ky. Oct. 30, 2013).
34. The use of federal money was important because the racketeering charge required an impact on interstate commerce. Bill Estep, "Jury Convicts All 8 Defendants in Vote-Buying Case," March 26, 2010; "Clay County Businessman, Wife Sentenced in Vote-Buying Scam," March 12, 2011; "Judge Rejects Attempts to Plead Guilty in Alleged Clay County Vote-Buying Conspiracy," October 31, 2013; "Five Remaining Defendants in Clay," November 6, 2013 (all in *Lexington (KY) Herald-Leader*).
35. Kentucky County Judge/Executive Association, "History of the Kentucky County Judge/Executive," http://www.kcjea.org/history_judge_executive.html.
36. Patrick Crowley, "Baesler, Bunning Race Has D.C. Agog: National Parties Target Senate Seat," *Cincinnati Enquirer*, May 31, 1998.
37. Donald A. Gross and Penny M. Miller, "The Kentucky Senate and 6th District House Races," in *Outside Money: Soft Money and Issue Advocacy in the 1998 Congressional Elections*, ed. David B. Magleby (Lanham, MD: Rowman and Littlefield, 2000), 188–92.
38. Jean Chung, *Felony Disenfranchisement: A Primer* (Washington, DC: Sentencing Project, April 2014); Martha Neil, "Jailed Ky. Judge-Executive Hasn't Resigned; Will He, Like Predecessor, Hold Job in Prison?," *ABA Journal*, December 10, 2012, http://www.abajournal.com/news/article/jailed_ky._judge-executive_hasn't_resigned_will_he_like_predecessor_hold_job.
39. John Cheves, "KY County Judge Conducts Business from Jail Cell," *Lexington Herald-Leader*, November 9, 2003, on *Free Republic* website, http://www.freerepublic.com/focus/f-news/1018091/posts.
40. US Department of Justice, "Knott County, Ky., Judge Executive Sentenced on Vote-Buying Conspiracy Charges," press release, March 16, 2004, http://www.justice.gov/archive/opa/pr/2004/March/04_crm_164.htm; James Dao, "Where Prosecutors Say Votes Are Sold," *New York Times*, August 29, 2004; Newsome v. Hall, 261 Ky. 52 (2005); Cheves, "KY County Judge Conducts Business from Jail Cell."
41. US v. Thompson, 501 Fed. Appx. 347 (2012); Dori Jhalmarson, "2 Felons Running for Knott Judge-Executive," *Lexington Herald-Leader*, January 29, 2010.
42. "Prepared Remarks of Attorney General Alberto R. Gonzales at the Anniversary of the Voting Rights Act," Lyndon B. Johnson Presidential Library, Austin, TX, August 2, 2005, http://www.justice.gov/archive/ag/speeches/2005/080205agvotingrights.htm.
43. "Study: Feds Prosecuted Only 38 Cases of Voter Fraud Between 2002–05, 14

Were Thrown Out," *ThinkProgress*, May 16, 2007, http://thinkprogress.org/politics/2007/05/16/12920/voter-fraud-study/.

44. Harold Meyerson, "The Cost of a GOP Myth," *Washington Post*, May 16, 2007.
45. Ryan J. Reilly, "Obama DOJ Keeps Bush-Era Name on Voting Integrity Effort," *TPM*, October 25, 2010, http://talkingpointsmemo.com/muckraker/obama-doj-keeps-bush-era-name-on-voting-integrity-effort.
46. State v. Brookins, 380 Md. 345 844 A.2d 1162 (2004). Also see Michael Weisskopf, "Baltimore: Politics as Usual Precinct Payouts Typify Election Windup," *Washington Post*, September 11, 1978.
47. *State v. Brookins.*
48. Ibid.
49. Ibid.
50. Howard Libit and Tim Craig, "Allegations Fly as Election Day Nears," *Baltimore Sun*, November 4, 2002, http://www.baltimoresun.com/bal-te.md.turnout04nov04-story.html.

CONCLUSION

1. Board of Commissioners of Clinton County v. Davis, 162 Ind. 80; 69 NE 680 (1904); see also State ex rel. Beedle v. Schoonover 135 Ind. 526, 35 N.E. 119 (1889).
2. Citizens United v. Federal Election Commission, 558 US 310 (2010); McCutcheon et al. v. FEC (2014) 134 S. Ct.1434 (2014).
3. Database search: Louisiana campaign finance contributions. *New Orleans Times Picayune*, November 5, 2013.
4. Peter Overby, "Hillary Clinton Supports Amendment to Get Hidden Money Out of Politics," NPR, April 17, 2015, http://www.npr.org/blogs/itsallpolitics/2015/04/17/400362239/hillary-clinton-supports-amendment-to-get-hidden-money-out-of-politics.
5. Mary Frances Berry, "Amending the Constitution: How Hard It Is to Change," *New York Times Magazine*, September 13, 1987; People for the American Way, "PFAW and 50+ Allies Ask Obama to Require Government Contractors to Disclose Political Spending," March 3, 2015, http://blog.pfaw.org/content/pfaw-and-50-allies-ask-obama-require-government-contractors-disclose-political-spending.
6. "California's Record Low Voter Turnout Stirs Anxieties," *Sacramento Bee*, December 1, 2014, http://www.sacbee.com/news/politics-government/election/article4237488.html#storylink=cpy.
7. Lindsey Cook, "Midterm Turnout Down in 2014," *US News and World Report*, November 5, 2014, http://www.usnews.com/news/blogs/data-mine/2014/11/05/midterm-turnout-decreased-in-all-but-12-states.

8. "House Dems with John Lewis as Lead: Dems Push New Voting Rights Bill," *New Orleans Times Picayune*, March 20, 2015.
9. Pew Charitable Trusts, "Understanding Online Voter Registration," brief, 2015, http://www.pewtrusts.org/en/research-and-analysis/issue-briefs/2015/05/online-voter-registration; Lloyd Leonard, "The Problem with Online Voter Registration," League of Women Voters blog, December 2, 2014, http://lwv.org/blog/problem-online-voter-registration; Shelby Sebens, "Oregon Governor Signs Sweeping Automatic Voter Registration into Law," Reuters, May 16, 2015, http://www.reuters.com/article/2015/03/16/us-usa-politics-oregon.
10. International Institute for Democracy and Electoral Assistance, "Compulsory Voting," May 13, 2015, http://www.idea.int/vt/compulsory_voting.cfm.
11. "Mandatory Voting In America? President Discusses Idea During Town Hall Meeting," March 19, 2015, Inquisitr.com, http://www.inquisitr.com/1938138/mandatory-voting-in-america-president-discusses-idea-during-town-hall-meeting.
12. "Mandatory Voting Won't Cure Dismal Turnout," *USA Today*, editorial, April 5, 2015.
13. Information provided by Ruth Greenwood, staff attorney, Lawyers Committee for Civil Rights Under Law, who happens to be Australian; Snagvotes promotes these fund-raising initiatives through the election sausage sizzle map, social media, and traditional channels. "It has been running since 2010 with the help of a number of contributors. The message is 'Get together with your community and enjoy a sausage on election day—a great Australian tradition.'" There are sausages sizzling and vegan lollipops—it's like a party. "Snagvotes—Election Sausage Sizzle," http://www.electionsausagesizzle.com.au/; http://democracysausage.org/.
14. Campbell, *Deliver the Vote*, 5; Richard Fausset, "South Carolina's Ban on Election Day Liquor Sales May Go the Way of Prohibition," *New York Times*, May 28, 2014, http://www.nytimes.com/2014/05/29/us/south-carolinas-ban-on-election-day-liquor-sales-may-go-the-way-of-prohibition.html?_r=0.
15. Chicago Quirk, "Vote Today, Get Free Stuff!" *Chicago Now*, November 6, 2012; information on Election Day "freebies" from past elections: Christina Fierro, "Election Day Freebies," *Daily Finance*, November 2, 2010, http://www.dailyfinance.com/2010/11/02/election-day-freebies-starbucks-krispy-kreme-chick-fil-a-and/.
16. Trushin v. State, 425 So.2d 1126 (1983).
17. Dermot Cole, "House Backs Refinery Subsidies as Supporters Warn of Hardships," *Alaska Dispatch*, April 18, 2004.
18. A program sponsored by the Tanana Chiefs Conference, Doyon Limited, and the Fairbanks Native Association (TCC/Doyon/FNA) was not approved and was re-

served for further inquiry. It operated in a more complicated fashion. The conference mailed a postcard to Doyon members before the election, offering to voters who submitted an entry on the 1994 ballot stub, or a similarly sized piece of paper, an opportunity to join in a drawing for one thousand dollars. Participants had to submit entries to their tribal council office by noon the day after the election. The other side of the postcard encouraged Native Alaskans to vote, saying "it is very important" to vote and that "one vote does make a difference," and encouraged friends and relatives to vote in the general election. Also, on the same side of the postcard, it said: "At this year's Alaska Federation of Natives convention, Native delegates from across Alaska overwhelmingly endorsed Tony Knowles for governor." Dansereau v. Ulmer 903 P 2d 555 (1995), note 11, on raffles, discounts, and free rides.

19. Day-Brite Lighting v. Missouri, 342 US 421 (1952); Karlan, "Not by Money but by Virtue Won?," discusses dangers, especially to economically disadvantaged groups, of vote-buying schemes and contrasts these schemes with voting incentive programs.

INDEX

WITHDRAWN
Damaged, Obsolete, or Surplus
Jackson County Library Services